# JODI MARIE MACKIN

*Meeting Mister Baston*

*Copyright © 2022 by Jodi Marie Mackin*

*All rights reserved. No part of this publication may be reproduced, stored or transmitted in any form or by any means, electronic, mechanical, photocopying, recording, scanning, or otherwise without written permission from the publisher. It is illegal to copy this book, post it to a website, or distribute it by any other means without permission.*

*This novel is entirely a work of fiction. The names, characters and incidents portrayed in it are the work of the author's imagination. Any resemblance to actual persons, living or dead, events or localities is entirely coincidental.*

*Cover Image provided by Period Images*

*Second edition*

*Editing by Emily Yau*

*This book was professionally typeset on Reedsy. Find out more at reedsy.com*

# Contents

| | |
|---|---|
| *Acknowledgement* | vi |
| Chapter One | 1 |
| Chapter Two | 9 |
| Chapter Three | 13 |
| Chapter Four | 18 |
| Chapter Five | 23 |
| Chapter Six | 33 |
| Chapter Seven | 45 |
| Chapter Eight | 52 |
| Chapter Nine | 60 |
| Chapter Ten | 79 |
| Chapter Eleven | 93 |
| Chapter Twelve | 110 |
| Chapter Thirteen | 118 |
| Chapter Fourteen | 128 |
| Chapter Fifteen | 136 |
| Chapter Sixteen | 149 |
| Chapter Seventeen | 156 |
| Chapter Eighteen | 166 |
| Chapter Nineteen | 181 |
| Chapter Twenty | 192 |
| Chapter Twenty-One | 197 |
| Chapter Twenty-Two | 202 |
| Chapter Twenty-Three | 210 |

| | |
|---|---|
| Chapter Twenty-Four | 216 |
| Chapter Twenty-Five | 221 |
| Chapter Twenty-Six | 226 |
| Chapter Twenty-Seven | 237 |
| Chapter Twenty-Eight | 244 |
| Chapter Twenty-Nine | 252 |
| Chapter Thirty | 258 |
| Chapter Thirty-One | 262 |
| Chapter Thirty-Two | 267 |
| Chapter Thirty-Three | 271 |
| Chapter Thirty-Four | 275 |
| Chapter Thirty-Five | 283 |
| Chapter Thirty-Six | 294 |
| Chapter Thirty-Seven | 298 |
| Chapter Thirty-Eight | 311 |
| Chapter Thirty-Nine | 319 |
| Chapter Forty | 326 |
| Chapter Forty-One | 333 |
| Chapter Forty-Two | 337 |
| Chapter Forty-Three | 346 |
| Chapter Forty-Four | 355 |
| Chapter Forty-Five | 361 |
| Chapter Forty-Six | 367 |
| Chapter Forty-Seven | 376 |
| Chapter Forty-Eight | 382 |
| Chapter Forty-Nine | 387 |
| Chapter Fifty | 391 |
| Chapter Fifty-One | 399 |
| Chapter Fifty-Two | 409 |
| Chapter Fifty-Three | 414 |
| Epilogue | 425 |

| | |
|---|---|
| *More* | 449 |
| *About the Author* | 450 |

# Acknowledgement

*It took me five long years of writing, rewriting, editing, and revising to get my debut novel out to you all (now I understand why "they" say never to publish your first book...), and I would just like to thank you all for your lovely encouragement and support!*

-Jodi Marie Mackin

# Chapter One

*Spring 1817*
*London, England*

Standing at the edge of the Middleton's ballroom, Lady Isabella Avery slipped behind an azure, velvet curtain. Firstly, because she was avoiding her future dance partner. Secondly, because she was avoiding her mother who was *with* said future dance partner. She sighed, glancing out at the dance floor from her hiding place with the cold windowpane at her back, thinking how odd she must look to the patrons outside on the terrace.

Every week her mother, the Duchess of Waverly, dragged her by her ear to these dances for one purpose: to pair her with Viscount Edward Middleton. And to make matters worse, Edward also expected to wed her.

Thanks to her mother.

A sparkling pink gown caught Isabella's eye. She watched

in envy as the young debutante danced a country reel.

Taking a small step around the edge of the curtain, she focused on the lady's satin-clad slippers, the way her feet pointed and arched with every step. She drew her gaze to the hem of the lady's skirt. The fabric bounced and swayed, catching the warm candlelight in the satin's shine.

Oh, how she loved dancing. If only she could find herself an agreeable partner. And if it were acceptable for two ladies to dance with one another, she would far prefer to dance with her sister. Her sister would not ogle at her breasts or place her hand far lower on her back than is proper. No... She and Violet would dress in their mother's old powdered wigs and hoop skirts. They would hold hands while they twirled until they were so dizzy they'd fall flat on their bottoms, as they used to when they were children.

"There you are!" Isabella's mother yanked at her upper arm, nearly tearing the delicate lace of her sleeve. "I have been searching for you for ages. Edward is hoping to claim the next set."

"My apologies, Mother." Isabella donned a wistful smile and hooked her mother's arm around her own. "Surely my dance card is full enough already?"

They stepped out onto the perimeter of the dance floor. "Your dance card can never be too full, darling. Not until Edward's name is on it at least once."

Isabella's nostrils flared. Spotting Edward's familiar dark golden hair, she steered herself in the opposite direction.

The duchess brought her spectacles up to the bridge of her nose. "While I have you, be a dear and help me find your sister. I have lost sight of her again."

*Oh, Violet... Why must you disappear?*

## Chapter One

Isabella let her eyes glance about the elegant ballroom. The wood floors appeared to be so recently polished it was surprising that not a single patron had fallen and broken their hip. Her gaze trailed further upward, to the balconies lining the two-story, sky-blue walls of the ballroom. She did not think Violet had a reason to head for the balconies. Her sister was much too fond of dancing and making herself a spectacle to hide in such a place.

And just there, in the far corner, standing next to a stone marble statue, stood her sister with… "Lord Taunton." The name slipped from her lips.

"What was that, dear?" The duchess turned to her, causing a blonde curl to fall out of place.

Isabella let out a low growl. Lord Taunton was not the sort of gentleman a lady should associate with. Not that Isabella gave a jot about societal standards, but really… Lord Taunton? Her sister ought to have known better. The gentleman was a drunkard and rumored to be the worst sort of scoundrel. He attempted to bed any and every woman he came into contact with. The list of his depraved acts had to be miles long.

Heavens help her if she would allow the ignominious lord to have Violet as one of his accomplishments. "She is there."

"Oh, thank goodness for your young eyes—but a lady does not point," the duchess promptly reminded her, slapping Isabella's outstretched hand.

Her mother squinted through her wire-rimmed spectacles. *A lady also does not squint…* but it seemed the duchess had forgotten that particular lesson on decorum.

"I feared she had found her way to the gardens again. Heavens help me if I have to save that child from another scandal."

Isabella's lips turned up at the corners. Her mother was always so worried over her children. "Then we must retrieve her. We do not want Violet socializing with a scoundrel such as Lord Taunton, do we?"

The duchess removed her spectacles and turned to her with a grim expression. "Perhaps you should fetch your brother and have him keep a closer eye on Violet."

She flashed her mother a reassuring smile and left her with a peck on the cheek.

Making her way through the ballroom, Isabella passed through a kaleidoscope of colorful patrons. Gentlemen donned their best and brightest waistcoats, their whitest and most crisp cravats. Ladies wore the latest in Regency fashion and no doubt had their dresses tailor-made for the occasion—ivory evening gloves, puffed sleeves, and gowns created with the finest of silks and satins.

She spotted her brother, Simon, dancing with a young, beautiful, fair-haired lady. Isabella made her way toward the couple, but a large, masculine hand took hold of her shoulder, stopping her forward movement.

"I've been searching for you all evening." Heat stained her cheeks at the man bold enough to touch her.

Isabella whipped around to face him.

*Edward.*

The very gentleman she had been hoping to avoid all evening. "Lord Middleton. How lovely to see you," she lied, dropping into an elegant curtsy.

Edward had danced with Isabella twice during the Harper ball last week and was seeking to do the same this evening. It was a gentleman's way of silently announcing his claim on

## Chapter One

a lady.

But Isabella did not want to be claimed.

Yes, Lord Middleton was handsome enough with his slicked-back dark-blond hair and piercing chestnut eyes, but if she matched with someone, the gentleman had to at least have a sense of humor, quick wit, and the ability to make her laugh.

Edward did not possess any of those qualities.

"How many times have I told you to call me 'Edward?'" he asked on a laugh.

"Quite a few times, my lord. But being as we are out at a public function, it would be rather inappropriate."

"True." Edward placed her gloved hand in the crook of his elbow. "Where are you off to in such a rush?"

"I was searching for my brother," Isabella replied politely, turning back to face said brother who was no longer in sight.

*Blast.*

The viscount led her along the perimeter of the room. "May I offer my assistance?"

"I do not wish to trouble you." *I'd rather you leave me so I may continue my task undisturbed.*

"It is no trouble, I assure you." Edward craned his neck, searching over the crowd. "Have you been enjoying yourself tonight?"

She had spent most of the evening dancing with gentlemen she did not particularly care for, and consequently, had attempted to hide behind curtains... "Oh, yes. The music is lovely."

"Indeed." He nudged her with his elbow. "You must promise me a dance after we locate your dear brother. You are the guest of honor, after all."

*Meeting Mister Baston*

This again. She glanced down at the frustratingly full dance card dangling from her wrist. "My *mother* is the guest of honor," Isabella corrected.

Edward gave a little one-sided shrug. "Either way, I am inclined to dance with the guest of honor's eldest daughter at least once this evening." He leaned closer. "But I'd prefer it to be more than once."

Isabella's brows shot up. "Do not forget about the guest of honor's youngest daughter. Violet would not want to miss out on a dance with you, my lord," she insisted, attempting to direct the conversation away from herself.

Edward's lids lowered, and his lips turned into the smallest hint of a smile.

A shudder ran down Isabella's spine. What that expression suggested she did not wish to know.

A flash of color caught her attention and brought her gaze to the west corridor. Lord Taunton entered the darkened space with Violet in tow. Meanwhile, the viscount driveled on about the music and the dancing.

Isabella had to think of a way to be rid of him.

"I believe I just saw your brother step into that alcove." Edward's voice regained her attention.

She did not need Simon anymore; she needed to reach that corridor. "No—" *But perhaps I can send Simon to fetch her?* "I mean... *yes*. Let us fetch him."

Edward led her to a curtained alcove far from the west corridor. "Reading," he announced as they reached the closed azure curtain. "I have a young lady here who has been searching for you."

The velvet fabric sailed open, revealing quite the bawdy display. Isabella's eyes fell to a gentleman in the corner

6

## Chapter One

fondling a stunning dark-haired woman. She was scantily clad in a dampened satin gown that clung to her vivacious curves. The woman took her long, slender fingers and raked them through the gentleman's auburn tresses.

It was disgusting—yet fascinating all at once.

*Disgustingly fascinating?*

She watched as the auburn-haired gentleman lowered his lips to the woman's bosom.

"And which young lady is— Bella!" Simon took a sidestep and blocked her view of the erotic display, snapping the curtains closed. He took a step forward, composing himself. "Middleton. Dear sister. How may I be of service?"

Narrowing her eyes, Isabella attempted to peek through the small opening of the fabric. "What were you doing in there? Who is that other man?"

Simon stepped into her line of view. He crossed his arms over the lapels of his perfectly tailored jacket. "Nothing and no one."

Isabella stifled her laughter. Oh, how she loved baiting her eldest sibling. "I am fairly certain I saw a young lady in there. Does Mother know of your scandalous activities?"

Simon's nostrils flared as he glanced between her and Edward.

"Come now, my lady. Let us not tease Lord Reading." Edward's grip tightened on her arm, and Isabella turned to face him. His expression was stern, almost as if he were giving her an order.

How dare he. Treating her as if he owned her already.

Isabella feigned a smile. "I am suddenly parched. Lord Middleton, would you be so kind as to fetch me some lemonade?" *Bloody bastard.*

## Meeting Mister Baston

Being the proper gentleman he was, Edward bowed and placed a featherlight kiss on Isabella's hand. "I will be but a moment."

Once Edward was out of view, Isabella turned to Simon and rubbed her sore shoulder with her fingers.

*A lady must always maintain a good posture. No gentleman wants a wife with rounded shoulders...*

Isabella's upper back fell into a more comfortable slouch. "We have a situation." Simon cocked his head in bemusement. "Violet disappeared with Lord Taunton." She kept her voice low so none of the nearby patrons could hear.

"What?" Her brother's fists tightened at his sides. "Where are they?"

"I saw them enter the west corridor." She placed her hand on his forearm. "Go. Quickly. Before someone discovers them."

Simon stomped off, leaving Isabella alone. A slight giggle came from inside the alcove, but before she could sneak a glance, Edward appeared at her side.

"Your lemonade, my lady." Edward handed her a small glass, and Isabella gulped the beverage down in two large swallows.

"Lovely." She swiped the back of her hand over her lips, enjoying the astonishment in Edward's eyes. "Thank you."

Edward cleared his throat. "Now that your brother has conveniently disappeared, may I have the next set, my lady?"

She glanced toward the corridor her brother had vanished through. She could not possibly excuse herself to follow Simon. So she sighed, placing her now empty glass on a small table, and accepted Edward's hand.

*A bloody waltz.*

# Chapter Two

Her dance with Edward had to be a waltz, and it seemed to have gone on for far longer than it should have. The entire time the viscount's hand was on her waist, she could only think of her sister and where on earth Simon was. They should have returned by now.

Once the set ended, Edward turned to her, his eyes dissecting her features. "Is something amiss? You seem a bit distracted."

She was *very* much distracted by the gentleman attached to her person. "Will you excuse me?" she asked, feigning embarrassment. "I find myself in need of the retiring room."

Before Edward could offer further assistance, Isabella removed herself from his hold, grasped the coral silk of her gown, hiked up her skirts and trotted across the room. She smiled inwardly at the way her mother would react if she saw such a thing.

The Duchess of Waverly had tried so hard to mold her two daughters into prim, refined young ladies, but Violet had always proved to be a troublemaker, and Isabella had interests in other, less feminine pursuits. She preferred archery, blade throwing, rifle shooting. Her unusual hobbies often caused her suitors to retreat. If only Edward knew she had a dagger strapped to her ankle at this very moment. What would his reaction be?

As Isabella drew near the west corridor, hushed voices caught her attention. She slowed her pace and released her skirts, careful not to invite any more unwanted scrutiny. She discreetly glanced over her shoulder to be sure no one was watching her, but someone was.

*Edward.*

She flashed him a smile before continuing forward.

Entering the corridor, the voices became more distinct, more masculine. She came upon two gentlemen arguing with one another. The dim candlelight made them difficult to see.

*"Get out!"*

Isabella knew that voice. It was Simon.

She quickened her stride and spotted Violet standing beside Lord Taunton. With one hand pressed against Simon's chest, the other grasping Taunton's arm, it appeared she was attempting to keep their brother from pummeling the life out of the other gentleman.

"What is happening here?" Isabella made her way over to Violet and dragged her to the side.

*"Nothiiing.* I swear!" Lord Taunton slurred while trying to keep his balance. He reached out for Violet, but Isabella tugged her sister away from the gentleman's grasp. "We were just having ffffun."

Isabella froze. What had Simon interrupted? Were Lord

## Chapter Two

Taunton and Violet closer than she originally suspected?

"Please, Simon, do not hurt him," Violet begged, tugging at the arm in Isabella's grasp, but Isabella's grip held firm.

"How much have you had to drink?" Isabella directed her question at the drunkard. She could smell the spirits on his breath from miles away.

"Only a little." The gentleman swayed and held up his fingers, his pointer finger and thumb spaced an inch apart. He barked out a laugh and combed his hand through his copper-colored hair. "Perhaps your sister would like to join us? We were having a lovely time before Reading interrupted."

A *lovely* time? Perhaps they were too late. Perhaps Taunton and Violet were already intimate.

"I believe I told you to leave," Simon seethed, his hands held in tight fists at his sides.

Having donned all black and standing three inches over six-foot, their brother, the Marquess of Reading, was an imposing sight. Most of the *ton* knew of Simon's short temper, but it seemed Lord Taunton was one of the few who did not.

Violet threw a dramatic hand over her eyes and sank to the floor, pulling Isabella down with her. Her coral skirts meshed with the rose-petal pink of her little sister's. With Violet's dark brown curls and Isabella's light golden waves, they as sisters could not be more opposite—both in appearance and in nature.

Violet was the more feminine of the pair, preferring dancing, singing, and the pianoforte... but was also the one who got herself into troublesome situations with gentlemen—present situation included—whereas Isabella avoided said gentlemen at all costs.

"Reading." Taunton threw an arm out, gesturing to Violet's distress. "You've gone and upset the lady." He took a few steps toward Violet, reaching his hand out to touch her.

Simon slammed his large fist into Taunton's jaw, causing the gentleman to stumble backward until he fell to the floor. The back of his skull hit the parquet with a loud *thunk*. "I told you to stay away from her!"

"Simon!" Isabella shouted in disbelief. Though, she had to admit, her brother landed quite the impressive blow.

Simon turned to her, shaking out his injured knuckles. "Get up and fetch Mother. We need to leave." Isabella blinked at him, unable to speak. Simon's blue eyes grew dark. *"Now."*

Isabella helped Violet stand and followed their brother down the corridor. She glanced back and saw Lord Taunton sprawled out on the floor—motionless. "Should I see if he is all right?"

"No," Simon seethed without taking a second look.

Normally, Isabella would have offered help, even if her brother demanded the opposite, but she supposed Lord Taunton deserved his unconscious state and soon to be bruised jaw.

## Chapter Three

Returning to their family's black lacquered carriage, it felt as though one could cut the tension in the air with Isabella's own sapphire-studded dagger.

The duchess sat opposite Isabella with her eyes squinting and lips pursed. One would think the duchess had not had to escape a scandal in the past, but alas, escaping scandal was an all too familiar occurrence for the Avery family. Just last week, Violet had almost been caught hidden away in a viscountess's gardens with yet another gentleman. Their mother had sent Isabella and Simon on a mad hunt to find her, and when they did, Violet was practically hanging off the gentleman's person. Simon had dragged her away and stayed by their sister's side for the rest of the evening.

Now Simon sat next to their mother, his arms crossed over his chest, dark brows furrowed over blue eyes, glaring at their youngest sibling.

Isabella slung an arm over Violet's shoulder and drew small, comforting circles on her sister's arm.

## Meeting Mister Baston

Violet had always been a romantic, a fact that had repeatedly gotten her into trouble. The inside of the carriage would have been unbearably silent if it were not for her sister's weeping—she really was not sure if the sound of weeping was worse than the tense silence coming from her family. So instead, Isabella focused her mind on the sounds of the journey itself, the clacking of the horses' hooves hitting the cobblestone streets of Mayfair, the roar of the wheels in movement.

Still, Violet's tears overpowered all until they returned to their white stucco townhome on Grosvenor Crescent. And if that was not enough, Isabella was assigned the duty of lecturing her young sister. *She will not listen to me...* Her mother's words chimed in her mind, but the words rang true. The duchess had spoken with Violet on more than one occasion, and her youngest sibling seemed not to take the advice given to her repeatedly.

*Never associate oneself with rakes, rogues, scoundrels, and the like.*

*Never find oneself alone with said rakes, rogues, scoundrels, and the like.*

*Never be discovered in a compromising position with rakes, rogues, scoundrels... or any gentleman.*

The first two, Violet had occasion to do many times. The third, she was yet to do: be discovered by members of the *ton*. Isabella crossed her fingers and sent a prayer skyward. Hopefully, there were no demons around to hear her thoughts tonight.

Though... It was better for her to do the scolding rather than Simon. Isabella shuddered at the thought. They would use Simon as a last resort.

## Chapter Three

She took in a breath and rapped once on the panel.

Violet's voice came from inside the bedchamber. "Enter."

Turning the handle, she opened the door just enough to peek her head inside. Her sister was lying under the floral bed covers with a book in her hand. "I hoped we could discuss what happened this evening."

"Oh." Violet closed her book and set it on the rose-inlaid table. "Of course." She motioned for Isabella to sit.

"What did Lord Taunton do?" Isabella asked as she shut the wood panel behind her.

Violet sighed. "It was nothing. Simon was... overreacting."

Catching that slight stammer, Isabella knew her sister was not being truthful. "Violet... Simon was enraged! He has *never* struck a gentleman in our company before."

"Oh, very well." Violet slapped her palms against the mattress and pushed herself into an upright position. "We were dancing, and I knew he had had too much to drink, but we were having so much fun. He then asked me to accompany him to the terrace..."

"*And...*" Isabella drawled, taking a seat on the edge of the bed.

"Well... as soon as we were out of sight of the other patrons, Lord Taunton became touchy." Violet dropped her gaze to her hands as they fidgeted with the bed covers.

"Explain, '*touchy.*'" Isabella was trying her damnedest to hide her discontentment.

Violet gulped. "At first, I found it humorous—the way Lord Taunton was stumbling about—but then he began pulling at my bodice and kissing my neck... which is when Simon discovered us."

"Violet!" Isabella threw a hand to her mouth and gasped.

## Meeting Mister Baston

"You are lucky it was our brother who discovered you! If it were *anyone* else, you'd have been forced to marry him! If Taunton would be gentlemanly enough to offer marriage—which I am highly doubtful he would. If he did not offer, you would be ruined and would marry no one!"

*Good heavens, I sound like Mother.*

Isabella took in a steadying breath and gave her head a mental shake. A lone tear rolled down her sister's cheek, and Isabella made an effort to sweep it away. "My apologies. I did not mean to shout."

"It is all right." Violet sniffed. "I know I am foolish."

Isabella let out a sigh and took her sister's hand. She hated seeing her sister cry—and she despised the way she had scolded her.

A tinge of guilt struck her heart. She decided her sister had had enough beratement for one day. "Come, you." Isabella slid across the feathered mattress and took Violet into her arms. "I will never lose sight of you again, and I will not let you destroy your life, you silly girl."

Violet chuckled. "How could I have thought to like Lord Taunton anyhow? He has ginger hair. How could any woman have an interest in a man with *ginger* hair?"

Isabella pulled away and smiled. "The gentleman's fault is not with his coloring."

"Nor with his expert kissing skills."

"Violet!" *She has learned nothing.*

"What? Tis true." Violet leaned forward. "You should try it sometime."

Isabella's eyes widened. "With Lord Taunton?!"

"Of course not." Violet leaned back against the embroidered cushion, twirling a lock of her hair. "He has already

## Chapter Three

proven himself a scoundrel."

"Are you still upset?"

Violet pursed her lips. "I suppose not." She gave Isabella a saucy look. "I have someone else I find interesting, and I dare say he finds me interesting as well... but Father would never approve."

If there were such a thing, she'd say her sister was the female form of a rogue, the way she so easily swayed from one romantic interest to another. With a sigh, Isabella gave her sister a peck on the cheek. "You are hopeless."

## Chapter Four

A shout woke Isabella early that morning.
Who on earth would be shouting at this ungodly hour? She peeked toward the closed curtains. The sun was not even shining through the cracks yet.

Whomever it was should certainly expect a scolding from the head housekeeper, for the head housekeeper would certainly get a scolding from her mother about such a disturbance.

Well, she supposed she ought get up and determine what all of the shouting was about.

Isabella crawled out of bed, pulled on her maroon silk dressing robe and meandered into the corridor.

"Help, please!" Anna, Violet's lady's maid, shouted from down the hallway. "She is gone!"

Anna? What on earth was she on about? Isabella's pace quickened until she found Anna in Violet's room. "*Who* is gon—"

She gasped when she saw the state of the bedchamber.

## Chapter Four

It was in shambles. The dresser drawers were pulled out and emptied. The doors to the armoire were open, and her sister's dresses were missing.

*Did Violet run away?*

Her sister often found herself in unfavorable situations, but she would not do something such as that. It would ruin the entire family. And she had just spoken to Violet before they retired for the evening. Surely Isabella would have noticed if anything had been amiss, if Violet were planning to leave...

Isabella's eyes fell to the toppled chamber candle. The covers were stripped from the mattress and were now settled in a sloppy heap on the floor.

Isabella brought her hand to her mouth as all of the clues began to fall into place in her mind. *"Oh my goodness."* Mayhap Violet did not leave on her own accord. Mayhap she was *forced*. But, if someone had taken her sister, how would the assailant have time to pack a trunk?

She gave her head a frantic shake. That did not matter. *Who* would have abducted Violet in the middle of the night?

*Think. Think!*

Isabella's mind was spinning in circles until she focused on one moment. One voice.

*I have someone else I find interesting, and I dare say he finds me interesting as well...*

There was another gentleman. Someone other than Taunton.

The duchess came rushing into the room wearing her lavender robe and slippers. "What on earth is happening here?"

"Y-Your Grace," Anna fumbled. "I was collecting the lady's washing and saw the room in this state and..." Anna's hand

*Meeting Mister Baston*

fluttered over her chest.

Glancing about Violet's room, her eyes came to the French doors that led to the terrace. She cocked her head to the side, noticing they were slightly ajar. "The terrace." Isabella pointed a finger to the opening.

"The terrace?" her mother echoed.

She grasped the door handle, and it wobbled slightly in her hand. "It is broken."

If Violet left on her own accord, why was the handle broken?

She stepped out onto the marble stone flooring and studied her surroundings. The tall green shrubberies in the corners of the terrace were situated perfectly in their clay pots. All seemed well.

Walking toward the edge, she began inspecting the perimeter, searching for anything that might be out of place. When she peered over the east side of the balustrade, she spotted a ladder. "Mother, look!"

The duchess came rushing over. "What on earth...?"

"Shall I send for the constable, Your Grace?" Anna asked, stepping onto the cold, stoned patio, her eyes red from tears.

"Yes." Her mother's hand flew to her heart. "At once."

"Wait!" Anna and her mother looked to Isabella. They needed to keep this situation quiet. If word were to get out about Violet's disappearance, it would ruin the entire family. With Violet's flirtatious reputation, the *ton* would assume she ran off to elope with a less than suitable gentleman. Which well may be true. "If we contact the constable, news of this will spread."

The duchess pursed her lips. "Yes... you are correct." She tiptoed toward Isabella. "But think of Violet's safety."

## Chapter Four

Yes. Violet's safety was of the utmost importance. Violet could have run off on her own accord, but with everything Isabella had seen in her sister's room, she very much doubted that.

Isabella took her mother's hands. The skin of her fingers were like ice. "Come, it is much too cold out of doors." They stepped through the French doors. "Father is a very influential man with powerful connections. He will handle this quietly."

And in all honesty... Isabella trusted her father more than anyone. Even the constable.

The duchess let out a breath. "All right. Your father has business at Ashbury, but we will send word to him."

"I will go to him," Isabella offered.

*"What?"*

"Ashbury is only a few hours' journey, and we need to discuss the organization of a search party," Isabella explained. "We cannot wait until Father arrives in London."

"Surely Simon would be a better choice. Going to Surrey on your own could be dangerous," her mother said while taking a seat on the edge of Violet's bed.

Indeed, whoever had taken Violet could very well be close by and could be planning a further assault upon their family. But Isabella did not care. She was more than willing to sacrifice her safety for the sake of her sister.

"Simon is not here." Her brother was most likely off at one of his gambling hells. "And who is to know when he is to return?"

The duchess was quiet for a moment, then sighed. "You are correct... Get dressed." She turned to the lady's maid. "Anna, see that the carriage is readied."

*Meeting Mister Baston*

Anna bobbed a curtsy and left the room.

## Chapter Five

The road to Surrey was bumpier than usual, which made it particularly difficult for Isabella to nap inside the conveyance. So this gave her hours to reflect upon where Violet was taken—or where Violet had run off to. She far preferred if Violet had run off with a gentleman to elope. Scandalous, yes. But at least Isabella would know her sister was safe.

Who would this mysterious gentleman be? It was not Lord Taunton. He was far too much of a carouser to want to settle down with a lady of the *ton*.

Violet mentioned another she had an interest in... A gentleman their father would not approve of. Who on earth could that be?

Isabella sighed... She was getting nowhere with her musings.

The carriage lurched to a stop, signaling her arrival at Ashbury Hall, her family's country home. The large symmetrical Georgian estate with a cobbled drive lined with tall, white birch trees was always her favorite out of her family's properties. Isabella stepped out before the coachman left his perch. She stretched her stiff and achy limbs before scurrying up the stairs and pushing open the heavy mahogany doors.

"My lady! What a surprise." Dunnley, their loyal and very elderly butler, cocked his head. "My apologies. I did not hear you arrive."

"Your hearing must be leaving you, my dear Dunnley." Isabella flashed him the smallest hint of a smile. It was the only thing she could manage on such a day. She placed a hand on the loyal servant's shoulder. "I need to see my father at once."

"Of course, my lady. He is in his study." Dunnley turned to make for the staircase. "I will guide you."

Dunnley always looked to escort Isabella around her own home. It was as if she was as forgetful as he himself was. He was a sweet man, but the old servant was most definitely getting on in years. "I know my way. Thank you, Dunnley."

Down the east hall, three doors to the left—she knew the Ashbury estate well, even though it had been a long while since she'd visited. *"Ugh!"*

Her body slammed into a man's hard chest, knocking the air from her lungs.

*What dastard does not look where he is walking?* Isabella collected a breath and closed her eyes. *Calm yourself. A lady does not curse or show anger...*

She took in the man's features, discovering that he was quite handsome.

He had a firm jaw, a straight nose, sported tousled auburn hair with a few days' growth on his face, and had eyes as green as emeralds.

## Chapter Five

Isabella tilted her head. There was something oddly familiar about him, with his cream breeches and perfectly tailored crimson jacket. He was, indeed, a gentleman. But how did she recognize him?

The well-dressed and well-muscled stranger arched a single dark brow.

*Say something, you ninny.* She cleared her throat, uttered "Who are you?" and winced as the not-so-polite words left her mouth.

"I should ask you the same question, Miss...?" The man was too well-dressed to be a servant. Perhaps one of her father's wealthier tenants?

She supposed it'd be civilized to introduce herself, but she did not have time for such pleasantries. "I am here to see my father," she explained. "Now, if you will excuse me..." As she moved to pass the man, he grasped her shoulder.

He offered her an arrogant smirk. "I do not think so. There was no mention of visitors in His Grace's diary today."

Isabella fumed. *Sorry, Mother...* There was no bloody way she'd behave as a proper lady around such a dastard. "Release me."

"Do not assume you are the first young lady to come barging through demanding she see her 'father.'" Isabella noted the added emphasis on that last word.

Were fortune-hunting widows seeking out her father's company? Oh, the duchess would not be happy to hear about that. "What on earth do you mean?"

"I know," he drawled. "The duke is a handsome man, and I can see why you feel the need to come here. I assure you, he is a loyal husband to the duchess, and he has no interest in *you...*"

"Wait... What are you speaking of?" The gentleman continued to babble while shoving Isabella back where she'd come from.

"Is Dunnley so elderly that he has forgotten what the duke's daughters look like?" he mumbled under his breath. "...lets any female wander in here because she claims to be the duke's daughter." The gentleman paused. "That butler really needs a new pair of spectacles."

How *dare* he speak of Dunnley in such a way? The servant had been with the Averys for decades. And this stranger believed he could speak such rude things about her family's beloved butler? Isabella rolled her eyes and abruptly turned toward her father's study. "You, sir, are a *muttonhead*." She let out a curse as she moved to pass him.

"A *muttonhead?*" he laughed, yanking at Isabella's wrist. She stumbled backward, and he forced her against the wall, pushing his forearm against her chest. "You are a determined little chit, are you not?"

Isabella's breath hitched at his nearness. His eyes... How were his eyes so green?

Isabella gave her head a mental shake. She should worry about how this man had just pinned her against the wall and not about whether his eye color was genuine.

Really? How did he not recognize her? Every member of the bloody *ton* knew of her family. Isabella was certainly the most well-recognized after her brother. Being the unmarried eldest daughter of the Duke of Waverly, she was a popular subject for gossip. Either way, the gentleman needed to remove himself from her person immediately.

Remembering what her father taught her about how to defend one's self, Isabella brought her arm between the

## Chapter Five

gentleman's forearm and chest. Twisting her body, she slammed her elbow hard into his abdomen, causing him to stumble backward.

Lifting the hem of her skirts, Isabella pulled the sapphire-studded dagger from its holster at her calf and shoved the man against the wall, drawing the dagger to his throat.

Isabella reached for the pendant hidden under her bodice, a family heirloom with the Avery crest etched into the hard metal. She yanked at the piece and held it in the air. "Lady Isabella Avery, the eldest daughter of George and Mary, the Duke and Duchess of Waverly."

The gentleman blanched and stared as Isabella tucked the pendant into her bodice. She lowered her dagger, keeping her eyes focused on the handsome stranger.

*Dastard. He is a dastard, Isabella. Not a handsome stranger,* her inner voice reminded her. Taking the man's silence as her cue, she continued onward to her father's study.

The duke peeked up from his work as Isabella stumbled through the door.

"Are you acquainted with that terrible man outside of your study?"

The duke laughed as he rose from his leather wingback chair. "Bella, what a lovely surprise." Her father eyed the door Isabella entered through. "You are referring to Alistair, I presume?"

So her father was acquainted with the gentleman, and he even referred to the vile creature by his Christian name. "Yes. He is awful." *And needs a shave.*

Her father quirked a brow. "A shave?" he chuckled. "It *is* Alistair, then."

*Had she said that aloud?*

Either way, she hoped to never see the poorly groomed muttonhead again.

"Actually... I have a reason for my visit today."

"Oh?" The duke's brow raised in question.

No matter how much Isabella wanted this visit to be a pleasant one, that simply was not the case. "It is Violet..." she started, fidgeting with the fabric of her blue skirts. "It appears someone has... taken her." *Or she ran off?* She still was not certain.

The duke slowly set his palms on the dark mahogany of his desktop. "Taken her?" he parroted. "Taken her where?"

"We are not certain."

The duke lowered himself into the chair. "Did she run off with a man? Was there a note?" he asked quietly, raking a hand through his graying hair.

Isabella shook her head. "I do not believe so. Her room was in shambles and..." *her wardrobe had been emptied.*

"And?"

Isabella took in a calming breath and brought her shoulders back. "The door handle to her terrace was broken."

Her father sat back in his chair, making the leather groan in protest. After a long moment, he said, "I assume you have sent for the constable?"

"No." Isabella made her way to her father's desk. "I thought it best if we handled it ourselves to avoid gossip. We could organize a search party," she suggested. Though the constable was unlikely to spread any gossip, the *ton* already had eyes on their residence. If one were to see the constable at their home, rumor would begin to spread—and quickly.

"Good idea. We must be discreet. Where is Simon?" he asked, bringing his fingertips to his temples.

## Chapter Five

"He went out again last night and was yet to return this morn."

The duke grumbled something under his breath.

Isabella tensed. Knowing her father, he would not take this next part lightly. "I thought I might lead the search—"

The duke met her stare. "Absolutely not."

"She is my baby sister, and I'd like to—"

"And *you* are my daughter," he snapped. "I will not have you gallivanting around with a search party!" Her father drew in a long breath. "It is dangerous."

But Isabella did not care how dangerous it could be. She only cared about bringing her sister home safe. She took her father's hands in hers. "You of all people know I can care for myself." Her mind went to the cold metal blade resting against her leg and the day her father gifted it to her as a young child.

"I can account for that," a familiar voice interrupted. "Were you aware she keeps a dagger hidden under her skirts?"

"Come in, Alistair." The duke sighed and motioned him inside.

Isabella's body tensed. *He was listening?*

Alistair stepped in and closed the door behind him. Who did this gentleman think he was? This was a private family matter, and he thought he could listen in?

"If you must be a part of the search for your sister—" her father paused and hope fluttered in Isabella's breast "—Alistair will accompany you to keep you safe," he finished.

Her heart promptly sank.

"I beg your pardon?" Both Alistair and she said in unison.

Isabella laughed, her hands falling to her hips. She was not even properly introduced to the gentleman, and her father wanted him to look over her? She could take care of herself, and the last thing Isabella needed—or wanted—was this Alistair person acting as her guard. "Keep me safe? I nearly cut him right outside of this room! You expect *him* to protect me?"

The duke crossed his arms over his chest. "He has served as my man-of-affairs and has been a close friend of mine for over a year now."

Over a year? Perhaps that is why the gentleman seemed familiar to her. Perhaps she had seen him before and just did not remember. But… men-of-affairs were old stodgy fellows who donned overly thick spectacles and spoke through their nose. Alistair could not be more than thirty years of age. "We have never been introduced."

"You rarely visit my study, dear," her father answered. "And Alistair is often away conducting business."

She supposed she did not interrupt her father's work as often as she did as a child. But surely they would have crossed paths at Ashbury Hall. Though their country seat was quite expansive, and she could go days without seeing a soul if she so chose.

"In fact," her father continued, "I do not recall a time you have visited my study in the last two years." He raised his palm to the air before Isabella could speak. "I assure you, Alistair can handle daggers, swords, rifles, *and* pistols."

"As can I," she grumbled.

"Yes you can," the duke laughed, "but I would be much more comfortable if Alistair acted as your guard, as your brother Simon can hardly look after himself, let alone you."

"And what of your duties here?" she asked, hoping perhaps her father might be too busy to join them on their search.

## Chapter Five

If that were the case, Isabella would easily be able to take charge of the search party without her brother even knowing what was happening.

Her father gave a shrug of his shoulders. "My duties will have to wait." He placed a small stack of folios inside the desk drawer. "Alistair, be sure Simon and Mr. Diggory are ready to depart by morning."

Her heart sank a little. "Diggory?" she asked with a tilt of her head. "The footman?"

"Yes." Her father nodded. "We could use a well-built man such as him on the excursion. Alistair—" the duke turned his focus to the gentleman that appeared at her side "—do you agree?"

"Of course, Your Grace," he said with an air of smugness.

Isabella reluctantly agreed to her father's terms and eyed the gentleman beside her who stood erect with his hands clasped behind his back.

What made him so capable and trustworthy her father would have him act as a guard over his eldest daughter? There was, of course, the obvious: he was a man and therefore was stronger and faster than she. His well-muscled form would shield her from any danger they may face.

Noticing her gaze, Alistair shot her a lazy half grin, his emerald eyes piercing her own.

Isabella's heart jumped, and she returned her gaze frontward.

It was *him*... The man behind the curtain. That was how he seemed so familiar to her. Not because of his employment with her father, but from the ball last evening. He was the auburn-haired man groping the woman inside the alcove.

Alistair was no gentleman.

## Meeting Mister Baston

Alistair was a rake.

## Chapter Six

The next morning, Isabella tapped her foot on the steps of her London home.

After she left her father at Ashbury Hall, the rest of the day passed in a flurry of bustling maids and footmen as they readied the family for departure.

"I do not understand how this happened." Her mother began pacing the expanse of the room. "Mr. Diggory!"

Callum Diggory, the footman, stumbled in from the servants' quarters, his gold-studded jacket hanging crooked over his frame, which Isabella found quite strange. Their servants were usually dressed immaculately. "Your Grace?"

"Where have you been?" the duchess scolded. "Go gather your belongings! You are to accompany the duke on his journey."

"Right away, Your Grace." With a stiff bow, the footman took his leave and returned down the steps to the servants' quarters.

"You must calm yourself, Mother, before you swoon,"

## Meeting Mister Baston

Simon insisted as he descended the grand marble staircase, but she continued her relentless pacing. "Has Father arrived yet?"

"No." Isabella sighed. "Though I suspect he will arrive shortly." She had already been waiting on the steps of the foyer all morning. How long would it take her father to finish his business at Ashbury? It was nearing noon already.

"I should have been more strict with that child." Her mother's voice cracked as she stared out the windowpane.

Simon took their mother's hand in his, his tall figure at complete odds with the duchess's small frame. "You could not have known this would happen," he whispered.

Her mother removed her hand from Simon's grasp and wiped away the tears from her reddened cheeks. Her eyes widened. "Your father has arrived!" Trotting toward the doors, the duchess waved her children over with frantic hands. "Come now, we shan't keep him waiting."

*Finally.*

Isabella exited through the front doors as the first carriage rolled to a halt. The cool late morning air slapped her skin, and she rubbed her bare hands together vigorously.

"Here you are, my lady." Her lady's maid appeared at her side, holding a pair of ivory gloves.

"Thank you." With a sigh of relief, Isabella donned the soft, kid-skinned gloves.

A second, smaller conveyance slowed with a half dozen footmen upon stallions trailing at the rear.

Before the groom left his perch, the duke stepped down from the black lacquered carriage. "Hello, my loves." He greeted them with a wave.

"George!"

## Chapter Six

Isabella watched as her mother raced to her father. With a ducal grace, her father brought her mother's gloved hand to his lips. "My Duchess."

Isabella's heartstrings pulled as she watched how her mother and father interacted with each other. They were a love match through and through, and Isabella could not help but hope for the same for herself one day.

"Please tell me you will find her, and she will be safe," her mother pleaded.

"We will find her," her father whispered, "and she will be safe." Releasing his wife's hand, he eyed his children. "I assume everyone is ready to depart?"

Isabella nodded once. She, indeed, had been prepared for departure since she left her father at Ashbury Hall the day prior.

Simon took his father's hand in his and gave it a hard shake. "We're ready to depart, Father."

The duke began relaying orders to the footmen, and if she were to be honest, Isabella paid little attention to the day's plans. They could well be traveling to seek help from the Prince Regent himself, for all she knew.

"Isabella is to ride with Alistair in the second carriage."

She perked up at the sound of her name. "Pardon?" she replied. Did she hear her father correctly? She was to ride with the muttonhead? Alone? Trapped in a small conveyance with him for *hours* on end?

This was to be her punishment for insisting upon accompanying her father.

"Have you forgotten?" Alistair poked his head out of the door of the smaller black carriage. "I am to be your guard."

Isabella turned to her father. "Why can I not ride with you?

*Meeting Mister Baston*

Surely I'd be safer with you and Simon. You do not need the entire coach to yourselves."

"Of course not." Her father motioned toward his conveyance. "It will not only be me and Simon. Captain Lucas and Mr. Diggory will join us. And you would not be safer with me. What if Violet's disappearance has something to do with me? What if I am targeted? It is best if you ride separately."

Isabella pursed her lips. She had not thought of that. But certainly, Captain Lucas was a better choice to act as her guard. He was a trained soldier in the British army. "You do not have any enemies," she pointed out.

"A duke *always* has enemies, whether or not he knows of them." Her father shrugged.

She shuddered at the thought, but all the more reason to ride with her father. "I should be in the carriage with you. To protect you."

Simon let out a laugh. "That is why Captain Lucas is here, little sister."

Isabella turned a sharp glare on her brother. "I can hit a tree with my throwing daggers from meters away."

Her brother scoffed. "Right. Because your daggers will be of any use against pistols."

Perhaps her brother was right. But stubborn as she was, Isabella crossed her arms at her chest. She would find a way out of this situation one way or another.

Her father knew being alone with a gentleman in a carriage was highly improper, especially for a nobleman's unmarried daughter. Her reputation would be ruined if any member of the *ton* were to find out…

"Mother." She turned to the duchess in a last bid of

## Chapter Six

desperation. "You see how improper this is..."

"What is improper, darling?" The duchess asked without removing her gaze from her husband.

Isabella rolled her eyes.

"I saw that," her mother said scornfully.

Of course, she had forgotten about her mother's third eye. "I cannot ride alone in a carriage with a gentleman while I am unmarried." How did a woman who worried over all that is proper and conventional not see the error in this?

"You do not have to worry about Alistair, dear. He is a perfect gentleman."

*A perfect gentleman?* Do perfect gentlemen press their lips against a wanton lady's bosom in the middle of social events?

Isabella's cheeks warmed as her patience wore thin. "It does not matter. If someone recognizes me—or witnesses us together—no one will have me. Who will I marry?" Her heart tripled its beat. Marriage had always been one of her mother's favorite subjects.

Her mother paused for a moment. "She does have a point, George. Should Bella not ride with you?"

Isabella let out a sigh of relief. If the duke would not listen to his daughter, surely he would listen to his wife.

The duke gave his head a prompt shake, and at that slight movement, Isabella lost all hope.

"We do not have time to make changes." He raised stiff fingers to his temples. "If you do not agree with the way I have arranged things, feel free to stay behind with your mother." With that, her father stalked away to his carriage.

Isabella's shoulders hunched over, and her mother swiftly swatted at her now curved spine. "Do stand up straight dear."

Isabella ignored her mother, which earned her a pointed

*Meeting Mister Baston*

look. "Do not pay much attention to your father. He is under duress."

They were all under duress. Her father's decisions were absolute nonsense, and the only reasoning she could work out in her mind was that her father was attempting to make this journey as miserable for her as possible so she might want to return home. But she would be damned if she would fall for her father's tricks. "Fine. Father may have his way." *For now.* "But I am not happy about it."

Leaving her mother with a peck on the cheek, Isabella stalked off toward her carriage.

"My lady…"

Isabella's body jerked at the sudden appearance of the dastard.

She promptly straightened her shoulders. "Do refrain from sneaking up on people."

"Request noted," the gentleman demurred.

Rolling her eyes skyward, she followed behind Alistair as they made their way to their modest conveyance. Alistair settled himself inside as the groom stood with his hand held out to her.

Isabella cursed under her breath as she saw Alistair staring out at her from within the carriage. His arms were crossed over his strong chest with an ankle lazily propped over one knee.

The groom smiled as he gave her his hand.

"Thank you." Isabella placed her hand in his and stepped into the carriage, taking the small cushioned seat opposite Alistair.

"Welcome to our humble abode, my lady." He welcomed her with a large, lopsided grin.

## Chapter Six

"I would supply you with a proper greeting, but alas, I am only familiar with your Christian name," she retorted, removing her gloves and placing them on the seat next to her.

"Mr. Alistair Baston."

"Good morning, *Mr. Baston.*" She could not help but mimic his tone. After all, her foul mood was to do with her being forced to ride inside a cramped conveyance with *him.*

A rake.

"I look forward to getting acquainted with you on our journey." He smiled.

"That makes one of us," she muttered, then winced as she realized she had said it aloud.

"Well," he laughed, "as the daughter of a duke, one would think you had knowledge of proper manners and etiquette."

She deserved that jibe. Though *he* certainly hadn't shown proper manners and etiquette during their first meeting—or during the ball. But Isabella did not comment on those facts.

"I assure you, I am not the muttonhead you accused me of being," he said as the carriage lurched forward.

Isabella sighed. She supposed she ought to make amends with Mr. Baston if she wanted this journey to be at all pleasant. "I do not think you a muttonhead."

"Well, that is a relief." He grinned.

Isabella eyed his pearly white teeth and noted that the gentleman must spend a great deal of time on his appearance. "Do you care much what people think of you, Mr. Baston?" Isabella asked dryly, trying her best to ignore his gaze.

"Of course. Being the spare to the heir, one must always keep up one's reputation."

She wondered what sort of reputation the gentleman held.

*Meeting Mister Baston*

After witnessing such a display in the alcove, it could not be a good one. "And what reputation would that be, Mr. Baston?"

"That of a worthless second son, of course."

"Oh, God," she groaned. "You are one of *those*."

Alistair cocked his head to the side. "One of what? One of those worthless sons?"

"Of course not!" *Drat.* She could not care less about titles and who was what to whom. "I mean to say, one of those men who felt sorry for themselves for being the second-born son, for not inheriting the glorious title and all that comes with it."

*Try being a lady of the* ton. *Ladies do not work, they do not inherit titles, and must marry for their livelihoods.*

Alistair snorted and, after a long moment of silence, leaned toward her. "Tell me, do you care what people think of *you*?"

She thought about all of the times her mother and governess would scold her when she did not act like a proper lady. "No." She was still scolded even to this day, but she would never be a proper lady with impeccable manners and etiquette

A life such as that was far too boring.

Alistair's smile widened, and he leaned back in his seat. "As the eldest daughter, one would think your family expects you to be married quite soon, yes?"

*Where was he going with this?*

"Yes." Her eyes narrowed.

"Then one would think you would at least *try* to get gentlemen to like you." He paused. "Being in your... third Season, is it?"

"How do you know it is my third Season?" she snapped.

Alistair waved a hand through the air. "Fathers talk."

## Chapter Six

*Of course.*

Isabella sighed and contemplated his words. "No. I do not *try* to get gentlemen to like me. It is insincere." She looked to the small floral reticule in her hands. "I am not so desperate to need to be insincere to find suitors." Not that she wanted to find suitors to begin with.

"Oh, I did not accuse you of being desperate."

Isabella arched a brow. It appeared Mr. Baston was intentionally baiting her. "Pardon?" she scoffed. "I had ten gentlemen call upon me just last week." She lied. Her only caller had been Lord Middleton.

Alistair narrowed his eyes into small slits. "Now you are being arrogant."

"I do not *try* to get them to like me. Some just—" Isabella cut herself off, realizing she was, indeed, sounding quite arrogant.

Alistair laughed.

"What I mean to say is if one starts off a relationship by *trying* to get one to fancy them, there would be no reason for a courtship. The entire relationship would be a lie."

"Hmmm." Alistair rubbed his fingertips through the stubble of his cheek. "Well, my lady, I cannot tease you about that."

Some time had passed since their petty squabble ended, and the carriage had grown quiet. Smoothing the wrinkles from her skirts, she glanced toward Alistair. He was slouched over asleep with his arms crossed over his chest. She looked to his hand and noticed the shiny gold ring on his ring finger. It was not a betrothal ring, being as those were displayed on one's left hand.

Isabella leaned forward in order to get a better look. There was a small etching throughout the center of the band. She leaned closer until her bottom was entirely off the bench.

It read, *'Matthias Baston.'*

"What are you inspecting?" Alistair muttered as he rubbed his eyes awake.

Blast and damn. He had caught her gaping. "Noth— *Oomph!*"

The carriage must have run over a bump, or a log, or perhaps a giant boulder, because their bodies flew into the air. They hovered over their benches for what seemed to be a full three seconds.

Alistair landed perfectly back onto his rear, but Isabella was not quite so lucky. Her body hurtled forward, her face landing on Alistair's lap, the part of his lap that was dangerously close to his—

"Oh dear," was all Alistair managed to say at the scandalous position they found themselves in.

Isabella gasped and looked at the gentleman in horror. *Bloody, bloody hell.*

She attempted to steady her body to lift herself, but the carriage jumped and rocked about as though they were driving through a stone-bottomed creek.

"Here," Alistair laughed and took Isabella's hand into his. "Let me help you."

She went to stand, but their conveyance hit yet another bump, and Isabella tumbled onto her knees. "Perhaps I should stay down here," she jested.

Where on earth was the driver taking them?

"Do not be silly." Alistair reached out to take her other hand. She accepted as she rose from the floor, waiting for another rock of the carriage to throw her off balance. "Thank

## Chapter Six

you."

"It was my father's," Alistair announced, causing Isabella to cock her head in confusion. "The ring. Assuming that is what you were inspecting."

"Oh, yes. My apologies—"

"It is all right," he laughed, looking at the gold ring.

*It was my father's...* Isabella registered the gentleman's words. He had used the past tense, which made her wonder if the gentleman's father had passed. What a horrible thing to lose one's father at such a young age. Alistair could not be more than thirty. She could not imagine life without her father. Isabella would guess that, out of all of her siblings, she was probably the closest to him.

When the road smoothed, Isabella turned to face Alistair. "Do you know where we are headed?" She had not paid attention whatsoever when her father was speaking earlier about the journey.

"Yes," he replied, keeping his eyes on the window.

Isabella waited for him to elaborate, but he stayed silent. "Do you care to *share* your knowledge with me?"

He snorted. "We are to stop in Amersham for the night, but our current destination is Derby."

"Derby?" she asked, baffled. "That is quite the journey."

"Apparently, Lord Taunton's mother told so-and-so she had not seen her son since the Middleton ball." He leaned forward, lowering his voice as though he were about to reveal some grand secret. "Their country seat is in Derby."

"My father believes Violet to be with that scoundrel?" She brought her fingertips to her chin. "But, why would he take her to his family's property in Derby? Would that not be a bit obvious?" If they planned on eloping, surely they would be headed straight for Gretna Green.

"He is not the smartest fellow." He paused. "And it is the only lead we have at the moment."

Violet would not run off with a scoundrel such as Lord Taunton, and the gentleman was a drunkard, *not* a mad man. She did not think they were together at all. Lord Taunton was not the sort of gentleman to whisk a lady of the *ton* away to Scotland so they may elope.

## Chapter Seven

Amersham Lodge. It was not as grand as Isabella was used to, but it had a cozy feel with its carved walls and stained-glass windows. Walking inside the dimly lit parlor, she held a small leather sketchbook against her chest.

She made her way to her brother's table in the center of the lounge and dropped her book opposite Simon's arm. It landed with a loud *thwack*.

Simon grimaced. "Oh, not that again."

When they were children, she'd often hide in dark corners, hoping to catch her family in their natural state. Posed portraiture was never an interest of hers. What fun was drawing a person if they were aware you were doing it?

"If you must sketch me, please do so from my good side," he jibed, motioning to the left side of his face.

"Arrogance does not suit you, dear brother." She pulled out the miniature of Violet from her satchel. "Father wants me to update Violet's portrait."

## Meeting Mister Baston

"Ah." Simon nodded toward the small image. "I suppose it is unwise to show around a miniature of a ten-year-old girl."

"Indeed." Isabella flipped to a clean page in her sketchbook. "Should you not be discussing tomorrow's plans with the group? Instead of sitting alone, sulking over a glass of spirits?"

"I needed a break from the bickering." Simon's blue eyes fell to his snifter.

Understanding filled her chest—and a desire to gulp down her brother's brandy in two large swallows, but such an act would earn them too many stares.

Isabella placed the tip of her pencil onto her sketchbook. She started by structuring the shape of Violet's face—not as round in the cheeks as she was at ten years of age. Isabella sharpened the cheekbones and gave her a more pronounced jaw.

*A face.*

Yes, it was easier to think of this drawing as "a face" rather than that of her sister. Isabella needed to be strong to finish the task assigned to her. She cleared her throat and began shaping the hair. It would be smart to draw a more mature hairstyle than what was in the miniature. Tight ringlets in two separate piles atop her head would not do. And who knew what the state of her hair was when she left—or was taken—in the middle of the night?

Isabella released a huff of breath. She did not know what to believe. What sort of person would break into their home and abduct their youngest sibling? To what end?

Her father stated that a duke always had enemies. But who would want to hurt them in such a way?

Perhaps it was Simon. He gambled, attended gentlemen's

## Chapter Seven

clubs. Who knew what he got up to during his long nights out?

Right. Back to sketching. She gave Violet a simple hairstyle: a loose coiffure with a few small ringlets around her temples and cheeks to frame her face.

Perfect. Now onto the eyes.

They were like ice. So pale and bright. Isabella was always jealous of her sister's eyes—so much more beautiful and unique than her own darker shade of blue. Not that color mattered. After all, she had only her charcoal pencil to work with.

A small drop of moisture landed on the corner of the paper. She swiped at her cheek. She had not realized she was crying.

Mayhap she should take a break and sketch something a little less painful to her heart.

Isabella studied the room and found her father standing over a table with Captain Lucas, staring down at a wrinkled map.

Captain Lucas was a married gentleman with a young son and another babe on the way. With his wavy dark hair and unruly sideburns, he was handsome in his own disheveled sort of manner—but not precisely what she wanted to draw.

The captain stepped around the table, bringing Mr. Baston into view. The gentleman sat next to the wall, swirling an amber liquid around in his glass. There was something melancholic in his air. He appeared so very alone in a room full of people.

*Worthless second son, of course...* Alistair's words echoed in her mind.

She supposed the scene laid out before her was fitting to her mood. Isabella sighed and flipped to a clean page.

Her charcoal pencil moved at a quickened pace, though still careful and delicate.

A lone table in a dark room appeared on the paper. A man sat in the only chair at its head, his hands gripping an almost empty glass.

Isabella looked up from the sketch to study Alistair's features. She brought the pencil to her lip as she examined the shape of his eyes. They were not perfectly round, more like almonds. His eyelashes were long and dark, making his emerald green eyes stand out all the more.

She dropped her gaze to his lips. The curve of his Cupid's bow, so perfect, it was as though the myth himself had created it.

A slow smile crept over his face, and she had to admit, he was indeed quite handsome.

*What is wrong with me?* She was never a woman to gape at a gentleman.

She glanced back to his eyes, which were suddenly staring deeply into hers. Isabella's body went stiff, causing her pencil to fall from her lip.

\* \* \*

Alistair had stepped into the cheroot-smoke-filled room inside Amersham Lodge. He scanned the many unfamiliar faces until he spotted his employer and Captain Lucas. They sat at a quiet corner table with a map of the surrounding counties laid out before them.

The gentlemen had stood before him, and Alistair greeted each of them with a bow. "Your Grace. Captain."

## Chapter Seven

"Ah, Baston!" George gave him a friendly slap on the shoulder. "Glad to see you survived my daughter's company."

"Only just," he'd laughed. Which was almost true. The lady was stubborn. "Captain Lucas, I hope I did not keep you with His Grace for too long. His talk of politics can prove redundant."

George snorted.

"I find conversation with Your Grace to be quite informative." The captain gave George a courteous nod.

Such a flatterer, that Lucas.

"At least one of you understands how to respect your superiors." George laughed and motioned to the empty chairs. "Let us sit, gentlemen. We have much to discuss."

They'd taken their seats as Captain Lucas pointed to an area on the map. "I thought we would set out from here. It is the quickest route to Bicester and we can stop at the farmhouses along the way to question tenants—and we shall be far enough out of London to keep this minor mishap away from the *ton's* eyes and ears."

Alistair disagreed. "Questioning the tenants will be a waste of time. How can they have seen Taunton and Violet together if they are always out working the fields? We should head straight for Derby."

"It is not about whether the farmers have seen Violet," Lucas said in hushed tones. "Mayhap someone has seen Taunton's carriage pass through. We must be thorough in our search."

"We must also keep this quiet. What is to stop the farmers from gossiping about the duke's visit?"

"Leave that to me." George cut in. "I will be sure they understand not to say a word about the situation. I also

*Meeting Mister Baston*

thought you could accompany Bella tomorrow morning while she shows Violet's portrait around the village. They may have stopped to rest here."

"Surely I could do that on my own," Alistair said. He did not need the lady following him about, making the task more difficult than it ought to be.

"Yes," the duke drawled, "but we must keep Bella happy. And what better way to keep a young lady happy than to make her feel useful?"

Alistair arched a brow. Such a peculiar idea. But he had to admit, the man was a genius for thinking of it. He nodded and wondered how the lady would feel having him as an escort, as she did not seem to enjoy his company within their carriage—which was quite a foreign feeling, he had to admit. He was much more used to women openly seeking him out for the pleasure of his company, rather than rolling their eyes every time they laid eyes upon him.

A servant had arrived with a crystal decanter of brandy and placed it in the center of the table. Alistair murmured his thanks and poured a glass of the amber liquid for each gentleman.

"Baston, how long will it take you to question the locals?" the captain asked.

He shrugged his shoulders. "Only a few hours, I imagine." Any longer and Lady Isabella may just cut him with her dagger.

"Perfect. We should be in Bicester before sunset, I presume." Captain Lucas stood and drew the route on the map. "From Bicester, we will travel north-west to Stratford-upon-Avon."

George had risen from his seat and placed his pointer

## Chapter Seven

finger on the map. "But, would it not be faster to head north to Rugby?"

Captain Lucas stepped around the table and placed himself next to the duke. "There is no direct route from Bicester to Rugby." He slid his finger across the paper. "We would have to travel east to Luton, then north to Rugby. It would be a much longer journey."

Alistair gazed down at his drink and swirled the brandy in his glass. He no longer listened to the gentlemen bicker about which direction to take the carriages. He glanced at the ring on his finger and thought of his father.

*I wear it to remind myself to be a better man than he ever was...* He looked up from his ring. Lady Isabella sat diagonally from his own table. She seemed to be writing—no, drawing?

Alistair had studied her for a few moments and watched as she brought the pencil to her lip—almost seductively. She was beautiful, of course, with her long golden hair that reached just below her bust, her glittering blue eyes and full pouting lips.

Alistair's eyes left her lips, and she began staring at him contentedly. Actually, not just staring... She had a sense of longing in her expression. And she was not looking into his eyes... Isabella was looking at something further down his face. His nose? No...

His *mouth*.

His lips curved up into a smile on their own accord.

Just then, their eyes met, and the pencil tumbled from its place on her lip.

Now, this was interesting.

## Chapter Eight

Isabella watched in horror as Alistair rose from his seat and strolled toward her in all of his masculine grace. She focused her eyes on the white plaster wall beyond Simon's shoulder.

Then, of course, her traitorous cheeks flushed as the gentleman settled in the chair beside her.

Alistair reached down to pick up her pencil and set it on the hard oak of the tabletop. Isabella let out a small exhale. "Thank you."

How could she have let the gentleman catch her gaping at him? Being the rake he was, he would surely get the wrong idea. She was merely studying his face for artistic purposes.

"Baston! Good of you to join us." Simon raised his glass in greeting.

Alistair nodded. "May I look?" he asked, reaching for her sketchbook.

"Oh! It is not finish—"

It was too late. The book was already in his hands.

## Chapter Eight

Isabella's heart raced as she watched Alistair study the drawing. She hoped he would not recognize himself since she had not finished his face. His hair was fully sketched, but he could not know it was his own hair.

Glancing over at the drawing, her eyes widened.

She'd drawn his father's ring. She hadn't even remembered adding it.

"Is this... *me*?" he asked, bewildered.

Isabella troubled her lower lip.

"Hand it over." Simon reached across the table and snatched the book out of Alistair's grasp. "Hmm." He thought for a moment. "The face is not finished, but it is most definitely you."

Isabella's cheeks were positively aflame as Simon tossed the sketchbook on the table. What was wrong with her? She *never* blushed.

Alistair picked up her treasured tome, taking one last look.

"It is very bleak, but still rather good." He handed Isabella the sketchbook. She plucked it from his hands. "I am quite flattered you would want to draw me, Lady Isabella," he teased.

She flipped the pages closed and gripped the book against her chest. "I am not finished," she seethed. One was never to gaze upon a portrait before it was completed.

"I see." He smiled. "Say, should you not be tossing daggers at trees, or shooting squirrels? Something *less* common of the female gender?"

Simon laughed.

*I have never and would never shoot an innocent little squirrel.* "I like drawing." One of the only feminine pursuits she actually enjoyed.

Alistair looked under the table toward her feet. She pulled her ankles under the carved oak chair in response. "Are you still carrying that dagger of yours?"

"Always," Simon answered for her.

"And I will use it again if I have to."

"Again?" Simon questioned.

Alistair chuckled. "She nearly stabbed me when she arrived at Ashbury Hall."

Simon scrutinized her with narrowed eyes.

Isabella glanced from Alistair to Simon, Simon to Alistair. "He deserved it!" Just as he deserved a slicing at this precise moment.

"Come now, what did Alistair do to deserve such treatment?" Simon asked.

Isabella scoffed. "Where shall I start? Keeping me from seeing our father?" She turned and narrowed her eyes on the gentleman in question. "Or putting his hands on me and thrusting me into a wall?"

Simon brought his chin to his chest. "What?" He turned to Alistair. "Baston?"

Ah, one could always rely on Simon to act as the overprotective eldest brother.

Alistair raised his hands, palms facing outward. "I do not deny it. There was a strange woman stomping through the duke's home. What else would you have me do?"

"Strange woman?" Isabella said at the same moment Simon shouted, "Bloody keep your hands to yourself!"

She huffed, crossing her arms over her bodice. *Strange woman... I am not a strange woman. Unconventional? Fine. Strange? Not at all.*

"It was nothing, Reading." Alistair reached across the table

## Chapter Eight

and took hold of Simon's drink. "I believed her to be an intruder, so I did as the duke expected of me." He brought the glass to his mouth and finished its contents in one swallow.

Simon snorted. "In that case, how did a lady such as my sister manage to best you?"

"She caught me off guard."

"Ha!" Simon slapped his palms onto the hard oak of the tabletop. "My little sister took down Alistair Baston. If only I had been there to see it."

"If she had not had her dagger, she would be trapped against that wall even now." Alistair turned to her and winked.

Isabella arched a brow. "I took out my dagger *after* I escaped your hold, Mr. Baston. Do not give a lady less credit than she deserves."

"A lady?" Alistair mimicked her own expression and arched his brow in return. "You are unlike any lady I have ever come upon."

"You are correct on that account." Isabella leaned closer to Alistair, her lips turning up into a cheeky grin. "I do not straddle gentlemen behind closed curtains or allow them to grope my breasts in the middle of societal events. How *did* you make it to Ashbury Hall so quickly after the Middleton ball?" Alistair's green eyes widened and his already chiseled features turned to stone. Good. He knew exactly what she spoke of.

"I-I haven't a clue what you are on about," he stuttered.

Simon burst into a laughing fit.

Satisfied with Alistair's reaction, Isabella slid her chair out from under the table. "If you will excuse me, gentlemen, I have work that needs seeing to." She could not finish

## Meeting Mister Baston

Violet's portrait while seated at a table with these two cumbergrounds.

Alistair rose from his chair and offered his hand. "I will escort you."

Unwittingly trailing her eyes over his well-muscled form, she settled on his gaze. "Thank you, but I can find my own way."

Alistair said nothing, still holding his hand out to her. She glared at him, waiting to see if the gentleman persisted. He did.

Letting out an unladylike groan, Isabella placed her hand in his.

"Do not stray too long. I rarely trust gentlemen to escort my sister, especially gentlemen such as you," Simon warned as Isabella rose from her chair.

"You need not worry about me." Alistair laughed.

"I shall count the minutes!" Simon yelled after them, waving his finger in the air.

Ignoring Simon's shouts, Isabella and Alistair left the room, arm in arm.

They walked down the hall, around a corner, and up the stairs until they reached Isabella's room. She turned to thank him, but her breath caught, not realizing just how close he was—a mere hand breadth away.

Attempting to take a step back, the heel of her satin slipper clashed with the door. She held the sketchbook against her chest as if to use it as a barrier between them. She was not sure why, but Alistair's presence made her uneasy. She tried to put words together to say... well, she wasn't certain, but she needed to say *something*.

Alistair took a half step toward her and reached for her

## Chapter Eight

sketchbook.

"What are you so afraid of?" he whispered, the sound of his voice a soft purr in her ears.

\* \* \*

Alistair understood a true gentleman would not search through a lady's personal items without her permission, but... he was curious. Curious how a strong-willed, stubborn-minded miss who wielded daggers with ease and watched as a gentleman fondled a woman could enjoy drawing.

His fingers grasped the top of Isabella's sketchbook, sliding it from her grip, and taking a moment to admire her long, delicate fingers. He flipped through pages of various sketched landscapes, animals and flowers, and paused at a portrait of the Duke and Duchess of Waverly.

The pair were standing in a ballroom surrounded by chandeliers and candelabras, both dressed in formal evening attire, the duchess's hands on the duke's shoulders, his hands at her waist. Tiny silhouetted figures on the dance floor surrounded them, and they had the widest of grins on their faces. "Beautiful," he breathed.

He searched through the last few pages until he reached *his* portrait. "Are you going to finish it?"

She snatched the leather book from his hands. "Perhaps," she murmured. "With someone else's face."

"Do not do that." He laughed. Was there a gentleman the lady had eyes for?

"Why not? I do not believe you deserve to be in my

*Meeting Mister Baston*

collection."

Leaning closer, he whispered into her ear. "I do not believe it matters whether I *deserve* it... You will want me in your precious little book either way." Alistair noted the way the lady's cheeks flushed, the way her breath quickened. He could sense her wariness of him—and he reveled in it.

If there *was* a gentleman, Alistair was sure she'd soon forget him.

Bringing his fingertips to her cheek, he forced Isabella to face him. "You are blushing."

Their eyes met. "It is not what you think." Alistair noted the slight tremble in the lady's voice.

"And what do I think?" He flashed her one of his inviting grins.

"I..." She troubled her lower lip, the sight sending a rush of blood to the front of his breeches.

"You were outside the alcove that night," he whispered. "Did you enjoy watching us?" He placed his mouth a hair's breadth from her own. "Watching me?"

The lady's breath trembled against his lips, and they stood there, together, for what seemed like an eternity.

"It is getting late." Isabella's eyes fell to the floor, breaking their connection.

Alistair took a step back, making space between them, and Simon's words trickled into his mind. *I shall count the minutes...* Not that Alistair had planned to charm his way into her chambers, though it would prove quite entertaining. Alas, she was his employer's daughter. Even he, rake as he was, appreciated she was off limits.

For now, he would just have to enjoy baiting her.

*What are you doing? She is the duke's daughter,* the little voice

## Chapter Eight

in his head reminded him again, causing guilt to sting at his chest.

He took her free hand and raised it to his lips. "Until tomorrow, my lady."

Isabella slipped her hand free of his grasp. "Do not think you can make me one of your playthings." She stabbed his chest with her pointer finger, the unexpectedness of the attack causing him to stumble backward. "I know what you are." She took a step forward. "I know what you *do*." Her blue eyes glared up toward him, her nose high in the air, and her face hard and stern. "And I will not let you ruin me, *Mr. Baston*." She spat out his name as if it was poison on her tongue, then disappeared into her room.

Alistair released a breath.

*I've never been so damned afraid of a woman in the whole of my life...*

Lady Isabella Avery just proved herself to be quite terrifying.

## Chapter Nine

Isabella spent the next few hours staring at the wooden beams that stretched across the ceiling of her room.

She replayed the memory of Mr. Baston's touch over and over again in her mind, still sensing the heat radiating from his body, discovering new details about the gentleman she had not seen before.

The small flecks of amber dancing around his emerald eyes. The slight hint of mint on his breath. The way her body changed when he was near. The way it became something new and full of life.

*He is a rake.* One whose purpose in life was to make ladies swoon. One of the seductive men mothers warn their daughters to stay away from. *Remember the ball?* Alistair's hands were all over the dark-haired woman. Did he use his rakish powers to seduce her into the alcove?

Disappointment squeezed in her breast.

*Were you hoping he'd be different?*

She dragged a pillow over her face. *Why do I care at all?*

*Chapter Nine*

If Alistair were a rake, her father would never have trusted him enough to act as her personal guard—*or* leave her without a chaperone in the gentleman's company.

Mayhap he was a secret rake. Or mayhap he was no rake at all... Perhaps he actually fancied her?

No.

No one fancied her aside from Lord Middleton.

Isabella groaned as she forced a cushion under her head and contemplated whether or not she would finish Alistair's portrait.

*You will want me in your precious little book...* Alistair's words from earlier in the evening came back to taunt her. She did not necessarily *want* his image forever burned onto the pages of her sketchbook. It was a drawing and nothing more.

Isabella let out a huff and flipped the pages of her sketchbook, returning to Violet's unfinished portrait. Alistair had occupied her thoughts enough for one night. She needed to finish Violet's sketch if she wished to aid in the search for her sister.

The next morning, Isabella sat in front of the bow-fronted dressing table, attempting to pin her hair back.

She was failing miserably.

With a grunt, she tossed the pins onto the table's surface. Her hair would just have to be left as is.

A loud knock came from the door—presumably, her brother to accompany her into town. Isabella took one last look in the mirror and smoothed out the pale-blue fabric of her muslin skirts.

Her mother once said the color made her sapphire eyes stand out all the more.

Which was rubbish.

## Meeting Mister Baston

Isabella's eyes could never compare to the ice-blue depths of her sister's gaze. When they were small girls, they would dress up in their mother's old gowns. Violet would always comment about the beauty of Isabella's fair hair and the deep blue color of her eyes.

*"You are far prettier than I, dear Bella. You will be sure to find a husband the moment you are of age..."*

It was true, Isabella's light hair and statuesque frame were more appealing to the gentlemen of the *ton*, but, ultimately, her unusual hobbies scared said gentleman away. She was never one to show off her more feminine abilities, such as sketching and dancing. Violet... she loved performing for others, as she should. Her sister's voice was angelic.

*"Oh, hogwash. Once they hear you sing and play you will be sure to have all the gentlemen falling at your feet..."*

With a frown, Isabella grabbed her cloak and opened the door. A pair of emerald eyes greeted her.

"Alistair!" Her hand flew to her heart. "Why..." *are you standing in my doorway appearing more handsome than yesterday?*

Donning dark leather boots, cream-colored breeches and a forest-green jacket which brought far too much attention to his strong shoulders, Alistair arched a single brow. "Why... have I not shaved yet?" He brought his fingers to the stubble on his cheek. "I have quite the baby face, you know."

With his sharp, angular features and masculine jaw, she highly disagreed with that statement.

He winked. Why did the gentleman always wink? Was it meant to be endearing? Was it meant to make a lady swoon? *Such tricks will not work on me,* she reminded herself.

"I... I was expecting Simon." Catching herself staring, she

## Chapter Nine

turned away from his gaze and twisted the key inside the lock.

"Your brother is to help plan our journey to Derby." Alistair held out an arm, and she placed a hesitant hand in its crook. *How long did it take to draw out routes on a map?* Surely she could master the art of shooting in less time.

"You look disappointed, my lady."

"I do not appreciate my father tying you to my person."

"I am not exactly tied to you. Although, I am not opposed to the idea." He smirked.

An image came to Isabella's mind of Alistair and herself bound together by their wrists.

Her cheeks burned.

Alistair brought his mouth to her ear. "A penny for your thoughts, my lady."

Her mouth fell open, and she whipped around to face the gentleman, their noses nearly colliding. "No amount of money will let you in on my thoughts, sir." Why was she thinking of such things anyhow?

"Ouch!" His hand flew to his chest, feigning a pain at his heart.

Endearing as it was, Isabella ignored the gentleman's sarcasm and yanked on her cloak. She motioned to the staircase. "Shall we?"

"My lady." Alistair bowed his head.

They made their way outside where a carriage was waiting, but something caught Isabella's eye. Her brother stood near the stables with both hands clenched in tight fists at his sides. Callum Diggory, the footman, stood opposite Simon, a smug grin pulling at the corners of the servant's mouth. Simon took his right hand and shoved it into Mr. Diggory's

*Meeting Mister Baston*

shoulder, causing the young man to stumble backward.

Were they in the midst of an argument?

"You had better get used to it, my lady." Alistair cut into her musings. "We will be spending a good amount of time together these next few days."

She furrowed her brows, wishing there was not a need to go on this journey in the first place.

"Traveling the country together," Alistair continued. "The long, *bumpy* carriage rides." He waggled his brows.

Isabella's thoughts jumped to the moment her face nearly landed in the gentleman's groin. Her entire body flushed at the memory.

The coachman held open the carriage door. Isabella glanced back to where her brother stood just moments ago—he and Mr. Diggory were gone—and she stepped into the hired hack and took her seat.

The vehicle was quite small, with one bench instead of the usual two, so Isabella was forced to sit next to Alistair.

"Hopefully this journey will not be quite as bumpy," he jested.

She pressed her lips together in an attempt to stifle a smile. It did not work. Though the gentleman beside her could prove to be aggravating, she would admit he was also quite charming at times.

"Ah, she smiles. And here I thought you'd become hard of hearing somewhere between your room and the carriage."

Isabella narrowed her eyes, relaxing her smile. "Do Simon and Mr. Diggory get on well?"

"The footman?" Alistair placed an ankle atop his knee, bringing his muscled thigh into contact with her own slender one. "Why do you ask?"

## Chapter Nine

Isabella eyed the fabric of his trousers and slid herself further from the gentleman. "They appeared to be arguing." About what, she hadn't a clue. Perhaps her brother lost a bet to the footman. Simon was always one to gamble, and more often than not, he did not see himself on the winning side.

"Hmmm..." Alistair turned to face her, causing their legs to touch once more. "Now that you mention it, Reading has been rather distant—and useless, if you ask my opinion." His knee matched the bounce of the carriage and landed atop hers with each bump. "He'd rather be off in his own company drinking spirits instead of assisting."

Perhaps Violet's disappearance affected Simon more than she'd thought.

*Thump. Thump.*

Isabella watched as Alistair's knee bounced atop hers. Her chest tightened with annoyance or... something else? She attempted to slide down the bench only for her shoulder to meet with the glass of the windowpane.

Alistair's knee landed atop hers once more. "Must you do that?" she gritted out between clenched teeth.

"Do what?" The gentleman cocked his head.

She slashed her hand through the air *"That!"* His knee grazed hers again. "You are taking up the entirety of the carriage."

Alistair flashed her a crooked grin. "My apologies, my lady. I did not consider you so innocent that you could not handle a brushing of knees." He returned his foot to the floor, putting a stop to his relaxed position.

*So innocent?* Isabella huffed. "It is not that." She lied. "I am not used to being so... so..."

"Close to a gentleman?" Alistair whispered, arching a dark

## Meeting Mister Baston

auburn brow.

*Yes.* "No." She crossed her arms over her chest. "I am not used to being cramped inside such a small carriage."

Alistair let out a bark of laughter.

"What is it?"

"It seems I have forgotten you are a duke's daughter," he said scornfully. "You must be so used to your fine carriages, with velvet cushions and room enough to seat six. It is a wonder you are in your third Season." He muttered those last words.

That is not what she'd meant at all! She was in her third Season because she chose to be. There were a great deal of suitors for her—that was, until they actually sat down and had a proper conversation with her, and learned Lady Isabella Avery was, in fact, *not* the fragile flower they expected her to be. "Oh? And life must have been so difficult for you, Mr. Baston?" she countered. "Being the son of a viscount, is it?"

Alistair turned to face the windowpane. "You have no idea," he mumbled.

The gentleman's voice turned again. Her heart sank. She much preferred him when he was the sarcastic, charming rake, or the mocking gentleman who would judge her for her privileged upbringing.

*This.* This sorrowful expression reflected upon the windowpane was far too much for her to handle. "*You* are still unmarried." She attempted to bring back the teasing man she'd spoken to moments ago. "And I do not recall you at any of the *ton* events." Apart from the last one, of course.

"Because I do not particularly enjoy mingling with such people," he said dryly.

## Chapter Nine

*Such people?* "Yet you work for my father."

"He is... different." He shifted in his seat. "Your family is different."

"How so?" she asked with a hungering need. When one called Isabella "different" it was not usually in a polite way.

"You have daggers strapped to your legs, for starters." There was a small hint of a smile reflecting through the windowpane. "A gift from your father. What man would give his young daughter a weapon as a gift?"

"It is just the one dagger," she pointed out. "And I suppose it is because my father is, as you said, different than most." Isabella suppressed a smile. She supposed being different was not such a bad thing, after all.

\* \* \*

*You are still unmarried...* Isabella's words echoed throughout Alistair's mind.

Yes, at seven-and-twenty, he was indeed at an age where one would look to settle down and have a family. But what need did he have for a wife? He was nothing more than a spare to the heir, which his father had reminded him of quite often. He was not a titled gentleman, and therefore, there was no urgency for him to have children. Unlike his brother.

Of course, Alistair wanted to have children...

Eventually.

The carriage rolled to a halt, signally their arrival at Amersham market. Alistair stepped out and offered his hand to Isabella. She laid her long, elegant fingers in his palm as she stepped down with perfect grace.

*Meeting Mister Baston*

Isabella dug around her satchel and yanked out her beloved leather tome that housed her sister's portrait.

"May I?" Alistair motioned for her sketchbook. "We can begin questioning the patrons at the market stalls."

Isabella brought her sketchbook protectively into her chest. "Violet is my sister. Surely I should be the one doing the questioning."

The lady's stubbornness came to light. She was correct on one part. Violet was her sister, but Alistair was the gentleman. He could not let the lady interview these strangers. Without a word, Alistair gave her a pointed look and motioned for the sketchbook once more.

With a flare of her nostrils, Lady Isabella handed over the precious tome.

Alistair eyed an old woman perusing the fruit stalls. Surely she would be easy enough to approach. "Stay behind me," he ordered. "Excuse me, madame." Alistair approached the old woman and flipped open the sketchbook to Violet's portrait.

The old woman turned to face him. She eyed the sketchbook and gave him a disgusted look. "I ain't posin' for ya. Go on and leave me be."

Alistair scoffed. As if he would want to sketch an old woman. Even if he had such a talent, he would use the ability to sketch beautiful *young* women. Preferably in the nude. "You misunderstand me, madame. I simply—"

"I said NO!" The old woman whacked him on the arm with her wicker basket, with surprising strength, and marched off into the market.

Unbelievable. He rubbed his sore arm and checked his jacket for tearing. A slow clapping came from behind.

"Amazing." Isabella continued her clapping. "How very

## Chapter Nine

impressive. Your interview skills are beyond compare. Are you positive you do not work for the brethren?"

*Minx.*

Isabella closed the distance between them and snatched the sketchbook from Alistair's hands. "My turn, Mr. Baston."

Alistair watched as Isabella approached the same grouch of a woman. He shook his head. Surely the lady did not believe she could get anything other than an argument out of the old hag.

"Pardon me." Isabella stood next to the old woman, attempting to get her attention. "I was curious as to where you bought your basket? It is truly a work of art."

The old woman pulled the basket close to her person. "M-my granddaughter made it for me. She truly is an accomplished young lady."

*Unbelievable.* They were there to gather information about Lady Violet, not to discuss the creation of wicker baskets. Alistair stood in his place near the lane as the two women conversed. He tapped the toe of his boot and waited until Isabella took out her sketchbook and presented it to the old woman.

A few minutes later, Isabella returned to his side with a cocky grin plastered over her features. "And?"

"Violet did not look familiar to her."

Alistair cocked his head in confusion. "Why are you still smirking?"

"Because." Isabella gave a little shrug. "The woman at least spoke with me without feeling the need to strike me with her basket."

*Bloody hell.* "You are enjoying this, are you?"

"I am." She gave a curt nod and stood with her arms crossed

*Meeting Mister Baston*

in that expectant way of hers.

She was waiting for him to say more.

"Yes?" he asked.

"Are you going to let me continue with the interviews?"

Stubborn. She was nothing short of stubborn. Alistair sighed, but ultimately agreed. "Fine. But I will be by your side the entire time."

The lady glanced about the bustling market. "Who shall we question next?"

Such an odd creature she was. Isabella held herself as a perfectly proper noblewoman, possessed an angelic-like beauty that surely made gentlemen fall to their knees, yet handled a dagger better than any street rough.

After visiting two bakeries, the butcher, a salon and the public market, the proud and confident Lady Isabella appeared discouraged. Having found no new leads on the whereabouts of her sister, Alistair decided a stroll through the village gardens would do her well.

"I do hope Violet is all right." Isabella sighed, watching her feet as she walked.

"As do I."

"I cannot help but believe this was all her doing." She let out a small chuckle. "Like some sort of scheme. Violet will show up perfectly well at home and laugh at us all." Tears swelled in her blue eyes. "When we were children, we would often play hide and seek at our country home in Surrey. Violet was— *is*," she corrected, "the greatest at finding the best hiding places. She once hid in a cupboard for *hours* and only emerged because she was in need of a chamber pot."

Alistair could not help but smile at her lightheartedness. He knew she was attempting to mask her worry. "We will

## Chapter Nine

find her." He placed his hand on hers and gave a reassuring squeeze. "I promise you."

Isabella studied their joint hands and sighed. "Do not make promises you cannot keep."

"I will keep it." He paused and flashed her one of his charming grins. "A gentleman never goes back on his word." Though the lady was correct. He could not guarantee they would find her sister.

Only having observed Lady Violet from a distance, Alistair could not be certain as to whether she was the type to sneak off and elope with a gentleman, but hearing of her free spirit, he would not be surprised if she'd done just that.

Stopping at a park bench, Isabella plucked a small yellow primrose from its place in the ground. "Do you expect she is hurt?" she asked, stroking the tiny satin petals.

Alistair gave her forearm a sympathetic touch. "It is best not to think of such things."

Isabella glanced down to where his hand lay. "Why is that?"

"I..." Alistair's words stuck in his throat. "I... *do not know.*"

*Dash it.* And here he thought he was a charming rogue who had a way with words.

She slipped away from his touch and brought her eyes to his. "Am I supposed to believe all is well? That she went off to visit our relatives in the north, and be done with it?" Her eyes narrowed. "We *need* to think of such things in order to figure out where she has gone. She could be in danger—all the more reason we should be out there searching instead of sitting here on this bench pretending everything is all well and good."

She threw the small flower to the ground and took in a deep breath. Alistair watched as she closed her eyes and tilted

## Meeting Mister Baston

her face to the sun. She was not wearing a bonnet, which left her hair to fall freely about her shoulders.

He fought the urge to reach out and take a lock between his fingers. Isabella's décolletage rose and fell as she slowly inhaled the fresh spring air. Alistair's pulse quickened, bringing a flow of heat straight to his groin—a sensation he was not prepared for.

Turning away, he straightened his shoulders and brought his eyes to focus on a distant tree. Yes, a tree should be just the thing to keep his thoughts at bay.

*The tree is tall. The tree is green—*

"Are you unwell?" Concern lingered in Isabella's voice. "You look a bit pale."

His body tensed. "No—" He cleared his throat. "I mean, *yes*, I am fine. Just woolgathering."

"About your father?" She placed a hand on his shoulder.

His father? Why would he be thinking about his miserable sire? He glanced down to where she had settled her palm, the warmth of her touch melting through his layers of clothing.

Alistair hastily rose from the bench. He took a few steps forward, trying to distance himself from the duke's siren of a daughter, and nodded in response to her question.

It was a lie, of course. He could not possibly tell her what he was *actually* thinking.

"Mr. Baston?" Isabella called out.

He shook his head to clear the devilish thoughts from his mind. What was wrong with him? He was acting like a green boy who had never spent time with a woman before, and Isabella was nothing special. She was a prim and proper lady of the *ton*. Well, mayhap not so proper, but still a lady of the *ton*.

## Chapter Nine

He had bedded plenty of women much more appealing than Lady Isabella. Pulling his jacket by the hem, he took in a deep breath and returned to the bench.

With a slight bow, he held out his hands in offering. "Shall we return?"

\* \* \*

Alistair helped her to her feet and pressed his mouth against the bare skin of her knuckles. Innocent as the gesture was, Isabella could not help but shiver from the gentleman's wet lips against her skin, only just realizing she forgot to don gloves. She stood frozen, her body incapable of movement. The pulsing in her fingertips was the only true evidence she was even still alive and breathing.

With flushed cheeks, her eyes fell to her feet. *Get ahold of yourself.* Dragging her gaze up, she forced her lips into a smile.

What was it about the gentleman at her side? Alistair confused her, excited her and annoyed her all at the same time. She'd spent a good deal of time with other gentlemen, all innocent of course, and they never caused her mind to run havoc.

Lord Middleton, who had called upon her more than once, was handsome enough to make any woman melt at his feet. But he was dull. She could not remember a time she had seen him laugh... *truly* laugh. He'd always been polite and proper during their outings. He never teased her, never made her so much as chuckle.

A pang of guilt niggled in the back of her mind. She should

not be pondering such things while her sister was missing. Her mind should be set on trying to find Violet, *not* the way Alistair filled her traitorous body with butterflies.

She slowly slid her bare hands from his grasp and started toward the carriage. Isabella shivered as the wind grew brisk. The clouds moved and covered the warm rays of the sun.

She hoped Violet was somewhere safe and warm. She hoped her sister was not lost somewhere out of doors without the basic necessities.

"It looks as though it may rain," Alistair announced from behind.

She grimaced. "The skies were blue not twenty minutes ago."

Alistair appeared at her side. "Welcome to England."

Indeed. A country where one could experience all four seasons in a single day.

They arrived at the corner of Chapel Street and Church Street, where the conveyance left them two hours earlier. "What is the time?" she asked as she rubbed her bare hands together, longing for warmth.

Alistair pulled a golden watch fob from his jacket and flipped open its face. "Ten past noon."

"He is late," she growled, growing more and more irritated—not with the weather, but with herself. Why did the gentleman so easily distract her from the task at hand? There was something about Alistair's touch, his emerald gaze boring into hers, that made her forget why they were here.

*It is his roguish charm.*

"Stupid. Stupid," she muttered to herself.

"What was that?" Alistair asked.

"Nothing."

## Chapter Nine

"Give him a few more minutes." He laughed, misinterpreting the reason for her irritation. "I am certain the man is on his way."

Tiny drops of rain sprinkled over Isabella's frock. She cursed under her breath.

"Here." Alistair tugged at the sleeves of his jacket. "Take this; you look frigid."

"Please, keep it." Her teeth chattered. "I have a hood and you do not." She could not possibly ask him to remove his only jacket for the sake of her comfort.

With one arm already out of his sleeve, Alistair made his way over to her—

"*No.*" Isabella took a step back. She did not need nor want the gentleman's pity. What she needed was to focus on the task at hand. "I told you; I am fine."

Alistair paused, his brows stitched together as he searched her features. "As you wish, my lady." He took a step back and slipped his arm inside his jacket.

Isabella sighed with relief and tugged the hood over her head to shield herself from the rain. Restless, she began to pace. Three steps to the left, three steps to the right. It was the only way to relieve the aggravation swarming within her chest.

She stared at Alistair. His wet auburn hair clung to his forehead. Droplets of rain traced the masculine planes of his face. His jacket, now damp, clung to the muscles of the gentleman's chest and shoulders.

She peeled her eyes away.

*Admit it. You are attracted to him.*

She was not. She could not...

Isabella tripped over her own foot and cursed.

*Meeting Mister Baston*

"You are going to roll an ankle," Alistair warned.

She broke her stride and turned to face him. "I am not going to roll—" The heavy rain turned into a downpour. "Oh, wonderful!" She crossed her arms over her chest. The fabric of her cloak and hood darkened as the rain soaked through, the ends of her hair damp and tangled.

Alistair threw his head back and laughed.

*He is laughing at me!*

The gentleman grasped her upper arm and began dragging her down the muddied lane. "What are you doing? Where are we going?"

"We are getting you out of the rain," he put simply.

The bounder. "I can take care of myself."

"Of course you can. But I am afraid your dagger cannot shield you from the rain."

Isabella sputtered as the rain dripped down from her hood. Was he teasing her?

They reached the overhang of one of the shops. "Better?" Alistair asked, releasing his grip.

*Actually...* "Yes, thank you. But," she added, rubbing her sore arm, "did you have to grip me so tightly? You may have left a bruise."

"Do you wish me to kiss it for you, my lady?" He made his words sound like a dare.

She took a half step backward and attempted not to focus on the charmingly boyish grin, which currently took up half of Mr. Baston's face. "Do not be ridiculous."

But he winked instead, which left her strangely disappointed.

The sound of a horse's trot came from the distance. "My apologies, Mr. Baston, my lady," the coachman said as the

## Chapter Nine

horses slowed to a stop. "One of the stallions became ill, and we had to ready a replacement."

"It is quite all right. Although—" Alistair flashed Isabella a devilish smile "—Lady Isabella may be coming down with a cold."

She turned to him. "I am certain I will be just fine." *Cheeky dastard.*

Alistair stepped inside the cramped carriage and situated himself on the bench next to her. Isabella lifted her hand to the window curtain, opening it just enough to let a small beam of light illuminate the dark space. She turned to follow the glittering ray when her eyes landed on a single purple daisy held gently in Alistair's grasp. "What is this?"

"It is for you," he answered as the carriage lurched forward.

One minute the gentleman was a dastard and the next he was charming. Isabella sighed. She would never understand him. "Where did you get it?" she asked.

He lowered the delicate flower to her hands. "The gardens. I thought you might appreciate it."

"You stole from a public garden?" With an enticing smile, she added, "How wicked of you, Mr. Baston."

"Wicked, indeed." He winked.

She reached out to pluck the daisy from his hand, her mood becoming slightly more pleasant. "Where were you hiding it?"

"Where do you imagine I was hiding it?" His eyes narrowed.

Unthinking, she glanced down to the hard muscles of his thighs, which strained his breeches. Catching herself, she quickly returned her eyes to his.

Alistair laughed. "What a filthy mind you have, Lady

Isabella. I swear to you, it was just hiding inside my waistcoat pocket."

Bringing a hand over her lips, Isabella felt her cheeks burn. "I swear I was not looking at *that*; I was just... looking." *At his well-muscled legs.*

Alistair raised his brows in response.

"I was looking, but not *focusing* on what I was looking upon." She lied. "Do you understand?"

"Oh, of course," he answered, with a sarcastic nod.

Isabella rolled her eyes, hoping he had not noticed the flush staining her cheeks. "Well, thank you. I appreciate you stealing this flower for me."

"You are very welcome, my lady."

Her eyes dropped to the delicate petals of the flower as a smile tugged at the corners of her mouth.

## Chapter Ten

Isabella woke with a burn in her throat. The morning light sent a wave of pain through her skull—if it, in fact, was still morning. Bringing her fingertips to her temples, she attempted to rub away the stabbing pain.

*Damn that Alistair.* He must have cursed her somehow. *Lady Isabella may be coming down with a cold,* he'd said.

"I am sure I will be all right, I'd said." Isabella mocked her past self. She'd been perfectly well yesterday—before the rain and before Alistair's cursing words.

Isabella rose up from her comfortable position, surprised by the unexpected knock at the door. She yanked the covers up to her chin. "Come in…"

The door swung open. "I see you forgot to lock your door again—" Simon winced. "Dear God. You look dreadful."

Isabella relaxed her posture. "Oh. It is you." Her hand then reached up to her tangled mass of hair. It was nice to know she looked as unpleasant as she felt.

"Were you expecting someone else?" Simon closed the

door behind him and made his way over to the decrepit wooden chair in the corner of the room.

"I was half expecting Mr. Baston to come through the door," she muttered.

"Baston?" He raised a brow in question. "Has Baston been seeking you out in your room?"

"Do not be ridiculous, Simon. Father has him follow me around like a puppy dog." She felt a tickle in her nose and sneezed into her arm.

"Yes..." Simon narrowed his eyes into thin slits. "Has he tried anything?"

Her cheeks grew warm. "No— I mean, not really."

"What do you mean 'not really?'" He stood from his chair and tightened his hands into fists. "Has he put his hands on you?"

"No!" *Yes*. He did touch her cheek and kiss her hand, but her brother need not be aware of every small detail.

Simon's blue eyes studied her for a moment. Then, returning to his position in the chair, he unclenched his hands. "If he does, I will kill him."

"You will do no such thing!" Isabella sniffled and reached for her handkerchief on the nightstand. She had no doubt her ill-tempered brother would harm any gentleman who made unwanted advances toward his siblings—as she had witnessed a few nights prior.

Raising a dark brow, Simon crossed his arms over his chest. "Nevertheless... Father sent me to fetch you since you have yet to come down for breakfast. But I can see you are ill. I will have a servant bring a tray up for you, and you will eat *all* of it," he ordered. "We do not need your illness setting our journey back any further."

## Chapter Ten

Isabella dropped a hand to her roaring belly. "I can eat, I suppose. But if I vomit, it will be your doing."

"*Lovely,*" he said with a roll of his eyes. "I shall send for some food." Simon stood from his seat and made his way to the door. His expression turning serious, he said, "Do tell me if Baston does anything to upset you."

*Upset* would not be the word she would use. Unsettle? Perhaps…

Exasperate? Most definitely.

Oh! She'd nearly forgotten. "Wait!" Simon paused before he reached the door. "What was your argument with Mr. Diggory about?"

Her brother stiffened. "Argument?"

"Yes. I saw the two of you arguing by the stables yesterday morn." Surely her brother had not forgotten.

"Do not worry yourself over it."

"You shoved him, Simon."

He turned to her, his expression stern. "I *said*, do not worry yourself. It is men's business."

Simon turned the handle and left.

Isabella raised her fingertips to her mouth and began biting her nails. Was her brother hiding something from her?

\* \* \*

Novel in hand, Alistair made his way back to his room. Since Isabella was bedridden for the day, their journey to Derby had been delayed.

His room was two doors down from the lady's, and he began to wonder about her well-being. He could not help but feel slightly guilty she caught the chill during their little endeavor in the rain. It was a silly thing to feel guilty for. Surely it was not his fault the carriage was late or that the weather had turned.

*Hell*, she may very well have been ill before all of that.

A pair of footsteps echoed from ahead. A servant turned the corner, carrying a silver food tray. It must have been for Isabella since she had not come below stairs for her morning meal.

"You, there." Alistair motioned the servant over. "Where are you headed?"

"Lord Reading requested a tray be brought up for his sister, sir."

"I will take that for you. I was just about to check in on her." He cleared his throat. "She being ill and all."

The young man narrowed his eyes. "And who are you to the lady, sir?"

"*Erm*…" Alistair tugged at his suddenly too-tight cravat. "I am her betrothed, of course," he lied.

After a long, scrutinizing moment passed, the servant bowed and handed Alistair the tray. "Of course, sir."

Alistair tucked his copy of *Gulliver's Travels* inside his jacket pocket and accepted the silver tray. He waited for the servant to turn the corner before he made his way to the lady's room. Using the knuckles of his free hand, he rapped on the center of the door.

"Enter." Isabella's muffled voice emerged from beyond the wood panel.

He turned the handle and opened the door enough that he was able to peek inside.

Isabella was sat upright in bed with her nose behind a book.

## Chapter Ten

It looked to be Miss Austen's latest novel, *Persuasion*.

He took a few short steps to enter the room and closed the door softly behind him, not wishing to alert her of his presence.

"You may set it on the nightstand." She motioned to the table beside her, her eyes trained on the leather tome in her hands.

Alistair obeyed without saying a word and set the tray on the table.

She flipped a page. "Thank you."

He bowed. "You are very welcome, *my lady*."

"Alistair!" Isabella slammed her book closed. "What are you doing in my room?"

"I thought I would check in." He flashed her one of his boyish grins.

"Well, good heavens, you could have announced yourself." She set the small leather tome on her lap.

Alistair walked to the chair at the foot of her bed. "Where is the fun in that?"

She watched him as he lifted the wooden piece and brought it closer to the head of the bed. Setting the chair in front of the nightstand, he sat down. "How are you faring?"

"Wonderful," she drawled.

Alistair chuckled and motioned to the silver tray. "Are you going to eat?" He would admit, she did look a bit disheveled, but it did nothing to distract him from the fact she was still in her night shift.

"Yes." She paused. "When you leave."

"You are not going to share?" He *was* quite hungry… again. And baiting Isabella was an entertaining pastime.

Isabella snorted. "I am quite sure you've already had your

morning meal."

"Yes, but I could go for a light snack." He leaned back in the wooden chair and set his ankle atop his knee. "Tis almost noon, after all." Isabella rolled her eyes and let out a harsh exhale of air followed by three small coughs. "You do not want to be alone *all* day, do you? It will be very boring."

"I have not been alone all day. My brother came to visit just before you. Besides—" she lifted her book to her chest "—I am quite enjoying this book."

"You would be the sort to read an Austen novel," Isabella was still a lady of the *ton*. So why did it surprise him to find her reading a dull romance novel?

Her eyes narrowed. "And what is wrong with Jane Austen?"

"Other than the fact her stories are tedious and predictable?" He shrugged. "She gives women false hope."

"False hope?"

He leaned forward. "False hope of a fairy-tale existence." His life had been far from a fairy tale. Such silly stories of family, love and hope just ensured a lady's disappointment once she stepped foot into society.

"These stories are hardly fairy tales. And how would you know?" She crossed her arms over her chest, which now brought his attention to the swell of her breasts. "Have you read any of her work?"

He raised his gaze. "This morning, actually. In the library." When he was attempting to find anything *other* than romance novels to read.

The lady scoffed. "One can hardly form an opinion of her work by simply reading part of a novel for a few short minutes."

He had actually been reading an Austen novel for a few

## Chapter Ten

*hours* rather than minutes. But he would never admit as much. Alistair gazed to the ceiling and smiled. "I cannot believe I am discussing Jane Austen with you."

She cocked her head to the side. "What would you rather discuss?"

*The fact that you are perfectly comfortable being ill in your night shift in front of a near stranger?* His eyes came back to focus on her. "What about the daggers you hide under your skirts?"

She rolled her eyes. "Are you *still* going on about that?"

"Yes," he laughed. "I have never met a lady who strapped daggers to her legs."

"It is just the one dagger." Isabella smiled and reached for the handle of the tray cover. "You really should not be here, you know."

No, he should not… Alistair yanked off the tray cover before the lady could reach it. "Oh, quite an array we have here. Eggs, pastries, meats, jam, and fruits." He smiled innocently. "Where shall I start?"

Isabella glared at him. "You may have *one* blueberry."

"Just one?"

"Just one," she confirmed.

"You are a greedy little chit," he jested.

"I am ill and must do all I can to get better." She lifted the tray from the nightstand and set it on her lap. "Which includes eating all that is on this tray."

She was unlike any lady of the *ton* he'd ever met. Most were polite figures of perfection with cold expressions and even colder hearts. "I doubt you can finish all of it on your own,"

"Watch me." She plucked a single blueberry off her tray

*Meeting Mister Baston*

and tossed it in Alistair's direction.

Alistair grabbed it from the air and popped the small berry into his mouth.

Isabella's head jerked to the door.

"What is it?" Alistair asked, noticing her change in demeanor.

She waved her hand through the air. "Shhh! Someone is coming."

They both stayed quiet and motionless as they listened to a pair of footsteps creeping closer...

"Bella? Are you decent?"

It was her father.

Alistair searched for a place to hide. There was under the lady's bed, but it was fairly high off the ground, and one could see underneath quite easily... There was also the window, which he could jump out of. They were only on the second story, and he could—

Isabella turned to Alistair with wide eyes. "Hide! Quickly!"

"Where?" Alistair whispered as he stood from his chair.

"One moment, Papa!" Isabella scanned over the small room, keeping her position under the bed covers. "In the wardrobe. Quickly!"

"Are you feeling well?" the duke asked through the wood panel.

"Very well!"

Alistair made it to the wardrobe in three long strides. He glanced at Isabella's door just as the handle started to turn. He opened the wardrobe and slid inside.

"You are eating? That is good to see," he heard as George stepped into the room.

"Yes." She paused. "I had very strict orders from Simon

## Chapter Ten

that I must not skip any meals today."

George laughed as his footfalls echoed through the room. "You are looking quite poorly. Not 'very well' at all."

"Thanks, Papa..." Isabella's voice came through the thin walls of the wardrobe, and Alistair's heart began to race. While crouched inside the small, confined space, his body warmed with nervous energy.

Alistair listened impatiently as the duke and his daughter discussed her meal, the size of her room, the comfort of her bed—all while he was trying to steady his breathing and calm his heart rate. He did not believe himself one that becomes nervous in small spaces, but perhaps he was, and now was not the best time to be discovering such a thing.

"Has Alistair been treating you well?" Alistair perked up at his name. "Or should I say... have *you* been treating Alistair well?"

"Well enough."

"*Bella...*" the duke said scornfully. "The lad is important to me, and therefore, I want you to treat him with the utmost respect."

Alistair's heartstrings pulled. He never knew his employer felt that way about him.

"He has had a difficult life."

His heart stopped. *Do not speak of it. Please do not tell her about my—*

"His father was a cruel man," George continued. "He blamed Alistair for the death of the viscountess."

*No, no, no.* Memories of his father whipping him with the horse crop began flooding his memory. The pain used to be like fire on his back. But Alistair took the frequent beatings with courage; he never let his father see him shed a single

## Meeting Mister Baston

tear, which definitely made his sire all the angrier.

*May the bastard rot in hell.*

"His mother died giving birth to him, and that is all his father saw when he looked at his youngest son. And he beat the poor lad for it. Daily. Can you believe it?"

"That is terrible." Isabella's soft voice came through the thin walls of the wardrobe.

"Yes, well... I should leave you to your rest."

Through the small crevice between the double doors, Alistair watched as the duke began creeping around the foot of Isabella's bed. He stood tall with his hands clasped behind his back and inched ever closer to the wardrobe Alistair was currently sat in.

"What is this?" The duke crouched down and picked something up from the floor.

"What?" Alistair heard Isabella's muffled voice.

"*Gulliver's Travels?*" George questioned.

Alistair held his breath. It must have fallen from his pocket as he slid inside his hiding place.

"It was here when I moved into the room," Isabella attested.

"Have you read it?" the duke asked. "It is quite good."

"Is it? Perhaps I will, then."

Alistair slowly exhaled as George disappeared from his limited line of sight. He listened as the gentleman's heavy footsteps marched toward the door. "I will leave you now. Get some rest."

Once the door opened and closed, there was a quick pitter-patter of feet crossing the floor. The double doors to the wardrobe flew open. Isabella stood in front of Alistair with a doleful expression, still wearing nothing more than her ivory night shift. Both of her arms were outstretched as she held

## Chapter Ten

open the two meager white doors. "Alistair, I—"

"Do not," he warned.

"But I—"

"It is all in the past," he reassured her. And he loathed discussing it. He especially did not wish to discuss his past with *her*.

Isabella's hands slid off the doors and fell to her perfectly rounded hips. "You need to speak about these things. You cannot let it all fester inside your mind."

Alistair huffed. Was she really going to keep on with this? "Does it look as though I am *'festering?'*"

Her eyes searched over his features. "Well, you do look somewhat... sweaty."

He gave her a pointed look. "May I get out now?"

"Oh, my apologies." Isabella took a step to the side and motioned for him to exit the tight space.

Alistair shifted his way around the hanging garments and stepped out. Isabella crossed her arms over her chest and waited. "What is it?"

She shrugged. "Are we going to talk about it?"

"I already told you." He took a few steps closer, stopping when they were almost nose to nose. "*No.*"

Isabella gasped when he grew near. Her décolletage rose and fell with each breath.

"I can think of many—" he brought his hand to her ear and tucked her tangled mass of hair behind the delicate shell. Sliding his fingers along her jaw, he tilted her mouth up to his own "—many other things we can do with our mouths."

*What are you doing?*

*Changing the subject of discussion*, he told himself.

Their breath mingled together as they stood in silence.

## Meeting Mister Baston

Should he wait for her approval? That was what a proper gentleman would do, but Alistair was no proper gentleman. And he needed this. He needed this kiss to distract himself from the images forming in his mind.

*'You killed her...' Thwack!*

*'You are useless...' Crack!*

Alistair squeezed his eyes shut, hoping the action would erase the images in his skull.

It did not.

He slid his hand to the nape of Isabella's neck and tangled his fingers into her blonde hair. Impatiently, he lowered his mouth, but a pair of hands pushed against his chest, and he stumbled backward.

Isabella stood before him with a finger pointed to the door. "Get. Out," she seethed.

His hands rose in the air as he surrendered to the lady's request. He marched toward the dressing table and picked up the discarded copy of *Gulliver's Travels*. "Back to reading it is, then."

Alistair opened the door and poked his head out to be sure there were no lingering servants. All seemed clear, and he quietly stepped out of Isabella's room, closed the panel behind him, then swiped a hand over his face.

*I truly am a bastard.*

With a sigh, Alistair decided a drink was in order. A very strong drink. He turned on his heel and began making his way to the tavern. His footfalls echoed with every step he took through the mahogany-lined hallways.

He let out a curse.

What was he thinking? Attempting to kiss the duke's daughter. Trying to use her as he would use any common

## Chapter Ten

whore. A meaningless tupping to distract himself from his miserable past, a past any other gentleman could easily forget or use to his benefit. Instead, Alistair used it to fuel his depravity. Yes, he had always been good with numbers and investments—which was how he came to work for the duke, after all—but he was even better at seducing women. And seducing women was far more effective at keeping his memories at bay.

But why her? Why the daughter of his employer? A prim and proper lady of the *ton*. Very well... mayhap not the most proper, but she was still an innocent nonetheless.

"*Oomph!*"

Alistair's chest collided with a large figure, causing his book to land on the hard wood of the floor with a loud thump.

"Watch yourself, Baston. I am getting old," the duke teased as he rubbed the muscle of his shoulder.

Alistair watched in a panic as George reached to the floor to rescue his copy of *Gulliver's Travels*. Trailing a finger along the engraved golden text, the duke looked over the spine of the book. "*Gulliver's Travels*, is it?"

"My apologies, Your Grace." Alistair winced at his use of the gentleman's formal title. He gulped and reached out to retrieve the leather tome.

"This must be quite the popular read." George gave him a pointed look, handing Alistair the book.

"Oh?" Alistair inspected its cover nonchalantly. "And why do you say that?"

"Bella had a copy *just* like that one in her room but a moment ago." George arched a brow.

Alistair gulped.

What would he say? *I found it in the library... It is a common book... It is a copy passed down from my great-grandmother and could not possibly be the same.*

No. He would say nothing. Saying nothing surely was the best option. Stay calm and casual. Act aloof.

He gave his employer a shrug of the shoulders and a slap on the back for good measure. As he stalked off, he felt the nobleman's glare burning at the back of his neck.

*He knows...*

## Chapter Eleven

The journey to Bicester was quite idyllic. The grass was so green it almost looked surreal. Charming thatch-roofed cottages were scattered along the roadside. Small hedgerows lined the roads, keeping the dozens of white sheep inside of their grazing sanctuaries.

The weather was unseasonably warm and unseasonably sunny for late April, a welcome change being as Isabella had been soaked by the cold rain just two days prior. The symptoms of her illness had almost vanished. Unfortunately, she still had the occasional cough or sniffle.

The beauty of the rolling hills was almost enough to make her forget the events that happened in her room the previous morn. In fact, the events of the previous morn were the reason she sat inside this carriage with her father instead of Mr. Baston.

She clenched the fabrics of her skirts in tight fists.

*Ohhh, that man.*

She could not believe he tried to kiss her.

But why not believe it? He was a rake, after all. And evidently, rakes preferred to bury their emotions in a woman's body rather than speaking of them.

*I can think of many, many other things we can do with our mouths...*

"Oh, I will kill him," she growled.

"Bella?"

She really needed to remember to refrain from speaking to herself while in the presence of others. She turned to her father. "Yes, Papa?"

He frowned, causing the lines around his mouth to crinkle. "Are you all right? Your behavior this morning has been rather... peculiar."

She glanced at her hands, which were clenching and wrinkling the delicate satin fabric of her skirts. Releasing her tight hold, she smoothed the rumpled green-and-blue checkered fabric. "I am quite well, Papa," she lied.

The duke arched a graying brow. "You have always been a dreadful liar." He paused and turned his lips up in a cheeky smile. "Are you avoiding him?"

Isabella scoffed. "Avoiding who?" Though she knew very well the 'who' he was speaking of.

"Alistair," he said with an air of confidence only a duke could manage. "You did not speak to him at breakfast. You threw him out of your carriage—"

"I did no such—"

Her father held up a silencing hand. "I am not finished. You are moaning and groaning to yourself, you are clenching at your skirts, and—" he held up a finger "—I know Alistair was in your room yesterday."

All of the blood rushed to Isabella's cheeks. How did he

## *Chapter Eleven*

know? After all the effort of hiding the gentleman inside of that flimsy wardrobe, her father had known all along? Though, to be honest, after Mr. Baston's actions with her the previous day, he deserved to spend the entirety of the week locked away in a grubby wardrobe.

As if her father was able to read her mind, he asked, "Does *Gulliver's Travels* sound familiar to you?"

She slouched in her seat. It was the book. Why had she allowed Alistair to take it? She should have burned it before allowing him the enjoyment of reading. After what he'd done, she should have burned Alistair alongside it.

*Take a breath. All is well.* "Nothing happened, Papa." *Other than the attempted kiss.* She flashed her father a reassuring smile.

"Then why am I here, in your carriage instead of him? I am getting far too old and fragile. You need a strong, young gentleman to protect you in case anything is to happen."

"You are not that old, Papa, and you are far from fragile." Yes, the duke was not as athletic as he used to be when she and her siblings were children, but other than his graying hair and slightly wrinkled features, her father looked much the same as he did ten years prior.

She crossed her arms over her chest. "Is it so wrong a daughter should want to spend time with her father?" Isabella looked to him with wide, innocent eyes.

Violet was always remarkable at doing such things. Like a puppy, she was. No one could stay angry with her for long once she'd given one her 'sad eyes'.

The duke's face was expressionless. Alas, Isabella's actions did not have the desired effect her little sister would have so easily achieved. Taking her father's hand in her own, she sighed. "Nothing happened. He was just checking up on me, I promise."

"If your mother knew of this, she would force the both of you to marry—"

"But," Isabella cut in, "she does not know of it." And there was no need for her mother to know of it, or anyone else. Her poor mother had enough to worry over.

"No... but I will need to speak with Alistair."

She straightened her posture. "No!" Anything but that. Knowing her father, he would have the gentleman out purchasing a betrothal ring this very day. "I will speak to him. I will tell him he can no longer visit me in my rooms unaccompanied." And he could no longer attempt to kiss her as if she were one of his courtesans at the Middleton's ball.

The duke nodded in agreement.

Splendid. Isabella relaxed her posture once more. She could handle such a task on her own.

The carriage slowed as they arrived at their first stop of the day: a large Tudor-style farmstead in the Chilterns, the residents of which were some of her father's many tenants. It was an asymmetrical build with heavenly green and maroon ivy creeping over the red brick of its west wing. It proved to be quite charming.

Isabella imagined herself and her sister at a young age attempting to climb the timbered rails along the house's white stucco exterior near the entrance. What fun they could make of it even now.

Once the conveyance rolled to a halt, the coachman stepped down from his perch and opened the carriage door.

Isabella rubbed her stiff joints and made to stand. Once she had exited the carriage, she massaged the tingly, stabbing

## Chapter Eleven

sensations from her bum, not giving a jot who was around to see.

Simon appeared at her side. "Have a care, woman. There may be scoundrels lurking about."

Scoundrels lurking about? In the middle of a country road? She highly doubted that statement. "The only scoundrel I see lurking about is *you*." She punched Simon's shoulder. He returned the sentiment.

"No fighting, children." The duke stepped down from the carriage and stretched his arms above his head.

"We all know who would win that fight." Captain Lucas exited the larger conveyance at the front of their party. Once on solid ground, the captain pointed his gold-handled cane in Simon's direction. "And no, I am not speaking of you, young man."

Isabella snorted and stuck her tongue out at Simon. She knew she'd always adored Captain Lucas for a reason.

*Right.* She would have to leave the teasing for later. Now was the time to focus. Isabella plunged a hand inside her satchel and pulled out her small leather sketch pad. Flipping open its pages, she paused at Violet's portrait.

*Hello farmer, sir. I am here conducting an investigation on the whereabouts of this young woman. She was last seen wearing a white, cotton nightshift...*

Isabella sighed.

Was she still wearing that? Violet could have changed her clothes, or perhaps the intruder threw his jacket over Violet's person. Or mayhap she was knocked unconscious and thrown into a sack.

She gave her head a mental shake. Her thoughts were becoming far too fantastical for her own liking.

"Bella, dear." The duke stepped into her line of vision.

"Hmmm?"

He held out a hand. "I shall handle this. You take this time to have your talk—" his eyes glanced about their surroundings "—with *you know who.*"

The talk? With Mr. Baston? Now?

"But... I am..."

"I am aware, and you've been doing an excellent job." He slid the sketch pad from her hands. "I am familiar with this particular tenant, and I would rather be the one to handle it." His gaze looked beyond her shoulder. "Alistair, my boy, do keep my daughter company while Simon, Lucas, and I talk with the farmers." His eyes narrowed at Isabella. "She has been known to wander."

*I do not wander...* All right... mayhap she did on occasion. She once snuck away from her governess to follow a squirrel around Hyde Park. The little bugger never did stay still quite long enough for her to sketch.

Alistair bowed in assurance. "I shall stay right by her side, Your Grace."

Her father, brother, and Captain Lucas made their way to the farmhouse. The footmen dismounted their steeds, bringing them to graze in a nearby field.

Isabella sighed. "Care for a walk, Alistair?"

"Of course, my lady," Alistair said in a rogue's murmur, which tickled her ear. He offered her his arm with a wink.

Isabella tried her damnedest not to let the gentleman's melodic tone have an effect on her nerves. She was barely acquainted with the gentleman. Why did he have such an effect on her? They began their walk down the narrow road along the hedgerow.

## Chapter Eleven

Should she just come right out and say it? *My father does not want you visiting my rooms unless you plan on proposing marriage. Therefore, I would appreciate it if we kept our relationship purely professional. You as my guard, I as your... your...* What was she to him anyhow? A damsel in need of protection? She'd be damned if she let any man bestow such a title upon her.

The bloody bastard hadn't even apologized for attempting to kiss her yet—not that she'd given him the opportunity to do so.

"I—" They both started in unison.

Isabella's nerves leapt at the sudden sound of his voice. Giving Alistair's arm a gentle squeeze, she urged him on. "You first."

He nodded, causing an auburn tendril to fall over his brow. "I wanted to apologize for last evening." He stopped both of them in their stride and took her hands in his. "I should not have treated you in such a way. You are a lady of the *ton*, the eldest daughter in a ducal family, the daughter of my *employer*. I tried to use you as a way to avoid speaking about my past, and it was wrong of me. It shan't happen again."

"Oh." Well, she certainly hadn't been expecting that speech, though she'd been hoping for it. She'd anticipated having to beat the apology from his lips. She'd expected him to say something... *rogue-like*.

She looked down to where the gentleman's thumb was rubbing soft circles against the palm of her hand. The light caress did strange things to her belly, and suddenly, she was very aware of how hard her heart was beating.

The small, circling movement of his thumb was like an unspoken spell. It was mesmerizing, pulling her deeper and deeper into a place unknown. Her breath caught. She slipped her hands from Alistair's grasp and turned away, effectively breaking that spell.

"Thank you," she whispered.

So... Alistair had apologized... Could she really stay angry with him now? She was the one who'd pressed him to speak about his past, after all.

Isabella turned to face him once more, his emerald eyes meeting hers. The dark green color of the outer ring reminded her of the spongy moss beds often found in the forests of her family's country seat. The flecks of yellow dancing around his pupil made her wonder what cruelty they'd seen—what cruelty *he* had seen, and how it may have changed him.

What was he like as a young boy? What was it like to live with an abusive father?

"Lady Isabella."

Alistair's smooth baritone brought her back from her musings. She blinked. "Yes?"

"You are staring." The gentleman's mouth turned up at the corners, giving her a peek at his almost too-perfect teeth.

"Was I?" *Yes, you ninny*. "I must have been lost in my own thoughts."

His smile grew wider. "Were you thinking of our kiss?"

And there it was. The rogue's words she'd been expecting. She gave him a pointed look. "May I add, it was not a kiss." She motioned between herself and Alistair. "*We* did not kiss."

In one swift motion, he swept out a hand and bowed regally before her. "You are indeed correct, my lady. I apologize." He lifted his gaze to her. "But... is it what you were thinking of?"

## Chapter Eleven

Isabella strode forward and reached out to force his outstretched arm back to his side. "You are insufferable."

"Thank you—"

"It was not a compliment." Isabella huffed and smoothed out the front of her skirts. "But speaking of kissing—or *almost* kissing—my father is aware of our time together in my room, and he said if it were to happen again, you'd better prepare yourself for a marriage... to me."

There. She'd said it. Now the bounder would have to stay out of her rooms and keep his roguish hands to himself.

He straightened and dragged a hand over the stubble of his jaw. "I suspected as much."

Isabella shook her head in disbelief. "You *knew*? You knew, and you did not tell me?"

"I said, 'I *suspected*.' And how could I have told you of my suspicions when you have been avoiding me all morning?"

*Avoiding him?* Yes, one could say she was avoiding the gentleman. What was a lady to say to her father's man-of-affairs after he'd attempted to use her to slate his lust and distract his mind? Or whatever it was rakes, rogues and the like did.

"I was not avoiding you." Isabella turned away from him and continued their walk uphill. "I was simply—"

"Tossing me out of the carriage?" Alistair was back at her side in three quick strides.

Her nostrils flared. And to think just moments ago he was proving himself to be a decent human being. How much more irritating could he become? "Call it what you will."

Isabella spotted an opening in the hedgerow. She darted to the opposite side, using the shrubbery as a barrier between them.

*Meeting Mister Baston*

There.

Perhaps some distance from him would better her mood. "I do not understand why you are even here to begin with. Simon could have looked after my well-being." Or better yet, she could have looked after her *own* well-being. Why did a lady have to be followed around by maids and escorts anyhow?

Alistair scoffed. "Your brother can hardly look after himself."

She let out a laugh. It was true; her brother was horribly irresponsible. He spent most of his nights losing bets at gambling hells, and she dreaded the day he was to take over as the Duke of Waverly. "Either way, you must promise not to visit my rooms again—unless you wish to propose marriage."

"I do not."

"Good." Not that she would accept him if he were to propose anyhow. They barely knew one another, and what she did know of his character was not at all impressive.

They continued their stride in companionable quiet, Alistair in the roadway and Isabella in the grass on the opposite side of the hedges—where they belonged, at an agreeable distance from each other.

And *not* touching.

She sensed Alistair watching her as she plucked the tiny leaves off the shrubs and fiddled with them in her fingers.

She looked up toward him.

He narrowed his eyes at her.

She returned the expression.

"My father's words, of course," she continued.

Why did the air feel so dense? And why did she feel the need to fill the quiet between them? "If it were up to me, I

## Chapter Eleven

would pay no mind to you visiting my rooms unaccompanied, and I most certainly would not expect you to wed me. Not that I *want* you visiting my rooms..." She was rambling. She *never* rambled.

"I understand," he assured her with a wave of his hand.

"I am sorry," she said, glancing to her fingers, which were still fiddling with the little green leaves of the shrub. "I have made this so very awkward."

Alistair tilted his head. "So you *do* want me to visit your rooms?"

"No! I mean—" *Stop. Talking.*

What was wrong with her? Was it the topic of marriage that had gotten her so... so... anxious? She'd never been so clumsy with her words before. Her cheeks began to warm. She opened her hand and let her small collection of leaves flutter to the ground.

"If you want me to visit your rooms, you need only ask." Alistair flashed her a cheeky grin.

"Ask?" No, no, no. He had this all wrong. He thought her wanton. "You have visited my rooms without my asking. That is why we are having this discussion to begin with." Her pace quickened as the slope of the grassy hill began its downward journey. Would she have to explain everything to him all over again?

She stopped mid-stride and pointed a finger toward his person. "*You* do not visit my rooms unaccompanied." She turned her finger toward herself. "*I* do not want you to visit my rooms tonight, tomorrow night, in a fortnight or *any* night." She let her hands fall to her hips. "My father, *your employer*, does not want you visiting my rooms unless you propose marriage, which you have already stated you—"

## Meeting Mister Baston

"Bella, *stop*."

She froze. Her stomach did a strange flip-flop motion inside of her belly.

Alistair arched a brow. "I jest. You do not need to explain it all again."

*He jests*. He was teasing her? This entire time? He let her prattle on like a fool, making her believe he truly thought she wanted him to visit her rooms.

"Bella?"

She brought her gaze up to meet his and there it was again: the flip-flopping of her belly when he said her name aloud. The sound of his smooth baritone raising gooseflesh along her arms. "You called me Bella. Only my family uses that name."

"I did." He raked a hand through the tousled strands of his auburn hair. "I was not thinking. I—"

"No." She lifted a hand in the air, stopping his forthcoming apology. "It is fine." She lowered her hand to once again toy with the hedgerow between them. "As long as I may call you by your Christian name as well."

He cocked his head as if befuddled by her request. "Of course."

She glanced up, and they shared a smile.

"Now, my Bella." Her heart fluttered at the endearment. "Are you going to return to *this* side of the hedgerow?"

Isabella flashed him a coy smile. It was good to return to the strange, back-and-forth teasing friendship that had developed between them these last few days. "I would—" she gave an overly dramatic sigh "—but it would mean we would have to go back in the direction we've come." Her eyes squinted as she surveyed the landscape before her. "I do not

## Chapter Eleven

spot any openings up ahead."

"Well, then." He loosened the cravat at his neck. Her eyes fell to the smallest glimpse of skin that had once been hidden by the cloth. It caused her pulse to quicken and she cursed that blasted feeling. "I will just have to come to you."

Isabella inspected the gentleman from behind the hedges. Alistair walked backward toward the opposite side of the narrow gravel road. He combed his fingers through his hair and pulled his gold-buttoned jacket at the hem. Alistair danced a little jig, shaking out his limbs before starting for the bushes.

Isabella gasped as she watched the gentleman sprint across the road with astonishing speed. He reached the hedgerow in mere *seconds*, and as soon as Isabella realized what he was about to do, she called out to him—"Alistair, wait!"—and realized it was a terrible mistake. As soon as she called out, Alistair glanced over to her and lost his footing. As he leaped over the shrubbery, his left foot caught on its edge.

Within a half second, he was facedown in the grass.

She knew, being a lady of noble birth, that the polite thing to do in such a situation would be to run over, offer help, and ask if he were injured. But Isabella was not a proper lady. She strapped daggers to her calves, fenced, and shot pistols.

So, she laughed.

She laughed with so much ferocity she nearly fell face-first into the grass herself. Tears began to stream down her cheeks, and as soon as she was able to breathe again, she finally asked, "Was that supposed to impress me?" She swiped a tear from her cheek. "Were you expecting me to swoon over all of your masculine glory after you scaled the bushes?"

Alistair lifted his head from its position in the grass and

## Meeting Mister Baston

hoisted himself up from the ground. He placed his hands on his narrow hips and tapped his foot. "This is funny to you, is it?" he asked.

"Yes," she managed to say mid-laugh, "it is." Alistair watched her as she wiped the tears from her cheeks and fought to catch her breath. "My God," she muttered. "My stomach hurts from laughing so much."

Once her breathing steadied, Isabella searched over Alistair's frame. A small section of his cream trousers were stained green from the grass, and there was a rather sizable tear just above his now scuffed leather boots. The gentleman also had a considerable amount of dirt smudged along his forehead. She chuckled and closed the distance between them.

"You have some dirt…" She motioned to his forehead and watched as Alistair vigorously rubbed his left cheek.

"No," she said, shaking her head. "Your forehead."

With her fingertips, Isabella reached out and began wiping away the dirt on his skin.

Her eyes met his, and just as she was about to pull her hand away, Alistair grasped her wrist with startling force, causing her heart to stop its racing rhythm. But after he held it in the air for a few short moments, he placed her palm upon his cheek.

Isabella gulped.

What was she to do?

She stared at him and blinked rapidly as the roguish gentleman in front of her closed his eyes and tilted his face, rubbing the soft stubble of his cheek against the palm of her hand. "What are you…?"

At first, he was moving her hand for her, but after a few

## Chapter Eleven

short seconds of observation, she wanted to *feel* for herself. She began gently stroking his cheek with the pad of her thumb. His hand grew limp around hers, not letting go, but holding on as her fingers explored the curves of his face. His eyes opened, and he watched her as she slowly traced the outline of his jaw. Her fingertips moved across his chin and up the opposite side of his face.

What was happening? They agreed not to have meetings in her rooms for the sake of propriety and now... Now, after she had refused his kiss the evening prior, she wanted to kiss Alistair more than anything in the world.

What was happening with this day?

She paused for an instant, her breath slow and shallow as her heart raced. Her eyes dropped down to his mouth, and she dragged the tip of her thumb along the outer edge of his bottom lip.

But they should not. They could not. The gentleman had made it clear he'd no intentions to wed her. And she did not want marriage anyhow. She was on this journey to find her sister, not to find a husband.

"Bella!"

Startled by the sound, they both froze in unison.

*"Bellllaaaaaa!"*

Isabella recognized the voice to be that of her brother. They both stood frozen. She blinked away her foolish haze of desire and yanked her wrist from Alistair's gentle grasp.

It must have been the rogue's spell that had been cast upon her. What else could possibly explain her foolishness?

"We should go," she stated, then moved past him. They would not want her hot-headed brother to witness them in such a position. Heavens only knew what he would do to

Alistair, though with the gentleman's build, she had no doubt he could easily defend himself from any fists Simon was sure to throw his way.

"Mr. Baston!" Simon shouted, making his way to them with quick, even strides. Once he came to a stop at the hedgerow, her brother looked over Alistair's person, from the top of his head to the very toes of his boots. "What is happening here?"

"Simon." Isabella cut in. "Nothing happened." She watched as her brother clenched and unclenched his fists. His face became the color of one of her favorite rose pink evening gowns. "Simon…" She took a step in front of Alistair, shielding him with her body.

"You filthy bastard!" Simon leaped forward, only to be halted by the green bushes acting as a barrier between them.

Alistair stepped around her, placing himself at the forefront. "Calm down, Reading. I did not touch her."

No… *She* touched him.

Blast and damn.

Simon motioned toward the gentleman's disheveled appearance. "Explain this, then," he fumed.

Alistair laughed. "I, unfortunately, took a tumble as I attempted to scale the bushes."

How quickly the gentleman went back to his usual carefree and cocky self, while she was still attempting to slow her pulse back to its normal cadence.

Simon turned to Isabella. "Is this true?"

"Yes, Simon." Isabella let out a relieved sigh. Heavens knew what would have happened if they hadn't had the shrubbery to protect them from her brother's temper.

The color faded from Simon's cheeks. He placed his hands

## Chapter Eleven

over his hips and shook his head. "What the bloody hell is wrong with you two? Why are you scaling bushes? Or failing at scaling bushes, I should say." Simon nodded toward Isabella's person. "And how did you manage not to dirty yourself?"

If she had a few more minutes in Alistair's arms, she could have easily found herself tumbling toward the grass. Dirtying herself, indeed.

Isabella shook the notion from her mind, and a tinge of guilt swelled in her chest. Could she have a wanton soul? What other explanation was there for her selfish acts? Her one and only focus should be finding her sister.

Isabella took in a steadying breath and plastered on a false smile. "I am much more agile and graceful than one Mr. Baston."

Alistair gave her a look, and without moving his focus from her, he stated, "Lady Isabella walked through an opening in the hedgerow. She did no scaling, or jumping, or leaping of any sort—*surprisingly...*" He muttered the last word under his breath, but she heard it all the same.

Simon cocked his head, and after a moment, waved his hand in dismissal. "I do not wish to know any more of your curious escapades." He turned and walked in the direction he'd come. "Come now. Father is waiting."

In all honesty, Isabella was relieved by her brother's interruption. Heavens only knew what would have happened if she and Alistair had been left on their own for any longer. He undoubtedly would have kissed her.

Her breath hitched. Or worse... *She would have kissed him.*

## Chapter Twelve

It was late in the evening when the party arrived in Bicester, a charming village known for its historic market center, which dated back to the sixteenth century. If they were not there on important business, Alistair would have enjoyed exploring its medieval church and old market square.

Making his way inside the inn's tavern, the smell of cheroots and alcohol filled his senses. It was just the environment he needed to get his mind off the Duke of Waverly's siren of a daughter.

*Blast it all.*

What was he thinking? The duke had all but threatened him to marry his daughter if he laid a hand on her, and what did he do? He laid a hand on her... *again*. Sort of.

When he felt the lady's bare fingers on his skin, he'd forgotten everything and just wanted more. Her delicate fingertips were not nearly enough, and so he'd grasped her hand in his and forced her warm flesh to rove over his

## Chapter Twelve

features, something he often did with the more humble women he bedded. He would guide their hand lower and lower... until finally they found what they did not know they sought.

But Isabella was different. She was an angel brought to him from the heavens, when all he truly deserved were the wicked women who so often sought him out. Those women he would someday meet again in hell.

Isabella was bold in her innocence as she'd taken control over the caress and explored his skin like no other had. She was pure and hadn't a clue what her touch did to his body.

Shaking the thoughts from his head, Alistair eyed a familiar young footman hunched over the pub counter. Surely a few drinks and some polite conversation would rid him of his remembrance. At least for tonight.

Alistair took a seat beside the young servant. "What are you drinking?" Hopefully something strong enough to get him soused.

The young man gave him a sideways glance. "Ale."

Rotted stuff, but it would do the trick. Alistair ordered two ales from the busty bar wench.

She set the mugs down before him with a wink. Normally, such a woman would catch his fancy. Normally he would invite the young woman with fiery hair and plump lips to his rooms, but guilt squeezed at his chest at the mere thought of it. No, not because he was on a mission to aid in the search for Lady Violet Avery—but because of a very different lady with long golden hair and eyes as blue as sapphires.

*Damn it all to hell.* He was thinking of her again.

Pushing one of the mugs toward the forgotten footman at his side, he greeted the young man with a nod.

*Meeting Mister Baston*

Diggory nodded his thanks then downed the ale in three large swallows.

Ah, of course. The footman that was handpicked by the duke to accompany them to Derby. And Alistair could now understand why...

The lad was young, yes—probably had not reached his twentieth year—but he was strong. It was difficult to assess his build while in a seated position, but Alistair gathered the young man had to stand at least three inches taller than himself. Possessing a slightly crooked nose and scarred knuckles, Alistair believed the servant participated in the underground fighting rings. He himself was not a stranger to such places, especially when he needed to release some pent-up anger. "Where are you from, Callum?"

"Buckinghamshire, sir," he answered coyly, his mousy brown hair sticking to the skin of his forehead. Callum brushed the strands away with his hand.

"Not so far from here, then."

Callum nodded. "Just a few miles to the east."

The barmaid refilled their mugs with the cheap ale. Alistair took a large swallow of the sweet amber liquid. "I cannot imagine this is the type of work you do often." Gallivanting around the country in attempts to find the duke's daughter. It was not something Alistair thought he would be doing when he started his position as man-of-affairs.

"No." He laughed and took a sip of his drink. Callum leaned in and said in a quiet voice, "But locating His Grace's daughter is important work."

Alistair lifted his glass in agreement and downed a large gulp of the brew.

"What do you think of Lady Violet?" Perhaps he would use

## Chapter Twelve

this time to find out more about Isabella's sister and where she could possibly be. "Have you ever conversed with her?"

Callum choked on his drink, spitting small droplets of ale onto the counter. "I... we... We have crossed paths."

Arching a brow, Alistair took in the young servant's reddened cheeks and sweat-beaded brow. He was nervous. Why would he be nervous?

"I ask because I have never met the lady." He turned on his stool to face Callum. "Do you think her the type to run away and elope?"

Callum scoffed. "I would not know. But..." Taking another sip of his drink, the servant glanced about the room.

Alistair urged him to finish. "But?"

"The lady has a reputation." The young servant downed the remainder of his ale. "She is a flirt and makes promises to men, but in the end, leaves them wanting."

So Lady Violet enjoyed toying with gentlemen of the *ton*. That could easily get a young lady into trouble, if she toyed with the wrong one.

But how would a servant know of such things? He supposed gossip could run rampant in a ducal household, but perhaps Lady Violet did not just tease the gentlemen of the *ton*. "Is that what she did to you? Left you wanting?"

"What?" Callum's hands squeezed into tight fists on the countertop as he shook his head. "N-no, of course not." The young servant jumped down from his stool. "I have to go." And promptly, he shuffled through the crowd of patrons.

Arching a brow, Alistair watched as the footman stumbled his way up the stairs toward the rented rooms, which he found slightly odd. Usually servants stayed in the stables, but perhaps the duke had rented the young footman a room of his own.

\*\*\*

Isabella lay in bed with Alistair flooding her thoughts. She assumed that finishing his bloody portrait would ease the gentleman out of her mind.

But her plan did not work. When they arrived at the inn, she immediately retired to her room, and she'd been staring at the gentleman's portrait ever since.

With a huff, she slammed closed her leather sketchbook and tossed it on the oak nightside table.

*If you want me to visit your rooms, you need only ask...* That statement echoed around the chambers of her mind, and glancing at the door, she noticed she'd left her door unlatched. Did she merely forget? Or was it her subconscious hoping Alistair would visit her?

"Do not be ridiculous. Alistair will *not* visit you tonight," she whispered to herself. They had agreed only a few hours ago that he would not. Isabella sighed and turned to snuff out the candle. She covered its flame with a tin lid, and the room turned to blackness. She needed to be rid of this damned rake's spell. Now she understood why her mother so often warned her of such gentlemen.

Footfalls echoed from the hallway.

Was it him? It could not be...

Isabella suddenly regretted her decision to keep the door unlocked. What was she thinking? She'd just been angry with him for attempting to use her body to forget the memories of his childhood. And now she *wanted* to see him again. Surely

## Chapter Twelve

she was suffering from a case of madness.

Peeking over the bed covers, she saw a tiny shadow of movement through the light of the keyhole. The door handle began to turn, and she quickly placed her head back onto her pillow.

Perhaps once Alistair found her asleep, he would leave. Or mayhap it was her father or Simon coming to check in on her.

The light from the open door shone over her pillow. She squeezed closed her eyelids as she listened to a pair of heavy footsteps entering the room. There was a short moment of silence before she heard two more heavy steps and the sound of the door clicking shut.

Isabella sighed in relief. He had left. Now she should get up and lock the door. She did not want Alistair—or whomever—to come again later.

She peered over the top of her bedsheets, and an alarm rang in her chest.

*Is he still here?*

Her vision was quite blurry, having difficulty focusing in the darkness of the night, but even with her blurred vision, there was no mistaking the large shadowy figure standing at the foot of her bed.

It was most definitely *not* Alistair... or her father or Simon. It was not even Captain Lucas. She was sure of it. This stranger was *enormous*. He had to be at least four inches taller than Alistair, and his figure was much bulkier. Her heart began pounding in her ears as her body sensed the impending danger.

*Fetch your dagger.*

Isabella threw herself toward the nightstand and reached

for the small drawer that housed her weapon.

Before she could grip its sapphire-studded handle, the stranger lunged at her. He landed on top of her and took hold of both of her wrists. He reeked of alcohol, and Isabella tried to free herself, but the man was too heavy. Too strong.

The blackness of night only revealed the whites of the stranger's eyes. She struggled against him and heard the sound of fabric against metal.

Was he unclasping his breeches?

Isabella let out a loud shriek, but the stranger's large palm came down hard over her mouth and abolished any chance for her to cry out for help. His hand left her wrists and began moving up the side of her leg, vigorously squeezing at the inner part of her thigh.

*She did not want this.* How could she make the man understand that she did not want this?

Isabella used her free hand to slap the stranger hard across the cheek. Again and again. She attempted to free herself as he took hold of her wrists once more.

Was God punishing her? Was he to torment her for the folly of leaving her door unlocked?

*Please. Please. It was a mistake.*

A mistake she would never make again—if she made it through this ordeal alive.

The stranger's mouth came down hard on hers, and she could taste the alcohol on his lips. Nausea turned her stomach. She kicked and flailed, trying desperately to get the brute off her.

The door flew open and crashed into the wardrobe, letting much-needed light into the room.

A second man appeared in the doorway.

## Chapter Twelve

It was Alistair.

A sense of relief pumped through her veins, but she had to keep fighting. Isabella lifted her head and bit the stranger's forearm, and the man let out a yelp of pain.

The next thing she saw was a large palm heading straight for her cheek. But before her attacker could land the blow, Alistair grabbed him by his collar and threw the large man to the ground. With the blur of movement, her eyes struggled to focus on the men. The stranger lifted himself to his hands and knees... but he was not a stranger at all. He was a footman.

It was Mr. Diggory, the very same footman her father insisted on bringing along.

Mr. Diggory managed a shove to Alistair's abdomen with a force that sent the gentleman crashing into the wall behind him.

*Do something.*

While the men were busy wrestling each other, Isabella snatched the marble clock from its place on the nightstand, and using its base, she bashed the traitorous servant over the skull.

## Chapter Thirteen

One moment, Alistair was on his way to his rented rooms, and the next, he was yanking young Callum off Isabella's bed.

He shook the images from his mind and looked to the lady who stood with a mantle clock held tightly in her fist. She was shaking. He glanced down to her décolletage where he noticed the neck of her night shift was torn. His brows came together, with a fury building inside of him. He let his gaze linger on that tear in the fabric.

*Callum touched her.*

No. He did more than touch her... he *forced* himself on her.

Without warning, the small marble clock that was once held in Isabella's grasp came hurtling in his direction. "Bloody hell!" Alistair ducked to the right, and the clock smashed into pieces against the wall behind him. "What was that for?!"

Isabella's hand flew to the tear in her night shift' "You, sir,

## Chapter Thirteen

are a *lecher*."

"Say again?" A lecher? What in God's name was she on about?

Isabella rushed over to grab the quilt at the foot of her bed and wrapped it around her body.

"And to think I wanted you here... You are just as bad as he is!" She motioned to Callum's limp form.

Alistair scoffed. "Pardon, my lady?" How could this ungrateful slip of a woman claim Alistair was just as bad as the man who attempted to defile her? Wait... she said she *wanted him here*? "Say that first bit again."

A blush stained her cheeks. "I said you are a soulless and heartless scoundrel!"

He picked himself up from the floor. "I just saved your life," he hissed.

"You were staring—" she glanced about the room and lowered her voice to a whisper "—at my breasts."

Alistair threw his head back and let out a sharp laugh. He crossed the room with three long strides. "Is that what you think?" He moved to set his palm on her shoulder, but the lady flinched. Lowering his arm to his side, he whispered, "The last thing on my mind right now is your breasts."

What type of man would he be to gape at a woman's breasts after she'd been attacked? He may be a good-for-nothing second son, but he was not a sick-minded bastard. Wait... "Were you— Did he..." How to say this? "Did he penetrate you? With his..."

"No!"

"All right!" Alistair could not believe how stubborn she was being. He took one last slow, tantalizing step toward her. "You do not want to know what would have happened if I had not come along, *my lady.*" His voice was low and grating, even to his own ears.

She shivered.

Alistair's glare left Isabella's eyes as he remembered the drunken servant lying unconscious in the middle of the floor. He sighed. "What shall we do with him?"

"What shall we *do* with him?" she asked. "Nothing!" Isabella made her way to the door of her room, which was still open and resting against the wardrobe. "I am going to fetch my father."

"What?" Alistair stepped in front of Isabella, forcing her to a stop. "You are not going anywhere dressed as you are!" His eyes glanced down to the quilt wrapped over her torn night shift. "I will fetch him."

Isabella huffed. "And I am supposed to stay here with the man who attacked me?"

He pursed his lips to one side. "You are right. I will move him out of the room and *you* will lock the door," he said to her with a pointed finger. Alistair made his way to the unconscious man in the middle of the floor. "Why was your door unlocked anyhow?"

Isabella shrugged. "I did not think of it. We do not lock our bedchambers at home."

"You are not *at home.*" Alistair let out an irritated sigh. "You are staying in rented rooms at an inn." He pinched the bridge of his nose and added, "With a pub full of drunken men."

Isabella dropped her gaze to the floor and said nothing. Perhaps she was finally beginning to understand the graveness of the situation.

Alistair crouched down next to the young man and began tugging at his feet. A sound of exertion escaped his lips as

## Chapter Thirteen

he leaned back and pulled the large footman with all of his strength.

Callum barely moved an inch.

Isabella chuckled at the sight, and Alistair shot her an irritated glance. "I do not see you helping."

"I am not in the proper dress to pull a man across the room." *Ungrateful chit.*

Alistair rolled his eyes and continued his fruitless efforts.

After a few more yanks of the man's feet, the left boot slipped off, and Alistair tumbled backward, landing on his backside.

Isabella attempted to hide her wide grin with her hand. "Here is an idea," she said, trying desperately not to laugh. "I will lift his arms and you will lift his legs. Surely both of us can manage to wiggle him out."

Alistair nodded in agreement and hoisted himself from the floor. He resumed his position at the man's feet, but instead of pulling, he grasped the footman's ankles and lifted.

"All right," Alistair started. "I will go this direction—" he motioned to the left with his head "—and you go that direction, then we will twist him around so we can both drag him toward the door."

Isabella dropped the quilt she had wrapped herself in and made her way to the man who had almost succeeded in defiling her.

She looked over the once loyal servant and shuddered. "How could he?"

Pain gripped at Alistair's heart as he remembered the spirits the boy had consumed in his company. And Lord only knew how many he consumed before Alistair had arrived.

*Oh, God.* This was all his doing…

*Meeting Mister Baston*

Isabella tugged at the young man's arms, lifting them from the ground, forcing Alistair to momentarily set aside his thoughts.

The pair began twisting the footman on his back until his side faced the doorway.

Alistair glanced toward her. She leaned forward, her long golden hair flowed over her collarbone, and her white, torn shift hung loosely from her breasts. He noticed the shine of a golden amulet resting against her bosom, the very same one she wore the first day they had met.

*I am not a sick-minded bastard, remember?* He tore his gaze away and focused his efforts on moving Callum's limp frame. "Now, come next to me, and we will pull him toward the doorway."

Isabella moved toward Alistair. With the footman's arms still in the lady's hands, they both began tugging at the young man's limbs.

*"Urrggghhh!"*

They pulled the footman with their combined strength, leaning forward, scooting their feet backward, moving closer and closer to the doorway.

"What the devil is going on here?"

Isabella and Alistair froze in their awkward positions with their rears high in the air. They both turned their heads to see the duke standing just outside the room, his arms crossed at his chest and his face red with anger.

They simultaneously dropped Callum's limbs and stood erect, turning to face the duke.

"Father!" Isabella squealed. "Err." She paused. "Well… you see…"

Alistair interrupted her fumbled words. "Your Grace," he

## Chapter Thirteen

said as he greeted George with a bow. "This servant made his way into Lady Isabella's room and attempted to defile her." *Best to put it plainly.*

"What?!" the duke boomed, which made Alistair flinch.

He took a step back as his employer entered the room, almost tripping over the unconscious servant on the floor.

"I heard a commotion on the way to my room and realized it was coming from here. When I entered, I saw this man on top of her as she struggled to push him away."

Isabella snorted. "I did not struggle..."

Alistair ignored her. "I was able to get Mr. Diggory off her... and he was knocked unconscious."

"Which was my doing," Isabella so amiably pointed out.

George brought his fingertips to his temples. "Why would Mr. Diggory do this?"

Because Alistair had not escorted the young man to his room, and instead, watched as the drunken footman wobbled his way up the stairs.

"And how did he get in here?" The duke settled a glare on his daughter. "Bella?"

She troubled her bottom lip. "I may have forgotten to lock my door."

George sighed. "What are we to do with him?" He motioned toward Isabella. "And what are we to do with you?"

"*Me?*" Isabella tightened her arms at her chest. "What have I done?"

George sighed. "I told you; you should not have come with us." He paused, trailing a hand over his cheek. "I will arrange for a carriage to return you home first thing in the morning."

"Papa, no!" Her hands dropped and formed tight fists at

*Meeting Mister Baston*

her sides. She took a step forward. "Please, Papa, I need to help find Violet," she pleaded. "I cannot sit at home waiting in agony for word from you."

"It was my fault," Alistair interrupted. Guilt swelled in his chest. He had to tell the truth. He was here to protect Isabella. *And I failed.* "I was sharing drinks with the lad and I—" *...allowed Callum to wander unattended.* "I saw he was becoming inebriated... but I did nothing."

After a long moment of silence, George spoke. "It was the young man's choice to attack my daughter, not yours."

Alistair shook his head in disagreement. "I take full responsibility—"

George raised a hand to silence him. "We will discuss this in the morning. Right now, I need you to help me move this young man out of my daughter's room. And *you*—" he motioned toward his daughter "—need to cover yourself."

Isabella's eyes widened, apparently having forgotten she was wearing nothing but a torn night shift. She yanked the small quilt from where she'd tossed it on the floor and began wrapping it around her body.

"Off to bed with you." George shooed her away with his hands.

"And lock your door," Alistair insisted, then cleared his throat, remembering he was in the presence of the duke. He bowed in Isabella's direction. "Erm, *my lady.*"

\* \* \*

Isabella had watched as Alistair and her father lifted the footman and carried him down the hallway.

## Chapter Thirteen

This time she was sure to clamp down the latch on the door before tucking herself into bed. No more drunken men were entering her room this night.

She closed her eyes and felt the cool night air tickle her chest. She peered down to the torn fabric of her night shift. Her hand reached up to righten the fabric—which was meant to be fixed at her neck—but it continued to fall over her breast.

The excitement of the evening was beginning to fade, causing the memories of the attack to spring forward in her mind.

She squeezed her eyelids tight, hoping somehow it would cause the memories to disappear, but Mr. Diggory's face was etched into her mind's eye: his dried, cracked lips coming down on hers; his rough, callused hands grabbing at her thighs.

When had he torn her night shift? She did not recall him touching her... *her breasts.*

*Oh, God.*

Diggory touched her. He put his filthy hands on her person. Thank God it was as far as he had gone.

No... She should be thanking Alistair. For when a woman knew a man intimately, whether consented or not, she was no longer an innocent, no longer a marriageable lady. All of society would consider her a wanton woman. *A whore.* And even though she was still a virgin, if word got out about what had happened here... she would be ruined.

She yanked the bedsheets over her chin and let out a sob.

What would become of her life if the *ton* were to find out? What future would she hold?

What would become of that monster, Diggory? She had

*Meeting Mister Baston*

no such knowledge of criminal law and knew no one who had—other than her brother, and he was no expert.

Their library at Avery House was fully stocked with books on the subject; even their home in London boasted a small collection of law books. But she was never interested in the subject; they were more for Simon's enjoyment. Isabella preferred poetry and Gothic novels—romantic stories of love and happily-ever-afters. Would there be a happy ending for her now?

*Calm down. Word will not get out. Rumors will not spread.*

Isabella took in a calming breath, which only led to thoughts of her sister.

What if Violet was attacked as she, herself, just was? Or worse, what if Violet was defiled? She could be sitting at an inn somewhere against her will. There would be no happiness for her young sister. She would live out the rest of her days sitting in their mother's drawing room, knitting cushions and speaking of grand adventures she would never have.

She would be known as the Avery Spinster. *Or worse...* The Avery Doxy.

*Stop it.*

Such musings would not help her find her sister. And now that her father wanted to send her home, she would no longer be able to aid in the search.

*And what would become of Alistair if she were sent home?* Would he escort her back to London? Or would he stay with her father and the others?

Her eyes opened at the thought.

Why did he so suddenly slip into her mind? She should not be thinking of *him* after she was just attacked, not when

## Chapter Thirteen

her sister was missing and perhaps may even be *dead*.

Dear God, these thoughts were poisoning her mind. Lord help her be at ease. *May You keep Violet safe, wherever she is.*

So instead, she remembered better times, when she and her siblings chased each other through Ashbury Hall's massive grounds; when Isabella would give Violet dance lessons in her bedchamber late into the night; and when Violet would sing her to sleep after suffering from a bad dream.

Isabella forced her eyes shut once again, stopping the tears from escaping. Turning over on her side, she let out a slow exhale of breath. Her mind turned to blackness until a pair of emerald green eyes appeared in the dark.

Alistair. And a familiar pang of guilt squeezed at her heart.

Alistair saved her. He rescued her from an attack that could have ended much worse than it had. And what did she do in return? She threw a clock at his head and accused him of being a lecher.

## Chapter Fourteen

Alistair and George moved the unconscious Callum into Alistair's room just down the hall. Both men stood over the servant. "What are we to do with him?" Alistair asked the burning question.

"Wait for him to wake," George replied.

Alistair looked up in surprise. "What?"

"Well, we bloody well cannot leave him on his own."

Alistair pursed his lips to the side and planted his hands akimbo. He hadn't a clue of how long Callum was going to stay unconscious, and he was already quite exhausted from the journey and the fighting.

*And the drinking.* According to his warmed cheeks, the ale had finally caught up with him. So he decided the best thing to do would be to help Callum wake from his comatose state.

So he kicked him. Directly in his abdomen.

Callum's body moved slightly, but he lay motionless on the floor with no signs of life—except for the fact he was breathing, of course.

## Chapter Fourteen

George looked to Alistair with curious eyes. "What was that?"

Alistair shrugged. "I am not standing here all night waiting for him to wake on his own accord."

George agreed with a reluctant nod and joined in Alistair's pursuit. The duke lightly nudged Callum's leg. He was not nearly as aggressive in his attempts.

"You have to kick him harder than *that*."

"I do not want to hurt him."

"You do not?" All Alistair wanted to do was hurt the young fool, and he could not understand how George could be so gentle-hearted. He narrowed his eyes, not caring that this man was his employer. "He nearly defiled your daughter. Did you forget that?"

George glared at him, the type of glare that made any man shake in his boots.

"Of course I have not forgotten," George said through gritted teeth. He then bashed his leather boot into Callum's arm with much more vigor.

That was more like it. The duke just needed a small nudge in the right direction.

Alistair took a deep breath and swung back his right foot, taking aim at Callum's abdomen. The man who tried to defile Isabella. The man who put his vile hands all over her. The footman who was here to protect, not *attack*.

He clenched his hands into tight fists at his side and thrust the toe of his boot forward. When Alistair's heavy boot came into contact with his gut, Callum let out a gasp of air and gripped his stomach.

"Good, he is awake." Alistair smiled, quite pleased with himself. He'd never felt so bloody angry in all his life... And all of this over a woman.

"Where am I?" Callum asked between coughs as he sat up, still holding his stomach in his arms.

"My room," Alistair answered dryly.

"Why?" the servant asked, searching around the room. His gaze fell upon Isabella's father, and his eyes widened considerably. "Oh."

"Oh?" Alistair mocked, crossing his arms over his chest. "So you *do* remember what happened?" The vile bastard.

*I should kill him.*

"Erm... Yes." Callum rose from his position on the floor, still swaying from his overindulgence of spirits—or perhaps from being knocked unconscious. "I-I apologize."

"You *apologize?*" Alistair shook his head in disbelief. He tapped his toe against the wooden floor in aggravation and raked a hand through his hair. He glanced over at George who was still yet to speak.

The duke was standing stiff with his hands at his hips, looking unsure of himself.

Alistair raked a hand through his hair a second time, this time pausing to yank at the thick strands, hoping the tension would ease his anger.

It did not.

Alistair took in a large breath of air, and with two long strides, he closed the small distance between himself and the footman.

Grabbing the lapels of Callum's gold-studded jacket, Alistair lifted him from the floor and shoved the servant against the wall. The back of Callum's skull hit the plaster in the process. A small painful groan left the servant's lips.

Alistair, quite impressed with his ability to handle a person

## Chapter Fourteen

much larger than himself, smiled and pulled the despicable letcher away from the wall, only to thrust him into it again.

"Your apology is not quite enough, I'm afraid." He stared into the footman's eyes. Though he was much taller and much bigger in girth than Alistair, the young man seemed terrified—like a small boy being bullied by someone twice his size.

He felt a sting of guilt swelling in his chest, but pushed it aside. This bastard was going to get what he deserved. Alistair released Callum from his grasp and took a step back.

Callum glanced toward the duke, then to the floor. "I did not realize it was her until it was too late."

George kept silent.

"And if it were not the lady, that would make it better?" Alistair was disgusted. How could he have shared drinks with such a scoundrel?

"No." Callum shook his head. "I just—"

His sentence was interrupted by Alistair's fist crushing into his jaw. Callum's head whirled to the side from the sharp impact.

"Alistair!" the duke cried out.

Strangely, the blow did not ease his fury. The only thing that would make him feel at ease again would be to hold Isabella in his arms and kiss away any scrapes and bruises she might have acquired.

Alistair rubbed the knuckles of his right hand—not that it made his soon to be bruised skin feel any better. It actually made it feel a bit worse. He straightened his shoulders and turned to face the footman, who was cupping his jaw. "*That* was for trying to fight me off in the lady's room."

Before the servant could look up, Alistair took hold of

Callum's shoulders and, with one swift movement, thrust a knee into the young man's groin.

A short burst of air left his lungs as he toppled over onto the ground.

"And *that*," Alistair continued, "was for the lady."

"Are you quite finished?" George boomed, with disapproval lacing his tone.

"I do not want to be," he said with a sardonic grin. Alistair looked down at Callum, who was curled up on the floor, cupping his groin in his hands. The lad deserved a much more brutal beating than what he'd received.

George brought his hand up and rubbed his chin. There was a moment of silence before he said, "I believe he is lying."

"Lying?" Alistair cocked his head in question. "Lying about what?"

"I think this young man knew precisely what he was doing." George took a step toward Callum, who was still writhing in pain like a coward. "I think he had this planned all along."

Alistair arched a brow. Perhaps the duke was correct, but what would the boy's motives be? What did he have to gain by defiling Isabella and betraying his employer? Or perhaps he had no motive. Mayhap the boy was perverse. "How many others?"

"W-What?" Callum peered up at him with confusion in his eyes.

"How. Many. Women. Have you forced yourself upon?" Alistair said through gritted teeth.

"None, I swear!" Callum screamed. "I-I mean this was my first time."

Alistair remembered his conversation with the lad at the pub counter. "Does this have something to do with

## Chapter Fourteen

your infatuation with Violet? You could not have her, so instead, you thought you might have the sister?" Alistair spat, disgusted by the idea.

"This is the first I've heard of this." The duke balled his hands into fists at his side. Finally a show of anger from the nobleman.

Alistair ignored George and focused his attentions on Callum. The lad's features turned gray.

*Got him.*

"You are angry Lady Violet did not love you. She flirted with you and gave you attention—gave a *servant* attention—then, when she denied your affections, when she ran off with another man, you wanted to enact revenge on her sister. Is that it?"

Callum's blanched features soon became red, and his mouth turned up into a sinister smile. "You have no idea—"

George closed the distance between himself and the servant. With one quick movement, he plastered the servant in the jaw with his fist—knocking him out cold.

*Bloody hell.*

Alistair watched as the duke shook out his hand and rubbed his knuckles. He wanted to applaud the nobleman. No… he wanted to kiss him. "Bravo, Your Grace." He gave his employer a friendly slap on the shoulder. "Now what?"

"We will send him back to where he came from."

Send him back to where he came from? Let the dog limp home to lick his wounds? Let the servant think over what he had done?

No…

Alistair would lock him inside of a cage like the brute he was. "What about the constable?"

George shook his head. "There is not much they can do."

Alistair glared at him in confusion.

George sighed. "He was apprehended before he could finish the… the *act*. Therefore, no laws were broken," he explained.

Alistair brought his injured hand to his chin, then shook his head. "He needs to be locked away, and it needs to be done tonight." If word got out of this, Bella would be ruined. Did the duke not understand that? She may not have been deflowered, but rumors could prove vicious to one's reputation.

After a short moment, George gave a reluctant nod. "I will see what I can do."

He will see what he can do? That was not good enough. "You are the Goddamned Duke of Waverly!" He was near royalty. He could raise an army and take over as king if he bloody well wanted to.

George took a step toward Alistair. "I am also your employer, and you will watch your tone with me, boy."

Alistair tightened his fists, enraged at how lax the duke was being.

"I am just as disgusted with the boy as you, but that is what he is… a boy. And a drunk one at that."

They were interrupted by a loud sound coming from where Callum lay on the ground.

He was snoring.

Alistair rolled his eyes and made his way to the sleeping footman. He used his foot to nudge at Callum's leg. "Wake up," he hissed, which only made the young man snore even louder.

At this point, Alistair's blood was boiling in his veins, and

## Chapter Fourteen

he wanted nothing more to do with the servant. He crouched down next to the young man and gave him a firm slap across the cheek. "Wake up!"

Callum blinked his eyes open in confusion. "Where am I?"

*Heavens help him.* Alistair grabbed the young man by the forearms and started tugging him to his feet.

George took it upon himself to grab Callum's jacket to help pull him up.

Once he was steady on his feet—as steady as a drunken and formerly unconscious person could be—George and Alistair each grabbed an arm and began pushing him out of the room.

George arranged for a carriage and two of the other footmen to take Callum back to London. He instructed the men to deliver him to the constable upon arrival with a sealed letter explaining the events of the evening.

With that, the young footman was gone. Alistair sighed with relief as he made his way back up the stairs and toward his rented room.

But before he settled in for the night, he stopped at Isabella's door, turned the handle, and smiled. Her door was locked as it bloody well should be.

He sighed and ran a hand over his stubble. *This woman will be the death of me.*

## Chapter Fifteen

Isabella woke the next morning completely famished. She'd actually slept quite well, considering the events of the previous evening—and considering her heart was fastened at the top of her throat throughout the majority of the night. Every small creek of the floorboards had her eyes flying open to check her door was still latched shut.

Fine… mayhap it was not the best sleep of her life, but it could have been worse.

She actually hadn't a clue of what time she fell asleep, as the marble clock that once sat on the nightside table was now in pieces on the floor.

The memory of her clutching said clock in her hands came forward, how Alistair had burst into the room like her knight in shining armor.

*These stories are hardly fairy tales...*

The words from her conversation with Alistair floated through her mind. She thought of when they discussed Jane Austen in her room. The woman may not have written fairy

## Chapter Fifteen

tales with knights in shining armor, but neither did she write of the most dreadful things a man could do to a woman.

If Jane Austen were to write Isabella's life story, how would it end?

She closed her eyes and let her mind wander. It was as if her entire life flew by in an instant. She saw herself as an old woman surrounded by her children, her sister and brother, and their children. There was a man standing beside her, laying a soft kiss on her knuckles.

It was Alistair.

He was much older and his auburn tresses had lost their hue, but it was him.

Her eyes flew open, and it was strange... She found she did not feel the guilt weighing on her chest like she usually did when thinking of the gentleman. Perhaps keeping Alistair on her mind would keep the dark memories of her attack from pushing forward.

She pulled the servant bell next to the door and ordered her morning meal, preferring to eat in her room. She was not quite ready for company just yet. She tucked herself under the bedsheets and took her copy of *Persuasion* off the nightstand.

She had only read a few pages when there was a light knock at the door.

Her heart jumped to its now familiar place in her throat. *What if it is Diggory again?* Isabella shook the thought from her mind. She had witnessed her father and Alistair drag the servant away. They would not have left the servant to wander the inn without retribution—and surely the young servant would not be inclined to knock.

Swallowing down the nervous lump in her throat, she

jumped down from her bed, her pulse increasing in speed with each measured step toward the door. Upon reaching the wooden panel, Isabella lifted the latch and opened the wood panel.

Of course, it was the maid arriving with her morning meal. Isabella let out an exhale of breath and motioned for the young servant to enter.

The girl set the tray down on the nightside table and turned to exit. She paused and looked over the remains of the expensive marble clock.

Once the maid finished cleaning the shattered pieces, Isabella gave her thanks and returned to her bed. The maid bobbed a curtsy and left the room, leaving Isabella to her own company. She took the tray from the oak table and placed it on her lap. Upon lifting the silver lid, her stomach let out an angry growl. She smiled and looked over her selection of boiled eggs, kippers, ham, and berries.

Kippers were not her favorite, but perhaps there was a stray cat she could feed them to outside.

She nibbled at the contents of the tray and was getting lost in the pages of *Persuasion* once more when another knock sounded. Her stomach recoiled at the noise.

For heaven's sake. Was she to always be afraid when someone arrived at her door? "Come in…"

Alistair poked his head in. "Good morning."

"Alistair." Isabella jolted up from her cushions, relief filling her breast. Her cheeks flushed as she remembered the tear at her neckline. She quickly pulled the bed covers over her bust. "Do come in." It was as though she'd conjured him from her thoughts and, this time, when the gentleman entered her room, she was actually quite pleased to see him.

## Chapter Fifteen

He stepped inside, leaving the door slightly ajar. "You did not come down for breakfast, so I wished to see if you were well."

The thought of Alistair worrying about her pulled at her heartstrings. "Oh, thank you."

Alistair made his way over to her bedside and motioned to the berries that she had just plucked from the tray. "I was afraid you may not have an appetite, but I can see you are eating just fine." He smiled.

"Famished actually." Why was he being so kind to her after the way she treated him? Who was this man? Certainly not the Alistair she had become familiar with over the last week.

Shoving his hands into his pockets, Alistair glanced about the room, swaying from his heels to the toes of his leather riding boots. Isabella arched a brow. Was he waiting for something? Or was he simply worried over her well-being?

"I should leave you—"

"No," she interrupted, then cleared her throat. *No? I want him to stay?* After the conversation they had about him staying *out* of her rooms, she should most definitely not want him to stay. Isabella's cheeks burned and she was suddenly overly aware of her rounded shoulders.

*Ladies do not slouch. Ladies sit up straight with elegance and poise...*

She wiggled herself backward and leaned her back against the headboard. "No, it is all right. Please sit." She motioned toward the aged embroidered chair to the right of her bed.

Alistair smiled and went to pluck a blackberry from her tray. Isabella watched as the gentleman reached for the small berry and gasped when she saw the state of his hand. She reached out and grabbed his fingers, inspecting the dark bruises and dried cuts that covered his knuckles. "Alistair! What happened?"

He tugged his hand away, but her grasp only grew tighter. "It is nothing," he assured her.

*He injured himself saving you.* A small piece of her heart fluttered at the thought.

"It is not nothing. You are hurt." Reaching over to the nightside table, she took her kerchief and dabbed it into a bowl of water. "Did someone clean these?" A ping of jealousy stabbed in her chest. Did he ring for a maid to clean his injuries?

She imagined some faceless woman tending to Alistair's wounds, inspecting the injured flesh with care and precision.

She rubbed at his dried cuts with the damp cloth with vigor.

*That faceless woman should have been me.*

Alistair laid his other hand atop hers to cease the motion. "I cleaned them. My hand is fine."

"Good," she whispered. Her eyes stayed locked where his hand rested atop hers, a jolt of energy charging between them. Was she the only one who felt it, or did he feel it too? Her breathing became heavy. It was as though a boulder were laying atop her chest as she attempted to fill her lungs under its crushing weight.

"Look at me." Alistair brought his knuckles to her chin, lifting her gaze to meet his burning emerald stare. "You are the one who is injured…" A glint of concern washed over his eyes.

"I-I am fine." She silently cursed the slight fumble of words as Alistair searched over her features.

"You have a bruise." His thumb traced along her lower lip,

## Chapter Fifteen

causing her breath to hitch. "Just there." He caressed the tender flesh. "Does it hurt?"

"Yes." Her voice came out as a barely there whisper. She had not known she had a bruise, but when Alistair touched her mouth, she felt the slight pain there.

*Do you wish me to kiss it for you, my lady...?* The rake's words came forward in her mind—

The door to her room crashed open as Simon burst inside. "Where is he?" he roared.

Alistair's hand fell from her cheek, and she mourned the loss of his gentle caress.

Isabella watched as her brother paced across the room, then realized Alistair was seated at the edge of her bed, and she still held his hand in hers...

She released her grasp.

*"I will bloody kill him!"* Simon stomped over to Isabella and grabbed her cheeks in both hands, tilted her chin toward the ceiling, and inspected the bruise on her lip. "Did he hit you?"

"No," she replied, trying to pull her face from Simon's hold. "It is nothing. It probably happened when he placed his hand over my mouth." *So I could not scream.* A shudder ran down her spine.

Simon released her and resumed his pacing. "A bruise is not *nothing*."

Alistair stood from the feathered mattress and grabbed Simon by the shoulder, stopping him in his angry stride. "He is gone."

"Gone?" Simon repeated with rage in his eyes.

Alistair's hand fell to his side. "Your father sent him to London last night."

"What?" Simon and Isabella asked in unison.

"Why did you not come to fetch me?" Simon asked Alistair. Alistair shrugged. "I did not think of it."

Simon thrust his finger into Alistair's chest. "You do not know what you have done." Isabella recognized the rage burning within her brother's blue eyes. Simon shoved the other gentleman. "I needed him here!"

"Simon!" Isabella leaped from the mattress and stood between the two gentlemen. "We still have other footmen to aid us. Calm down."

"Stay out of this, Bella." Simon gritted his teeth. "You have no idea…"

Isabella stared at her brother. Regret, fear, and fury flashed within the depths of his eyes. "What are you speaking of, Simon?"

When her brother did not answer, Alistair stepped around Isabella. "No idea about what, Reading?" he demanded.

Simon glared at her, then suddenly strode over to the cushioned chair, and before taking a seat, he paused, glancing at Isabella's meal tray. All anger left Simon's person and he returned to the carefree, rake of a brother she loved. She shook her head in a state of confusion.

Simon reached over, lifted the tray off the mattress and set it comfortably on his lap. "I really wish…" he said as he began popping small berries into his mouth, "that you would have let me—" he paused for a brief moment to swallow "—*strangle the bastard.*"

She and Alistair shared a look. Isabella shrugged her shoulders in response. She was just as confused as Alistair most likely was. She remembered the day she saw Simon and Mr. Diggory in the midst of an argument at Amersham Lodge. Perhaps there was more to that exchange than her

## Chapter Fifteen

brother had initially told her.

Simon glanced at Isabella and began shoveling kippers into his mouth with a small silver spoon. He gulped. "You are not dressed yet?" he asked.

Her cheeks flushed with embarrassment. "Err... I was not expecting company," she explained as she fingered the ripped scrap of material at her bust.

"It is eleven in the morning," her brother replied with a mouthful of eggs.

Isabella glanced back toward Simon who had just taken a bite of her toast, then back to Alistair who was studying her with a hint of a smirk on his lips. She should not be looking at Alistair's lips. Looking at his lips caused her to *think* of his lips, and she should not be thinking of Alistair's mouth while Simon was in her company.

*I should not be thinking of Alistair's mouth at all!*

Oh, but she did. It was the charm that oozed from his frame. Those bright emerald eyes that reeled her in time and time again. The dark stubble on his jaw that called to her. His thick auburn tresses that made her want to dive her fingers deep into his mussed hair.

*What is wrong with me?*

She focused her gaze back to her brother, who studied her curiously. A blush formed over Isabella's cheeks at being caught gaping at Alistair. She shot her brother a look. "Well, leave so I can change into proper dress."

"Of course." Simon stood from the chair and set what was left of her meal back onto the floral bed covers.

Simon made his way into the hallway and paused to lean against the door frame. "Are you coming, Baston?"

Isabella looked to Alistair, where he still stood with the

*Meeting Mister Baston*

same flirtatious smirk. He was the one to break eye contact by turning to leave. Before the door was fully closed, Alistair poked his head in. "Enjoy your breakfast, my lady."

After finishing what was left of her breakfast, which was very little after Simon had helped himself to it, she washed herself of last evening's predicament and changed into her pale green muslin dress.

Isabella took one last look in the mirror and frowned. It was time to confront her father. She turned to the door, but something was not quite right. Glancing back toward the nightstand, she remembered her dagger laying within its drawer.

She attached the leather holster to her calf and slid the weapon into place. "Much better."

Entering the tavern, she found her father with Captain Lucas, Simon, and Alistair. Each held a glass of dark liquid in their hands—as though they needed more spirits after what had happened.

She was hoping for a one on one conversation with her father, but mayhap her brother would agree with her on staying. "Have you gathered your belongings, dear sister?" Simon asked in a derisive tone.

*Or mayhap not.*

"Good morning, gentlemen." She greeted them, ignoring her brother's query. She must stay positive if she wanted to stay with the party. She must be strong… for her sister. She glanced at Alistair, who nodded his head in greeting.

"Lady Isabella." Captain Lucas stood from his chair and gave a gentlemanly bow. "You are looking quite well—" he cleared his throat "—considering… the… the *events*."

Her eyes widened. "Good heavens, does everyone know?"

## Chapter Fifteen

"It is difficult to keep something such as that a secret, my dear," her father said. "Especially now we are down three footmen. Happenings such as that do not go unnoticed." The duke stood from his seat and positioned himself in the chair at the head of the table. "Move down, Simon, so your sister may sit."

Simon scooted himself into the chair beside their father, leaving the seat across from Alistair free. Captain Lucas sat as she did, and Simon grasped his glass of spirits, yanking it toward himself.

"A little early for spirits, do you not agree?" Isabella cocked her head as she settled into her chair.

Simon narrowed his eyes and brought the glass to his lips. "Obviously, I do not agree." He took a large gulp of the auburn liquid and set the glass back on the table.

Captain Lucas chuckled. "I do hope you thanked Mr. Baston here for rescuing you from that unfortunate situation."

She gave Captain Lucas a reassuring smile. "I did."

"She did not," Alistair corrected.

Of course she did! Did she not? Isabella glared at the gentleman and kicked his foot under the table. Alistair jumped slightly, surprised by the impact, and tossed her a shameless grin.

She had planned to apologize to Alistair for her behavior toward him yesterday. She felt dreadful for the way she had treated him. *You do not want to know what would have happened if I had not come along...*

Alistair's words echoed through her mind, causing a shudder to move throughout her body. No, she did not wish to know what would have come of her, and she acted so ungrateful for the gentleman's rescue.

*Meeting Mister Baston*

Swallowing her pride, she looked straight into Alistair's eyes. "Thank you, Mr. Baston." She spoke more softly than anticipated.

Alistair gave a curt nod. "You are very welcome, my lady."

"So," Simon drawled. "Are you ready to keep Mother company at home while we men continue our duties here?"

Isabella moved her focus to her father. "Papa." She smiled sweetly. "That is what I wished to discuss—"

"There will be no discussion," her father countered.

"Papa, I am perfectly well!" Aside from her bruised lip, there was not a scratch on her person. "It will not happen again."

"It will not happen again because you will be at home, tending to your mother."

Gritting her teeth, she said, "Mother does not *need* tending to."

Her father took a small sip of his brandy. "Of course she does."

Isabella most assuredly inherited her stubbornness from her father. "Well, then, if I have to leave—" she motioned toward Alistair "—then so does *he*."

Alistair choked on his beverage.

"If I am not here for him to look after, then he will be of no use to you." She confidently crossed her arms over her chest.

George scoffed. "I am sure I will find other uses for him." He paused for a moment. "Especially now we are down three footmen."

*Think... Think!* "Who will show around Violet's portrait?" Isabella asked, more out of desperation than anything.

"I am certain Alistair can handle that on his own," her father replied, picking up the day's newspaper.

## Chapter Fifteen

"It is faster when I help him."

"Simon can help him."

"No, I plan the routes," Simon nearly shouted.

Whose side was her brother on anyhow? Clearly not hers.

Her father unfolded the newspaper and glanced through the pages.

She was losing her father's attention and the argument. She needed something better... Surely if Isabella were to leave then... then... Isabella's eyes widened. *Of course!* "If I leave, then someone will surely need to escort me back to London. It only makes sense for that someone to be Alistair. We are already down three footmen; do you really want to lose another?" she blurted.

There was a long moment of silence. Her father simply stared at her until Captain Lucas cleared his throat. "I do not believe we can afford to lose another able-bodied man on this mission, Your Grace," he said as the true captain he was.

The duke scowled at Lucas.

Oh, how she loved Captain Lucas! She'd always known he was an intelligent and wise man. Isabella tightened her arms over her chest and smirked. She could not bear sitting at home while everyone else was searching for Violet. As an older sibling, it was Isabella's duty to look after her sister—and she'd failed.

*Now it is my duty to find her.*

The table went silent. Isabella glanced from Simon to her father, her father to Captain Lucas, Captain Lucas to Alistair, waiting for *someone* to reply.

"I do value Lady Isabella's assistance during our outings. She is much more sociable and charming than I, and she is able to get more information out of the townspeople," Alistair directed toward her father.

The duke looked up from his paper and focused on Alistair. He pursed his lips and glanced to his daughter, and then back to Alistair. "If *anything* else happens…" Isabella's heart lifted. *He is going to let me stay.* "If Bella so much as trips over her own slippers…" the duke continued, turning his focus on Alistair. "You are unemployed."

Alistair's smile dipped, and he gulped audibly. "Of course, Your Grace."

Isabella jumped from her chair, causing the legs to scrape against the wood floor, and kissed her father on his cheek. "Thank you, Papa!"

And thank *you*, Mr. Baston.

## Chapter Sixteen

The wildflowers rolled past the carriage window in a blur of purple and yellow. The scene reminded Isabella of her sister, the way Violet would run and dance through the rolling fields of their country estate—the carefree spirit that had always gotten her into trouble.

*"Mother wants us to play Graces." Young Violet tossed aside the set of sticks and small hooped ribbon. "I would rather dance. What about you?"*

*Isabella imagined herself using the sticks for a round of fencing instead, but dancing would be fun too. She stood from her spot in the grass. "There is no music," she noted.*

*"Do not worry yourself over that, sister." Violet took her hand and pulled Isabella into a waltz stance. "I will be the music." Violet hummed a slow 1, 2, 3 rhythm.*

*"A waltz? Father will never permit us to waltz."*

*"Not now." Violet scoffed. "But when I make my coming out, I most definitely will dance a waltz."*

Of course, just a few moments later, their governess had

found them dancing that forbidden waltz on the lawn, and she'd had them studying French for an extra hour that day.

Despite their interests being so different, they'd always been close. Violet was more interested in music, art, and singing, while Isabella always preferred more masculine pursuits.

"Bella?" Alistair broke into her musings inside the small conveyance.

She turned to focus on him. "Yes?"

"Are you well?" he asked, worry clouding his eyes.

*No. I am not well.* This was the first time she had acknowledged that truth.

Thoughts of Alistair had flooded her mind so frequently over the last few days, she had not worried much over Violet—the very reason she and Alistair were traveling around England to begin with.

"I am well," she lied. "Just tired." *Sometimes, lying is easier.*

"I can imagine." A small frown emerged on his lips. "After the evening you endured."

The memories of that night made her wince. She supposed now would be a good time to properly thank him for saving her life... Or at the very least, for saving her virtue.

Isabella moved from her bench and sat in the empty space next to the gentleman. "It could have been worse. *Much worse.*" She turned away from his gaze, feeling very much like a terrified little girl. Why was it so difficult to let go of her pride and thank him? "If you hadn't been passing by that very moment..."

He clasped his free hand over hers, causing those little butterflies to dance in her belly. "I will never let anything happen to you again," Alistair said quietly. He brought her

## Chapter Sixteen

knuckles to his lips and watched her through hooded lashes. He slowly kissed each digit.

Her breath caught at the intimacy of the moment, and tears pricked her eyes. Her heart stood as frozen as a statue as his fiery gaze met hers. The inside of the carriage seemed to shrink, being smaller and more cramped than it was just moments ago. She swallowed past the lump forming in her throat, swallowed past the indisputable need for the gentleman to kiss away all her worries and fears.

But her mind thought better of it. She could not distract herself with gentlemen and investigate her sister's disappearance all at once. Isabella slid her hand out of his, and she took in a much-needed breath of air.

\* \* \*

What was he thinking? And why had he been asking himself said question so often as of late?

*You were thinking you wished to kiss away the sorrowful expression on the lady's face.* But instead, he'd kissed her knuckles, each one more tantalizing than the last. And, being the soulless cad he was, he could not stop wondering what it'd be like to kiss every last inch of her skin.

*Christ.*

Perhaps he should bed a woman, now that they'd arrived in town. Not only was the woman in front of him an innocent lady of the *ton*, but she was also his friend's sister and—to make matters worse—his employer's daughter. She was untouchable. And he was trapped inside a tiny conveyance with this siren more often than was proper. It would drive even the most virginal son of a vicar to perverted lust-crazed fantasies.

"Excuse me," a small voice came from below Alistair's line of sight as something tugged on the hem of his jacket.

A small boy, around the age of ten or so, looked up at him with sad eyes. His cheeks were coated in dirt and his shirt far too big for his tiny frame.

An orphan, he guessed.

"Is that a watch?" the boy asked, motioning toward the fob hanging from his breast pocket.

Alistair crouched down to the boy's level and smiled. "Indeed, it is. Would you like to see it?"

The young boy looked to the ground and nodded.

"Well." Alistair reached into his pocket and pulled out his timepiece. "One day, if you work hard enough, you will be able to buy a watch such as this one." He softly clasped the young boy's hand, and as he was about to drop the coins into his palm, he heard Isabella laugh.

It was soft and magical, and he could not help but look over at her. That was when he saw the second boy, just as dirty and small as the other, reach inside her reticule. "You!" Alistair shouted. He stood from his crouched position and slipped his watch back inside his pocket.

With two quick strides, he reached Isabella's side and grabbed the second boy's arm before he had the chance to run off.

"What do you think you are doing?" He scowled at the orphan, who seemed to be around the same age as the first boy. He had short, messy brown hair, reddened cheeks, and pale skin speckled with dirt and freckles.

The boy looked up, his dark hazel eyes filled with guilt as

## Chapter Sixteen

tears began to form within their depths.

"What is this?" Isabella asked in surprise as she looked toward the small arm that was in Alistair's grasp.

"He was going to steal from you," Alistair replied, still holding tightly onto the urchin's forearm.

The boy hesitated for a moment, having a difficult time keeping eye contact. "Erm... Joseph, my lady."

A smile played on her lips as she slipped the boy's arm out of Alistair's grasp. "Where are you from, Joseph?"

"The orphanage, my lady."

Alistair's heart broke a little, and he watched as Isabella pulled a few coins from her coin purse. She laid them into the boy's hand, folding his fingers gently into his palm. "I hope this will help."

The young boy thanked her, and as he turned to leave, Alistair noticed that his pocket felt a bit lighter than it had a few moments earlier.

His left hand flew to his chest and felt for his timepiece. It was gone. He looked to Joseph, who had been studying him from a few feet away. Just as Alistair took a step forward, the boy stuck out his tongue and darted down the crowded lane.

To think he was starting to feel sorry for the bugger. He gritted his teeth. *"That little..."*

"Pardon?" Isabella asked, most definitely unaware of what the young thief had just done.

"He stole my timepiece," Alistair responded dryly.

Isabella's hand flew to cover her mouth.

"Are you laughing?"

"No."

*She was.*

His eyes narrowed. "Is that funny to you?" he asked, trying

to sound irate, but he could not bring himself to be angry with her.

Isabella shook her head again, and her hand fell from her lips. "Perhaps a little," she admitted.

The smile creeping over Isabella's lips took his breath away. It should be unlawful for a woman to be so beautiful—his stomach lurched at his own thoughts. He had really better get such thoughts under control. He had no place by her side. She, the daughter of a duke and he... a mere nothing.

As they made their way to the edge of Market Square, Alistair spotted their groomsman sprinting toward them. He halted in front of them. "There is news, my lady," he said in labored breaths.

"News?" she asked. "News of my sister?"

"Yes, my lady." The groomsman gave a curt nod. "There may have been a sighting of her in Newark-on-Trent."

"That is quite close to Derby," Alistair noted.

"What do you mean *may* have been a sighting?" she asked the coachman, confusion clouding her voice.

"Well." He cleared his throat. "The duke's informer said the young woman looked very much like Violet."

She glanced down to her fingers, which were fidgeting with the cloth of her skirts. "I see."

"Your father ordered that we leave straight away. Your belongings are already packed into the carriage. He is waiting just outside of town, and we are to meet him there."

This was wonderful news. The sooner they found Lady Violet, the sooner Alistair could be rid of his friend's enchantress of a sister. He could go back to his rakish ways and clear Isabella from his mind. It was unnatural for him to lust after a proper lady of the *ton* anyhow. Unnatural and

## Chapter Sixteen

unwise. "Let us make haste, then."

## Chapter Seventeen

The driver made way, not bothering to stop so that Isabella might speak with her father before departing. Isabella desperately wished to speak about the letter her father received.

Was Violet alive? Was she taken hostage? Was she out shopping for gowns and ribbons with her secret betrothed, going on with her life as normal?

Out of those options, the last would be optimal. Yes, mayhap her running away would ruin the Avery name, but at least Violet would be happy and in love. There would be no need to worry over her well-being any longer. And of course, their parents would still support Violet. Oh, yes, they would most definitely be cross, but Isabella knew her parents would not stay angry forever.

She sighed. Unfortunately, her questions would not be answered for at least another four hours, so she was forced to sit and wait. She looked to Alistair for distraction, but he'd been gazing out the carriage window since they had

## Chapter Seventeen

departed.

Perhaps sleep would do her well, being as the gentleman beside her did not seem to be in a talkative mood—and she had long ago finished reading her novel.

Sleep soon took her, but she was awoken by a sudden jolt. She blinked her eyes open and yawned. Her vision had not completely returned, but she realized the carriage must have run over something quite large.

Once her vision cleared, she noticed her cheek resting on something. She looked down and saw Alistair's arm.

She also became aware of the fact that her arm was wrapped about the gentleman's well-muscled bicep. Lifting her head, she quickly pulled away.

Alistair flashed her a boyish grin. "Sleep well?"

"Why did you not move me?" she asked, irritated with him—and with herself for enjoying the way his strong arm felt in her embrace.

"I would have had to wake you." He turned to face her. "And you just looked too damned charming to wake," he said with a wink, which caused her heart to skip a beat.

She shot him a look. "How long was I sleeping?"

"About five hours," he answered with a dry tone.

"*What?!*"

"I jest." Alistair lurched forward as the carriage rolled to a stop. "*Fewer* than five hours." He smirked.

She rolled her eyes. "I wonder why we've stopped?" Opening the curtains, she added, "We're still in the country."

"I am not certain." He too gazed out the windowpane. "I will take a look."

Alistair opened the carriage door and stepped out, offering Isabella his hand once he reached the ground. Isabella accepted his offer just as he let out a curse.

"What is it?" She followed his gaze to the back wheel of the carriage, which was cracked nearly in half. "Oh, dear…"

How on earth could that have happened? She looked down the lane they had traveled, but there was nothing in the road that would have caused such damage.

The coachman stepped down from his perch to inspect the damage. "Terrible luck, that is."

Alistair nodded and stood with his hands at his hips. He took a quick look at their surroundings as the footmen dismounted their horses.

Isabella sighed and brought her fingertips to her forehead. "This is not good." There was no time for such hindrances, and there was no telling how long Violet was planning to stay in Newark-on-Trent.

First her illness and now this. It was as if the universe was hell-bent on working against her.

"Hey!" Simon shouted with a wave in their direction as his long legs hopped down from the conveyance.

"Is yours damaged as well?" Alistair called out to Simon, who was currently inspecting the back wheel of their larger conveyance.

"Not looking good!"

George stepped out from his carriage and knelt beside Simon. He shook his head, looking quite disappointed.

Isabella followed behind Alistair as he made his way over to her family.

"Bloody hell." Captain Lucas cursed as he exited.

*Bloody hell, indeed.* "What happens now?" she asked no one in particular.

After a moment of silence, the duke stood from his

## Chapter Seventeen

haunches. "I am afraid we will have to camp here for the night."

"What?" Camp in the road? Isabella scoffed. "Surely you are not serious, Papa." She had never slept out of doors before. Her mother forbade it. They could not just stay... *here*. Their journey had been delayed enough already.

"I am afraid we are still miles from the nearest village. And it is much too late to start walking." George motioned toward the sky, which had a purple and orange hue.

*Walking?* "We have plenty of horses to—"

"Yes," her father interrupted. "And two broken carriages full of luggage, which will need to be taken with us."

She could not give a jot about her belongings if it meant being reunited with Violet all the sooner. "Perhaps—" Alistair stepped between Isabella and her father "—I can escort Lady Isabella to the nearest inn?"

"Absolutely not." George pointed a finger toward her person. "You had your chance to return home. You will not be receiving any special treatment, and you will camp out with everyone else."

Isabella stepped between Alistair and her father. "I do not care about that," she said, silencing him. "What of Violet? We were supposed to arrive to wherever we were going by tonight."

"Newark-on-Trent," Simon supplied.

"Yes," she huffed, shooting Simon an annoyed glance. "Thank you."

Placing his hands on his hips, the duke let out a sigh. "We will just have to pray she is still there tomorrow."

"Perhaps I may ride ahead?" Captain Lucas stepped in. "If I find her, I will send word."

## Meeting Mister Baston

Isabella perked up at the captain's offer, but her father shook his head. "I would rather we stay together as a group. We do not know what is out there. Someone could be waiting for us to split up."

*We do not know what is out there...* Her father spoke as if this were some dark gothic novel. This was real life. She let out a heavy sigh. There was no arguing with her father once he made up his mind. "Well, I do hope we have blankets..."

Simon held his first two fingers in the air. "Two tents." Then he shot her an amused grin. "And about two hundred twenty-two blankets just for the lady. We all know how much you enjoy complaining of the cold."

Isabella crossed her arms over her chest. "I do not complain of the cold," she lied.

"Yes you do," Simon countered.

"No, I don—"

"Enough!" her father boomed. "Stop behaving like children."

Fine. She occasionally complained of the cold. But who did not? She just hoped, wherever Violet was, she would not be left out to sleep in the cold this night.

\* \* \*

While the footmen were busy setting up tents of their own, Alistair began to work on Isabella's small cloth shelter.

"Where will you sleep?" Isabella's voice came from behind him.

"Right here." Alistair motioned to the spongy, wet grass, which was soaking through the knees of his cream breeches.

## Chapter Seventeen

"Out here?" she asked, her eyes filled with concern.

"I do not mind it." He continued to hammer the small wooden stake into the soft ground. "I used to camp out with my father and brother as a child."

She furrowed her brow. "Did you enjoy it?"

He gazed up at her and smiled. "Very much so." It was the *only* activity he enjoyed doing with his father.

"My mother would never allow the girls to camp out with my father and brother. I do enjoy being out of doors, but—" she motioned to the damp dirt "—sleeping on the ground cannot be very comfortable."

He pulled out a second stake. "It is not," he laughed. "But I suppose that is part of the fun."

Once their campsite was set up, Alistair settled into his makeshift bed next to the warm, crackling fire. Looking to the stars, he smiled. *I could get used to sleeping out of doors...* The silence of night filled him. Peace embraced him.

He'd often gone out to lay under the stars after a particularly brutal day with his father. There was something about the darkness and the silence that would help him to forget the pain from being whipped. The cool grass on his tender skin had been bliss, a godsend after days such as that.

"Oh!" Isabella stumbled over Alistair's torso as she peeked through the opening of her tent. "What are you doing?"

He glanced toward her. She was on all fours, hovering over his hips. "I *was* stargazing, but you've seemed to block my view." *With an even pleasanter view of your décolletage.*

Isabella rested on her knees and looked up toward the stars. "They are quite beautiful when one is outside of the city."

Alistair watched as the glow of the fire danced over Isabella's cream white skin. *She* was even more beautiful outside of the city.

"But it does not explain to me why you are lying outside of my tent..."

He shrugged and placed both hands at his nape for support. "Neither your father nor I wanted a repeat of last night's events."

Without a word, Isabella vanished inside. She reappeared and tossed a feather cushion at his face.

"How thoughtful of you, my lady." He laughed as he placed the small cushion under the base of his skull.

"You are welcome. Now..." Isabella settled on her stomach at the entrance, using her elbows to prop herself up. "Tell me of your family, Alistair."

*His family?* "I believe you know all you need to know. I never knew my mother, and my father loved my brother more than he loved me."

She rolled her eyes skyward. "Not *that*."

Alistair let out a soft chuckle. "What would you like to know?" That his father enjoyed beating him on a regular basis? That his loving sire blamed Alistair for all that went wrong in his life? Wait... she was already aware of that.

"What did you do on these camping excursions of yours?"

Camping was the only time he had spent with his father that seemed somewhat normal. His father enjoyed being out of doors so much that it must have made him forget his hatred for his youngest son. "Swimming, fishing, hunting, hiking." He paused and turned onto his side to better see her. "Archery." He winked.

"You enjoy archery?" Isabella cocked her head in that adorable way of hers. "I do as well."

"*Nooo.*" Alistair sarcastically placed his fingertips over his

## Chapter Seventeen

mouth. "*You?* A lady who enjoys threatening gentlemen with daggers also enjoys shooting arrows?"

She slapped his knee.

"My mother would never allow me to go camping." Isabella placed a hand over her cheek and lowered her voice to a whisper. "It would ruin my expensive dresses."

"But she allowed you to practice archery and wield dangerous daggers?" What a strange family they were.

"*And* shoot pistols," she added. "But no, not at first. My father and I had to hide it from her." She smiled to herself. "One day, Mother caught me swinging around an antique cutlass in the garden." She paused and stared off into the distance. "I never heard her scream so loud."

A grin formed over his lips as he brought the scene to light in his mind.

"What about your mother? You know nothing of her?"

Alistair flinched at the question. He despised speaking of his mother... but Bella was asking, and the gentlemanly thing to do would be to answer truthfully. "Just that my father blamed me for her death."

"I am sorry," she whispered, her hand still at her face.

His father had not always shown his hatred toward him. He used to think he was treated differently because he was the second son. Because he did not need to learn the responsibilities of being a viscount. Because he was not as important as his brother, Colin.

But Alistair's suspicions were made clear one day when he was out shopping in the markets with his father and brother. He was twelve years old at the time, passing by a small table with vases and glassware out for display. His sire had been in a particularly foul mood that day, so when Alistair tripped on his own feet and fell into the table, he'd watched in horror as a large white and gold French vase toppled over and shattered into pieces, causing a good portion of the glassware to fall and break as well.

The viscount had taken hold of his shoulders and shook him. He shook and shook him and screamed, *What is wrong with you boy?! You are useless! Why could it not have been you? Why did you have to kill her?!*

From then on, he could not help but blame himself for his mother's death. His father had reminded him of the fact nearly every day since.

"Alistair?"

Isabella's voice brought him back to the present. "Hmm?"

"It is not your fault your mother died." She searched his gaze.

Alistair tore his eyes from hers. "But it was. If I was never born, my mother would still be alive."

She placed her cold hand over his. His heart lifted slightly from the shallow depths of his chest. "Do not say such things."

A long moment of silence passed between them, and hearing nothing but the low crackle of the fire, Alistair closed his eyes and readied himself for sleep.

"Alistair?"

His eyes jolted open. "Yes?"

"How did you come to work for my father?"

He let out a low yawn and answered simply. "We met at a gentlemen's club."

"A club?" She sounded puzzled.

"Yes, a club." He smiled to himself. "Where gentlemen go to drink and enjoy the company of other gentlemen. Or just to drink and enjoy their own company."

## Chapter Seventeen

Isabella snorted. "I know what a club is."

After a few moments, she called out his name again.

"Yes?"

"That is how you met him," she stated. "But how did you come to *work* for him?"

*Christ, what a curious little minx she is.*

"He started speaking of his work and how he needed a new man-of-affairs. So I offered my help. Being as I was nothing but the viscount's *brother,* I really had nothing useful to do with my time."

"Oh…"

"Oh?" he mocked.

She repeated herself in a more aggressive tone. "*Oh.*"

A ghost of a smile played at his lips. No sneering remark from the lady? He inhaled the cool night air and closed his eyes—

"Alistair?"

*Good God.*

He peeked over to where she still sat at the entrance of her tent. If she did not remove her enticing form from view, he would have to take her into his arms and lay her down inside that monstrous tower of fabric. "Bella?" he growled.

She gave him a wolfish smile. "Goodnight."

He let out an exasperated sigh. "Goodnight, Bella."

Such an odd creature she was. But Alistair could not deny that he enjoyed hearing his name come from the lady's lips. And the next time she brought up his mother or his father, he would just have to silence her with a kiss, and Alistair had a feeling that this time, the lady would not refuse.

*Go to sleep, Baston.*

## Chapter Eighteen

A rustling noise woke Alistair. He squinted between the two cloth flaps at the tent's entrance to where Isabella had fallen asleep. Her bright hair swept across her pillow, and he watched as her chest rose and fell in the peaceful rhythm of sleep. He looked toward the carriage, careful not to make a sound.

He spotted a shadow of movement under the conveyance.

It sounded like footsteps—not heavy enough to be a man's, but what would a woman be doing creeping about the woodlands in the middle of the night? He shook the idea from his head and closed his eyes.

It was just a rat... *An uncommonly large rat.*

*Crunch.*

Whipping around, he peered toward the carriage once again, and he swore he saw a pair of small feet running about the broken wheel.

Were they being robbed? Here? They were in the middle of nowhere. Alistair threw off his covers and rose from his

## Chapter Eighteen

makeshift bed.

"What are you doing?" Isabella's drowsy voice asked.

She was kneeling down behind him with his dark burgundy blanket covering her head. He must have flung it over the lady when he stood. He smiled at the sight. "My apologies."

She slid the blanket off and eyed Alistair with suspicion.

"There is someone here," he whispered.

She scowled. "Yes, there are quite a few people here."

"You know what I mean." He watched as she rose from her comfortable nest. "What do you think you are doing?"

She flashed him a devilish smile. "Following you."

"Like hell you are." Alistair watched as Isabella stepped out in her night shift. The woman was as stubborn as a mule. "Fine," he hissed. "But stay by my side and stay quiet."

They tip-toed their way to the broken carriage when Isabella let out a fearful gasp.

Alistair whipped around to face her. "What is it?"

She pointed toward their conveyance. "Look."

Alistair's eyes followed her outstretched hand toward a shadow in the window. He dropped to his haunches and pulled Isabella down with him. Now there was no doubt in his mind a thief had stolen into their camp.

"Who is it?" she whispered.

"It seems to be a child."

"Why would a child be out of doors in the middle of the night?"

He shrugged. "I do not know." The nearest village was miles away. There must be a small farm or cottage near.

Taking Isabella's hand in his, Alistair proceeded forward. Their bodies huddled near the ground as they took small, quiet steps, like tigers stalking their prey—only, there were

*Meeting Mister Baston*

not any tigers in England.

Alistair reached out to grip the silver handle of the door and took a steadying breath.

One… two… three!

He yanked it open and— Nothing. It was strange…

Alistair poked his head inside and inspected every corner of the vehicle, but it was empty. He shook his head in disbelief. Both he and Isabella saw someone. How could there be no one?

Isabella tugged at his hand. "What is it?"

He shrugged. "There is no one here."

"What?" She tore her hand from his grasp and popped her head inside. "How can that be? We both saw… something."

"I do not know." He reached out to take Isabella's hand again. "Come, we should go back to sleep."

Isabella followed him back to her tent. "As if I will ever be able to sleep knowing there may be a thief lurking about."

"I will be right outside your tent," he assured her.

He watched as she nestled herself under the blanket, then just as he was about to return to his bed, Isabella called, "What if it is Mr. Diggory?"

Alistair's heart sank. It could not be. Callum was monstrous, and the shadow and the footsteps seemed to belong to a child. Why would the traitorous footman return anyhow? To finish what he'd started?

Rage built in Alistair's chest, and he cursed under his breath. Lord above, if he ever faced that bastard again, he would kill him.

"Callum is shut away in London by now," he assured her. He knelt down in front of her and set his palm on her cheek. The touch set his skin aflame. "Whatever it was, I will be just

## Chapter Eighteen

outside your tent. Now sleep, my Bella."

He wanted so much to hold this woman in his arms and draw her worries away.

\* \* \*

Ignoring the rumbling of her belly, Isabella took aim at the target Simon had carved into the bark of the tree before her. She took in a breath and exhaled slowly, silencing everything around her.

*Using your thumb and forefinger, hold the blade about an inch from the shaft. Hold your opposite arm out to aim—then throw...*

Her father's long-ago lesson echoed around the walls of her mind.

She brought her wrist back to her shoulder and slung her hand forward. The dagger soared through the air until the tip of the blade pierced the bark of the tree with a soft *thunk*.

The sapphire-studded dagger hit just a few centimeters from the center ring.

"Nicely done!" Simon applauded from behind her.

Her shoulders slumped forward. *I can do better.*

Simon took her place in front of the tree and pulled out his gold-encrusted dagger. He aimed, and inhaled and exhaled just as she had. A few seconds later, her brother hurled his dagger through the air.

*Thunk.*

It hit the second ring from the center—just an inch from Isabella's dagger.

"Damn," he muttered to himself.

"Well done, Simon." Their father approached and studied

the carved-out target. "Though still not as proficient as your sister," he teased.

Isabella grinned at Simon, who then shot her a narrow-eyed glance.

She had always bested Simon at throwing blades, but as for pistol shooting, he had her beat. She just could not figure out how to aim those damned contraptions. Not that she missed the target. She never missed the target, but she repeatedly hit far off-center. While throwing daggers had always come naturally to her.

"Let us see you try, Father." Simon placed a fist on his hip and eyed the duke.

George arched a brow and strode forward. He stared Simon in the eye. "I never back down from a dare."

Simon smirked. "Excellent."

Isabella knew how it would end. Their father had always been outstanding at all things. He was the one who taught her all she knew, whether it be archery, knife throwing, pistol shooting or cricket.

She watched as he pulled Simon's dagger from the tree and took about ten steps back. He paused for a moment, lifted his arm to aim and—

*Whoosh, thunk.*

Perfectly center.

Simon ran to the tree to inspect their father's work. His jaw dropped at the sight of it. "Unbelievable." He turned to face their father and laughed. "You did not even aim." He stood next to the tree with his jaw hanging open.

Isabella chuckled. Her brother looked as though he'd just witnessed the end of the earth as they knew it. "I believe you are the worst of us all."

## Chapter Eighteen

Simon closed the distance between them with hurried strides. He crossed his arms lazily over his chest. "Get yourself a pistol, then we will see who is worst."

"Absolutely not!"

They jerked their head toward their father in unison. He seemed to have been listening to her and Simon's bickering.

Isabella was not disappointed to hear their father's protest though. In fact, she knew her brother would best her at shooting. And she also knew she did not fancy being bested by her brother today.

Or tomorrow.

Or any day, really.

Her hand fell to her stomach as it let out an angry growl.

"Hungry are we?" Simon eyed her, amused.

She pursed her lips to the side. "I hope Alistair remembers to bring food."

"As do I." Simon pulled his dagger from the tree bark and placed it inside of his jacket pocket. "I can seldom make it two hours without eating, let alone an entire day."

Isabella rolled her eyes skyward. What was it with men and food? They inhaled each meal as though they hadn't eaten in months.

She smiled at the memory of Alistair attempting to steal the blueberries from her meal tray. The butterflies ran rampant through her belly—*because I am famished*, she told herself. Not because she longed for the gentleman's company.

Isabella made her way to the tree and yanked her blade from its place on the target. She inspected the shine and silver of the blade for traces of damage, then not-so-discreetly hiked up her skirts and slid it into place on her calf. It was wonderful not having to worry about manners and proper etiquette. It was one thing she loved best about being in the countryside.

When she looked up from her holster, she watched as two men on horses approached.

Alistair had left with the footmen to retrieve supplies, but this was not his group. "Wait here," Simon ordered as he stalked off to join their father. She did as she was told, no matter how much it killed her.

Straightening her skirts, she studied the group of men. One of them mentioned something to her father which made him lower his head in dismay. Then Simon let out a black curse.

Isabella took an errant step forward. If only she could understand what they were saying… but Captain Lucas spotted her movement and stayed her with a raise of his hand.

Blast and damn.

The longer she stayed there, observing the gentlemen's conversation instead of partaking in it, the further her mind strayed.

Was Alistair injured? Did these men find him bleeding on the side of the road? She shook away that thought. No… for if they found a battered Alistair, they would have instructed him to return to camp. And to add to it, Alistair hadn't traveled alone.

The men dismounted their steeds and unloaded their equipment. The duke turned to Simon and Lucas, and they spoke among themselves in hushed tones.

*Go now. Speak to them.* With frustration bubbling beneath her skin, she stalked toward the group. She refused to stay put any longer.

Reaching the group of gentlemen unnoticed, Isabella stood

## Chapter Eighteen

with her arms crossed over her chest. She cleared her throat.

All three men turned their heads around to face her.

"Does anyone plan on telling me what is going on?"

The duke turned to both Lucas and Simon. They exchanged looks. Lucas gave a shrug of his shoulders and Simon just glowered.

The duke sighed. "Wait here, gentlemen."

Her father grasped her arm and led her a few feet away. He motioned for her to take a seat on a fallen tree before her.

"Well?" she prompted.

Her father let out an even heavier sigh. "The men who approached… they are the footmen who traveled with Mr. Diggory to London."

"Oh?" Her body froze at the sound of the servant's name. And from her brother's and father's reaction earlier… she did not believe this news of Diggory would be good.

"He… escaped."

She stared at her father as last eve's shadow appeared in her mind's eye. Could the rustling have been him? But… Alistair said it was a shadow of a boy, not a young man of Mr. Diggory's size.

"Bella?" Her father's voice brought her back to the present. "What is wrong?"

"I…" *Tell him. Your father needs to know.* "I… Alistair and I," she amended, "believed we saw someone sneaking about last night."

"What?" The duke stiffened. "Why did you not mention this earlier?"

"We did not find anyone, so I thought perhaps we imagined it." Or perhaps it was an animal. Or anything but Mr. Diggory.

## Meeting Mister Baston

The duke paced. "You still should have told me. *Alistair* should have told me."

"The food has arrived!" Simon shouted as he ran off in the direction of a small cavalry.

It was Alistair, but something was not right. As the group of men approached, she could see a footman was injured. She turned to Alistair and gasped. He was bruised as well.

Isabella left her father's side and reached Alistair just as he jumped down from his mount. Ignoring her, he unloaded small sacks, tools, and a carriage wheel. How they found that she hadn't a clue. "Did you steal it?"

"Steal what?" Alistair asked, with his back turned to her.

"The carriage wheel."

She moved to his side, but the gentleman still refused to face her. "How did you get it? And why are you injured?" She waited, her heart beating a frantic rhythm in her chest.

"A farmer was nice enough to lend it to us." He untied the brown sacks from the saddle and set them on the ground. "It may not be a perfect fit, but it is better than nothing."

She stood, tapping the toe of her slipper against the ground. He had not answered her second question, she noted. With an impatient huff, she grasped the sleeve of Alistair's dirtied jacket and forced him to turn.

"Good heavens, Alistair." She brought her hand to touch the fresh cut above his bruised brow. The heat of his skin radiated onto her bare fingers, and she dropped her hand to her side. "Were you mugged?"

Her breath hitched as he lifted her hand to his lips and brushed a kiss across her bare knuckles. "A small misunderstanding," he whispered as her hand slipped from his grasp. "You need not worry."

## Chapter Eighteen

"What sort of misunderstanding?"

Alistair lowered his face to hers, and his breath tickled her ear. "A misunderstanding," he repeated. "About you."

Isabella's heart tripled its beat. "Me?" She watched him for a moment and studied his powerful hands as he unknotted the sacks.

He glanced back at her as she rid herself of her dazed state. "Are you going to tell me what happened?" She crossed her arms at her waist. "Or leave me in suspense?"

His lips curved into a crooked grin. "I'd prefer to leave you in suspense."

She arched a brow and waited.

"But being as you can kill me with that dagger of yours…" He sighed. "I did not agree with how one footman spoke of you."

"Which one?" As soon as the question left her lips, she remembered the injured footman. She focused on the small crowd of men surrounding one particularly bloodied and bruised servant.

Her fingers flew to her lips on a gasp. "My goodness." Upon closer inspection, it looked as though the servant had been trampled by a stampede of wild stallions—and was most definitely in need of a doctor. "What could he have said to earn him such a beating?"

Isabella waited as Alistair released the second bag from the saddle. They found a place to sit, and Alistair pulled out a scone, before handing it to her. She took a small bite out of the pastry and eyed Alistair anxiously. She had not forgotten that he still had yet to answer her question.

He pulled the second scone from the sack and took a large bite, his eyes focused on hers. She jerked her chin forward,

## Meeting Mister Baston

signaling her impatience.

Alistair smiled. "It is not something that should be repeated to a delicate lady, such as yourself."

She tilted her head and shot him a look. "I am certain my delicate ears can handle whatever it is you have to say."

Alistair took another bite of his pastry and glanced to where the men stood across the road. "If you must know…" He inched his body closer to her own.

"I must." Her cheeks burned as she attempted to ignore his nearness.

He nibbled on his scone and said, "This may make me more uncomfortable than it will make you."

She let out an unladylike snort. "All the better, then."

"Do you enjoy seeing me uncomfortable, my lady?"

She could not recall a time she had ever seen the gentleman uncomfortable… but she supposed she would not mind, being as he had made *her* uncomfortable several times. "Yes."

His eyes widened, and he threw his head back in laughter. "You are direct."

She tore off a small piece of scone and tossed it inside her mouth. "There is nothing wrong with one speaking one's mind."

The edge of his mouth curved up into that boyish grin that did funny things to her heart. "No, I suppose there is not." He winked and wiggled himself closer until he was just a hair's breadth away.

Isabella gulped at his nearness, causing the gentleman to tilt his head in question. "You are crowding me," she blurted out.

He chuckled and leaned into her. "I do not want anyone to hear our conversation."

## Chapter Eighteen

Mocking his movements, she leaned toward him and whispered, "And if someone sees us sitting this close, *they* will converse about *us*."

Alistair glanced toward the chattering group of footmen. "They already do."

Heat flooded her cheeks. The servants gossiped about Alistair and herself? Had they been spreading rumors about her and the gentleman? Should they not worry over the fact that Violet was nowhere to be found? Should they not focus on the reason they were on this journey to begin with?

She straightened her shoulders. "What did they say?"

Alistair turned to face her once again, and she could see the hesitation in his green eyes. He cleared his throat. "First," he whispered, "Marcus asked if there was anything romantic between us." His eyes fell to her lips, and she lifted her fingers to cover her bruised mouth.

Did Alistair *want* something romantic to happen between them?

*Do I want something to happen?*

What else did the servant say? "What—" Her thoughts were left unspoken as Alistair brought his forefinger dangerously close to her lips.

"No interruptions. Understand?"

Careful not to lean into his almost-touch, she nodded.

He returned his hand to rest on his lap and continued, "I said no, of course."

"Of course?"

Alistair glared at her.

Right... she was meant to stay quiet. Why she posed his statement as a question, she hadn't a clue.

*Because you fancy him.*

No—that was silly. How could she have feelings for a gentleman when her heart was so consumed with worry over her sister?

"They then accused me of—" Alistair paused "—laying with you… inside your tent."

*Laying with me?* She let out an unladylike snort. How absurd… How could the servants imagine such a thing?

*Because it is not so absurd. You fancy him, and he fancies you.*

She needed to silence that irritating voice inside of her head.

"At first, I was fine with it,"

Her eyes widened.

"With the time we spend together, I would not blame one for assuming."

Those proverbial butterflies fluttered around her stomach. Alistair was fine with rumors that they had lain together? Or he was fine with them laying together?

Her cheeks flushed. She should not be thinking of such things—they should not be discussing such things—but before she could stop their scandalous conversation, Isabella noted a change in Alistair's demeanor. He curled his fingers into the palms of his hands.

"But then," he continued and furrowed his brows, "Marcus spoke of putting his filthy hands on you." After a moment, Alistair relaxed his fists. "He spoke of trailing his hands along your waist…"

His eyes fell to her midsection, and her pulse quickened. She needed to stop this. Alistair leaned closer. "How he would…"

His words trailed off into nothing as his face inched closer to hers. Was she imagining his nearness? Or was he leaning

## Chapter Eighteen

in to *kiss* her? Her senses seemed to dull, and her vision blurred. Her limbs grew weak, and she could not make sense of what was happening.

It was as if she was floating on a cloud. Isabella's eyes fluttered closed as she tilted her chin up to receive him.

*"I cannot."* The heat of Alistair's whisper caressed her lips. "I cannot."

She opened her eyes to discover Alistair standing several feet away.

Disappointment filled her chest.

*Why are you disappointed? Did you want your father's man-of-affairs to kiss you?*

She did. And she should not.

"Cannot what?" she asked, mentally shaking the haze that clouded her mind.

Alistair dragged a hand over his face. "I cannot get myself to repeat the rest."

"What the bloody hell happened?"

Isabella whipped her head toward Simon as he stomped his way over.

Did he see her and Alistair together? How he had been just a mere inch away from her lips?

"Baston!" Simon reached Alistair's side. "Are you going to answer me?"

"Did you ask a question? I must have missed it," Alistair quipped.

"Did you and the servant get into a bloody battle over who would eat the last scone?"

A sigh of relief escaped Isabella's lungs. Simon did not notice a thing. Her brother was preoccupied with food, as he always was. She shook her head.

"Something like that." Alistair gave her a knowing look, and her heart skipped a beat.

"Is that food?" Simon asked, reaching for the brown sack in Alistair's hand.

Alistair yanked the small bag from Simon's grasp. "Yes, but you must promise to share."

Simon placed his fist on his heart. "I promise."

Alistair tossed the brown sack of food at Simon. Her brother caught the bag and marched off toward the carriages, shouting, "Gentlemen, we have food!"

Once Simon was at a distance, Alistair continued where he left off. "I jumped off my mount and tackled Marcus off his. Once the other footmen could pull me off—" he motioned to his injured brow "—that is when he did this."

"I am so sorry."

His focus turned on her. "There is no need to apologize." He knitted his dark brows together and clenched his fists once more. "No one will ever touch you again. I will make sure of it."

## Chapter Nineteen

Alistair wondered if it was the subject of his retelling of events that had caused him to lean in so close that he had felt her breath on his skin. Until he was so close it caused her cheeks to flush. Until he was so close he wanted to devour her with his mouth.

Or was it more than a rake's lust for a beautiful woman?

Either way, his conscience had gotten the better of him. If he had kissed Isabella in front of so many witnesses, he would have had to marry her, and a lady such as Isabella would never be happy with a gentleman such as him. He would never be able to afford her all of the grand luxuries she was so used to.

They were introduced not a fortnight ago, yet so much had happened between them. Dare he say that they were friends? And with their flirtations, he could easily see their relationship growing into something more.

*Listen to me... Why am I thinking such things?*

After all, he was quite certain that the last thing on Isabella's mind at the moment was marriage. Marriage to *himself* especially. She was the daughter of a rich and powerful duke. And he was…

*Nothing.*

Ack! Listen to him. The lady was attacked just two nights prior…

*I am a bastard.* A selfish, pitiful bastard.

He needed to rid himself of Isabella's company before he did something incredibly stupid—which was quite difficult since he was currently sat with her in the newly repaired carriage.

"Thank you."

He looked to Isabella, her voice cutting into his musings. Her lips were turned down at the corners, and he tilted his head in question.

"Thank you," she repeated, and her mouth curved into a ghost of a smile. "For not letting those men speak ill of me."

He turned to face her. "No one will ever speak of you or touch you in that way again," he promised, referring to the incident with Callum. He then flashed her a quick, lopsided grin to lighten the mood. "Unless you'd like them to, of course."

Her smile quickly faded, and her jaw tensed. He threw his head back in laughter. The lady was definitely not amused by his quip. And more quickly than anticipated, the rake in him reemerged. Alistair lowered his elbows to his knees and clasped his hands together, inspecting her carefully.

Isabella started fidgeting with the fabric of her skirts, and Alistair began to feel a bit mischievous.

It was always great fun to make her uncomfortable. After all, what else was one to do on long, cramped carriage

## Chapter Nineteen

journeys?

Isabella cleared her throat and glanced about the carriage, trying her best to avoid his gaze.

"Are you feeling well?" he asked, noticing the slightly deeper shade of pink currently staining her cheeks.

She boldly caught his gaze. "Just a bit warm, that is all."

His eyes narrowed. "It is quite warm for April," he said, leaning back on his bench.

"It is warm in here," she repeated defensively.

"Right." He gave a sarcastic nod.

"*It is.*"

He shrugged. "I never said otherwise."

\* \* \*

*It is warm.*

Or at the very least, *she* was warm, and it took all of her strength not to snatch the bloody sketchbook out of her satchel and fan herself with it.

Why did the gentleman have to be so damned vexing?

*Unless you'd like them to...*

And why must he look at her in such a way? With his taunting grin and piercing emerald gaze? How could a lady *not* react to him?

She crossed her arms over her chest as a show of her indifference.

"Nothing to say?" He placed an ankle atop his knee, causing her eyes to wander to the front fall of his breeches, and her cheeks flushed even more—if such a thing were possible.

She turned her focus to the window. "And what would you

have me say to such a statement?"

"Anything you'd like."

Isabella took a breath in to regain confidence. What happened to the fearless and unconventional woman she was before this auburn-haired stranger burst into her life?

"I know what you'd have me say, Mr. Baston." She swept her gaze over his features, pausing at his grinning lips.

Alistair arched a brow

"You would have me say that the only man I want in my arms—" she leaned forward "—is *you*."

He blinked, and she confidently returned her focus to the window, satisfied with the fact that she had rendered the gentleman speechless. If he wanted to play games, well then... she had no choice but to play along with him—

The carriage skidded to an abrupt halt, and her body flew into Alistair's arms. She was hard-pressed not to notice the irony in that. She gripped his shoulders as the sound of screaming horses pierced her ears.

*Something is wrong.*

Panic rose in her chest. "Why did we stop?" Perhaps the new carriage wheel was not properly fitted?

"I will have a look." Alistair guided her onto the bench and pushed open the carriage door. He quickly stepped out onto the ledge and then pulled himself back inside, yanking the door closed behind him.

"What is it?" Her heart thudded loudly in her chest. He dragged a hand over his stark white complexion. "Alistair?" Something was most definitely wrong. She had never seen him so pale.

His hand dropped to his lap. "Our driver. He is dead."

Before Isabella had time to fully register Alistair's words, a

## Chapter Nineteen

sharp *pop* flooded her senses.

*Pop! Pop-pop!*

Her eyes widened, her heart jumping into her throat. "Alistair? What is happen—"

"Get down!" Alistair tugged on her wrist and pulled her to the floor.

*Pop-pop! Pew!*

The popping sound was familiar, and she now realized it was the firing of pistols. They were under attack, and she did not understand why. Highwaymen, perhaps? Isabella had heard tales of such men and knew they usually only wanted money and goods.

*Be strong. Be brave.*

There was soon another eruption of gunfire, and Isabella shrieked. She threw her arms over her head and ducked toward the floor of the conveyance.

She did not feel brave; she felt helpless. No—she *was* helpless. And what of her father and brother? Captain Lucas? Had they been injured?

Alistair knelt down beside her and took Isabella's face in his hands. "You are safe with me."

The intensity of his eyes was strong—dark depths of protection and promise.

*I believe you.*

His hands fell from her cheeks, and she mourned the loss of his soothing touch.

"Is someone shooting at us?" a small muffled voice came from somewhere nearby.

"Who said that?!" It sounded like the voice of a child. She looked around as much as she could from her crouched position. It was impossible to see anything from her place on the floor.

"It sounds as though the voice came from inside the carriage."

Inside the carriage? How was that possible? There was simply nowhere for a child to hide.

Alistair turned toward the velvet bench and slid his fingers under the cushioned seat, lifting it to reveal a hollow space within.

Positioning herself on her hands and knees, Isabella slowly peeked over the edge of the bench and gasped. There was a small boy inside.

It was the orphaned boy from the market, she realized. "Joseph?"

The young boy looked up to her with a toothy grin. "Hullo."

"You!" Alistair reached inside and grabbed the collar of the boy's white linen shirt. "You are the one who stole my watch."

Good heavens. They were under attack from highwaymen, and Alistair was worried over his watch? "This really is not the time, Alistair!" she shouted over the sound of wailing horses and pistol fire.

The orphaned boy began toying with his right wrist. "Aha!" Alistair grasped the boy's arm and yanked the golden timepiece that dangled from his small wrist. "This is mine," he growled through gritted teeth.

A bullet pierced the upper wall of the carriage. "Alistair!" Isabella's eyes darted to the small beam of sunlight now burning through the bullet hole.

Alistair quickly placed the watch inside his breast pocket. "We need to leave."

"*What?!*"

## Chapter Nineteen

"We need to—"

"I heard you!" *Bloody hell.* Where would they go? Running out into a sea of flying bullets did not sound like a good plan.

"Now!" Alistair demanded, taking hold of her arm.

Joseph lifted himself from the hollow bench and scrambled to open the carriage door.

Alistair took the handle and opened it with ease.

"Follow me." Alistair slowly stepped out, dragging her behind him.

The orphaned boy jumped out of the conveyance and took off running.

Isabella's heart raced. What would become of the poor boy? *What if he is killed?*

The pair crept alongside the carriage hand in hand. "Keep low," he whispered.

*Whooooosh-pop.*

"Christ!" Alistair fell backward into Isabella, causing her to stumble. An arrow was lodged into the carriage wall just a few inches from where Alistair had been standing.

*Who in God's name still uses crossbows?!*

"Run!" he shouted. And before she knew it, Alistair was dragging her alongside him.

She turned to look toward the coachman's perch. An arrow was lodged into his chest.

*My God.*

Tears flooded her vision, and everything began to pass by in a blur. She blindly followed Alistair through rearing horses and footmen aiming their weapons toward an unknown enemy.

How does one wake themselves from such a nightmare?

They finally reached her father's coach. *Where is he?* And

where was Simon? Captain Lucas?

As if the heavens had answered her query, her father stepped out from his conveyance, his eyes widening at the sight of her. "Bella, get back!"

Instantly, Isabella lost her footing. Her legs swept high into the air as all oxygen left her lungs.

*Am I falling?*

She looked down to see a pair of arms wrapped about her midsection, and all became clear. A man had grabbed her. And not just any man—a masked highwayman. What did he want with her?

"Alistair!" she yelled to the gentleman who was still running toward her father.

The highwayman was pulling her backward into the tree line. She kicked and flailed her limbs in an attempt to escape the stranger's hold.

Time seemed to slow as Alistair sprinted in her direction. He pulled his arm back, balling his hand into a tight fist. Isabella squeezed her eyes closed and ducked her head, just as Alistair's fist smashed into her captor's jaw.

The man's grip on her loosened, and she was able to free herself.

He stumbled, and Alistair made to strike him once more, but her attacker struck first with a swift kick to Alistair's abdomen, knocking him to the ground. The man's eyes met hers with an animalistic fierceness, and Isabella froze, unable to move as she watched the assailant inch closer.

He was the hungry wolf, and she the petrified lamb.

*What do they want?*

There were at least a dozen masked men running about camp. It was the strangest thing though… the men were not

## Chapter Nineteen

rummaging through the carriages or their belongings.

Were they planning to kill everyone first? Surely they could take what they wanted without loss of life.

The man's heavy strides increased in speed, and Isabella panicked. *What should I do? Let him take me?*

*Your dagger*, the small niggling voice in her head reminded her. Without thinking twice, she removed her dagger from its place at her leg. The masked man was now only an arm's length away. He made to step closer, his eyes burning like wildfire, and she had to decide.

She had to decide whether to let this man take her, or if she was going to defend herself, just like her father had taught her. But she was out of time; the man made to reach for her, and she had to choose…

Isabella's pulse pounded wildly as she took the tip of her dagger and plunged it into the man's chest. She squeezed her eyes shut and twisted the sharp metal between his ribs and pulled. Slowly, she opened her eyes to see the flame in the stranger's eyes had died. Blood seeped through his clothing. Her stomach recoiled at the sight of it, the dagger slipping from her grasp.

*What have I done?*
*I killed him.*

A masculine hand took hold of her wrist, and she whipped her head around to see Alistair standing beside her. He was shouting something, but she could not make out what it was. He sounded as though he was at the end of a long tunnel. A tunnel from which she could not seem to escape.

Her ears rang as a loud burst of gunfire pierced her senses.

She attempted to make her way toward her father's coach, but Alistair's grip was too strong. "My father!"

She could not leave him. She sought out her father in the sea of chaos before her and found him. He held out a pistol, aiming it toward the tree line.

*Pow!*

But it had not come from his gun.

Her father clenched his stomach and slowly fell to the ground. "Papa!" Isabella tore her wrist from Alistair's grasp and rushed to him. "Papa!" She gasped and fell to her knees. "Have you been shot?" Blood began to seep through his waistcoat, and at that moment, she knew he had.

Her father took her hand in his, blood soaking her palm.

*No...* She placed his hand against his wound. "Y-you must keep pressure on it." Her voice shook as she struggled to hold back the flood of tears.

*Be strong.* Her father had always told her to be strong, and now, she had to be strong for him.

The blood seeped through their intertwined fingers as she pressed her father's wound.

*He is going to be all right*, she told herself. He will not die. He. Will. Not. But the amount of blood currently soaking through her father's waistcoat told her differently.

"You must leave," her father said through labored breaths.

Isabella shook her head. "Not without you."

*Never without you.*

Alistair appeared and knelt down beside her. "Alistair." George coughed. "Do what you must to keep my daughter safe."

Alistair's brows came together, and he nodded.

*No...*

Captain Lucas and Simon appeared in front of them. The captain knelt down and replaced her hand with his own,

## Chapter Nineteen

putting pressure on her father's wound. "We need to stop the bleeding."

Simon knelt down beside Captain Lucas. "Father, I have something to confess."

Her father took in a ragged breath. "What is it, son?"

"These men... they are not highwaymen." But before Simon could finish, the popping of gunfire returned, and her father fell unconscious.

Alistair pulled her to her feet. "Wait!" Isabella screamed. Did Simon know these men? But before she could ask, Alistair dragged her in the opposite direction, forcing her to run alongside him.

Together, they ran from her father. Ran from her brother. The gunfire.

They ran from *everything*.

## Chapter Twenty

*These men... they are not highwaymen...*

Her brother's words repeated over and over again in her mind. Why would he think that? What did he know? If only Alistair had let them stay a few moments longer. If only her father hadn't ordered them to leave.

"Take this." Alistair held out a small gold ring.

She tilted her head in question. "What is this?"

"We are no longer Mr. Baston and Lady Isabella," he said, slipping the ring onto her betrothal finger. "We need new identities, for the time being."

*New identities?* "What do you mean? We have to return to my father. My brother... Captain Lucas. What of them?" Her father could still be lying in the mud bleeding. Her brother and the captain may have been injured as well. They could not just leave them. It had been hours since the attack. Surely the footmen were able to fight them off. Surely—

"Bella..." He brought his hand to her cheek. It was cool against her flushed skin. "Your father... the highwaymen."

## Chapter Twenty

Alistair let out a huff. "There was so much blood—"

"What are you saying?" she asked in a low whisper, not really wanting to know the answer.

Returning his palm to her cheek, he said, "With an injury like that... I am sorry, Bella, but there is no possible way he could have survived it."

A shiver ran up her spine, and she began to slowly shake her head. What was Alistair speaking of? That her father was... He could not be...

Heavens help her; she could not even *think* the words, let alone say them. Tears pricked at her eyes. "You are wrong."

Alistair framed her face with both of his hands now. "I am so sorry, Bella."

Her throat began to squeeze shut, her breathing growing heavy as it became more and more difficult to take in air. She shook her head, tears streaming down her cheeks. *"You are lying!"* With both hands, she shoved at Alistair's chest, causing him to slam into the wall of the hired hack they were currently riding in. "It is not true!"

It could not be true. Her father was perfectly well. He was speaking to her. Simon and Captain Lucas were aiding her father before she and Alistair had fled.

*"Shhh..."* Alistair crooned as he pulled her into his warm embrace. "We do not want to alarm the coachman."

"What about Simon and Captain Lucas?" Her voice came out as a raspy sputter.

"We shall pray that they escaped and are safely on their way back to London."

Pray? Yes. She supposed that was all they could do. "And Violet?" What will become of their search? They could not simply abandon her sister.

*Meeting Mister Baston*

Placing his mouth against her temple, he whispered, "We will find her, I promise you. But first, we must get you to London."

Isabella sat staring out the window, still with Alistair's arm wrapped about her. Her tears had long since dried, and no matter how much she wanted to cry, she just could not.

Alistair rapped on the ceiling of the carriage, signaling for the coachman to stop. "We will rest here for the night," he said quietly.

*What town are we in?* She did not know. She did not *care*.

The small golden ring was loose on her finger. It was funny how badly her mother wanted to see a betrothal ring on her finger, how important it was for her daughters to find husbands.

It did not matter now. *Nothing* mattered now. Who would want a dejected, melancholy and forever grieving twenty-something for a wife anyhow? "Where did you get it?" Isabella motioned toward the band around her finger.

"There was a jeweler in the first village we stopped in." He gave her a sympathetic smile. "We are now Alec and Anna of Devonshire—for the time being."

She managed a tight laugh. She would rather be *anyone* other than Isabella Avery.

They entered the small inn just as the sun began to set. The Dusty Mare. What a terrible name for an inn. Isabella glanced about room. There were dated English oak tables and chairs scattered about the space, with a counter directly in the room's center. The room was dark, cramped, and dusty.

Suddenly, the name, The Dusty Mare, seemed quite fitting.

With her hand in the crook of Alistair's elbow, he led them

## Chapter Twenty

to the counter where a bar maiden was wiping down its surface. "We need a room for the night." He cleared his throat. "Preferably with two beds."

The woman looked up from her work, her eyes a striking shade of turquoise blue. "Havin' a quarrel are ya?" She placed her elbows on the bar, letting her plump breasts spill over her bodice.

"Something like that." Alistair flashed the woman a charming smile, and a strange sensation filtered through Isabella's body.

*Jealousy.* How could she be jealous of this woman? Though she was quite stunning, with luscious black hair that nearly reached her waist, full lips, and luminescent skin.

Isabella could not help but glare at the woman now, feeling suddenly possessive over the gentleman standing beside her. Perhaps it was because Alistair was a close friend of her father's. And with her father gone, perhaps even Lucas and her brother too, Alistair may be the last gentleman left in her life worth caring for.

"Sorry to say, we only have the one room." She glanced at Isabella, looking unimpressed. "With the *one* bed." She winked at Alistair.

"I suppose that will have to do." He accepted a key from the woman and paid for the room with whatever coins he managed to carry with him.

"Enjoy ya stay," the woman demurred as they made their way to the staircase. "It is the second door on ya left."

Their room housed only one small bed, an unsteady night table, a wardrobe, a cracked mirror, and an old wooden chair. "Well, this is quite cozy," Isabella said dryly.

Alistair took a seat in the flimsy chair and began unlacing

his muddied boots. Isabella caught her reflection in the mirror.

She looked dreadful. The hem of her dress was stained almost black from their journey, her hair was tangled and windblown, and her eyes were red from the tears. She sighed and sat down on the lumpy feather mattress, which was in desperate need of fluffing. She watched Alistair with curious eyes as he removed his topcoat and cravat.

Alistair caught her gaze. "Would you like me to undress elsewhere?"

Her lips curved into a smile. "Where? In the hallway?" She waved a tired hand through the air. "Do not be ridiculous." She let her shoulders fall against the mattress and gazed up to the white stucco ceiling, pretending the little specks of dirt were stars in the night sky.

She listened as Alistair's fingers unclasped the buttons of his waistcoat. It was odd sharing a room with him, intimate even… but she did not have the strength to feel embarrassed or scandalized by the situation. She did not have the strength to worry over her reputation either.

At least she had Alistair. He would keep her safe. Keep her sane.

"I am sorry about your father," she heard him say. But instead of acknowledging him, she let her eyes flutter closed, and she soon found sleep.

## Chapter Twenty-One

The Duke of Waverly. His employer and close friend. *Isabella's father.*

Could he really be... gone?

And those men—the highwaymen that were not highwaymen. They hadn't demanded anything of them... None of it made any sort of sense.

Alistair rubbed the sore muscles in his neck. His eyelids drifted open to the sight of Isabella standing in front of the mirror in nothing but her chemise and corset. Their gazes met in the reflection of the glass.

"Alistair?"

He immediately averted his eyes. "I-I am so sorry." He lifted himself from the chair and began making his way to the door.

"Wait!" Isabella shouted. Alistair halted his movements. "I thought you were asleep."

He focused his gaze on the wood panel ahead of him. 'I was."

"Of course."

There was a long, awkward silence. "Is there something you needed from me?" Surely she did not need him to be present while she undressed.

"I am actually in need of some assistance."

"I will fetch a maid for you." He reached for the door handle—

"No, please. I-I would rather not be left alone."

His hand dropped to his side, and his heart ached for her. "All right."

"I need... I need assistance removing my corset. The laces are tangled."

His breath hitched. *She needs what?*

"Please." Her voice sounded raw. Drained. He could only imagine how she was feeling. "I am tired, and it will take but a moment."

He glanced over his shoulder. His eyes ran over the white, crisscrossed laces of the lady's corset, causing his pulse to quicken.

*You should not do this.*

No... he really should not.

Alistair's footfalls echoed softly off the wooden floor. He stopped just inches from Isabella's back, and her hair still somehow smelled of lavender.

"You just have to pull—"

"I know how." His voice came out raspy and unfamiliar.

When Alistair was in university, being young and reckless, he would often visit brothels and scandalous clubs with his schoolmates, as was normal for young men of that age, and he removed a good many corsets at the time. But, this was different. Isabella was an innocent.

## Chapter Twenty-One

Purity in every form of the word.

The short sleeves of her chemise hung loosely at her shoulders, the corset tightly cradling her small waist. Suddenly the memories of the ambush, of his friend's death, seemed to fade.

He reached out and swept her long golden hair over one shoulder, and a freckle appeared from under the long curtain of silky strands. He touched the laces of her corset, pulling and untangling until the small bow popped free. He slowly loosened the laces up the arch of her back.

She was the most beautiful woman he'd ever seen.

"Thank you." Her voice was soft and sweet in his ears. But he lingered. His gaze traced over the curve of her waist to the bare skin of her neck and shoulders, to the newly discovered freckle just above the soft lining of her chemise.

"Alistair?"

He found himself lowering his mouth to her cream white skin, but their eyes met in the mirror, and he froze. Her usual lively sapphire eyes appeared so very gray.

Her father had just died, and her sister was nowhere to be found. What was he doing? Alistair inhaled a steadying breath and turned to face the front wall of the room.

He listened as Isabella stepped out of her corset and slipped under the bed covers.

"You may turn now."

He turned to see her sitting up in bed, with the dusty blue fabric pulled up to her waist, and he tried not to notice the thin fabric of her chemise. The stiff mahogany chair seemed to call his name from across the room. He paused beside Isabella to blow out the candle on the nightstand and lazily sat in what felt like less of a chair and more like a pile of sharp sticks. The chair screeched in protest.

Some time later, after his eyes drifted closed, he heard Isabella mumbling in her sleep.

*"Papa…"*

Alistair's heart wrenched inside of his chest. She was dreaming of her father.

"I could not… save…" Her teeth began to chatter and she groaned as if she were in pain.

Perhaps… perhaps if she felt his presence, it would calm her. He could not just sit by and listen to her struggle and shiver all night.

He stood from his seat and slid quietly under the covers beside her. Even in the darkness of night, he could see the tears glistening off her cheeks. He wiped them dry with his shirtsleeve and cradled her against his chest. She sighed, and her shivers quickly dissipated. She nuzzled her nose into his neck, and he pulled her close, placing a featherlight kiss on her forehead.

Isabella stiffened in his arms. "Bella, are you awake?" He watched as her eyes moved underneath her closed eyelids.

*Is she still dreaming of her father?*

How he wished he could take her pain away. How he wished he was the one to be shot instead of George. Alistair kissed her cheek. "Everything will be all right. I promise."

Isabella let out a sleepy moan as her eyes struggled to flutter open. The light from the moon shone into the room to where he could see the white of her eyes. Then something came over him. A strange pulling at his heart. An ache in his chest.

He needed to kiss her.

She angled her neck in order to look into his eyes. "Alistair?" she murmured.

## Chapter Twenty-One

"Shhh." He watched as she struggled to keep her eyes open. "I am here." With his forefinger, he tilted her chin up just slightly. He placed a sweet and tender kiss on her mouth. Her lips were warm and wet from her tears. He swept his tongue along the soft, salty flesh.

Isabella let out a soft gasp, and with a hesitant movement, she placed her palm at the base of his skull. Her eyes closed fully as she let out a quiet moan.

He was not sure what had come over him. He just knew he needed to feel her in his arms, against his mouth.

Alistair deepened their kiss but made sure to still be gentle. He wanted her to know that she was safe with him, that she would *always* be safe with him. Reluctantly, he pulled his lips from hers before Isabella woke fully and threw him out on his ass.

God, how he wanted to kiss away all of her pain, but he knew he could not. And so he just held her close to his chest and laid his chin atop her head.

Soon, she had fallen back to sleep, and for what seemed like hours, Alistair just held her, listening to her rhythmic breathing.

*I could hold her like this forever.*

## Chapter Twenty-Two

Alistair knew it was wrong of him to slip into bed beside Isabella. She still had her reputation to look after, and if someone were to discover their true identities... the lady would be ruined.

Unmarriageable in the eyes of society.

*I would marry her.*

Alistair surprised himself with the sudden thought, and for some strange reason, the idea did not scare the bloody hell out of him.

But his father's voice came to mind... pushing back his hopeful musings. *You will never be good enough... You will never account to anything...*

The Duchess of Waverly would never let her daughter marry a second son. Isabella needed to marry someone with a title, a gentleman who could bring even more wealth and power to the already powerful Avery family.

And with George gone, he no longer had a reason to stay with the Averys. Once Alistair returned Isabella to her

## Chapter Twenty-Two

mother, he supposed he'd have no choice but to return to his bachelor lodgings in London.

Alistair let out a small chuckle as he realized he was sat at the modiste, contemplating marriage to a lady who would never have him.

A lady whose father had just died right before her eyes. Marriage would be the *last* thing on her mind.

*And should be the last thing on mine...*

"What is it? Is it the dress?"

Alistair glanced over to Isabella, who was holding an emerald-green cotton dress against her frame.

"It is quite hideous."

He flashed her a charming grin. "Nothing could look hideous on you, *dear wife.*"

Did Isabella's face light up? Or was he simply imagining it?

She began swaying her hips back and forth, causing the fabrics of the skirt to swish around her ankles.

"It does not matter anyhow. I will only wear it for the journey to London." Isabella sulked over and sat on the cushioned chair beside him. She let out a melancholy sigh and asked, "How much money do we have left?"

He hated seeing her in such a way.

"Not much." Being as they had left almost all of their belongings back at the carriage. "But enough to get us back to London without a problem."

Isabella let out a sudden bark of laughter. Startled, Alistair turned to her, but she was not laughing, he realized. She was crying.

Sobbing.

Noticing his concerned gaze, she dropped her face into

*Meeting Mister Baston*

her hands. "Oh, I am sorry." Her shoulders jumped with each jittery breath. "I a-am trying so very hard to stay strong."

"Oh, Bella…" Alistair wrapped an arm about her and pulled her close. "You are the strongest woman I have ever met." It was true. "It is all right to cry. It is normal to feel pain. Especially during times such as these."

"Is everything all right?" the clerk asked from the desk.

Alistair nodded. "Jacket, coat and trousers for me. Dress and slippers for the lady." He took Isabella's quivering hand in his and placed a gentle kiss on her knuckles. "Come." He eased her up to her feet and led Isabella to the counter, the tears still wet upon her cheeks.

The clerk eyed them with sympathy. "I am sorry to ask—" the woman motioned toward their muddied attire "—but what happened to ya?"

Alistair handed Isabella his kerchief to wipe away her tears. "Our carriage got stuck in the mud, and we tried to push it out ourselves," he lied.

"Terrible luck, that is." The clerk took the garments from Alistair's arms. "I know just the thing to cheer up the both of yous." The woman looked to Isabella with bright eyes. "The town is holding its weekly dance tonight. You should come. It is a public one so there's no need for ye to worry over invitations."

As lovely as that sounded, Alistair knew they needed to return to London. Isabella was in no position to attend a dance after what she had just endured. "Thank you, but—"

"That would be lovely," Isabella answered for them.

There was a sudden glint in her eyes, and he gave her a look. "But we have not the proper attire to attend a dance, *dear*." He laced that last word with a warning.

## Chapter Twenty-Two

Isabella glared at him. Did she *want* to go to the dance? After everything that had just occurred?

"Don't ya worry yourselves over that!" The clerk's eyes brightened. "We have plenty of fine pieces for you to wear here. I can easily have them readied by tonight."

Even if they were not on the run from highwaymen, they simply could not afford the additional garments. "I am afraid we cannot afford—"

"After what yous endured, it will be on the house." The woman lowered her voice to a whisper. "As long as ya return the pieces when yer through."

He supposed getting the current events off Isabella's mind would do her some good. And they were to spend another night in the village anyhow…

Alistair sighed and gave the clerk a curt nod.

\* \* \*

It was selfish not to return to London immediately, but Isabella did not *want* to return to London. She could not simply give up on the search for her sister—especially after what had happened at the campsite.

With the ambush and Simon's words, she knew Violet did not simply run off and elope with a gentleman. She was taken. She was in danger.

The not-highwaymen and her father's *death* was proof of that. How did Alistair not see it? How could he want to simply return to London and leave behind her sister as if nothing had happened?

She supposed, if they returned to London, she could

*Meeting Mister Baston*

question Simon about how he knew those men. But when the clerk told them of this dance, she thought it the perfect opportunity to lose Alistair in the whirl of patrons so she could then return to the campsite.

There had to be something there. Something that would give her more information about Violet's location.

"Would you like to dance?" Alistair's query interrupted her musings.

*Dance?* She supposed it would only be normal for Alistair to assume she wanted to dance... at a *ball*. Isabella scanned the crowded room.

She had never been to a public dance hall. It was much smaller and more informal than all the private balls her family had ever attended. The floor was scuffed hardwood instead of polished marble, the servants were clad in black instead of the liveried servants donning white powdered wigs, and the patrons seemed much more lively and... *happy*.

There were no high society standards here. No one turned up their noses at those of a lower station. Silk and lace were not the norms. Instead, the ladies wore simple cotton dresses.

It was refreshing.

But alas, she was not here to dance; she was here to escape. *But Alistair does not know that...*

Isabella placed her hand in his, and he led her across the faded parquet flooring toward the dancing couples, just as the sound of violins began to fill the room. They stood across from one another, and Alistair bowed, signaling the start of the reel. Isabella curtsied in return, and they began to dance.

As they moved toward one another, she felt the tightness in her chest begin to dissipate. Slowly, her heart began to live again. Dancing seemed to have that effect on her.

## Chapter Twenty-Two

She met Alistair's gaze, and it was as though her life began anew. She completely forgot about the past and only focused on the present.

His eyes were piercing into her shattered soul, causing a rush of heat to flow to her cheeks. He placed his hands in hers and pulled her close. Their bodies moved together in perfect rhythm, which was quite surprising—she was not thinking about the steps or the 1,2,3,4 count that was meant to keep her from stumbling.

All she could focus on was the slight pressure of his hands against hers and his inviting emerald stare.

"What are you thinking about?" he shouted over the lively music.

"Nothing." Her voice came out breathless. "Just your eyes." She winced, but luckily, they switched partners, which gave her time to compose herself before returning to him.

Alistair took hold of her hand again, his lips curving into an enticing smile. "What about them?"

"I..." She paused for a moment, attempting to collect her thoughts. "I never noticed how green they were." Which was a lie.

"Are they?" He stepped forward, and she stepped back. "I never paid much attention to them. Do you like them?"

She missed a step, and he quickly righted her.

*Yes.*

His mouth grew into an amused grin. "Do you?"

*Did I say that aloud?* Her pulse began to quicken. "W-Why would I not like them?" She twirled outward, giving herself some much-needed space between them, even if it were only for a few seconds. She spun inward, returning to his side, and Alistair said nothing. "Not that I prefer your eyes over others. I just believe they suit you well."

*You are rambling.*

"Do you study my eyes often, Lady Anna of Devonshire?" he whispered next to her ear.

She gasped as he lifted her into the air and carefully lowered her back down. She bit her lip, unknowing of how to respond.

Alistair's eyes fell to her mouth for a moment. *Does he want to kiss me?*

Or rather, *would I let him kiss me?*

"Yes— I mean, not only *your* eyes," she amended. "Everyone's eyes are fascinating."

He tilted his chin to the air. "And what is so fascinating about mine?" he asked with a hint of false arrogance.

She pressed her lips together in thought. "Because they are so green, as I said." *He will never accept such a plain answer, you ninny.*

Alistair cocked his head in a sort of endearing way. "There must be more to it than 'because they are so green,'" he teased.

Indeed, that voice in her head was correct. Yet again. "Well." She swallowed nervously. "They are not *only* green." She squinted her eyes in order to study him closer. "You have a gold ring that wraps around your pupil... and there are also small specks of blue and bronze mixed in with the green."

"That is very... specific."

Isabella shrugged, feigning nonchalance. How had she never noticed the variety of colors in Alistair's eyes until now?

The music began to slow, and he released her from his hold. She was breathless as she realized their dance had been the first time she could relax and truly be herself with Alistair.

## Chapter Twenty-Two

She was... having *fun*. And she could not help but want to spend the entirety of the night dancing with him.

She shook that nonsense from her mind. She was here for one reason and one reason only... to continue the search for her sister.

## Chapter Twenty-Three

The dance had seemed to improve Isabella's mood. And Alistair had to admit that holding her in his arms during their dance had him in a much pleasanter state of mind as well. The feel of her form in his grasp was almost enough to make him forget how dangerous it was to delay their journey to London.

But it was so gratifying to see her smile again.

Once they returned to London, Isabella would be in mourning. Her grief would no doubt take over once again. Here, at the dance hall, they were different people. A married couple. Not a single person was familiar to them. It was just her and him and the low hum of music.

"I am quite parched now," he heard Isabella say. "Are you?"

"Quite." He winked.

A blush stained her cheeks as she glanced toward the beverage table. "Shall I fetch the drinks?"

Before she could escape him, he took hold of her small wrist and placed her hand in the crook of his elbow. "Surely

## Chapter Twenty-Three

it is the gentleman's duty to fetch drinks for the lady?"

She pursed her lips. "I can manage on my own."

He stayed her by tightening his squeeze on her hand. "I insist." It was still too dangerous to let the lady wander off on her own, even in the middle of a public ball. They did not know these people. Any of them could be working with the men who attacked them.

Once they reached the beverage table together, Alistair poured them each a glass of port.

"Oh, I could not."

"Oh, you could," he assured, holding the small crystal glass out to her. The alcohol would be good for her—it would help raise her spirits after such a devastating loss. And to be honest, he could use the drink as well.

Her eyes gazed over the dark liquid. "I am not allowed, Alistair."

"Alec," he corrected. "And it is allowed for *married* ladies."

It had taken a moment for her to decide, but Isabella eventually accepted the glass and downed its contents, letting out a pleasure-filled moan.

His manhood swelled beneath his breeches.

*Lord, help me.* He silently sent a prayer skyward. If she let out another sound like that, he would have to ravish her in front of the entire dance hall.

"That was delightful." She reached for the decanter, and Alistair quickly moved it from her reach. "Hey!"

"I think one is enough." He laughed. He wanted to raise her spirits, not get her inebriated.

"I am still thirsty." She frowned like a child who had just lost their favorite toy.

He arched a brow and tauntingly sipped at his port. With a

bitter glare, she crossed her arms over her chest then reached for a glass of lemonade instead.

"I think I shall go out on the terrace for some air." Isabella turned to leave, but Alistair stepped in front of her.

"Not alone."

She scoffed. "I will be but a moment." She moved to step around him. Alistair blocked her stride.

"No."

"Why are you being so difficult?"

"Why are you trying to rid yourself of me?" Alistair asked on a low growl.

Isabella let out a choking noise. Her mouth opened and closed before she said, "I do not know what you mean."

She was a terrible liar. "Oh, you do." Alistair shot her a menacing glare. He needed to figure out why she was so eager to be rid of him, and he could not do that in a room full of people.

In one slow swallow, he finished the contents of his drink and set the glass down. "Come with me." His voice came out low and grating.

"Where are we going?"

He did not answer. He was too fixed on finding a quiet place to discuss her sudden strange behavior.

As they reached a dimly lit corridor, Alistair began to check each door to see where they would lead. He turned a handle. *Locked*.

He tried a second door. *Locked*.

"Where are we going?" she asked again, a bit more urgently. "What if someone sees us?"

Alistair stopped mid-stride, which caused Isabella to crash into his shoulder. He brushed a knuckle over her cheek.

## Chapter Twenty-Three

"No one will see us," he whispered, attempting to mask his irritation.

Her skin glowed against the candlelight, and small flecks of fire danced in her deep blue eyes. Desire pumped through his veins, and the image of her lips on his filtered through his mind. He remembered the taste of her mouth when he had kissed her for the first time.

*This is not the time, Baston.*

He gave his head a mental shake. He led her around a corner and spotted an oak panel ajar at the end of the hallway. After he peeked inside to be sure there were no lingering couples, he guided Isabella into the small office and closed the door behind them.

\* \* \*

Isabella's heart thudded frantically in her chest. She was not quite sure why Alistair was leading her into dark and quiet spaces. Well... she had an idea of why, but surely Alistair would not dare think to ravish her... in a dance hall of all places.

*After my father has just been killed.*

Alistair locked the door behind him.

"What are you doing?"

A devilish smile formed on his lips. "Nothing." He shrugged.

"Then why are we here, Alistair?" she whispered, attempting to hide the concern in her voice.

Alistair slowly inched his way toward her. His eyes burned with an emotion she had never seen in him before. He cocked

*Meeting Mister Baston*

his head to the side. "You wanted to come to the dance... then you try to run off on your own. You are attempting to be rid of me. Why?"

She took a step back with heavy breaths. "I am not," she lied. She knew very well she was trying to be rid of him so she could return to the campsite. Return to her father. But, Alistair could not know that. If he did, he would drag her inside the next hackney and head straight to London.

He stepped forward, his large and powerful form making her feel small and weak.

Isabella continued her retreat until the backs of her thighs were pressed against the large mahogany desk at the center of the room. "Alistair?" He was but a hair's breadth away now, trapping her with his gaze.

"*Alec*," he corrected for the third time.

But, she did not want Alec.

She wanted Alistair.

The man in front of her was a stranger with burning desire and anger in his eyes.

He slowly removed his ivory evening gloves and dropped them carelessly to the floor. "You are a terrible liar." His voice was smooth and seductive, reeling her in with every one of his words. "And so damned beautiful."

She leaned back and grasped the edge of the desk, attempting to put as much distance between them as possible. "I-I." she stumbled, unable to break away from his gaze.

He reached out and traced the outline of her jaw with the tip of his forefinger. The slight touch raised goosebumps on her arms. It sent a wave of heat down to her core.

*This is wrong.*

Was he Alec, playacting the role of her husband? Or was

## Chapter Twenty-Three

he Alistair, and this was simply a side to him she'd never seen before?

Whatever it was, she could not help but want more of it. *More of him.*

His hand moved to the nape of her neck, cupping it with his palm.

"Please," she whimpered, remembering their chaste kiss back at the inn, the kiss she had thought was a dream. But now, as their mouths drew closer... she knew it had not been a dream.

It seemed as though gravity was pulling them together, closer and closer, until his warm lips were pressed against hers, causing her body to stiffen. But something quickly ignited within her—a strange, searing passion she had never before experienced.

Alistair reached around with his free hand and pressed it against her lower back, pulling her body into his.

*This is wrong*, her conscience repeated. *Wrong, wrong, wrong.*

Isabella ignored the little voice in her head and pressed her body wickedly against his. Their lips began to move perfectly in sync with one another. She reached around and lost her fingers in his wonderfully tousled auburn hair. She yanked at the strands, unsure whether she should push the gentleman away or pull him closer.

## Chapter Twenty-Four

Alistair's desire was beginning to grow wild. Reckless.

Isabella felt so perfect in his arms, and she just tasted so damned *good*. He could not even remember why he had brought her into this room to begin with.

He expected the lady to be hesitant at first, and perhaps even pull away, but as soon as she ripped at his hair, he knew her need for him was just as great as his need for her.

She parted her lips, allowing his tongue to slip inside and explore every inch of her beautiful mouth. The very same mouth and lips that had drove him mad since their first stop at Amersham Lodge. The same mouth he had just the smallest taste of the evening prior.

Isabella arched against him as he slid his hand down her waist, pausing every so often to grasp at her gown. He could not help but want to tear the fabric from her body. But he could not.

*He would not.*

## Chapter Twenty-Four

He remembered why he had escorted her to this room... He had meant to question her, to scold her for trying to leave his side again and again. But now—now he needed this kiss.

He wanted to show her what they could have together. What they *already* had together. To prove that they were compatible in every sort of way. To prove passion was far better than a title.

To make her forget all of the pain she'd just endured.

*God, how I want this woman.*

"Bella," he groaned against her pink lips. He moved his mouth to the smooth skin on her neck, tickling, tasting and teasing her with his tongue.

*Christ.*

She smelled of lavender and soap again, sending another wave of desire through his body. His heart began to beat erratically within his chest. He growled, tightening his grip on her small waist. He lifted her up and up until her bottom was perfectly perched on the edge of the mahogany desk.

The hunger inside him grew more urgent—more *ravenous*—and he was on the verge of losing control.

Alistair returned his lips to hers. He slipped his hands down her legs until he reached the hem of her skirts. He yanked at the fabric, bringing it up and over her knees until it pooled at her thighs.

The smooth hosiery covering her legs felt like heaven against his fingers. He nudged against her knees, forcing her legs to spread so he could settle his body between them. The palms of his hands reached the end of her hosiery, and the feel of her bare thighs caused a rush of blood to flow straight to his manhood.

He needed more of this. More of *her*.

Just as a lion craved the taste of blood, Alistair craved the taste of her... the taste of the slick folds of her womanhood on his tongue.

He tore his lips from hers and admired her disheveled appearance.

Large strands of Isabella's hair were freed of their pins, her pink lips now red and swollen. The sight of her made his pulse race. He grabbed at her bottom and pulled her into his heat.

She grasped on to his shoulders to steady herself.

His fingers slipped past her undergarments, digging into the skin of her buttocks with a need to explore every inch of her body.

She moaned against his ear, causing him to press her tighter against his hardening shaft. "Alistair," she groaned in between breaths. He crushed his lips over hers, his thumbs tickling the tops of her thighs.

Isabella grasped at his wrists. "Alistair..."

"Bella." His fingers moved closer to her feminine center, and he crushed his lips to her neck. He touched the soft thatch of curls between her legs—

"Alistair, stop!" Isabella pushed against his chest, causing him to stumble backward.

She quickly hopped down from her place on the desk and rightened the fabric of her gown. "What do you think you are doing?" Her voice came out shaky and breathless. "Is this why you brought me here?"

*Christ.*

He made a promise to himself. *To her*—that he would not lose control.

He failed.

## Chapter Twenty-Four

And worst of all, he failed Isabella in a time of need. In a time of support. She needed his comforting words, not his lust-filled body.

Alistair swiped a hand over his face, attempting to catch his breath. What was he to say? He brought her to this room to scold her, and instead, he ravished her?

He felt like a complete bastard. Her father had just died, and he should have known better. They should have never attended this bloody dance.

"Look at me!" His face whirled to the right, just as the lady landed a ferocious slap across his cheek. His skin stung from the hard blow.

*I deserved that.*

Their eyes met. A wrenching pain filled his heart as he watched the tears form in her eyes. He hadn't meant for this to happen, and he definitely had not wished to make her cry.

Isabella closed the distance between them. "Just when I was thinking you might be different—" she motioned to the room "—you do this."

Shame filled his gut. "I-I lost control…"

A tear swept down her reddened cheek, and she took in a deep breath, before saying, "You took advantage of me—"

"No, I did not mean to…" He took her hand in his. She instantly pulled away.

"My father just died." She turned her back to him. "My father just *died*, and you took advantage of my emotions."

"Please, Bella," he pleaded. "That was not my intention. I wanted to know why you kept trying to run off on your own!"

"Because I want to find my sister!" she shouted, her frame rigid, her fists shaking at her sides. "I knew there would be a large group of people at the dance and… I wanted to lose you—" she turned away "—so I could return to the camp on my own."

So that was it, then? A pain filled his chest. And there he thought Isabella was enjoying their dancing, was enjoying a night away from everything that had happened. He raked a hand through his hair. "Bella, I—"

Isabella's voice quavered. "I want to leave."

"I would have gone with you if you had just told me."

She let out a bitter laugh. "No you would not have."

She was correct… He would have taken her straight to London. It was too dangerous to return.

For a long moment, Alistair could not move. He could not speak. All he could do was stare at the woman in front of him. The woman he wanted to spend all of his time with.

The woman he had just lost.

## Chapter Twenty-Five

Isabella could not sleep.

She felt betrayed. How could Alistair take advantage of her so? Yes, it was her atrocious idea to attend the dance, but she never expected Alistair to kiss her. To *touch* her.

Perhaps he had thought she wanted this to happen. And perhaps she did, but the timing was all wrong. *So very wrong.*

She sighed and glanced toward Alistair's sleeping form. He'd made up a bed on the hardwood floor from spare pillows and blankets. His arms were crossed tightly over his chest with his knees curled into his abdomen.

He looked cold. And even in the darkness of the night, she could see the red streak on his cheek from where she had struck him.

*He deserved it.*

Did he not?

That kiss had made her forget everything for a brief moment. For those few sweet seconds in Alistair's arms, she had forgotten about her father's death, and of her sister's disappearance. How could she give in to such passion during a time of grief?

Perhaps it was this grief that made her enjoy the touch of a gentleman. But, not just any gentleman…

*Alistair.*

Guilt swelled in her belly each time her thoughts lingered over his kiss. Grief squeezed at her heart each time she remembered her tragic loss—and the thought of how her mother would take the news.

The next morning, she was no longer afraid to be on her own anymore, so Alistair waited downstairs as Isabella readied herself for the day's journey. After bathing away the week's dire events, she donned the cotton dress Alistair had purchased the day prior. Her head tilted slightly as she inspected her reflection in the cracked mirror. Her bruise had finally disappeared.

And how had she not noticed that the emerald fabric of the dress was the very same shade as Alistair's eyes?

The fit and quality of the fabric was not the best, but perhaps it was the color that had drawn her toward the dress in the first place.

There was a rapping at the door. "Yes?"

"Are you ready to depart?" Alistair's voice was muffled behind the wood panel.

Isabella slowly turned the handle and poked her head through the slight opening. "I am ready."

He motioned to the stairs. "The carriage is waiting, my lady."

Her heart sank to the floor. Were they back to being formal with each other? She did not want what had happened

## Chapter Twenty-Five

last evening to have an effect on their friendship, but she supposed it was inevitable. How could they act as they usually did after sharing such an intimate moment, then such a heated argument?

Two hours had passed since they started the miserably quiet journey to London. Isabella could feel the tension between them, the awkwardness that was never present before... *the kiss.*

She wished they could both forget it had ever happened. But how could she expect Alistair to forget what had happened if she herself could not?

Isabella closed her eyes and sighed as she recalled the way her skin burned from Alistair's touch. The way her heart fluttered with the anticipation of his lips touching hers. The way her hand stung and tingled after she'd struck him.

She turned to sneak a glimpse at him.

His body was turned slightly away from her with his arms crossed rigidly over his chest as he stared out the windowpane. He appeared stiff, as if he were attempting not to notice her presence inside their small conveyance.

Her eyes fell to the reddened skin of his cheek, and guilt squeezed at her chest.

*But why should I feel guilty?*

*He* kissed her. *He* touched her... in a place no man had a right to, unless he had planned to marry her.

*Alistair is a rake*, she reminded herself. And he more than proved that truth the night prior. Rakes did not marry. Rakes took what they wanted from women and discarded them once they had gotten their fill.

"Isabella?"

Alistair's voice startled her from her angry stupor.

"Yes?" she said tightly.

Alistair turned to face her. "I..." He paused for a moment and settled his eyes on hers. "I wanted to apologize. For last evening."

"*I see.*" But rakes did not apologize... "And I suppose you wish me to apologize for lying to you? For striking you?"

His posture stiffened, and he cocked his head to one side. "I am not looking for an apology from you. *I* am the one who kissed you in a time of grief. I am the one who lost control." Alistair's eyes fell on his lap, and her treacherous heart ached for him to kiss her again, longed to be held in his arms, no matter how immoral it was.

No.

It was wrong. *He* was wrong.

"Bella." He reached out and took her hand in his. The sound of her name across his lips made her heart triple its beat.

"Yes?" she whispered.

"I am sorry." He gently rubbed her knuckles with the pad of his thumb. "I am so, *so* sorry. I just want this, whatever we have together, to go back to how it was... before..."

Before his lips touched hers? Before he pulled her close and ground his manhood against her feminine place? Before she knew what it was to *feel*...? Shame filled her gut, and she pulled her hand away. Fury lodged itself deep in her chest as she realized he was never going to marry anyone.

*This is what rakes do.*

They reeled you in again and again until you finally gave them what they wanted, and Isabella would never fall for such trickery again.

Looking out to the dark city streets, she knew they could

*Chapter Twenty-Five*

never go back to how things were.

## Chapter Twenty-Six

Arriving at her family home in London, Isabella longed to see her mother, but dreaded the state she might be in after hearing the news of the duke's death—presuming her mother had already received word.

And what of Simon and Captain Lucas? Had they returned safely? Were they inside the house comforting Mother? Had they continued to search for Violet? Her throat squeezed. Had they escaped the ambush at all?

She had not thought Simon and Lucas could also be dead. But, now, seeing her home in the darkness of the night made her realize just how dark and dangerous her life had become. And so she sat inside the carriage, unable to move, unable to breathe as the weight of her life fell onto her shoulders.

Alistair had already stepped down from the conveyance, awaiting her exit. She was not sure how long she'd been sitting in frozen silence.

Isabella drew in a shaky breath, allowing her repressed emotions to break through the wall she seemed to have built

## Chapter Twenty-Six

around them. Hot tears began to stream down her face, causing her vision to blur. Every breath she drew burned her lungs. Her entire body shook from the overwhelming feeling of sorrow, and she began gasping for air as if she were drowning.

Alistair rushed to her side and wrapped her tightly in his arms, her cheeks wet against his strong chest. The feel of him made her cry even more.

"Shhh..." His breath caressed her ear. "It is all right. I am here with you."

She was not ready; it was too soon. "I-I cannot," she managed to get out between sobs.

"I am here," he whispered. "I will not leave your side. I promise."

She buried her face in the lapels of his coat, listening to his heart's steady beat through the many layers of fabric. The warmth of his body soothed her, calmed her.

"Shhh," Alistair crooned. He gently stroked her hair with his hand, and her breathing began to slow. She was no longer gasping for air, no longer drowning.

"I am here," he whispered." I am here with you."

His words, his touch, brought forth the memories of their kiss. His tongue invading her mouth. His hands sliding beneath her skirts.

Callum's calloused fingers gripping painfully at her thighs. Her screams lost beneath the weight of his hands.

Her father's blood-soaked shirt.

The blood dripping from her beloved dagger.

Rage pooled beneath her chest. "I do not need your comfort." Isabella pulled away from Alistair's hold. "I do not need anyone."

She did not want to leave the carriage, but she knew it was time.

Swiping the tears from her cheeks, Isabella jumped down from the steps of their conveyance.

And all too soon, she found herself standing in the dimly lit foyer of her family's townhouse. It felt strange being there, even though she had only been away for less than a fortnight.

"Bella?"

The familiar voice calling her name made her heart halt its beat. She quickly turned to catch a familiar face.

"Simon!" She took him into her arms. "I was so worried about you." Relief soon filled her.

"Worried about me?" Simon asked, returning Isabella's embrace. "Where were you? We have been awaiting your return."

"I thought it best to hide out in a nearby town for a day or so," Alistair cut in from behind. "In case the highwaymen attempted to follow us."

Simon's eyes moved to focus on Alistair. "Of course." He gave a stiff nod.

Isabella looked between the two gentlemen, sensing the tension between them. Her brother was always far too protective over her, though she understood why—especially with what happened to Violet.

Isabella released Simon from her hold. "Nothing happened between us, Simon," she lied. "Is that all you can think about?"

Simon's cold gaze quickly vanished as he turned to her. "Mother is sitting with Father in his bedchamber. They will wish to see you."

"Father?" Isabella's heart jumped. "He is here?" *Alive?*

Simon let out a small chuckle. "Of course he is here. Where

## Chapter Twenty-Six

else would he be?"

With the coroner perhaps? Or at the mortuary? These last few days she had been mourning the death of her father. She had delayed their journey home, and he was... *alive?*

Isabella left Alistair in her brother's company and quickly made her way upstairs. She softly knocked on the door of her father's bedchamber. She was not quite ready for what she would find on the other side of the panel.

Just because Father was alive did not mean he was alive and *well*.

"Enter." Her mother's soft voice came from inside the room. Isabella slowly turned the handle. The room was dimly lit by candlelight, which bathed the muraled walls in an eternal glow. Her mother was sat on the large four-poster bed in the center of the room, brushing back her father's graying hair with her palm. Her father looked serene as he slept, healthy even, but she could not be certain.

"Bella!" Her mother looked at her and abruptly stood from her place on the edge of the mattress. "You are all right! I was so worried." Her mother crossed the room to greet her.

"I am fine." Isabella held her mother gently in her arms. "How are you faring?"

"Oh, you know how I am." Her mother pulled away and looked over to her husband. "I tend to become a bit emotional when these things happen."

"And how is he?" Isabella's pulse increased its beat as she waited for her mother's reply. *Please be well...*

Her mother made her way to her father's side. "George!" Her mother began tugging at his sleeves. "George! Bella is home."

Her father slowly blinked his sleepy eyes awake.

"Papa!" Isabella sprinted to his bedside. "Oh my God—"

"That mouth, Bella!" her mother scolded.

Ignoring her mother, Isabella sat on the edge of the duke's bed. "I cannot— I thought— You are…"

"Calm down, Bella." Her father smiled and laid his hand atop hers.

"You do not understand, Papa." Isabella shook her head frantically. "These past few days… I thought you were dead."

"*Dead?*" George threw his head back in laughter. "You cannot be rid of me that easily."

"But…" *There was so much blood.* "But, how?"

"Captain Lucas." The duke paused to clear his throat. "Captain Lucas has some medical training—"

"Captain Lucas! How is he?"

"I will let you be," her mother interrupted as she exited the chambers.

After the door closed behind her, George explained with great detail how Captain Lucas saved his life by extracting the bullet with his bare hands and stopped the bleeding by—

"*Papa!* I do not need to hear of every gruesome detail."

Her father squeezed her hand. His eyes fell to the small betrothal ring on her finger. He inspected it carefully. "Is there something you need to tell me?"

"Oh." Isabella slid her hand from his grasp. "Do not worry; it is not real."

"Why would I worry?" His face glowed. "I would be delighted!"

She rolled her eyes skyward. "Now you are beginning to sound like Mother," she scoffed. "Alistair thought it best to pose as a married couple while we hid for a couple of days."

George nodded in agreement. "Smart man."

## Chapter Twenty-Six

Alistair *was* a smart man.

Guilt squeezed at her heart as the memory of Alistair's kiss came forth in her mind again. Was it wrong of her to deny him because of her sister? Also her father—whom she presumed dead at the time?

*With an injury like that... I am sorry, Bella, but there is no possible way he could have survived it.*

*He* had told her that her father was dead. She supposed she could be angry with him for that... but the kiss? Could she truly stay angry with him over a kiss? A touch?

*Yes, I can.*

She had every right to be angry. He took advantage of her while she was in mourning. And she was in mourning because of what *he* had said.

"What will come of Violet?" Isabella asked.

Her father let out a raspy breath. "Captain Lucas will continue the search while I recover." His palm cradled her cheek. "While *we* recover."

*We...*

She supposed, after all that had happened, the stress was enough to drive any person mad. Isabella was lucky to be in possession of a strong disposition. Any other gently bred lady of the *ton* would surely be abed for weeks, traumatized after nearly being raped.

After being attacked by highwaymen, or whatever one chose to call them.

After *killing* a man...

Isabella tried to ignore the shudder that ran up her spine. Images of blood dripping down her dagger clouded her mind. It was all too much. She placed a small peck on her father's cheek. "It is late. I shall let you sleep."

*Meeting Mister Baston*

She closed the door behind her, leaned her back against it and took in several slow, deep breaths. *Be strong. Do not let this one moment take over your life. Your father is alive and recovering. Your brother and Captain Lucas are safe.*

Her heart steadied its cadence and she supposed, no matter how angry she was with him, she should at least tell Alistair that her father was well. She made her way to the blue drawing room, where the men of the house usually gathered.

There was a small flicker of candlelight illuminating the hall just outside of the blue room. Isabella peeked inside, and there he was, alone, staring down at his beverage. He donned almost the same expression she had seen when she had sketched his portrait at Amersham Lodge.

She knocked softly against the door frame, causing his body to flinch slightly.

"Bella." He looked up in surprise. "Do come in."

"I hope I am not interrupting anything, Mr. Baston." It almost seemed too intimate to call the gentleman by his Christian name while they were alone in her parent's home, while they were still indifferent toward one another. After all, Isabella had never accepted his apology, and she was not certain she was ready to.

He tilted his head slightly, then took a small sip of his drink. "Back to formal greetings now, Lady Isabella?"

There was something different about him—a strange glint in his eyes; the room heavy with the smell of spirits.

She slowly made her way across the room and took a seat on the beryl-blue sofa. "We are no longer sleeping under the stars, Mr. Baston." She gave him a sad smile.

"Or sharing a bed at a dusty old inn, my lady," he teased.

Isabella glanced toward the open doorway. "Hush. Some-

## Chapter Twenty-Six

one may hear you."

He sketched a regal bow, spilling his drink in the process. "My sincerest apologies."

She pursed her lips. There was definitely something wrong with him. "The reason I sought you out was to tell you that my father is—"

"...doing well. I know."

"How do you know?"

"Your brother told me." Alistair set down his glass on a nearby table, surprising her by taking the seat beside her. "It is wonderful news." He took her hand in his. "I am so very happy for you."

Isabella looked down to Alistair's hand. She could not just return to their teasing friendship after what he had done. "Of course. I do not know why I did not think of that." She slowly slid her hand from his grasp. "How long do you plan to stay?"

Her mind hoped that he would return to his bachelor lodgings in London. It was so difficult to be around him—awkward even. This rake who made her heart flutter. This rake who touched her so intimately, but had no intention of marrying her. This man who sat before her now and acted as though everything was normal between them.

Alistair frowned at his now empty hand. "I was hoping to stay long enough to see your father recovered."

A slight feeling of disappointment rose in her chest. "Of course."

"Of course," he mimicked, a wolfish grin appearing over his features. "Not that I have any clothes to wear for a prolonged stay."

How could she tell him that she wished for him to leave?

She needed space from the gentleman before her, and yet, she did not have the courage to tell him so.

"I am sure Simon can lend you something of his, at least until your valet can bring over some items of your own."

Alistair rose from his place beside Isabella and surprised her by offering his hand. "My lady?"

Isabella arched her brow and inspected the whites of the gentleman's eyes. They were covered with little red veins that crept toward his pupils. His eyelids were heavy and puffier than usual. "Are you drunk?" she asked, even though she already knew the answer. But how could he possibly get drunk in the short amount of time she had been away?

Alistair extended his hand even further. "You did not answer my question."

"Did you ask one?" She placed her hand in his anyhow, allowing him to help her to a standing position. Almost out of instinct.

Alistair placed his hand on the small of her back and slowly pulled her close, and Isabella could almost forget about the gentleman's betrayal.

*Almost.*

She just watched carefully as Alistair took her hand and placed it on his shoulder, gently guiding her to and fro.

He stepped to the left, then to the right.

*Are we dancing?*

"You are a splendid dancer, my lady." He nuzzled his nose into her hair, and she could smell the alcohol on his breath. Mr. Diggory's breath smelled similar when he attacked her. "When may we dance again?"

"We are dancing now." She craned her neck away from the gentleman's nose.

## Chapter Twenty-Six

He chuckled. "One needs music to truly dance." He began to hum a 1,2,3 beat.

She really ought to cease this nonsense, but Isabella had to admit, there was something calming about the gentleman's quiet humming.

She screeched as he quickly twirled her outward and pulled her in, causing her to slam into his chest. "You are definitely drunk."

"Did you know," he drawled, "that your brother owes an exorbitant amount of money to Blackburn?"

Isabella stumbled. "What? Who is Blackburn?" And why did her brother owe him money?

"Sorry to have left you for so long—" Simon walked into the room with a bottle of whiskey in hand. He arched a brow at the dancing couple.

"Simon!" Isabella attempted to remove herself from Alistair's grasp, but the gentleman tightened his hold.

"The song has not yet concluded, my lady." Alistair continued their dance.

She turned her head toward Simon, whom she expected to be rather angry, but instead, her brother was hunched over a chair, shaking with laughter.

Alistair pulled her to the left.

"What did you give him, Simon?"

Her brother wiped the tears from his eyes. "Just some of my special brandy," he said between breaths.

Alistair circled her about the room.

"Special brandy? And who is Blackburn?" Isabella arched a curious brow.

Simon's grin faltered at the mention of the name. "How do you know of Blackburn?"

235

*Meeting Mister Baston*

"Ah, yes! Blackburn!" Alistair shouted next to Isabella's ear, causing her to flinch. "The bane of every gambler's existence."

"Gambler?" Isabella tried to pull away from Alistair's hold, but he continued their 1,2,3 step. "Simon, have you been gambling again?"

"Of course not!" Simon raised the bottle of whiskey into the air. "Come, Alistair, I have something even better for you to try."

Alistair ended their dance with a bow and a soft kiss to her knuckles. With irritation flushing her cheeks, she surged over to her brother. "Simon," she urged. "If there is something you are not telling me—"

"There is always something I am not telling you," he quipped, pushing her out of the room.

"Simon!" Isabella fought against her brother, but he was far stronger than her petite frame could handle.

"Goodnight, dear sister." Simon placed a kiss on her cheek and not so delicately shoved her through the doorway. "The gentlemen have whiskey to drink."

The heavy wooden door closed before her. She let out an aggravated sigh. There was no use questioning her brother about this Blackburn fellow in his inebriated state. Perhaps she would try to question him and Alistair separately on the morrow. And perhaps this Blackburn fellow could be a clue in the case of her sister's disappearance…

## Chapter Twenty-Seven

There was a loud thud just outside Isabella's bedchamber. Her pulse doubled the speed of its rhythm as the familiar feeling of panic rose in her chest.

Could it be Mr. Diggory? He had escaped, after all, and no one knew where he could have gone. He was a servant in her family's household for many years and probably knew of every hidden corner in their London home.

Looking over to her nightside table, Isabella's heart sank.

Her dagger was not there. She had dropped it after— She squeezed her eyelids shut. She could not even think of the words anymore. She did not want to.

After a moment or two of silence, Isabella had calmed herself enough to rise from her bed and inspect the noise. She peeked into the dark hall and, to her surprise, she saw the silhouette of a body lying in the middle of the ornate rug.

With slow even strides, she closed the distance between herself and the figure. As she drew closer, she noticed the slightly reddened strands of the gentleman's hair shining in the candlelight.

"Alistair?" she asked quietly. What was it about this gentleman? When she wanted his company, he was there. And when she *did not* want his company, he was still there.

Isabella knelt down next to him and brought her face closer to his. "Alistair?" He was facedown against the burgundy rug, both hands sitting lifelessly at his thighs. "Alis—"

"Hmmm?" A small grunt escaped his mouth.

Isabella let out a gasp. "Alistair? Are you all right?" she asked, smoothing his tresses away from his face.

He slowly opened the one eye that was not squished into the fabric of the carpeting. "Bella?" His eye closed. "I am trying to sleep."

He smelled strongly of spirits. "You cannot sleep in the middle of the hallway," she urged, tugging at his shirtsleeve. "Get up."

"Urghhh." He began to slowly lift himself from the floor. "Fine."

"Here." Isabella put Alistair's arm around her shoulder in an attempt to steady him. "Let me help you." Even though the gentleman deserved to be left on the floor.

The sudden weight of his body caused her to stumble. She righted herself and began to lead him toward the guest wing. "This way. I will get you to bed."

Alistair swayed back and forth along the corridor, tripping over his own feet. His misstep caused her to stumble once again. Perhaps the gentleman could take a room in the family wing. The guest wing was much too far for her to drag him all the way there.

Isabella turned them back toward the family bedchambers,

## Chapter Twenty-Seven

and Alistair began to lead her to her bedroom. "No, no. This is *my* room. You cannot sleep in there."

"Is it?" Alistair poked his head through the doorway. "I have always wanted to see your room."

She was not quite sure how to react to such a statement. "Erm... Perhaps tomorrow."

Alistair frowned, and she continued their forward movement down the hall.

They reached the jade room just two doors down from her own. Alistair stumbled inside and fell front first onto the mattress, letting his lower half hang off the edge.

She struggled to stifle a laugh, but as soon as she turned to leave, a strange noise came from Alistair's mouth. She leaned over to inspect him more carefully, and the sound escaped again.

"Oh!" Her hand flew to her chest as she came to the realization that he was snoring.

There was something charming about him in his helpless state. He made her feel needed. Useful. Although, he most likely would not remember any of this.

Isabella sighed. It was proving very difficult to stay angry at the gentleman, especially when he was in such a helpless—and quite amusing—state.

She cocked her head to the side and studied his form. His position did not look very comfortable. Perhaps it would be best to somehow rearrange his limbs and put him under the bed covers. After all, she would not want the gentleman to catch a chill during the night.

Isabella fell to her knees and carefully began unlacing Alistair's boots. She placed them to the side and eyed his feet.

## Meeting Mister Baston

*Should I remove his socks as well?*

She tilted her head in thought. The only time she slept in socks was during the winter season. Also, who would want to sleep in socks they had been wearing all day?

She yanked the soft fabric from Alistair's feet. Standing from her crouched position, she began work on removing his jacket as it looked quite restricting and most definitely would be difficult to sleep in.

That is when a bell rang in Isabella's head. Something mischievous began forming a picture in her mind's eye.

*Should I?*

Isabella examined the gentleman before her. A devilish smile formed on her lips.

*Why, yes. Yes, I should.*

It was the perfect way to get back at the gentleman for his lapse in judgment at the dance hall. And perhaps—if she were able to pull off such a prank—she would consider them even.

Isabella flipped Alistair onto his back and began unbuttoning his waistcoat. She searched over Alistair's features. He looked so at peace in his sleep. She softly laid her fingertips on the coarse stubble of his cheek. She slid her fingers along his jawline, much like she had done when they were alone in the countryside.

Alistair's hand quickly caught her wrist, and she gasped at the sudden movement.

His lids were still tightly closed, and after a moment, his arm relaxed and fell to his chest. He mumbled while he did so.

She moved to unbutton his waistcoat and loosened the folds of his cravat. A small dusting of hair peeked out from

## Chapter Twenty-Seven

his white cotton shirt, and her heart began to thump loudly in her chest.

Perhaps the prank was not such a good idea, after all.

*No.* No, she would go through with it.

With trembling hands, she slipped the cotton fabric over Alistair's head, slowly revealing the hard muscles of his abdomen and chest. She troubled her lower lip as her eyes followed the thin trail of hair leading from his navel to the waistline of his cream breeches.

"Bella." Alistair let out a soft moan, causing her eyes to rush to his.

*Still closed.*

She released a calming exhale of breath and reached toward the gentleman's brown leather belt. She paused. Would it be inappropriate to remove his trousers?

*Yes. Definitely, yes.*

Everything about what she was currently doing was inappropriate.

The nagging voice in her head advised against her actions, but oh, how humorous it would be for Alistair to wake in the morning with no clothes to be found. He would have to ring for a servant completely in the nude.

Ignoring her conscience, Isabella removed the gentleman's belt.

She pulled the bed covers out from underneath Alistair's large frame and unbuttoned the front fall of his breeches. Her pulse quickened as she hesitantly reached to open the flap.

She flipped open the fabric only to reveal thick dark hair underneath. *He was not wearing undergarments?!*

Her hands flew over her eyes as she stood from the edge

of the mattress.

This was a *terrible* idea. What was she thinking? She should have left immediately after laying him down. She began making her way to the doorway and paused. No. Alistair deserved this treatment. After a moment of hesitation, she turned and marched to the end of the bed. The sooner she finished this, the sooner she could leave.

She carefully tugged at the ends of his trousers, which proved quite stubborn to remove.

Isabella yanked and pulled until she was finally able to slip them over his feet, and when she saw the bareness of his legs, she gasped and ducked to the floor.

*Coward.* "I am not a coward," she whispered to herself.

Taking a deep breath, she brought her hands to the edge of the mattress and pulled herself upward until she was able to peek over the top. Since the gentleman was already in the nude, it would not hurt anyone to take a look... for educational purposes.

Her eyes narrowed. The *appendage* was different to what she had expected. She supposed it was similar to what she'd seen on the many famous carved statues—with one significant difference.

The hair.

She was not expecting hair.

But she should not be thinking of such things, and she could not help but come to a comical realization that the *appendage* reminded her of a hefty garden slug peeking out from the hedges.

It was time to leave. Isabella sighed and pulled the bedsheets over Alistair's naked form. She hurriedly collected his clothing in her arms and searched the wardrobes and

## Chapter Twenty-Seven

chest of drawers for any extra articles.

Once the room was sufficiently cleared of garments, Isabella returned to her chamber and slouched against the wood panel behind her.

How exactly would she be able to look at her father's man-of-affairs in the same light after this?

## Chapter Twenty-Eight

The next morning, Alistair woke inside one of the many bedrooms of the Averys' London home. A small ray of sunlight escaped through the jade green curtains and landed on his forehead. The burning heat of the sun had caused small beads of sweat to form at his temple. He quickly turned his body away from the burning light, which caused his head to scream with pain.

"Ah!" His hands flew out from under the satin bedsheets to rub at that place just above his brows. With an aggravated grunt, he pushed himself into a sitting position. The silky fabric of the bedsheets caressed the skin of his buttocks. He peered down at his naked form.

*Where are my clothes?*

He stood, pulling the bedsheet with him. He wrapped the soft fabric around his waist and made his way to the servant bell.

Before he could pull the bell string, there was a quiet rapping on the door.

## Chapter Twenty-Eight

Slowly opening the white panel, he peeked his head through the opening. The hallway was empty.

*Odd.*

He closed the door, and a short moment later, there was another knock. With quick hands, he yanked at the door handle.

"Are you searching for something?" a small, familiar voice came from a few feet away.

A young boy stood at the end of the hall, wearing the latest in high society fashion. Alistair narrowed his eyes at the small pile of garments the young boy held in his arms.

Alistair took a step forward. "I believe those are my clothes you have there."

He continued to advance, which caused the young boy to retreat, a fiendish smile creeping over his face.

There was something eerily familiar about the lad, with his dusty brown hair, hazel eyes, and rosy freckled cheeks. He threw out his arm to yank the trousers from the boy's grasp.

The boy pulled away, laughing.

*That laugh...*

It was the orphan from the market, the orphaned boy that had hidden inside their carriage. "Joseph?" Alistair narrowed his eyes.

The boy's hazel eyes widened, and he swiftly turned and darted down the hallway.

*Great.*

Now he was without clothes, and somehow, the little thief had followed them to London.

"Mr. Baston."

Alistair flinched.

*Meeting Mister Baston*

"May I be of some assistance?"

Alistair turned to see George's valet standing at his side. The servant glanced down at the blue satin bedsheet that currently covered the bottom half of his body. "Erm, yes." He flashed the servant an awkward smile. "It seems I am in need of a pair of trousers."

"And a dress shirt, waistcoat, jacket, and stockings, sir? Some boots, perhaps?" the valet asked with his hands perfectly clasped behind his back.

"Right." Alistair cleared his throat and peeked down at his naked toes. "Thank you."

"It is my pleasure, Mr. Baston." The servant turned and made his way down the long corridor.

*Cheeky bugger.*

After Alistair dressed, the butler escorted him to the yellow drawing room, which to his surprise, was drowning in an elegant sea of flowers.

"Mr. Alistair Baston." The servant announced his presence to the room.

Three familiar faces looked up from their current sources of employment: Simon's newspaper, the duchess's embroidery, and Isabella's open leather-bound book.

"How good of you to join us, Mr. Baston!" The duchess rose from the gold sofa.

He gave a slight shake of his head. "Please, no need to halt your activities on my behalf." Alistair stepped into the room as the butler made his exit.

"Oh, nonsense." Mary motioned to the empty space beside her. "Please, do sit. I have not seen you in an age."

"Good of you to join us, Baston," Simon added with a peculiar grin.

## Chapter Twenty-Eight

Alistair gave a polite nod and made his way over to the small, embroidered chair across the room.

"Do sit by me," the duchess said as she patted the cushion in between herself and Isabella. He sat, attempting not to sit too close to Isabella, who was looking radiant, but no doubt was still angry with him.

"Good morning, Lady Isabella." He glanced toward her.

"Good *afternoon*," she corrected, keeping her sapphire eyes glued to the pages of her book.

"My apologies. I did not realize how late in the day it was." He never tended to sleep later than mid-morning, but he supposed spending the night drinking with the marquess made him more tired than usual.

"Rough night?" Simon asked from the back corner of the room.

Alistair narrowed his eyes. "A bit, yes." How was it that Simon seemed perfectly well, while he himself felt like the fires of hell had torn through his skull. It proved how often Alistair got soused compared to his friend.

"Oh, dear. You must be famished. I will call for tea and sandwiches," Mary said as she rose from the sofa once again.

"And biscuits!" Simon shouted.

"Thank you." Alistair clutched his hand to his rumbling stomach. "May I ask what all of the flowers are for? I can barely see over all of the roses."

"They're from callers, my dear," the duchess answered as she tugged the bellpull. "Bella received quite a few gentlemen callers while you were away. Violet as well," she said, lowering her voice to a whisper. "Everyone believes Violet is visiting relatives in the north." The duchess brought a kerchief to her nose and sniffled. "I do hope she is all right."

*Meeting Mister Baston*

"I am so sorry—"

"No, no." The duchess waved her kerchief through the air. "It is not your fault. Now…" She straightened and curled her lips into a small smile. "Let us return to a more pleasant subject. Where were we? Oh, yes, the flowers. Sometimes we receive more than this. My Bella is considered the beauty of the county, perhaps even all of England."

"Mother, please." Isabella groaned, hiding her face even deeper within the book.

"Though the courtships never last," Mary continued, ignoring Isabella's protestations. "I do not understand why."

Perhaps those gentlemen were not what she wanted? Perhaps they were not good enough for her? Alistair tightened his hands into fists. Isabella had waves of gentlemen coming from every corner of the country who were better suited and better titled, and even *they* were not good enough for her.

Mary waved a hand at her daughter. "Oh, do not be so modest, and stop hiding behind your book."

Isabella glared at her mother.

"You will receive more callers today. I told Lord Middleton we were expecting your return very soon," Mary said, returning to her seat.

Isabella let out a bitter moan.

Mary then focused her attention on the maid standing in the doorway. "Some tea and sandwiches if you would, Bethany."

The young maid bobbed a curtsy.

"And biscuits!" Simon reminded.

"And biscuits." The duchess shook her head, then turned back to Isabella. "I do not understand your indifference toward him. He is a perfectly fine gentleman."

## Chapter Twenty-Eight

Isabella did not reply. Instead, her eyes met his for a brief moment. The pain from his nails digging into his palms reminded him that his fists were still clenched. He slowly relaxed his hands, trying not to bring attention to himself. Was Lord Middleton a suitor of hers?

"Tell me," Simon drawled, leaning against the back of the gold sofa. "Did you sleep well, Baston? I retired a bit before you."

Alistair turned to meet the marquess's amused stare, finding the sudden change of subject somewhat odd. "Quite well." Which was not a lie. He did sleep well—so well he could not remember the majority of the previous evening.

"I feared you were going to lose consciousness in the blue room before I left." He laughed.

"Simon!" Mary said scornfully. "There is no need for such talk around us ladies."

Ignoring his mother, Simon turned to Isabella. "What about you, little sister?"

"What about me?" Isabella asked, her nose still in the pages of her book.

"Did you not fear Mr. Baston would fall unconscious, right there in the blue room?" Simon's smile grew sinister. "You *were* a witness for a few short minutes."

Isabella slammed her book closed and mouthed something toward her brother.

"Or was it a few long minutes? I do not remember." Simon's tone grew derisive.

What was he getting at? Alistair did not remember Isabella being present in the blue room. The last he knew, the lady was abovestairs having a visit with her father.

Isabella's cheeks reddened. "I haven't a clue what you are

## Meeting Mister Baston

on about."

"Of course you do." Simon nudged Alistair from behind. "You remember, do you not, Baston?"

"Actually, I do not." He shrugged. "I believe I had a bit too much whiskey."

Simon threw his head back and laughed. "Perhaps I shall remind you?"

"Simon. That is enough," Isabella warned.

Mary looked up from her embroidery. "What are you two bickering over now?"

"Nothing," the siblings said in unison.

Alistair arched a brow. Did something happen between himself and the lady? Surely he'd remember.

"You children will be the death of me." The duchess sighed and set her project down on a nearby table. "Do excuse me; I must check on your father."

Alistair stood, as did the duchess, and gave a regal bow.

As soon as the duchess left the room, Isabella tossed her book toward Simon, hitting him directly in the forehead.

"Ow!"

"Perhaps *you* should remind us all who Blackburn is?" Isabella seethed.

Simon rubbed the top of his skull. "I haven't a clue what you are talking about."

*Blackburn?* "The Marquess of Blackburn? The owner of—" Simon launched Isabella's book in his direction, clipping his shoulder. "Ouch!"

"Hold your tongue, Baston!"

Isabella looked between Simon and himself. She jumped to her feet. Now standing on the cushions of the sofa, she outstretched a finger. "You *will* tell me!" She pointed between

250

## Chapter Twenty-Eight

the two of them. "Or I shall throttle you both!"

What was so important about Blackburn? Why did Simon not want to speak of the degenerate Lord? He remembered the name being mentioned the previous night, but for the life of him, he could not remember the significance. Alistair glared at Simon, who gave him a pointed look in return. "Lord Blackburn—" Simon began to sputter, but Alistair raised his voice over the gentleman "—owns the Fox's Den, a gaming hell."

The marquess looked as though he wanted to drive a dagger through Alistair's chest.

"A gaming hell?" Isabella looked to her brother, her hands falling to her hips. "You owe a gambling debt, then?" Simon looked to the floor but said nothing. "Does Father know of this?"

His own words resurfaced in his memory. Simon must have told him about his debt to Blackburn in the blue room the evening last. This could be a lead. Perhaps Blackburn had a part in Lady Violet's disappearance? "How much?"

Simon's gaze turned to the window. Defeated. "Three thousand pounds."

"Three thousand pounds!" Isabella jumped from the sofa and marched over to her brother. "You must tell Father at once! If you do not tell him, I will." She pushed her brother through the doorway leading out of the room. As soon as Simon stepped out into the hall, Isabella slammed the door to the drawing room shut, leaving the two of them well and fully alone.

## Chapter Twenty-Nine

It was strange how quickly life had seemed to go back to normal since returning to London.

When Isabella had risen that morning, she had sought out Joseph, the orphan boy from the market. Her mother had informed her that Simon, Captain Lucas, and her father happened upon him after the attack and decided to bring the boy home to London. She informed little Joseph of her plans to prank Alistair, leaving out many unimportant details, of course, and handed over Alistair's bundle of clothing.

It would not do well for a maid to find a pile of the gentleman's garments discarded across Isabella's bedchamber.

Somehow, Simon had then heard about Isabella's clever plan and had little Joseph run to Alistair's room to wake the gentleman.

And so Isabella found herself in a drawing room full of bouquets and other offerings from gentleman callers, and her mother still had it in her mind that she was to marry Lord Middleton.

## Chapter Twenty-Nine

But after all of that, Isabella had come to the conclusion that she had to put aside this feud with Alistair—at least for the next few minutes. Yes, he had mistreated her. Yes, she had seen him well and fully naked just the night prior. She was still angry with him, of course, but none of that was important right now. Not when her brother just revealed this latest information.

Pushing herself off the door, she approached Alistair with caution. "Alistair?" He squinted his green eyes at her, as if he knew what she was about to suggest. "We must visit the Fox's Den. This Blackburn fellow could have information about Violet and before you say *no*—"

"No."

"But we must!"

"Absolutely not. Your father would never agree to it. The Fox's Den is no place for a lady, and Blackburn is not the sort of gentleman one wants to make accusations of. He is dangerous."

"My sister could be in danger!"

Alistair stood from his place on the sofa and gave her a pitiful look. She did not need his pity. She needed his help. She crossed the room and took his hand in hers. She gave his palm a soft squeeze. "*Please*," she pleaded.

The gentleman let out a long sigh. "*I* will go to Blackburn. And I will also write to Captain Lucas and tell him of this new information."

It was not exactly what she wanted. She pulled her hand from his grasp, not quite ready for the gentleman's touch. Not after his betrayal. Not after she saw the rippling muscles of his stomach and chest. Not until her sister was found. "Thank you."

She stepped around him and returned to her place on the sofa. He stood where she had left him for a few moments, staring down at his now empty hand—the hand that had touched her so freely. She tried to swallow back the lump of guilt in her throat. Why should she feel guilty for thwarting his advances? Even if it was a simple touch of the hand meant to comfort her, she did not need his comfort.

Not any longer.

Isabella picked up her book and tried to find where she had left off. In truth, when Alistair entered the room, she could not pay any sort of attention to her reading. Every time she looked at the gentleman now, all she could see was his strong, naked form; all she could feel was his kiss and the anger it brought her.

Alistair moved to sit beside her. "You have been very distant this afternoon."

Unable to meet his gaze, she pulled her book closer to her nose. "I do not know what you mean. I have been right here."

"Did I do something wrong?" He turned her chin up with his fingers. "Other than… before."

There he went, touching her again. She could feel his warmth through the kidskin of his gloves. How did her body still react to him when she wanted so badly to be angry?

She shook her head. "No, of course not."

His hand left her chin. "Are you feeling well?"

"Quite well." She nodded, still avoiding eye contact.

"Good." Alistair's hand fell to his lap, and her gaze leaped to the front fall of his breeches.

She had not meant to; it was just difficult not to think of, after… "You remember nothing of last night?" she asked, eyeing him from behind the pages of her book.

## Chapter Twenty-Nine

"No." Alistair's eyes narrowed. "Should I?"

She shook her head frantically. "No."

"No?"

"No. I mean I-I..." Isabella could not help but stumble over her words. Thankfully, Alistair began to speak again.

"I am not even certain how I managed to undress and get into bed." He laughed, causing her cheeks to go aflame. "My apologies. That was an inappropriate thing to say."

She smiled awkwardly. "It is all right."

Alistair laid his hand atop hers, and she met his gaze. His eyes were greener than the country grass—so bright and beautiful—and in that moment, it felt as though her heart had ceased beating.

"Did something happen between us?" His voice came out sweet and endearing.

Isabella parted her lips to speak but found that she could not form words. Part of her wanted to tell him of their dance in the drawing room. The other part of her wanted to keep it her own little secret.

She also knew the one thing she would never, *could never*, tell him. "I put you to bed last evening." Her hand quickly flew to her lips.

*Bloody traitorous tongue!*

Alistair's jaw dropped open. "What?"

"You-you were unconscious in the middle of the hallway. I could not very well leave you on the floor."

The gentleman leaned toward her. "You..." He paused to glance at the closed door. "You undressed me?"

She troubled her lower lip and nodded. There was no point in denying it now.

"Did we?" Alistair made a hand gesture, pointing between

the two of them.

*Lay together?*

"No! No, of course not."

"Then why...?" His words trailed off.

Was she going to have to go over every explicit detail with him? "I thought it would be uncomfortable for you to sleep in your traveling clothes." It was a half truth, to say the least.

"Did you...?" *See anything?*

"No," she lied. "I covered you, of course."

"I see." Alistair rubbed his fingertips through the dark stubble on his cheek. "I suppose I should thank you, then."

"You are welcome," she said with a quick nod of the head.

"Speaking of a lack of clothing, someone stole mine this morning."

Isabella held back a smile— "Oh!" Joseph burst into the room and jumped on Isabella's lap. "Hello, Joseph," she laughed. "Do you not look dashing?"

"Mrs. Chambers told me you came home last night." He smiled and winked.

Oh, he was a natural prankster already.

"Did she? And how is our governess treating you?" she asked, trying to sound serious and not at all like she was trying to hold back a burst of laughter.

"Good."

"Very well," Isabella corrected.

"Did I miss something?" Alistair cut in, his expression confused.

Isabella glanced toward him. Of course, he was not present when her mother informed her of the little orphan boy she had taken under her wing. "Simon found him at the ambush and brought him home."

## Chapter Twenty-Nine

"I very well could not leave him behind," Simon added, waltzing into the room with the maid close behind.

*Did he tell Father of his debts?*

Joseph turned toward Simon and beamed. "I hid his trousers, just as you told me to." The boy's smile quickly faded. "Oops."

Isabella pressed her lips together, attempting to stifle a laugh.

Simon quickly crossed the room and lifted Joseph off her lap. "That's my boy!" He laughed and spun the orphan around in the air.

"That was *your* idea?" Alistair growled.

"All of us actually," Simon said casually.

Alistair looked to Isabella with narrowing eyes.

"Oh, look! The food has arrived." Simon quickly changed the subject and stole two biscuits from the meal tray the maid had just set on the table. "Thank you, Bethany." Simon winked, causing the young girl to blush.

Isabella let out a small chuckle. It was going to be lovely having a child in the house, especially if he was going to torment Alistair during his stay. She leaned against the cushions and let out a sigh of relief. Things were starting to feel as though they were falling back into place, especially with the latest information about Simon's gambling debts.

That was, until her mother walked through the doorway with Lord Middleton attached to her arm.

## Chapter Thirty

*This is going to be awkward*, Isabella thought as her eyes landed on Alistair. His face was white as snow. "May I announce Edward, Viscount Middleton?" The duchess beamed and tugged Lord Middleton's arm closer to her waist.

Her mother had always adored Edward, she being a close friend of his mother's for years, and of course, a match between Isabella and Edward had always been a favorite subject of conversation.

The duchess turned toward her. "What a delightful surprise, do you not agree, Bella?"

She faked a smile. "Splendid."

What a terrible situation to be caught up in, being in the same room with two gentlemen competing for her affections.

Alistair had made his intentions clear with his kiss. Edward, on the other hand, had been attempting to court her for nearly two months, mostly because her mother continuously invited the gentleman over for tea.

## Chapter Thirty

"I am so happy to see you, Edward!" Joseph sprung to his feet.

Isabella rolled her eyes. It seemed Edward had already won the affections of little Joseph. Her mother would never give up hope on a match between them now.

"Good to see you as well, Joseph." Lord Middleton smiled down at the young ward, a blond lock falling over his brow. He quickly swept it back with his fingers, all the while glancing toward Isabella.

Her stomach clenched.

*I would like to run away now.*

"You already know Simon" Her mother motioned toward Simon as she guided Edward into the room. "This is Mr. Alistair Baston, my husband's man-of-affairs and dearest friend of the family."

Alistair stood from the sofa to offer his greetings.

Her mother offered the gentleman tea, but instead of accepting her mother's offer as Isabella expected, Lord Middleton shook his head in refusal.

"Actually—" Edward cleared his throat "—being that the weather is so fine, I was hoping Lady Isabella would join me for a walk through Hyde Park."

Isabella's heart dropped into her stomach. Meanwhile, her mother practically jumped out of her skirts at the mention of an outing. "Oh, what a lovely idea. Is it not, Isabella?"

She saw a flash of fire burn in Alistair's eyes. Turning away from the gentleman who had not only violated her but made her think her father was dead, she faced Lord Middleton and gave him a wistful smile. "I'd be delighted. I could use a bit of fresh air."

Why yes, she supposed making Alistair jealous on purpose

*Meeting Mister Baston*

was unbecoming of her, but he deserved to be hurt. Just as he had hurt her.

"Simon, be a dear and accompany your sister," her mother instructed.

The marquess leaned back lazily in his chair, taking a small bite of a cucumber sandwich. "Surely Alistair would be the better choice? He has been her chaperone for nearly two weeks now."

Did her brother mean to torture her? Most likely. If Edward was not present, she would most definitely have thrown a second cucumber sandwich at his fat head.

"Do not be a lazy cow," the duchess said, and Isabella could hardly hold in her mirth. "Alistair is not a guard dog, and beside all that, he and I have much to catch up on."

She really did not want to be on an outing with a gentleman with her hotheaded brother by her side, even if said gentleman was only Edward. "Why do I not ask my lady's maid? Perhaps she would enjoy a walk through the park as well?"

Her mother agreed.

"I will just need to fetch my shawl," she said, standing from her place on the sofa. Alistair stood just as she did, and she noticed the glimmer of pain in his eyes.

Guilt rose up into her chest. Mayhap she should not have agreed to an outing with the viscount. Alistair was not to blame for thinking her father dead.

*There was so much blood...*

Isabella shook that horrid memory from her mind and instead thought of a much pleasanter one. Could the gentleman really be blamed for going as far as he did with their kiss? After all, she had kissed him back, and if she were

## Chapter Thirty

to be honest, she did quite enjoy the kiss in the moment.

"Isabella!" Joseph quickly rose from his spot on the floor before she had a chance to take a step. "I nearly forgot. I have something for you."

"Do you now?" She was so happy that her parents had decided to take in the young boy. Who knew what would have happened to the orphan otherwise?

Joseph pulled a small, sapphire-studded blade from inside his jacket pocket.

Isabella froze, not quite sure what to say. She thought she'd never see her dagger again, and even though it was a precious gift from her father, she was unsure whether she wanted the weapon back in her possession.

A trail of blood appeared on the dagger in her mind's eye. The moment when she pulled the dagger from her attacker's body. The moment it had fallen into the dirt below. "H-How did you find it?"

"It was on the ground," Joseph explained. "I cleaned it for you. There was a lot of blood and dirt on it."

With a gasp, Isabella yanked the weapon from the boy's hands.

"Blood?" Edward asked on a mirthful laugh.

She let out a nervous chuckle. "Children and their imaginations." She crouched down and placed a peck on the boy's plump cheek. "Thank you."

Now she just had to hide away her dagger before departing for Hyde Park. She did not want the memories from the ambush creeping into her mind again.

## Chapter Thirty-One

Isabella tilted her head toward the sun so she could feel the warmth on her skin.

Oh, how much she loathed wearing bonnets, but her mother would not let her leave the house without one. *A gently bred lady must never be seen out of doors without a bonnet...* Her mother's words came back to haunt her time and time again.

There was just something about the warm afternoon air that reminded her of the day she and Alistair had handed out Violet's posters.

She could not believe Simon recommended Alistair as her chaperone. How very uncomfortable that would have been, especially being that they had yet to officially reconcile after their argument at the dance hall. Alistair did not qualify as a chaperone anyhow. He was not a married gentleman nor a relative.

Isabella was brought back to the present when she heard the voice of another.

## Chapter Thirty-One

Edward. He had asked her something about being well today. "Yes, thank you," she blurted.

"You *look* well," Edward added with a demure smile.

"As do you." She flinched. Would the gentleman consider her statement as being flirtatious?

*Most likely.*

His eyes grew bright. "How was your journey up north?"

Up north? *Oh, of course.* Her mother had told all of the *ton* that she and Violet had decided to take a trip to Yorkshire. "Quite cold. And very quick. I felt as though I spent an entire fortnight in the carriage just to get there and back."

Edward chuckled. "Yes, I can imagine. It was good of you to accompany your sister on such a long journey." He paused for a moment. "Is Lady Violet well?"

Isabella's heart sank. How she wished she knew more about her sister's well-being. Hopefully, Captain Lucas would send word soon. "Very well," she lied. "My sister adores the north."

"When will she return?"

*Tomorrow? Next week? Never?* "She is unsure. Perhaps in a few weeks."

He cocked his head. "Is she having a Season in York as well as London?"

"Sort of." She lied again. It was strange how easy it was to think up false stories. She supposed it was better to fantasize than to reflect on the grim reality.

Edward's features grew dark. Venomous. "And Mr. Baston? He joined you on your trip to Yorkshire?"

*Was the gentleman jealous of Alistair?*

"Yes." She gulped. "As did my father and brother. Mr. Baston is the duke's man-of-affairs, after all."

## Meeting Mister Baston

"Of course."

They followed the path as it veered to the right. Isabella stepped on a wet patch of leaves, causing her foot to slip backward. "Oh!" she yelped as her body lurched into his arms.

"Are you all right?" His large hands grasped her arms, steadying her.

"Yes, thank you." Her eyes met the gentleman's brown depths. He gazed down toward her with heavy lids.

Edward was a handsome man—there was no denying it—but even as the gentleman lowered his mouth, closer and closer to her own, Isabella felt nothing but terror.

What was a lady to do? Surely, she could not be seen being kissed by the viscount in the middle of Hyde Park for all of London to see.

But it was too late. Edward's lips crushed against her own. His kiss was so hard that she almost lost her footing. Luckily, he soon broke away. A gust of wind tousled his golden hair, and he gazed upon her as if she were the only woman in the world.

And she felt nothing. No erratic heartbeat. No shaking of the knees.

Edward loosened his grip on her arms and slowly slid his hands down the length of them.

Isabella held her breath as the gentleman took her hands in his. Her stomach dropped to her feet as Lord Middleton knelt before her.

*No, no, no, no.*

She glanced toward her maid, who stood just a few meters away. The young servant held her hands over her mouth in shock.

## Chapter Thirty-One

Passersby turned their heads in her direction, pointing and whispering.

News of her outing with Edward would be in the gossip sheets in a matter of days.

"I know we have not spent an extraordinary amount of time together, but I feel as though we would make a great match…"

"Lord Middleton—" His name left her lips on a faint whisper. They would not make a great match. Edward was so very traditional in his beliefs and appearances, and Isabella was unconventional in every way.

"Every moment I have spent with you has been incredible," he continued. "As you know, I will inherit my father's title. I will be able to give you the lifestyle you are used to, and I believe we can be incredibly happy together."

Guilt squeezed her chest. Edward sounded incredibly sincere. But was he in love with her? She was not so sure…

"Isabella, will you please do me the honor of being my wife?"

"I… I…" A betrothal between herself and Edward would undoubtedly make her mother very happy. Even her father would approve of the match. Edward was from a good family with wealth and a title, after all. But what of her own happiness?

What of Alistair?

Yes, she was still slightly angry with him… but they would reconcile. In fact, as soon as she was home, she was going to apologize for being angry with him. She was going to apologize for striking him. Mayhap even tell him that she *had* seen him naked the previous night.

*No… Keep that part out.*

"I..." But Alistair was still a rake... Should she bet her life's happiness on a man such as Alistair? And who was to say she would be happy with him anyhow? She would admit there was an attraction there, but marriage? She still was not convinced he would change his rakish ways if he indeed wanted to marry her, or just *kiss* her... "I will have to think on it, Edward. I have only just returned home, and this is all so much..."

Edward rose from his knee. A melancholy smile crossed over his features, and he placed a soft kiss on her gloved hand. "I understand. I will give you all the time you need."

## Chapter Thirty-Two

Alistair stepped inside the cheroot-smoke-filled room, the loud roar of patrons overwhelming his senses. His eyes had to adjust to the dimly lit space overflowing with gambling tables and scantily dressed women.

Only a few weeks ago, Alistair would have felt perfectly at home in gaming hells such as this one, the Fox's Den. Only a few weeks ago, Alistair would have been delighted to join the Marquess of Reading at the card tables. He would have been thrilled at the idea of tasting the finest of gins with a whore seated upon his lap. Now... Now he was absolutely appalled by the sight of gentlemen throwing their fortunes on the green velvet gaming tables, lying with whores while their wives and children were at home. But today he was there for one reason, and that was to confront Blackburn about Simon's debt and the disappearance of Lady Violet.

"I am here to see Blackburn," Alistair said to a surly guard who stood in front of a staircase located at the back of the

*Meeting Mister Baston*

room.

"Do ye have an appointment?" the guard asked in a strong Cockney accent, his overly muscled arms crossed over his chest.

So the blackguard was indeed here, which was a start. "No," he said simply.

"Blackburn don't see no one without an appointment."

Alistair arched a brow. "It is about a debt owed." Surely Blackburn would not turn down a meeting about a debt, even if it was not scheduled.

After a moment of contemplative silence, the guard unlatched the red velvet rope crossing over the staircase. "Come with me."

He was ushered up the dark, narrow staircase and led to the end of a corridor to a set of double doors. The man rapped twice with his knuckles.

"Enter," came a brooding voice from behind the heavy wooden panels.

The guard entered the room and closed the door behind him. After a few mumbled words, the man returned. "He will see ya."

Alistair entered, the large guard closing the door with a loud *thunk* behind him. Blackburn sat behind an ornate mahogany desk with gold carved into its edges, and papers atop it piled neatly into stacks. With one gloved hand, he scribbled a signature onto some parchment and set it aside, which Alistair found quite odd. Did the gentleman have an unsightly mark on his right hand? An old injury he did not want to be seen? Grabbing another paper, Blackburn looked over its contents. Without looking up from his work, the gentleman asked, "Your name?"

## Chapter Thirty-Two

Alistair took a step toward the set of sapphire velvet chairs placed at the front of the marquess's expansive desk. He cleared his throat. "Alistair Baston." He noticed the lord did not even offer him a seat before getting straight into business.

Blackburn tugged open a drawer and pulled a brown leather notebook from the space. He flipped through its pages for what seemed like ages. Alistair tried his damnedest to stay calm and collected. He was on a bit of a time crunch since the Duchess of Waverly had invited him to dine with the family later that evening, and he wanted time to speak with Isabella beforehand. He did not want them to be cross with each other anymore—even though she did go on an outing with Middleton.

His blood boiled at the mere thought of it.

*Focus, Baston.*

"I am not seeing your name among my patrons…" Blackburn continued scanning the pages. His black hair was neatly slicked back, gleaming in the candlelight.

"I do not owe the debt," Alistair clarified.

"Ahhh…" Blackburn looked up from his desktop for the first time since Alistair had entered the room. His obsidian eyes gleamed with dark amusement, and Alistair noticed that the lord had an unseemly scar that reached across the top-right portion of his face. "Wishing to buy off an account, then? What is the name on the account?"

"Simon Avery, the Marquess of Reading." This seemed to give the gentleman pause. "Familiar with him, are you?"

He let out a mirthless laugh. "You can say that." He waved out a hand. "Sit."

Alistair took a seat in one of the expensive velvet chairs. Blackburn was obviously not coy about showing off his wealth. Not only was he titled and the owner of the Fox's Den, but he owned many other establishments, including a recently purchased opera house in London. Blackburn was a man of many... *interests*, if one were to say it politely.

Blackburn steepled his fingers, all amusement leaving his features. This was the Blackburn he knew of, the Blackburn all of society was terrified of. "What do you know of Reading's debts, then?"

"I know he owes you an obscene amount of money."

"And?"

"And I know it is not below you to do something unlawful to get said money from him."

Blackburn leaned back in his chair, a smile touching the corner of his mouth. "And what is it you believe I did to Reading?"

"His youngest sister is missing, and I believe you have something to do with her disappearance." Alistair's heart thumped in his chest. It was one thing to come into Blackburn's establishment and demand a meeting unannounced. It was altogether another to accuse said man of kidnap.

The gentleman narrowed his black eyes. "All I will say is that the marquess knows a great deal more about the disappearance of his sister than he is likely letting on."

*Simon...* Had Simon been the key to finding Lady Violet all along?

Alistair felt the first glimmers of hope building inside him. But alongside hope came anger... No, fury. If he found out that Simon had been lying to him... to *everyone* this entire time, Alistair was going to kill his friend.

He was going to beat him bloody.

## Chapter Thirty-Three

After traveling to his apartments to change into his evening clothes, Alistair returned to Avery House. It was high time to seek out Reading, that traitorous bastard he had thought was his friend.

Upon arrival, he was immediately led to the blue room, where the marquess in question was playing billiards.

"Baston!" Simon set down the cheroot that was hanging from the corner of his mouth. "You've returned. Care to join—"

Alistair grabbed the gentleman's lapels with tight fists. The lying was going to end here and now. Isabella had suspected Simon was hiding something, and Blackburn confirmed it. "What do you know of your sister's disappearance?"

Simon's face went white. "No more than you do. What are you on about, Baston?"

"You are lying." Alistair yanked the cue from the gentleman's grasp and tossed it across the room. "Tell me the truth."

Simon scoffed, but Alistair did not relinquish his hold.

*Meeting Mister Baston*

He tightened his fists on the lapels of the other man's fine evening jacket. He yanked him closer until their noses were nearly touching. A low growl escaped him

He had had enough of the lies. If Simon knew something, he was going to speak.

After what seemed an eternity of the two of them staring each other down, his friend let out an aggrieved sigh. "Fine. But you have to give me your word that you will say nothing of this to my family."

How could Alistair make such a promise when he hadn't a clue of what Simon was going to confess? He supposed he could give Simon his word, but that did not mean he could never refute said word. "Fine."

After Alistair released the marquess, Simon stalked over to the sideboard and poured himself and Alistair two fingers of whiskey. "You are going to need this," he said, handing Alistair the drink.

Simon fell into a nearby shell-backed chair, slouching as he let his head fall back, eyeing the painted cherubs on the ceiling. "You went to Blackburn, did you not?"

"I am not the one under interrogation." Alistair took a sip of the whiskey and leaned a hip against the billiards table. He was too highly strung to do anything but stand.

Simon gave him a sideways glance then sighed. "Blackburn hired the footman to kidnap Violet. That is all I know."

"Which footman?"

"Callum."

Callum? The one who attacked Bella? "He was with us. How could he have taken your sister?"

"I do not know." Simon leaned forward in his chair, gripping the glass in both hands. "I just know Blackburn

## Chapter Thirty-Three

paid Callum to take Violet somewhere. When Bella saw me arguing with Callum, I was trying to get him to tell me where he was keeping her."

"So... Derby? Lord Taunton? You knew it was not him. You knew we did not have to travel to Derby, but you let us waste time? She is your sister! And you had us following the wrong lead!" Alistair could not believe what he was hearing. Simon knew... He *knew* Lady Violet was not in Derbyshire, yet he allowed his father to travel there anyway. He allowed his sister to wallow away wherever she was without telling anyone what he knew.

What of the ambush? Did Blackburn orchestrate that as well? "The ambush..."

"I am assuming it was for me. Blackburn would not hurt Violet... but he would hurt me."

And how did Simon know Blackburn would not injure his sister? How did Simon know the footman would not? After all, the footman attacked Isabella. He could have very well attempted to defile Violet... and without anyone to protect her, would probably succeed.

Alistair let out a black curse.

"Does your father know of this? Did you tell him of your debt?"

Simon looked down to the glass of spirits in his hands, which he had yet to drink. He stayed silent.

Alistair's blood began to boil. He needed to hit something... *someone*. But instead, he downed what was left of his whiskey and slammed the glass onto the billiard's table, nearly shattering it. "All the time we have wasted..."

"I know. I thought I could handle it on my own."

Violet kidnapped. The duke shot. Bella nearly raped. All

for a three thousand dollar debt? It was no measly amount of money, to be sure, but certainly not enough to kill a man over. "How much is the debt?"

Simon looked up from his glass. His face had gone from pale white to gray. "Just over seven thousand."

"Seven thousand!" Alistair began to pace. "That is a small fortune! How did you manage to gamble away that much money?" One could buy a cottage in the countryside and live a comfortable life with seven thousand pounds. One could buy *multiple* cottages in the countryside with seven thousand pounds. "Christ…"

"I need to fix this."

"*We* need to fix this."

There was no bloody way Alistair was going to let Simon handle this on his own. He had made the situation much, much worse by hiding the information from his entire family. No… If Simon would not tell the duke about the debt, about Blackburn and Callum, then Alistair would.

They had to track down Captain Lucas. Lord only knew what wrong direction the gentleman was going in. Callum was the one they needed to find. And Blackburn was the one who was going to tell them where he was.

"Mother has guests over for dinner, and the dinner bell is going to ring at any moment. This will have to wait until later tonight."

Blasted hell. How was Alistair expected to mingle with the other guests and act as if everything was normal when all of this information had been thrust onto him? How would he hide this from Bella? She was still angry with him over the kiss. If she found out he was hiding *this* from her, she would loathe him for all eternity.

# Chapter Thirty-Four

The dinner bell rang, signaling the family to make their way to the formal dining room. Simon let out one last breath before putting on the proverbial mask. The marquess stood from his seat and gave Alistair a hard *whack* on the shoulder. "Time to mingle," he said with a grin.

How was the bastard so good at switching off his emotions? Turning a blind eye to everything he had just confessed, everything he knew about his sister and her disappearance?

Alistair would just have to learn from the marquess this evening. He tugged at the hem of his evening coat, flipped out the tails, and stepped out into the corridor.

Upon arrival, the footmen pulled out the extravagantly carved dining chairs and waited for the family to claim their seats.

"Come sit by me, little man," Simon instructed the young orphan boy with a friendly wink. Children usually ate separately from the family at such elegant dinner parties, but he supposed the Averys were not a typical family.

Alistair searched the room for a familiar blonde head of hair. When he found her, he noticed she had changed into an enticing evening gown. The fabric was made of crimson satin that turned the angelic beauty he had seen that afternoon into an enchanting seductress.

He should greet her... but Alistair found himself unsure of what to say. He, of course, had to act his normal self—contrary, sarcastic, and he should most definitely poke fun at her whenever the opportunity arose. But was that normal for them now? Their friendship had come to a standstill when they had left the public dance hall.

Should he instead ignore her completely? After all, he did have certain secrets to hide, and he did not want an accidental slip of the tongue—though that was unlikely. Alistair was *very* good at keeping secrets.

Their eyes met. A flash of terror, and then she turned away. Odd.

Not exactly the reaction he was expecting, but he supposed it was better than anger. Perhaps he should find a seat near Reading or the duke, whom he was surprised to see away from the confinements of his bedroom.

"Good of you to join us, Alistair." George raised a crystal wine glass into the air as Alistair took the seat beside him.

"Good to see you out of bed." Alistair mimicked the duke's movements. "I know we are good friends, but visiting you in your bedchambers was becoming quite awkward."

George let out a mirthful laugh and took a sip of his wine.

There was a movement of air, and Alistair looked beside him to where Isabella had surprisingly taken a seat on the soft, purple velvet of the chair.

## Chapter Thirty-Four

"You look quite fetching this evening, my lady," he whispered.

Without looking at him, she said, "Thank you. As do you, Mr. Baston."

He could not help but smile at her efforts to ignore him. Surely if she did not want his attentions the lady would have sat elsewhere.

"You stole my seat," she announced.

This made him snort. "Did I?"

"I always sit next to my father."

"My apologies, then. You are welcome to sit on my lap."

She choked on her wine.

It seemed as though their friendship had resumed its course. Perhaps acting his normal self around the lady would not be so difficult, after all—as long as he could keep his conscious at bay, and being the rake that he was, that should not prove difficult in the least.

"Where have you been?" she asked, delicately dabbing a kerchief at the corner of her rouge-tinted lips.

*Bloody hell...* Should he lie about where he had gone? Or should he tell the truth and lie about the outcome?

Truth... then lie. The more truthful the details, the easier it would be to keep his story straight. "I visited Blackburn. Where have *you* been?"

"You know very well where I have been," she scoffed. "I cannot believe you went without me."

"We can discuss it more after dinner."

"Where?"

"Meet me in the library," he whispered. Then at least he could lie to her in private instead of in a room full of people.

Once all of the guests were seated, the liveried footmen

served the table creamy clam chowder, momentarily distracting him from the lady seated beside him. He could not help but notice Simon and young Joseph exchanging whispers from across the table.

Alistair slowly sipped at his soup and caught the young orphan's eye.

*Are they planning another prank against me?*

He would have to watch himself each time he visited the Avery household from here on out.

Returning his attentions to Isabella, he asked, "How is your soup, my lady?"

She narrowed her eyes as she spooned the chowder into her mouth. "Very nice, Mr. Baston. How is yours?" She gave an innocent smile, drawing attention to her lips.

Alistair leaned close. "Quite delicious, my lady."

"I would hope so, being as it came from the same pot," she quipped, swallowing a spoonful of cream and clams.

He pressed his lips tight in an attempt to stifle his laughter. "I believe they are plotting against me." He tilted his head toward the marquess.

"They are *always* plotting against you."

"Are they?" He grinned. "Well, it seems I am in need of a protector, then."

The lady pursed her lips to the side. "Have you forgotten that I had a part in their previous plot?"

With a shrug of his shoulders, he whispered, "There is no one else."

"My mother is perfectly healthy," Isabella replied with a mocking shrug of her own.

Alistair chuckled. "Your mother is far too busy doing… *duchessy things.*"

## Chapter Thirty-Four

Isabella leaned toward him. "Duchessy things? Hmmm... That is a problem, then."

"And your father is wounded," he continued. "So that only leaves you."

The lady tilted her head in thought, causing a blonde tendril to fall over her brow. "Very well," she murmured. "How shall I protect you, Mr. Baston?" Isabella's eyes glistened with intrigue, and a wave of desire spread through Alistair's body.

He could think of many, *many* different ways in which she could protect him.

Before he had a chance to respond, the duke tapped a silver fork against his wine glass. The room quieted within seconds, and George slowly rose from his chair, gripping his recently wounded stomach. "My lovely Isabella," the duke started, smiling down at his beautiful daughter. "I have a gift for you."

Isabella straightened her shoulders as a footman walked over with an outstretched arm. The servant was holding a mystery item delicately wrapped in a white linen cloth.

The footman bowed as the lady slid the object from his hand. As the servant returned to his station, Isabella slowly unwrapped the cloth to reveal a leather tome.

"My sketchbook!" She gasped, and the widest, loveliest grin Alistair had ever seen appeared over the lady's features.

"I had one of the footmen fetch the belongings we had... erm... *forgotten* in Yorkshire." The duke motioned toward the leather book in his daughter's hands. "Your sketchbook happened to be one of them."

Yorkshire? Ah, yes... He supposed the duke did not want all of society to know about the highwaymen and the ambush,

*Meeting Mister Baston*

though it *would* make for a great heroic tale that the *ton* could talk about for weeks.

Isabella pulled the aged tome into her chest, and Alistair noticed the small glimmer of tears form in her sapphire eyes. "Oh, thank you, Papa! I thought I would never see it again."

Before taking his seat, George gave his daughter a gracious nod.

"May I see, Lady Isabella?" Joseph asked from across the table.

"Perhaps after dinner." Isabella smiled curtly.

Everyone returned to their meals—everyone except Isabella, who, he noticed, began flipping through the pages of her sketchbook, becoming lost in her own musings.

She turned another page, and a flash of purple slid out from within its pages. Alistair reached down to retrieve the object, and as he returned it to her, he realized it was a dried flower.

A purple daisy, to be precise—the exact purple daisy he had plucked from the public gardens in Bicester.

*She kept it all this time?*

The thought tugged at his heartstrings. Their eyes met, and Isabella's breath hitched. She slowly reached out and retrieved the delicate bloom, carefully returning it to its home.

*She cares for me.*

She had to... Perhaps the lady did not know it yet or did not know how to express her feelings for him, but at that very moment, he knew.

Alistair discreetly took her hand in his under the dark mahogany table. A blush stained Isabella's cheeks, but she did not pull away. Instead, her lips curved into a secret smile

## Chapter Thirty-Four

only meant for him.

"Bella, dear!" the duchess shouted from the other end of the table. "You never did tell me how your outing with Lord Middleton went."

The guests quieted their chatter, and Isabella's face went white. She discreetly tugged her hand from Alistair's grasp.

Damn that Middleton. The gentleman was not even in attendance, and he still managed to ruin everything.

"Fine, Mother," Isabella replied between clenched teeth.

"It is a shame he was not able to join us this evening. He is such a darling fellow, do you agree?"

"Yes, Mother." Isabella brought a spoonful of soup to her lips and slurped.

"The countess tells me he plans on proposing to my dear Bella soon," the duchess announced to the room. "I was sure he would have done it today in Hyde Park—"

"Oh, he did!" An older woman with fiery red hair nearly jumped from her chair. "I did not want to say anything—but now that it is out in the open—I witnessed the entire thing!"

Alistair's heart felt as though it had dropped into the pit of his stomach.

Middleton and Bella? *Engaged?* It could not be true.

Alistair turned to Isabella, but she kept her eyes purposefully on her soup, studying it as though it had spawned three heads.

"Engaged!"

"Congratulations!"

"Splendid!"

The room filled with cheerful congratulatory remarks from the guests. He even heard the duke murmur something along the lines of, *'not without my permission...'*

*Meeting Mister Baston*

Alistair sat in his chair as the room began to spin. His hands felt clammy, his stomach tied into knots. It was too much. He had to leave.

"If you will excuse me," Alistair said as he abruptly stood from his chair, his knees knocking the table, nearly spilling his wine. He left the room as quickly as he could without stepping into a full-on sprint. His hands clenched into fists.

Their meeting in the library was going to prove quite interesting, indeed.

## Chapter Thirty-Five

Once the ladies had moved to the drawing room and the men to the blue room, and after more than a few minutes of congratulatory praise, Isabella managed to slip away unnoticed.

Why did her mother have to bring up her outing with Lord Middleton? She knew the announcement had made Alistair furious, even though it was not true. But how would he have known it was not true?

Dinner had been so lovely at the beginning. Yes, she was a bit annoyed that he had disappeared without a word, but she knew now that he had only left to visit the Fox's Den... *without me*. Perhaps Alistair still thought Isabella was angry with him over the kiss.

Which she was not—though she hadn't exactly *told* Alistair that she was no longer angry with him. But now, unfortunately, *he* was angry with *her*. She made her way inside the dimly lit library and—

"Eeek!"

*Meeting Mister Baston*

Just as Isabella stepped inside the library, something, or rather *someone*, took hold of her arm and yanked her inside. The *someone* then promptly slammed her back against the wooden shelves behind her. "Ow!"

"My apologies…"

A flash of regret appeared in Alistair's bright green eyes, but they soon darkened to a shadowy moss color that Isabella had never seen before. It was not desire. This was something else.

"I suppose I do not know my own strength. I did not mean to…"

"It is all right." Isabella gave him a weak smile, attempting not to think of the red marks that were no doubt forming on the backs of her shoulders.

She should throttle him for handling her in such a careless manner.

Alistair released her from his grasp and took a step backward. "I need to speak with you."

"Then speak with me," she seethed. "There was no need to throw me into the bookshelves."

He gave her a sympathetic look before he said, "Explain yourself."

Isabella sputtered. "Explain myself?

"I believed you to be uninterested in him…" His hands fell to his sides as he began to pace. "Are you punishing me for the kiss?"

"What? No, of course not. I am no longer angry with you over that."

"Really?" Alistair paused mid-stride. "You seemed completely enamored with *Lord Middleton* just this afternoon."

"I am not enamored with him," she scoffed. "I was merely

## Chapter Thirty-Five

being polite."

"I saw the way you looked at him in the drawing room." He glared. His mossy eyes turned to smoke. "The way you hung on his every word."

"I thought we were supposed to be discussing Blackburn?" Alistair had gone completely mad. She looked at Edward no different to how she would look at a tree. Discussing his visit to the gambling hell was far more important.

Alistair waved a hand through the air. "I learned nothing from Blackburn." He began pacing with quick and determined strides. "Tell me of this Lord Middleton."

"Alistair." She took a step forward. She could not help but find the situation slightly amusing. "Are you jealous?"

"Am I jealous?" He paused himself in his stride and raked an aggravated hand through his hair. "Am I *jealous*?" he repeated. She saw a fire ignite within his eyes, like all of that moss had just been set ablaze.

It excited her.

Alistair closed the distance between them, causing Isabella's breath to hitch as he stopped just a hair's breadth away. "Suppose I *am* jealous?" he murmured. "Is that wrong?" He brushed his thumb over her bottom lip. "Is it wrong to want you all to myself?"

No, she supposed not. Was it wrong of her to want him too?

*Yes. Think of your sister.*

But she did not want to think of her sister. Not at this moment anyway. Not while her pulse was pounding with need. Not while Alistair's eyes were filled with lust. She had always wanted what was best for her sister. She had always tried her best to be there for Violet. No matter what her

*Meeting Mister Baston*

sister did, good or bad—and it was mostly bad.

It was time for Isabella to think of herself for once in her life. It was time for her to let herself have what she wanted.

What she needed.

And at this very moment, she needed Alistair.

Her eyes fluttered closed as she inhaled the scent of him—sandalwood and mint.

Her limbs grew weak as he continued to brush the pad of his thumb along her bottom lip. Over and over.

"Kiss me," he whispered.

Her eyes flew open. "What?" She supposed she wanted to kiss him, guests in the house be damned… but she had expected him to kiss *her*, and she certainly had not expected him to ask.

With his thumb and forefinger, he tilted her chin up to face him. "*Kiss me.*"

She glanced toward the open door, her confidence slipping. What if one of the guests happened to wander into the library? Or worse… What if Simon or her father walked in?

Alistair inched closer, his eyes burning into hers. "Are you going to marry the viscount?"

"I…" Her voice was barely audible, shaking under his scorn.

"*Say it.*" He cupped her jaw tightly, forcing her to look at him. His hold on her did not hurt her or frighten her. It *did* cause her heart to thud against her chest.

She should be afraid, but instead, she was mesmerized. "I…" Her words trailed off as Alistair brushed away a strand of hair at her temple.

"You must know… that when we are not together, all I think of is you. You next to me, against me, below me, atop

## Chapter Thirty-Five

me." The space between her legs pulsed with warmth on hearing his words. She did not know what they meant; she just knew she wanted more. "You are in my heart. You are in my very soul." He inched closer again, so close that her breasts were now pressed firmly against his rib cage. "I know you feel this... this pull we have between us."

She did. It was undeniable and, oftentimes, quite frustrating.

Her knees began to weaken, and so she gripped the shelving behind her, hoping it would be strong enough to keep her standing.

"I know the way your heart jumps when I step into the room."

*How could he possibly know that?*

"The way your pulse quickens when I am close." Alistair brought his mouth close to her ear and whispered, "That swirling feeling in your core when you feel my breath against your skin."

Isabella gasped, causing the gentleman's lips to curve into a devilish smile.

His hand trailed along her neck, causing goose pimples to rise over her flesh. "The things I want to do to you," he murmured, more to himself than to her, then moved his hand to the small of her back, pulling her into his heat. "The viscount would not know what to do with you. He cannot handle your free spirit as I can." He brought his mouth closer to her, until their lips were merely a breath away. "Kiss me."

She should tell him that she was not engaged to Edward, but for some strange reason, she could not speak. It was as though Alistair's words had rendered her mind useless. All she could do at that moment was touch him. Isabella hesitantly raised her fingers to the stubble of his cheek, much like she had back at the farm. Slowly, she moved upward and toyed with his luxurious auburn stands.

All she had to do now was close the distance between their lips, settle her mouth onto his... so why was it so difficult?

Her throat felt as though it were closing, like her heart was going to explode out of her chest. She closed her eyes... *Just do it. Kiss him.*

The heat of his breath on her skin was torture. Her feminine place pulsed with wicked anticipation until she could take no more of it.

Her lips met his in a spark of light and color that swirled behind her eyelids.

There was a connection between them so magical, so beautiful and amazing, and so many other words that she could not possibly think of in that moment.

Wanting more of him, she yanked at his hair, pulling Alistair closer—needing him closer. She was tired of fighting him, tired of fighting herself.

It had felt like years since their night at the dance hall, and she had been so angry with him.

Angry with herself.

For this one blissful moment, she wanted to be wrapped in Alistair's arms and forget everything.

She opened her mouth to him so he could kiss her more deeply, and after a moment of pure perfection, he pulled away, leaving her breathless.

Alistair gazed down at her with one of his boyish, lopsided grins that made her heart melt. "I need you."

*He needs me?* "What?"

His smile widened. "You have no idea how much I want

## Chapter Thirty-Five

you."

Before she could utter another word, he kissed her again. Her head fell back as he moved his lips to her neck.

"I long for you," he whispered. "So deeply."

"What?" It was all too fast. She could not keep up with his words.

He began to suckle at her flesh. How could she possibly think straight with Alistair doing whatever he was doing to her neck?

"Is 'what'... the only word... in your vocabulary?" he asked slowly, between kisses.

She felt him smile against her skin, and it made her want to smile in return. If only it were a perfect world. A perfect life. "I..."

Alistair's kisses came to a halt. He nipped at her shoulder, holding her tightly against him. "You..?" he asked, teasingly. "You..." he repeated with a boyish grin. Happiness lit his eyes. She had never seen him like this before, and she had to admit, she quite enjoyed it.

Before Alistair could say anything more, she heard a noise in the hallway. Isabella placed a finger over his lips. "Shush... Footsteps," she explained.

Fast, feminine and with purpose, those footsteps could only belong to one person.

Her mother.

"Bella!" the duchess called out from the hallway. "Are you in the library?"

Alistair and Isabella quickly dropped to the floor, scrambling to pick up six—no, seven—books that had fallen from the shelves during their... *moment*.

Once the books were put away, Alistair stole a newspaper

off a nearby table and took a seat in a burgundy lounge chair.

Isabella's hands flew to her head. "Alistair, my hair," she whispered with urgency. Their kiss was not as passionate as the one at the dance hall, but she knew her hair did not look as it ought to.

Alistair jumped from his position and sprinted over to her. He instantly brushed loose strands behind her ears and began…

*Patting her head?*

Oh, good heavens.

The gentleman looked frantic. "My hands are shaking too much," he admitted.

Isabella quickly shooed him away and yanked a book from its place on the shelving. She placed herself on the window seat and opened the leather tome to a random page, attempting to steady her breathing.

"There you are, dear," her mother said as she entered the room.

Alistair stood as the duchess entered.

"Oh." The duchess turned her attention toward the gentleman. "Alistair, you are here as well."

"Yes, Your Grace." He stood tall and confident with his hands clasped behind his back.

The duchess studied him carefully for a few moments then gave her shoulder a small shrug. "Wonderful." She paused, glancing at the book in Isabella's hands. *"Watkins Biographical Dictionary?"*

She gave her mother a sideways look. "I beg your pardon?"

Her mother motioned toward the book Isabella held in her hands. "When did you start studying dictionaries?"

She glanced toward the book she held and, indeed, it was

## Chapter Thirty-Five

*Watkins Biographical Dictionary.* "I thought I would expand my mind," she explained, hoping she sounded truthful and not at all suspicious.

"Right..." The duchess paused and gave her head a shake. "Well, make haste. Captain Lucas has sent word of your sister, and we are to have a family meeting."

"Violet." Isabella jumped from her place on the window seat, nearly stumbling when her slippers landed on the floor. She still felt a bit out of sorts from Alistair's kiss. "What of the guests?"

"I have arranged for a game of blind man's bluff, so they will be quite occupied, I assure you. Though some of the ladies were quite disappointed when I informed them that Simon and Alistair would not be joining in the festivities until later in the evening. Either way, we are to meet in George's office. And, Bella, dear—" her mother gave her a peculiar look "—do not overexert yourself with the reading of dictionaries. Your cheeks are as red as a strawberry." And with that, her mother left.

Isabella brought her fingertips to her cheek. They were, indeed, quite warm.

Alistair fell back into the lounge chair and let out a long exhale. "Are you really engaged to the viscount?" Alistair asked from across the room.

Isabella slammed her book closed. "Will you keep your voice down?"

Alistair stood from his chair and began stalking toward her like an enraged panther. She could not help but pull the dictionary close to her chest in the hopes of using it as a shield against him. They had just gotten word of her sister, and this was really all Alistair could think of?

## Meeting Mister Baston

His rage was terrifying but also oddly attractive. Isabella let out a gasp as Alistair pulled her close, her dictionary tumbling to the floor as he dragged her to the opposite side of the library.

"I will not lower my voice until you tell me why you are marrying him." He said each word through clenched teeth.

She pulled away from the gentleman's grasp. "I never said I was marrying Edward."

He cocked his head in confusion. "Then why does the entirety of the *ton* think you are engaged to that buffoon?"

"Firstly—" Isabella took a step toward him "—Edward is not a buffoon." She knew Alistair was upset, but there was no need for name-calling. "Secondly, the entirety of the *ton* does not think that—only the guests that you see here tonight." Though as fast as gossip moved through this part of London, the entirety of the *ton* would hear of her '*engagement*' soon enough.

"Oh, and that makes it better?" Alistair scoffed, raking a hand through his hair. After a moment, he closed the distance between them and took her hand in his once more. "Tell me this... Is my lack of title a problem for you?"

"What?" Isabella gave the gentleman's hand a reassuring squeeze. "You must know I do not care about such things."

"Truly?"

She gave him a soft smile. "*Truly.*"

"So you are not—"

But before Alistair could finish his question, she answered, "I am not engaged to Edward. He asked, but I refused." That was not altogether true; she had told the viscount that she would think on it. But Alistair was upset enough as it was, and she did not have it in her heart to tell him the full truth.

## Chapter Thirty-Five

"Come." She placed a light kiss on Alistair's knuckles. "Let us see what the captain's note has to say."

## Chapter Thirty-Six

It was difficult to think straight after she had almost been caught kissing Alistair in the library—by her own mother, no less. But there was finally news from Captain Lucas about her sister, so she had to clear the lust-filled haze from her mind.

"Come in, come in." Her father waved herself and Alistair inside his office. "Do close the door behind you, Alistair."

"Your Grace." Alistair complied with a gentlemanly nod.

Isabella took a seat on the velvet green sofa next to her mother, who happened to have the oddest sort of expression on her face. "What is it?"

"Nothing, dear." Her mother glanced toward Alistair, then back at Isabella. The smallest hint of a grin appeared over her lips.

Alistair went to stand next to her father and brother, greeting them with a curt nod. Simon looked uncharacteristically fidgety. Her brother was always so lax and carefree, even when it came to important familial matters. She wondered

## Chapter Thirty-Six

whether he had ever told Father of his gambling debts.

She very much doubted it.

"Now that we are all here," George started, "I must tell you that I have received news from Captain Lucas in regards to Violet's whereabouts." He opened the folded missive in his hand, scanned over the contents, then tossed it onto the carved mahogany desktop. "She has been spotted in Guildford... with a man."

"Guildford?" Simon gave his head a bemused shake.

"Lord Taunton does not have any relatives or property in Guildford that I know of..." The duchess perked up beside Isabella. "What sort of man was she seen with? Did he look as though he was part of the aristocracy? Or a country gentleman perhaps?"

Her mother thought Violet had simply run off with a gentleman, which could be true from what information they now had. "Have they eloped?" Isabella asked. If Violet had eloped, she would not be accepted by the *ton*, but she could easily lead a happy life in the country with her new husband, and perhaps, in a few years, they could return to London—once the gossip had dissipated.

"I am afraid I do not know the answers to either of your questions," her father said. "The note I received was very brief, but we will be leaving for Guildford first thing in the morning."

"*We?*" The duchess crossed her arms at her chest. "*You* are injured so *you* will be staying right where you are."

The duke clutched his hand at his stomach, almost as though he'd completely forgotten he'd just been shot a few days prior.

"What of the guests? Should we end the party?" Simon

asked.

The duchess waved her hands through the air quite animatedly. "No-no-no. We will entertain them like everything is completely well and good. We would not want any of them suspecting something is afoot."

Isabella was impressed with how well her mother was taking all of this. Any other mother in her station would surely have swooned at least three times by now— "Wait." Something was not right. Simon's words came to mind. *These men... they are not highwaymen.* "Simon." She turned to her brother. "What of the men who attacked us? You said they were not highwaymen…"

Simon's body went stiff, but a moment later he relaxed—almost as if she imagined it—and he returned to his normal aloof self. "Obviously, I was mistaken, dear sister."

"You seemed quite adamant about it."

Simon and Alistair shared a look, before he turned his attention back on her.

*Odd.*

"Bullets were flying through the air. *Father was shot.* I could have thought anything at that moment."

Simon's gaze pierced her own. He wanted her to stop asking questions, but she was Isabella Elizabeth Avery, and her sister's life might be in danger. "Father? What do you think of this?"

The duke looked between his two children. He let out a sigh before settling in the large leather chair behind his desk. "Captain Lucas made no mention of the highwaymen in his note. If the ambush was of some importance, I am sure the captain would have mentioned it." He turned to Alistair. "Alistair, you will stay here for the night," the duke instructed.

## Chapter Thirty-Six

"There is no sense for you to return home now. We will send word to your valet about readying your things."

Alistair gave a curt nod.

"Simon, you will accompany Alistair. I trust you know what must be done since my dear wife demands I stay home." He gave the duchess a look, and she gave him an impish smile in return. Simon nodded his understanding. But, wait—

Isabella turned to face her father with wide eyes. He had not forgotten about her, had he? Surely he did not expect her to stay behind.

She could not.

*She would not.*

Noticing Isabella's expression, the duke sighed. "Alistair, I trust you will keep my daughter safe?"

A sly smile crept over Isabella's lips. There was not a chance she would miss out on retrieving her sister.

## Chapter Thirty-Seven

The day had proven slightly disappointing. Isabella had been hoping Captain Lucas had had more information about Violet's location other than *"she was seen in the market."* Surely Captain Lucas could have discreetly followed Violet and her mystery gentleman in order to find where they were staying?

And men were supposed to be more educated than women... The older Isabella grew, the more that statement seemed to be untrue. She flipped through her sketchbook and paused at the portrait of her sister. *"Where are you?"* she asked herself quietly. They were so close to finding Violet, but after today, it still seemed so very far away.

Sleep. Yes, sleep would most definitely help pass the time. It was nearly ten in the evening, after all, and she had already been tucked into bed in her rented room for quite a while. She closed her sketchbook and was moving to return it to its place on the nightstand when she noticed an object slip from its pages. Now pressed and dried, Alistair's purple daisy lay

## Chapter Thirty-Seven

atop the bedcovers.

She picked up the small flower and pressed it to her lips. What was she to do with Alistair? He was not too thrilled with her accompanying them to Guildford, and after Callum's attack *and* the attack at their campsite, she supposed she could understand why.

Not to mention he had professed how he cared for her at a most inconvenient time. Yes, she had grown to care for him too, and *very well*, she would confess her attraction toward the gentleman over these last few weeks, but could there be more to their friendship? She was not sure she could allow herself to feel such emotions until her sister was home, which hopefully would be very, very soon.

\* \* \*

After a long and unsuccessful day in Guildford, Alistair's body was exhausted, but his mind... well, that had not seemed to quiet since the group had settled into their rooms at the inn.

He was very much worried about Isabella. He made sure to book a room across from her own, and he even went as far as to ask the innkeeper for the spare key to her room. After the ambush, the near-rape and now knowing that the highwaymen were most likely sent by Blackburn, Alistair could not afford to take any risks. If Reading had not been there, Alistair would have insisted that he stay in the very same room as Isabella. He cared for her; he was not sure when it had happened, or how, but he cared for her, and he was not going to let her get hurt again.

## Meeting Mister Baston

In all truth, Isabella should have stayed in London with her parents, but they all knew how stubborn the lady was, and they had thought it best to bring her along on the journey, rather than risk her sneaking off to Guildford on her own. The duke and duchess had already had one daughter disappear on them; they did not need the other to do the same, even if it was for completely different reasons.

Alistair took a large sip of his whiskey then brought two fingers to his temple and rubbed. It was after midnight, and he really wished he could just stop thinking and go to sleep. Perhaps if he just *saw* the lady before he went off to bed—to ensure himself of her well-being—then perhaps his mind would be at ease.

He let out a curse, jammed his free hand into his pocket, and pulled out the key to Isabella's room. "Just a peek," he told himself, setting down his glass on a nearby table. A peek would not hurt anyone, and it would make him feel a hell of a lot better about her being alone in the room all night.

Alistair reached for the handle of his door. Quietly, he stepped into the hall, which had just one small candle lighting its entirety. He crossed the hall to Isabella's room and reached for the door.

It was locked, as it should be. The lady seemed to be learning from her previous mistake, which made him feel somewhat better—but *only* somewhat.

He took hold of the small candelabra that was being used to light the hallway, and brought it close to Isabella's door. He assumed she would be asleep by now, and he did not want to risk waking Simon by knocking. He slipped the key inside and turned the lock, then quietly stepped in.

The room was very still. The only sound came from

## Chapter Thirty-Seven

Isabella's breathing, which made him feel at peace. Luckily, Alistair remembered to take off his boots or he most definitely would have woken her. He took his time crossing the room on his stockinged feet, taking the opportunity to watch Isabella as she slept.

Which sounded quite alarming, if he were to be honest. Perhaps he was mad. Perhaps *she* had driven him mad. For what other reason could there be for a rake like himself to feel the need to check on a lady's well-being before letting himself sleep?

But by God, she was lovely. Her golden hair spread across the pillow in loose waves, and he could not help but reach out and tuck a lock of silky strands behind her ear. He sat at the edge of her mattress and watched as her décolletage slowly rose and fell.

He could stay here forever. Watching her sleep was almost as erotic as kissing her, and damn, did he want to kiss her—but he was not there for that.

Out of the corner of his eye, he saw a hint of color. He set down the candle on the nightstand beside the bed. Reaching out, he noticed it was the daisy he had given her, the very same one that fell from her sketchbook at the dinner party.

She had brought it with her to Guildford. What did it signify? Surely this confirmed she had feelings for him. She may not know how to tell him of her feelings, not yet, but one day, Alistair thought ruefully, she would.

He turned to place the delicate flower atop her sketchbook so it would not get damaged in her sleep. Just then... something yanked at his shirt collar, causing his hand to knock the candelabra off the small table and onto the floor.

The room turned to black.

*Meeting Mister Baston*

"Leave quietly or I will cut you." Isabella's voice came abruptly from his side. She had him caught by his shirt collar and seemed to be pressing what felt like a dagger to his throat.

Well… It seemed to Alistair that he had severely underestimated the lady's ability to protect herself. She moved and pulled the strands of hair at his skull, yanking his head even further back. "That hurts…"

The blade fell from his throat as the lady gasped. "Alistair?"

He heard the clink of metal on wood. Hopefully, that was the sound of Isabella setting down her weapon. "Ow!" She gave his hair another painful yank.

"Are you mad? I could have injured you," she snapped.

"You would never," he whispered playfully.

The mattress moved as Isabella squirmed around. "How did you even get in here? I know I latched the door this time."

"I have my ways." He heard her move, then her finger poked him in the eye. "That would be my eye."

She quickly pulled away. "My apologies." A pause. "I cannot see a thing."

He laughed. "That would be because I knocked the candle when you attacked me."

"Hush. I will light another." He felt her reach across the bed toward the nightstand.

He stayed her hand with his. "It is all right. I can see a little, and I'd rather not have anyone see the candlelight coming from your room. Here." He brought her fingers to rest on the stubble of his cheek. "Now you can see me."

Her breath hitched as she moved her delicate fingers across his face. "I really *can* see you."

Alistair could have sworn he heard her smile. It was the way the words came out all breathy and sincere.

## Chapter Thirty-Seven

His vision finally began to adjust to the darkness. There was moonlight coming through the window in her room. It was not much, but it was enough. He watched as she rubbed her palm over his growth. As she traced the outline of his lips with her thumb, he let out a breath he hadn't realized he had been holding.

Her face was alight with wonder. A half smile appeared at the corner of her mouth as she explored his face, her eyes staring out at nothing in particular. "You really cannot see a thing, can you?"

"Night blindness," she explained.

How strange. He supposed his vision was not the best at night, as was the case with most people, but he could at least see the shine of one's eye, the white of their teeth or even the outline of a silhouette. "My apologies for waking you. I wanted to be sure you were safe." He stayed her hand and took her thumb into his mouth. His tongue swirled around the tip. Isabella let out a gasp as he released the delicate digit, reveling in her reaction to him. "I had to see you... touch you."

Alistair had not planned this, but now that he was here, alone with Isabella in her locked room—where no one could interrupt them—he thought, why not? Now was as good a time as any. He would not take her virginity—no, he was not that much of a cad—but he could show her how much he wanted her. How much she could want him.

His hand stole around her waist, and he pulled her close.

"Alistair!" She gasped, attempting to chide him, but as soon as his lips touched her neck, she relaxed in his arms.

He kissed her neck down to her collarbone, to the swell of her breasts, and then she just simply melted into him.

*Meeting Mister Baston*

\* \* \*

Isabella had tried so very hard to scold Alistair for sneaking into her room, but as soon as his mouth was on her neck, she was lost.

Oh, very well, she perhaps could have tried harder to scold him, to turn him away after he took her thumb between his lips, but she simply did not want to. She wanted to know what came next. She had thoroughly enjoyed their kiss in the library, and surely they would have continued if her mother hadn't intruded. She never knew kisses could be so enjoyable, especially after the one she shared with Edward… in the middle of Hyde Park where anyone could—and probably did—see them.

*Really, what had he been thinking?*

But with Alistair, it was different. Thrice now they had shared a kiss, and their kisses had made her feel things she had never felt in the entirety of her life.

A gasp left her as Alistair's mouth dropped to her breast. He kissed her through the thick fabric of her nightgown. Then he did the unthinkable. He yanked at the neckline of her nightgown until her breast was exposed to the air. His lips closed around her nipple, and she nearly screamed.

It was an odd sensation, she thought, as Alistair licked and sucked the tip of her breast. He brought his hand to her soft mound and began kneading the flesh there.

*Odd…* but she most definitely enjoyed it. She brought her hand to the nape of his neck and held him there as he kissed and licked and sucked for what seemed to be ages, but he clearly was not there long enough because she let out a

## Chapter Thirty-Seven

disappointed moan as soon as his mouth left her breast.

There was a moment of silence, of stillness, until he breathed, "My God, you are beautiful." And she felt quite jealous because she could not see a thing, and all she wanted in this world right now was to see him.

She reached out until she found the soft linen of his undershirt, realizing he must have removed his waistcoat and jacket before entering her room. She silently thanked him for it, because as she pressed harder, she could feel his firm chest, the rippling muscles of his abdomen, and God help her, she wanted to see him. "I want to see you."

"Later." His voice rasped as she felt the fabric of his shirt disappear beneath her fingers. "Right now, just feel." He took her wrist in his hand and guided her until her palm landed on the coarse hairs of his chest. She dragged her hand downward until she felt the smooth skin of his stomach. Heavens, how could he be so solid, yet so soft at the same time?

Her hand trailed down and down and down until she felt the tops of his trousers. Instantly, she pulled back, too frightened to dare go any further.

"It is all right," he whispered, and soon he was on top of her. His legs cradled her thighs as his hands dropped to each side of her face. She could feel him moving closer, the weight and power of his body becoming more and more evident.

His lips claimed hers. She opened her mouth to allow his tongue to enter inside. They had kissed thrice now before this, which now made her feel more confident in her kissing abilities, and she was quite certain she knew what Alistair liked.

His tongue touched hers, causing her to let out a moan

of desire. She snaked her hands around his neck, pulling him closer until she could feel his bare chest against her bare breasts. The sensation sent waves of pleasure down to her very center.

His fingers began trailing down her stomach, over the fabric of her nightgown until he reached her most feminine place. Her hand instinctively flew to his wrist, nervous about what he was going to do with those fingers.

"Tell me if you like it." Alistair's smooth baritone wrapped about her senses. "Tell me what makes you feel good."

Isabella gasped as Alistair touched his fingers against her sensitive nub and began caressing her outer folds. His fingers were not touching her flesh, only the outside of her clothing, but it still felt too personal… too intimate. No one had ever touched her there. Not even herself.

And, *dear heaven* was it wonderful, and if that made her a wanton for admitting it, then so be it.

"Tell me…" Alistair's other hand moved to cup her breast, which somehow, made her feel even more *down there*. "Do you like it?"

It was so difficult to concentrate on what he was asking. He was doing so many things at once: his lips on her neck, his hand cupping her breast, his fingers making swirls at her center. "Yes," she managed to breathe as her legs fell open on their own accord.

Her hips bucked against him as she attempted to move closer, to increase the friction that was driving her wild.

Alistair closed his lips around the tip of her breast as he began stroking with more intensity the space between her thighs. Her head lolled backward at the feel of it. Then something happened. Her hips began to move with the

## Chapter Thirty-Seven

rhythm of his hand. Her fingers dug into Alistair's neck as she began squirming and bucking beneath him.

*God*, she was so close to… to something. She did not quite know what, but she knew it was unlike anything she had ever experienced before. "Alistair," she whimpered as his mouth left her nipple and moved to the shell of her ear.

"I want you, Isabella. Let me show you."

Her heart skipped a beat. She thought she wanted him too. She *had* to if she was letting him do so many wicked things to her body. But it was impossible to form a proper sentence as his fingers continued to move at her center. All she could do was dig her nails into his skin, wanting him to stop, but needing him to continue. Her body was so confused, so alive with the pleasure she was receiving.

Alistair reached under the hem of her nightgown, bringing his hand up and up and up until he reached her center. This time it was skin against skin. No barrier keeping his fingers from entering her. Which is what he did.

He was *inside* of her, causing her to let out a sharp cry. For something so strange, so unfamiliar, it should have frightened her. It should have hurt her, but it did not. Somehow, it felt even better than before. Even more wicked.

Alistair made her feel so very devilish and innocent, all at the same time.

"You are so wet. I cannot wait to be inside you."

Was he not already inside of her? She did not know. She did not care.

Alistair removed his hand from her center, and oh, how she wanted to scream, but before she could, he grabbed her hips and angled her a different way. His body fell atop hers, and she was amazed at how right it felt to be under him. It was as

*Meeting Mister Baston*

if they were made to fit together, like two pieces of a puzzle. He ground his hips against her, and she felt the evidence of his arousal through his trousers. He pressed his hard length against her feminine place. "I want you so damned much."

"Take me," she begged, not quite knowing what it meant, but Alistair thrust himself against her center, again and again. The sensation of the fabric rubbing against her folds caused a scorching heat to flow throughout her body. Her hips instinctively moved in sync with his, and she had to bite her lip to keep herself from crying out. How did everything he did to her feel even better than what he had done before?

Her sensitive skin burned slightly from the friction of his trousers, but she did not care. Somehow, it made her feel all the better.

"This is how much I want you," he murmured. He left a fiery trail of kisses between her breasts, along her stomach. He placed one last kiss just under her belly button and— *Oh my God*.

He was kissing her... *down there*.

Isabella's hands flew to her sides, and she gripped the bedsheets with tight fists. "What are you—"

She gasped. He had reduced her into nothing but a puddle of sensation. She could not speak. Could not think. This was all too much for her. Yet... she somehow found herself wanting more. Was this why rakes and rogues were considered so dangerous?

Alistair's hands pushed against her inner thighs, spreading them further apart, gaining him even greater access to her womanhood.

He swirled his tongue around her slick folds, and a tortured moan slipped past her lips. Her hand flew to his hair, pushing

## Chapter Thirty-Seven

him deeper, craving more of his expert ministrations.

His tongue was doing wickedly wonderful things, and she could not... She did not know...

"I cannot," she mumbled. She did not know what she was trying to say, but Alistair did not stop, and she did not want him to.

Her eyes flared as she felt Alistair's teeth sink into her flesh—a quick nip before plunging two blunt fingers inside. Pleasure rippled through her center, causing her to grit her teeth. Isabella's hips bucked against his hand until her inner muscles clenched around his touch, and she threw her head back in a silent scream of pleasure.

Alistair placed one last kiss against the skin of her inner thigh. After a moment, she called out his name with ragged breaths.

Alistair inhaled a breath of air. Turning to face her, he pulled the blanket up and over her waist. "Yes?"

"What just happened?"

He leaned over and kissed her shoulder. "I made love to you."

*Made love?* Oh, no... Surely she would not come to be with child? Isabella felt her cheeks redden. Sometimes she wished she were not such an innocent—well, she supposed she was not all that innocent anymore. She turned to face the gentleman beside her. "Was that... Did we...?" Isabella's already flushed cheeks burned even more. "Is that what married couples do?"

Alistair chuckled. "That—" he placed a lingering kiss on her cheek "—and much, much more."

Isabella adjusted her nightshift and pulled the soft fabric over her breasts, suddenly aware of how bare she was in front of him. "Am I going to be with child?" she whispered. Surely not, but she had to know for sure.

It was still too dark to see, but she was sure he smiled. He pulled her tightly to his chest. "That is *not* how couples have children," he laughed.

"Then how—"

He placed his forefinger on her tender lips. "*Shhh.*" He lowered his voice to a whisper. "You will find out soon enough." He placed a kiss atop her forehead before pulling away. "I should go."

As much as she did not want Alistair to leave, she knew he could not stay. Heavens only knew what her brother would do to the gentleman if they were caught together like this. "I know," she groaned.

He buried his head into her neck and let out a ragged sigh. She wrapped her arms around him and held him there for the few short moments Alistair allowed.

## Chapter Thirty-Eight

The dining room at Winterforge Inn was laid out with an elaborate array of freshly baked pastries, eggs in three different styles, kippers, ham, and toast.

Isabella was the first to arrive for breakfast. Her lids were heavy with exhaustion. Between what had happened between herself and Alistair, and her excitement of hopefully being reunited with Violet, she had barely gotten any sleep.

Isabella hummed a tune as she made her way to the sideboard.

Yes, she was tired, but she could not help but feel different. More like a *woman*.

Her entire adult life, gentlemen had cut their courtships with her short, usually upon discovering Isabella's unusual hobbies, such as dagger throwing and archery, or they were fortune hunters who only wanted to marry her for her dowry and familial connections.

There were gentlemen such as Edward Middleton—agreeable in every way except for the fact she had not felt for them

*Meeting Mister Baston*

the way they had felt for her.

And then there was Alistair… He had made her feel things she had not known were possible. The gentleman's touch alone was enough to make her knees buckle. He had made her feel enticing and enchanting and happy. No—she was beyond happy. Some might call her besotted, infatuated, smitten or enraptured, but Isabella knew there was no need for such fancy wording.

She was simply made love to.

*And this is why mothers warn their daughters about rakes, rogues, and scoundrels.*

But Alistair was different. He *actually* cared for her.

He had told her so himself.

Rakes, rogues, and scoundrels do not *care* for the women they bed. Therefore, Alistair was *not* a rake.

At least not anymore.

"What has you in such a giddy mood?" Simon appeared beside her. He yawned as he reached for a sizable portion of soft-boiled eggs.

Isabella began filling her plate. "The possibility of seeing Violet, of course." Which was not entirely a lie. She was excited to see her sister, albeit a bit nervous. Was Violet happy and safe? Or was she in danger? She hoped for the former, of course.

Simon arched a brow. "It is far too early for anyone to be in such a pleasant mood, especially if one considers the circumstances."

"Please stay far away from me for the entirety of the day." Isabella grimaced as she watched her brother begin topping his plate with kippers. "Your breath will be rancid for hours."

"Hmm…" He paused, his spoon midway to his plate. "I

## Chapter Thirty-Eight

suppose you are right." Simon promptly plopped the horrid little fish on top of his already excessive pile. "I was hoping to make my breath rancid for *days*, not hours."

Simon grinned, and Isabella let out a sound of disgust. She promptly brought her plate to the empty table and claimed a seat, wondering how long it would be before Alistair would make his way down.

One would think a gentleman would take less time to get ready for the day.

And suddenly, he was there. Alistair walked through the doorway, and Isabella's heart dropped to her stomach. The unexpected feeling caused her to abruptly rise to her feet.

She froze, unknowing of how to greet the gentleman who had just made love to her. "G-good morning." She winced at her slight stumble of words. Lord, he looked especially handsome this morning. There was a glow to his skin, his auburn hair was particularly tousled, and the stubble of his jaw begged to be touched.

Alistair stood proud as if their encounter the previous evening *hadn't* turned his world upside-down. "Good morning."

Isabella glanced to her brother, who was an unfortunate witness to the awkward display.

"What is happening?" Simon asked. His eyes moved quickly between Alistair and herself.

"Nothing," she bit out.

Simon narrowed his eyes. "You do know the *gentleman* stands for the lady as they enter a room... not the other way around?"

The question sounded rhetorical, but she shot back an answer nonetheless. "Of course I do." She took her seat, and

*Meeting Mister Baston*

Alistair made his way to the sideboard.

"How did you sleep—"

"Fine!" Isabella yelped, causing her brother's kippers to fall from his fork.

"I was speaking to Alistair." Simon arched a brow.

"Oh."

*What is wrong with me?*

One moment she felt beautiful and confident, the next she was a blubbering fool full of those nervous butterflies fluttering around her belly.

She was acting completely mad.

Alistair took the seat across from her. "Better than usual." He answered Simon's query, and Isabella noticed a ghost of a smile hovering over the gentleman's lips.

The fork fell from her grasp, landing loudly on her plate. Simon and Alistair cast their gaze in her direction. "Oops…"

Simon gave his head a bemused shake. "I, myself, could not sleep a wink. Far too anxious for today. I trust Captain Lucas's word and believe we will have Violet home safely by the week's end."

"As do I," Alistair agreed, and Isabella tried her damnedest to avoid his emerald stare as he spoke. She may very well drop her fork again.

Or swoon in her chair.

*Good heavens*, she really did not think she was one to *swoon*.

"I am certain you will want us out of your hair as soon as possible." Simon laughed, finally finishing the last of his kippers. "I am not sure I could withstand watching over my sister all this time."

Isabella shot her brother a mean glare.

"She *has* been rather difficult." Alistair winked.

## Chapter Thirty-Eight

*Heavens help her.*

\* \* \*

The day had started off quite strangely for Alistair.

To be more precise, *Isabella* had started off the day quite strangely, and he could not help but revel in her awkwardness. And it was quite obvious to him the effects his lovemaking had had upon her.

Not to say that making love to Isabella Avery had not had its effect on him as well. In fact, he seemed quite unable to concentrate on anything but how stunning Isabella looked in white. So pure and angelic, and he decided at this very moment, white was his favorite color on her—was white even considered a color? Most gentlemen in his acquaintance loathed ladies in white. *Too virginal and innocent*, they said.

Though he supposed Isabella was not quite so innocent after their intimate encounter. No... It was not some mindless tupping. *I made love to her*, he reminded himself. And he felt forever changed. He did not know what was going to happen after they returned to London with Lady Violet. He *did* know that he could not see himself returning to the life of a rake. The thought of any other woman in his bed besides Isabella made his stomach turn. And the thought of Isabella with any other gentleman besides himself... well, that made him feel as though he could spit out hellfire through his nostrils.

Isabella's gaze met his from across the table, and time seemed to slow.

The striking blue of the lady's eyes was otherworldly. It

reminded him of a particular excerpt from an Icelandic exploration journal he had read years before.

*Where the skies dance and the ice is as blue as—*

"Baston!"

Alistair winced as a small piece of bread loaf struck his nose. "What?!"

"Refrain from drooling over my sister before I strike you," Simon warned with a second, much larger, chunk of bread in hand.

*I was not drooling...* He was simply admiring.

Alistair glanced toward Isabella and noticed her cheeks redden. Looking back at Simon, the gentleman glared at him as if he were some vile creature that needed to be slaughtered. Alistair responded with a simple, "I haven't a clue what you speak of..." and the marquess readied his throwing arm.

"Calm down, boys," Captain Lucas warned, grabbing Simon's wrist. "I am not here to act as your nursemaid."

When did the captain arrive? Good heavens, he really must have been lost in Isabella's eyes far longer than he cared to admit. "That is too bad. I think you would make an excellent nursemaid." Alistair grinned.

The captain pointed a finger toward his person. "Do not be an ass."

"Yeah, do not be an ass, Baston." Simon leaned back in his chair. The gentleman popped a small berry into his mouth, just as a large slice of ham slapped him across the cheek.

The entire room whipped their heads around to face Isabella. Whispers from the other patrons filled the room.

The lady gave an innocent shrug of her shoulders. "You threw food at Mr. Baston, so it is only fair for someone to throw food at you."

## Chapter Thirty-Eight

The marquess wiped away the residue from his face. "A harmless bit of bread. Not a slimy cut of meat."

Alistair crossed his arms over his chest and let out a chuckle. The woman he loved had just defended him with a cut of ham.

He nearly choked.

The woman he... *loved?*

He cared for her more than any woman in his acquaintance. He made love *to* her, but could he, in fact, *love* her?

Captain Lucas cleared his throat. "If you are quite finished, I'd like to discuss the plans for today."

"We are finished." Simon scowled.

"Good." The captain stood from his chair and clasped both hands behind his back. "I was thinking today, rather than staying as a group, we would split into two. One group can start at the end of Market Street, the other on the opposite side. Then we can simply meet back in the middle." The gentleman dragged a hand down his dark sideburns. "Alistair, you will group with me. Isabella and Simon—"

Isabella let out a groan.

Simon set down his fork. "Thanks."

Alistair did not particularly fancy spending the entire day with Captain Lucas—not that he disliked the gentleman, but he'd much rather be partnered with Isabella. Though he supposed, now that he'd had a taste of her, it'd be damned difficult to keep his hands to himself.

"You two are not married," Captain Lucas cut in, directing his statement toward Isabella. She crossed her arms over her chest. "And unlike your father, I will not let you go gallivanting around by yourselves."

Why did Alistair suddenly feel as though he was a nine-year-old boy instead of a man of seven-and-twenty?

"We would hardly be alone in a market," she countered with glaring eyes.

"Come, sister. Am I really that difficult to be around?" Simon asked with an innocent quality to his voice.

"Yes," Alistair and Isabella answered in unison.

## Chapter Thirty-Nine

Isabella rolled her eyes. Her brother jovially took her arm in his as they strolled through Guildford's market. "Come now, today is a good day."

"And what makes today a good day?" she mocked.

Simon playfully pinched her cheek, and Isabella slapped his hand away. "The weather is fine." He lifted a hand to the sky. "The sky is blue, we are to bring our little sister home, and my eldest sister is soon to be married—even if the man is a bore."

*Married?* Isabella's heart pounded in her chest. Simon could not possibly know of the night she shared with Alistair. Surely he would have thrown a fit, pummeled Alistair with his fists... anything before suggesting marriage. "While I do appreciate your positive outlook, big brother, I cannot help but argue that one, you cannot know we will find Violet today..." *But how she wished to.* "Two, you definitely cannot know that I am soon to be married. And three, Alistair is not a bore."

*Meeting Mister Baston*

"Alistair?" Simon narrowed his eyes. "I was speaking of Middleton, the gentleman you are engaged to…"

*Oh, Christ…* Her traitorous tongue deceived her yet again. "I… I am not engaged to him. I simply said I would think on it."

Simon chuckled. "Well, that is not what the entirety of the *ton* believes."

Heaven only knew what the scandal sheets said of her and Middleton after their outing in Hyde Park. Surely if her mother's dinner guest had witnessed Edward's proposal, then the lady certainly had noticed their fleeting kiss.

As if her family needed more scandal.

And like a hound sniffing for his next meal, Simon lifted his nose to the air. "Scones!" He looked to her with large eyes. "Do you have any money?"

"You did not bring your own money?" she scoffed.

"I forgot." Simon gave a shrug of his shoulders.

Isabella shook her head. It was a wonder her brother did not weigh as much as a mule. "You just ate."

"So?"

"So," she echoed. "You cannot possibly be hungry."

Simon shook his head and made a tsk sound. "A man is *always* hungry, and you'd do well not to forget that."

Isabella rolled her eyes. Reaching into her reticule, she scrambled around for pin money. She pulled out two coins and placed them in her brother's hand.

While Simon meandered about the stalls, Isabella surveyed the market and its patrons. The market was almost as noisy as the cramped streets of London. Her nostrils flared in protest as a passing horse trampled through a pile of manure.

*And just as filthy.*

## Chapter Thirty-Nine

Once Simon had finished feasting on his scones, they continued to work their way toward the center of the market, all the while turning their heads this way and that, being sure to keep an eye out for anyone who resembled Violet.

There were several dark-haired ladies meandering about, but they were all too old, too thin, too... *not* thin.

Isabella let out a frustrated groan. She did not want to give up hope, but it was difficult not to. And there in the distance, she spotted Alistair. How had they made it to the center already?

She sighed, and her shoulders sank. She really hated feeling so pessimis—

Isabella's heart stopped.

There was a girl... And suddenly Isabella was unable to move, unable to breathe.

"What is it?" Simon laid a gentle hand on her shoulder.

"I thought I saw..." She did not see the girl's face because it was covered by a dark hood.

*A black hood.*

What woman would wear a black hooded cloak in the middle of a sunny afternoon?

It was quite unusual. Even grieving widows would not don fully hooded cloaks at the end of April. And there was something about the way the lady walked and carried herself, something in her mannerisms, that had reminded her of Violet.

Isabella pulled away from Simon's soft grasp and weaved through the crowded street as quickly as she could manage. But there were so many damned people.

"Where are you going?" she heard Simon shout from behind, but she did not dare turn back.

*Meeting Mister Baston*

"Bella!"

At the sound of her name, the cloaked figure stiffened. *She stiffened!* It could not have been a coincidence.

Quickening her pace, Isabella pushed through the crowd until she was finally close enough to rip the lady's hood away from her head.

A young dark-haired woman with striking blue eyes whipped around to face her.

It was Violet.

"Oh… Bella."

Isabella's breath caught. "Oh? We have been searching everywhere for you, and all you have to say to me is 'oh?'"

The anger quickly left her as she looked over her little sister's features.

*She looks thin.* And pale…

"Violet…" Isabella reached out to touch her sister's face, just to be certain what she was seeing was real. Her cheeks were hollow, and her hair appeared dirty and tangled. "Violet, I cannot believe it is you." Isabella wrapped her arms around Violet as hot tears began to blur her vision.

She could not possibly explain how wonderful it felt to hold her baby sister in her arms, her baby sister who had been missing for over a week.

But it was clear to her now that Violet was in trouble. Whether she ran off on her own accord or not, she was clearly unwell.

"What are you doing out here?" Isabella moved back to study Violet's features. Her lips were purple and chapped… *or were they cut and bruised?* And her eyes… they were empty. Yes, they were still the ice-blue Isabella had always been envious of, but there was something lacking.

## Chapter Thirty-Nine

The light was gone.

"Why did you leave? Were you forced?" Isabella could not help but run her hands over her sister's frame, checking for injuries and anything else unusual she might find.

"I am fine." Violet pulled away and continued to look over the apples in the cart in front of her. "You should leave. It is not safe."

Not safe? The knot in her gut tightened. "What do you mean? Who is here with you?" Isabella took Violet's hand again. She looked down and noticed Violet was not wearing gloves. Her nails were dirtied and unkempt.

"What the hell did he do to you?" Simon burst through the crowd and cupped Violet's face in his hands. "This is all my fault."

Violet's panicked eyes darted back and forth between her siblings. "Please do not make a scene," she whispered.

Simon let out a cold laugh. "Do you really think I care about making a scene?"

"Please Simon," Violet pleaded. "You are hurting me."

Did her brother not see that Violet was unwell? Mayhap not... His rage was too blinding.

After a moment, Simon finally let his hand fall from their sister's arm, but the fire still flashed within his depths.

"May we please speak somewhere..." Violet paused to rub her arm. "...somewhere less crowded?"

She was right. The passersby were staring, whispering and pointing. Surely the Marquess of Reading would be recognized if he continued quarreling in the streets of Guildford.

"We will have plenty of time to talk in the carriage ride *back* to London," Simon spat.

"Simon," Isabella cut in. "Let her speak—not here."

Simon's eyes darted between herself and Violet, and thankfully, he nodded his head in agreement.

Violet led them just a few paces away to a small lane off the main road. She turned to face them. Her face had gone completely white. "They are watching." Her eyes widened. "Always watching."

Isabella's heart dropped into her stomach. She had never seen her sister like this.

"There are guards in my room." Violet looked past Isabella's shoulder. Her eyes were vacant and cold. "They never stop watching me," she whispered.

*So, Violet did not run away?*

"Then how are you here—" Isabella took her sister's hand in hers "—on your own?"

Violet's empty gaze returned to her own. "How am I to leave? With no money, no connections…"

"We are here now," Isabella reassured.

Footsteps came from behind, and Violet's body jerked at the sound. Simon and Isabella turned to see Alistair and Captain Lucas approaching.

She turned back to face her sister. "It is all right. They are with us."

Captain Lucas nudged Isabella aside and took Violet's face between his hands. "Are you hurt, child?"

Her sister did not appear to be injured, but there was definitely something amiss. She was not herself, though Isabella supposed, if she herself had been abducted and locked away for weeks, she would not act as she normally would either.

Violet's gaze moved past Isabella once more. Not answer-

## Chapter Thirty-Nine

ing the captain's query, she simply stared off into the distance.

Isabella followed her little sister's line of sight, and that is when two scraggly men appeared from around the corner.

Her heart started beating wildly in her chest, and not the sort of beating it had done when Alistair made love to her. Flashes of blood, screaming horses, and the sound of bullets entered her mind. Goose pimples raised on her flesh as if the temperature had suddenly dropped ten degrees.

"Alistair." Her voice cracked, and so she tried again. "Alistair!"

Alistair turned to her, immediately noticing the two men approaching their group.

The larger of the two men pulled out a baton and began bashing it against his palm. A perverse smile crept over his features. Meanwhile, the scrawnier man reached into his jacket pocket. He flashed Isabella a toothy smile; two of his teeth were as brown as the dirt they stood upon.

"It is time to leave." Alistair took hold of Isabella's arm and yanked her forward. It was an all too familiar sensation.

*You must leave... Do what you must to keep my daughter safe.*

The ambush at the campsite replayed over and over in Isabella's head.

*It was all happening again.*

## Chapter Forty

When Isabella thought of a reunion with her sister, she had hoped it to be a happy occasion.

Violet would be on the doorstep of a charming cottage in the countryside, calling for her husband to meet her family. Mayhap she would have been hiding out at some dusty roadside inn with a forbidden lover. Mayhap Violet would have been hiding out with *multiple* forbidden lovers.

Anything would have been better than this.

Isabella took hold of Violet's hand, dragging her down Jeffries Passage where their carriage was waiting.

Alistair was to their front, leading them toward the carriage, while Simon and Captain Lucas followed at their rear.

A shot echoed through the narrow alley, and Isabella realized she had left her dagger inside the carriage. She could not bring herself to begin carrying it on her person again—not yet. But, oh, how she wished she had it now.

Not that a dagger had any chance against a firearm.

Isabella glanced behind and saw Captain Lucas aim his

## Chapter Forty

pistol toward the two men chasing them.

*Pow!*

Another shot rang loudly in her ears.

As they neared their conveyance, the coachman hopped down from his perch and scrambled, opening the carriage doors just in time for Alistair to jump inside.

Isabella not so gently shoved Violet through the door as Alistair yanked her sister inside. She quickly followed suit and stumbled into the carriage, making room for Simon and Captain Lucas.

Just as Captain Lucas stepped in, the carriage lurched forward and hastily picked up speed.

"Simon!" Time seemed to slow as she watched her brother run beside the conveyance, struggling to keep pace.

Extending his arm, Captain Lucas reached through the carriage door. "Take my arm, lad!"

The wind howled through the open door. Isabella's hair flew in every direction, making it almost impossible to see. She lurched forward, nearly knocking into Captain Lucas. "Simon!"

Alistair drew her backward onto his lap, wrapping her tightly in his arms. Simon leaped onto the carriage steps, grabbing on to the captain's arm, and Isabella nearly collapsed with relief as she watched her brother enter the speeding conveyance.

He sat across from her on the upholstered bench with a crooked grin, acting as though they all had not just been shot at. "Worried I would not make it, dear sister?"

"Yes!" Yes, she was very much worried!

Isabella relaxed her back against Alistair's chest, taking in deep breaths to help steady her heartbeat. Her tangled mass of hair fell to her shoulders as Captain Lucas pulled the door closed.

They had done it. They had rescued Violet without injury. *We are alive.*

"You should have let me stay," Violet whispered from beside her. "He will hurt you."

Simon stiffened. "He already hurt us. He ambushed our carriage, killed our coachman, and shot our father!"

"Reading," Alistair warned.

Hadn't their sister gone through enough? "She does not need to hear this right now." Isabella slid from Alistair's hold and took Violet in her arms, hoping to give her some sort of comfort.

"Father was shot?" Violet sat lifeless in Isabella's arms. "I am sorry. I did not know."

Isabella took Violet's face in her hands, brushing away a few strands of hair that had fallen over her brow. "Do not apologize. None of this is your fault."

"I am the one who needs to apologize." Simon leaned over and placed a hand on Violet's shoulder. "You are not to blame. *God only knows you are not to blame.*" Simon combed a hand through his mussed hair, his features turning a slightly grayish hue.

The group sat in reciprocal silence for some time. Violet had long fallen asleep, her head against Isabella's shoulder. She tucked a few strands of her sister's dark hair behind the shell of her ear.

Violet's eyes fluttered open at the movement.

"I am sorry." Isabella met Violet's gaze. "I did not mean to wake you."

"How much longer?" Violet asked on a sleepy mumble.

## Chapter Forty

Isabella looked to Captain Lucas.

"An hour or so," he answered for her.

Violet pulled herself upright and peered out the window. "I suppose I should tell you... It was Callum Diggory. He made me go with him that night."

Isabella shook her head. "But Callum left with us that morning." It could not have been Callum. The servant was with her family for nearly the entirety of their journey to Derby.

"He held a knife to my throat and said he would hurt you if I did not go with him."

*Violet sacrificed herself for me?* Isabella's stomach clenched at the thought. Did the servant attack her little sister just as he had attacked her?

Though Violet would not have had Alistair to save her.

"We did not travel far. I believe we were still in London when he dropped me off somewhere. He blindfolded me in the hackney, so I am unsure of where he took me. He left me in a room with two men.

"The men who chased us."

Isabella thought back to the morning they had left London to begin their search for Violet.

*Where have you been? Go gather your belongings!* her mother had ordered. *You are to accompany the duke on his journey.*

*Right away, Your Grace...* Callum had entered the room, appearing so very disheveled and out of sorts.

She sighed. If only she had noticed something was amiss with the servant sooner, they could have questioned him. They could have perhaps found Violet before she was taken to Guildford. There were still so many unanswered questions, and she hated having to question her sister when she was clearly distressed.

Why would Callum do such a thing? What was his motive?

"What was his reasoning for taking you?" Captain Lucas asked the question for her. "Did he ever mention it?"

Violet turned to face the captain. "He did not say." She toyed with her mangled skirts. "I thought mayhap he needed money and would demand a payment from Father before returning me home."

"Surely he would have left a note if that were the case?" Isabella asked no one in particular. There was no note left in Violet's room. Mother had not received any letters through the post.

All that was left was Violet's empty bedchamber.

*Simon's gambling debt...*

"Simon," she called out. "What of your gambling debt? Did you not say you owed a Blackburn fellow money?"

Alistair had said he learned nothing from visiting Blackburn, but the man could still have something to do with all of this. This Blackburn fellow could have orchestrated the entire plot.

It was the perfect motive.

"Yes, Reading." Alistair crossed his ankle atop his knee. "How much did you owe Blackburn again?" There was a slight sound of contentment in Alistair's tone.

Glancing about the carriage, Simon placed his hand over his chin. "Only a measly—" he contemplated for a moment "—seven hundred pounds. Surely not enough to warrant a kidnapping."

Why was her brother acting so strangely? "Seven hundred?" she wondered aloud. "But you told Alistair you owed him three thousand."

## Chapter Forty

"Right." Simon's baritone nearly increased a full octave. "Seven hundred... three thousand. Somewhere around there."

"Lord Blackburn is not one to take debts owed to him lightly." The captain cut in.

"Father knows of the debt, and the debt has been paid," Simon insisted. "Now, let us move on to a different theory, shall we?"

Isabella wondered whether her brother could be lying, then quickly tossed away such musings. This was Simon she was speaking of. Yes, he was a rogue and enjoyed gambling a bit too much, but he would not lie about such things. He would not knowingly put their little sister in danger just to keep himself from such embarrassment.

Placing a hand over her sister's, Isabella asked Violet again, "Are you sure he said nothing about his motive? Perhaps the two men who were acting as your guards? They may have let something slip out."

Violet yanked her hand from Isabella's grasp and turned to her, glaring. "What will you have me say? Would you like me to tell you how they had me tied to a bedpost for nearly two days with no food or drink? Would you like to know how the guards spoke to me? How they spoke ill of our family? How they watched me?" There was a long pause before she continued. *"How they hurt me?"* Violet rubbed the red marks on her wrists, which Isabella did not notice until this very moment.

Tears pricked at her eyes, but Isabella hurriedly composed herself. She needed to stay strong for her sister as Violet would not want anyone taking pity on her, no matter how much she had suffered.

But that pity quickly turned to rage as she remembered how Callum had attacked her that night. She wondered whether Violet's guards had done the same. And if there was no one there to aid her, had they attacked her—hurt her—more than once?

The group ceased their questioning for now and instead allowed Violet to rest for the remainder of the journey.

# Chapter Forty-One

George slowly made his way to his desk, one hand over his wounded abdomen and the other reaching for his leather buttoned chair.

"I cannot thank you gentlemen enough." The duke let out a pained groan as he took his seat. "You returned my daughter to me unharmed."

As far as they and the doctor could tell, Violet sustained no serious bodily injuries. But Alistair knew the youngest Avery sibling *had* been harmed—physically *and* mentally, even if one could not see the damage with the naked eye. And God only knew how long it would take the young woman to recover from such an ordeal.

"There is no need—" *to thank us*, Alistair tried to say, but George raised his hand in the air to silence him.

"Of course, I need to thank you." George grunted. "You risked your lives for my family. And for that, I should pay you both a very large sum of money."

Alistair opened his mouth to refuse such a payment, but

George raised his hand again. "But," the nobleman continued, "I know you'd both refuse it."

Both Alistair and Captain Lucas chuckled. How could Alistair possibly accept such a gift for saving a life? For saving Isabella's sister and his employer's—nay, his *friend's*—daughter?

"I will find a way to sneak the monies into your salaries; you can count on that," George chided, and Alistair gave a playful shake of the head. "Alas, it has grown late, and I am tired." The duke paused, turning his attention toward Lucas. "But I must ask one more thing of you, dear friend."

"Of course." The captain nodded.

The duke's expression grew dark. "Return to Guildford. Find Callum." He paused, seeming as though he was contemplating his next words. "...*And get rid of him.*"

Captain Lucas inclined his head. "Consider it done."

Alistair's heart jumped. He did not expect the Duke of Waverly to order the boy to be killed, especially after how the nobleman had responded to Alistair beating the daylight out of the servant after he had just attacked Isabella. The duke was so dubious in his efforts of punishing the young footman. And now...? He swallowed down the lump in his throat, wondering just how well he knew one of his dearest friends.

"I would like to join the captain." Alistair turned to the gentleman standing beside him. "If you do not mind?" Normally, Alistair was not one to want a man killed, but Callum hurt Isabella—nearly defiled her—and abducted her sister, and being a man of honor, he would not let such occurrences go unpunished.

But there was also Blackburn... He needed to pay for

## Chapter Forty-One

his crimes as well, being as he was the one that arranged everything: hiring Callum, the once loyal servant, to abduct the family's youngest daughter; ordering Callum to defile Isabella; and organizing the ambush on their carriages. He was more in need of punishment than anyone.

All because of Simon's debts and secrets... Everything had happened because of *his* recklessness, and the gentleman needed to confess his sins to his family. It was the ethical thing to do.

He, of course, could tell the duke everything. Here and now. But that was not his place.

Simon needed to be the one to do it, and the gentleman needed to make amends, especially with Lady Violet.

Alistair was getting a headache just thinking of how his friend Reading could possibly make it right with his sister.

Or *sisters*, for that matter.

Isabella would be furious with her brother once she was aware of the truth.

"I am not sure if I like that idea, Alistair." The duke interrupted his musings. "You are my man-of-affairs; I need you here. I do not want you doing my dirty work."

"That is what I am for." Lucas turned to him with a serious expression.

He supposed George had a point, and seeing that Lucas had fought for king and country, the gentleman had experience with... *such things*.

But he needed to do this. He would not feel right with himself otherwise.

"I am sorry, Your Grace. But there is no talking me out of it. And there is something you are not aware of..." Alistair was not going to tell the duke *everything* his son had done,

*Meeting Mister Baston*

but he needed to at least know about Blackburn.

"What is it?"

Alistair raked a hand through his hair. "Simon owes debts to Blackburn, and I have reason to believe it was Blackburn who was behind all of this, not Callum."

Letting out a loud groan, George reclined in his seat. "And what gives you *reason* to believe such things?"

"You will have to find that out from your son."

George steepled his fingers atop the desk, and after a brief moment, said, "We must go after Blackburn as well."

Captain Lucas inclined his head. "I agree, and I could use Alistair's help if we are to go after *that* scoundrel."

George grumbled. "Fine. But do not dally. I want this to be quick."

Alistair gave a bow and turned to leave. He must inform Isabella of his departure— "And do not tell Isabella of our plans." George's words stayed him.

He supposed the duke was correct on that score. Isabella need not know of this. Spitfire that she was, the lady would most definitely want to join them in such a pursuit.

He need not inform Isabella about his plans, dangerous as they were, but he did wish to see the lady before he and Captain Lucas left for Guildford.

If anything went wrong with their mission, this could very well be the last time he might ever see the woman he loved. And he, indeed, loved her. There were simply no other words to describe his deep affections toward the lady. And as soon as he returned from Guildford, he would do what was right by her.

*I am going to marry her*.

# Chapter Forty-Two

Isabella was in an exceptionally pleasant mood. Life had felt like it was almost back to normal.

*Almost.*

Her father was home—injured, but home, and he was able to leave his bedchamber for longer periods of time. But most importantly, her sister was safe.

As Isabella entered the breakfast room, she was delighted to see her father seated at the table.

"Papa! It is so good to see you down for breakfast." She placed a quick kiss on his cheek before taking a plate from the sideboard.

"And it is good to be *able* to come down to breakfast, my dear," he replied, jabbing at the eggs on his plate.

"Oh," Simon drawled. "I suppose I do not get a '*good to see you, dear brother?*'" He slouched, his shoulders back, and feigned a frown.

"*You* have not been injured," she scoffed as she piled her plate full.

*Meeting Mister Baston*

"Ease up on the eggs, dear sister."

Isabella tossed Simon a mean glare then returned her attention to the sideboard before taking the seat closest to her father.

"Good morning, family." Her mother placed kisses on her and Simon's cheeks. "How lovely it is to see the entire family down for breakfast." She turned to retrieve a plate from the sideboard. "Well, not the *entire* family. Dear Joseph is upstairs with his governess and—" her lips turned down at the corners "—Violet wanted to rest and take breakfast in her room."

"She just needs time to herself, my love." The duke gave his wife a reassuring smile. "I promise, she will be back to her old self very soon."

Isabella sank down in her chair. She was hoping to see Violet at breakfast, but she supposed her father was right. Her sister needed time to recover from the torment she had endured.

"Yes." The duchess toyed with an elegant curl that flowed over her collarbone. "She is quite the resilient young lady." Giving her head a small, but delicate shake, all of the sorrow disappeared from her mother's features. "You are up quite early, Bella dear."

Isabella could not help but smile at her mother, who tried so very hard to stay strong for her children. "I am always awake this early," she lied.

"Perhaps it is because she knows Baston will be calling upon her today." Simon tossed Isabella a flippant smirk, causing her to drop her fork with a loud *clank*.

"The gentleman has been spending a great deal of time with you; it is only natural for him to develop feelings."

## Chapter Forty-Two

The duchess glanced toward her while spreading orange marmalade on a slice of toast.

Isabella grimaced. She had been home but a day, and her mother was already trying to match her up with yet another gentleman.

"The *gentleman* has been spending a good amount of time with *all* of us," she said smoothly and forked in as many eggs as she could fit into her mouth.

Indeed, Alistair had come to her last eve asking if she would like a promenade through Hyde Park, but her mother need not go all matchmaker on her.

She and Alistair were *friends*, and friends spent time together and promenaded through parks together.

*And make love, and steal kisses in the library, and...* Isabella quickly shook those dangerous musings from her head.

"I know you are engaged to Lord Middleton, but I happen to think Mr. Baston fancies you, my dear." Her mother smirked as she took her seat at the breakfast table.

Her cheeks warmed. "Mother, please." She had nearly forgotten about Edward and how all of London thought she was engaged to the viscount.

Her father picked up the newspaper and started flipping through it—an obvious attempt at keeping out of the discussion.

"I happen to *know* Mr. Baston fancies her," Simon added, leaning back in his chair.

*How could Simon possibly know?*

"Really?" Their mother gasped. "Did he mention something to you?"

Isabella's grasp tightened around her fork as she shot her brother a look that said *do not dare*.

## Meeting Mister Baston

Simon ignored her and turned to face their mother. "He did not have to." He shrugged. "I have witnessed it with my own eyes."

The duchess brought her toast to her lips. "What do you mean?"

Isabella stitched her brows together and kicked Simon's shoe in order to get his attention. "Simon, do not," she mouthed, and he winked at her in return.

The last thing she needed was her mother meddling in her and Alistair's friendship. She wanted their relationship to blossom as naturally as possible. If Alistair did, indeed, plan on proposing, she did not want him to feel pressured by her mother.

"Well..." her brother started, and Isabella could not help but let out a low growl.

He could not possibly think about telling their parents about her dancing *alone* with a drunken Alistair in the blue room—

"There *was* that time in the blue room..."

*He was!*

Without thinking, Isabella flung her fork at Simon's face, hitting him square in the forehead. Their mother would have them married by nightfall if she were to find out!

"Bloody hell!" Simon began rubbing the red mark on his skin.

"Isabella Elizabeth! What on earth— Oh!" The duchess's hand flew to her mouth as she watched Simon throw a handful of eggs toward Isabella.

"Arrgghhh!" Isabella jumped from her seat with her fists tight at her sides. "You!"

Her mother abruptly stood from her seat, glancing from

## Chapter Forty-Two

son to daughter, daughter to son, son to husband. "George!"

The duke folded his newspaper down and peered at his wife. "Yes, dear?"

"Your children are behaving like... like children!"

"They are your children too, my love," he countered.

She had had quite enough of her family's meddling. "If you will excuse me," Isabella started as she yanked bits of egg from her hair. "I will be in my room getting this—" she frantically motioned to her head "—out of my hair."

"Wait!" her mother shouted. Isabella really was not in the mood to be scolded by her mother...

The duchess relaxed her posture and threw Isabella a demure smile. "I think you also fancy Mr. Baston."

After cursing softly to herself, Isabella rushed from the room.

Must she always be the victim of her mother's matchmaking schemes? Though she supposed Alistair was the most agreeable suitor Isabella had had in the last two Seasons.

"Sister."

Simon's voice came from behind. Isabella turned to see her brother chasing after her from the breakfast room. "Simon?"

He pulled on his lapels as soon as he reached her and readjusted his dark velvet jacket. "Might I have a word?"

"Of course." Isabella motioned down the corridor to a corner that was out of sight of the breakfast room.

"Perhaps... in my study?" Simon grimaced. "It is a bit of a complicated matter."

"Very well." Isabella motioned Simon to lead them to his study. She hoped this discussion would be quick since she agreed to meet Alistair at Hyde Park after breakfast, and she had yet to remove the egg from her hair.

She followed Simon into the study, and he quickly closed the panel behind him. He leaned against his desk and raked both hands through his dark hair.

Isabella knew there was something bothering him. "What is it, Simon?"

"It is Blackburn."

Isabella cocked her head. "Blackburn? Is he harassing you over your debts?" It was unlike her brother to come to her for guidance. She presumed he went to their father or mayhap his friends.

He pinched the bridge of his nose. "Yes. I-I mean no." Letting out a low growl, he pushed off the desk and began pacing the room. "He is not hassling me any longer, though he was for quite some time…"

"So you paid off your debts, then?" Isabella brightened. This was excellent news!

"No."

*No?* "You have told Father about your debts?"

"Yes—I mean no. But this is why *you* are here."

Simon was not making much sense. "You want *me* to tell Father of your debts?"

He paused himself in his stride. "No. I want your advice on how to tell him of it—how to tell you and… Violet."

"Me?" Simon was acting very strange, indeed. "I already know of your debts, brother."

Simon sighed, walked to the sideboard, and poured himself a few fingers of amber liquid. He swirled the contents in the glass then took one large sip. "It is all my fault," he said in hushed tones. "*Everything* is my fault."

Isabella went to his side and squeezed Simon's shoulder. "If you want my help, you must tell me what is the matter."

## Chapter Forty-Two

"That is the problem." Simon hunched his back against the wall and slid down until his bottom sat on the floor. "*I* am the matter. *I* am the problem!"

Isabella began to feel worried. Her brother was never prone to histrionics. He had a temper, yes, but was never one to wallow in self-pity.

Or one to pity himself at all, for that matter.

"Violet is going to hate me. Mother and Father will never forgive me." He took another long swallow of his beverage and brought the glass to his forehead, rolling the cup back and forth across his temple.

"Mother and Father will forgive you. It is only a measly sum of—"

"No!"

Her brother's shout caused Isabella to flinch.

"No, you do not understand." He continued rolling the glass over his skin. "Everything that happened to Violet is *my* fault."

Isabella's hand flew to her mouth. *I knew it!* "It was Blackburn? He had Violet abducted?" That *bastard.* How could he do such a thing over such a small amount of money? How could he do such a thing over *any* amount of money? What kind of monster was this man? "It is not your fault, Simon. You could not have known he would do this."

"I did. I did." Simon's voice came out as a sob, his eyes tightly shut.

"You did not." Isabella's heart ached for her brother. He could not have possibly known his gambling debts would bring such chaos to their family.

Simon slammed his glass on the wood floor with a loud *clank,* amber liquid spilling over its edges and onto his

*Meeting Mister Baston*

hand. "I. Did. Know. I knew everything he was planning… Everything. And I did nothing."

Isabella stood, her hand slowly falling from his shoulder. "You knew?" Isabella's voice shook. Rage, hurt, betrayal—all filling her insides at once.

Her knees became weak, and so she grabbed on to the large mahogany desk to steady herself.

"I knew Callum was recruited by Blackburn to take Violet. I knew precisely where and when he would be taking Violet. I knew everything."

Isabella's head whipped toward her brother.

*He knew everything?* Now his words made sense. His arguments with Callum made sense. "You knew where they were keeping Violet, and you did nothing?!" Isabella whirled around to face her brother, her skirts whipping in a frenzy. "You had us travel all over the country searching for Violet when you *knew* precisely where she was being kept?!"

"Yes."

"To what end?!"

Simon dragged himself off the floor, his body limp with despair. "I did not want Father to know of my failings, and I wanted to try and raise the funds myself. I did not think Blackburn would take it so far. I did not think he would have Callum attack you or have highwaymen ambush our carriages."

"But kidnapping Violet and holding her against her will was perfectly acceptable?" Tears pricked at Isabella's eyes. How could her brother be so cowardly? How could her brother betray their family so for the sake of his pride?

"I thought it would only be for a day or so, as a warning—"

*Crack.* Isabella's palm stung from the hard impact on

## Chapter Forty-Two

Simon's cheek.

Her brother's hand flew to that now red and irritated skin. "You struck me!"

And she would gladly strike him again if her hand did not hurt so much. Ignoring her brother's shocked expression, Isabella turned to leave.

"Where are you going?"

"*You* will tell Father everything and apologize to Violet. *I* am off to meet Alistair in Hyde Park, and I am going to tell him everything you just told me."

"Alistair already knows."

Her brother's words stopped her in her stride. "What?" she asked without turning around.

"I told him already."

Isabella's throat began to swell, and she struggled to breathe. A stinging heat pulsed through her being as rage began to build in her chest.

*How long has Alistair known? And how could he not tell me?*

## Chapter Forty-Three

Standing alongside the Serpentine, Alistair stared at the single white daisy he held in his hand.

He'd never courted a lady before—not to say Alistair had plans to properly court Isabella. He did things to the lady that most definitely warranted a special license—but after seeing the elaborate floral displays in the Averys' drawing room, it was obvious to him that gentlemen presented flowers—or similar such favors—to ladies they were interested in courting.

The last thing the lady needed was more elaborate floral arrangements.

That was why Alistair had chosen a single flower, but would Isabella be unimpressed with his single white daisy? Or would she be delighted by the fact that he remembered her favorite flowers were, in fact, daisies?

*Stop overthinking, Baston.*

He brought his gaze back to the Serpentine. Its waters, usually a murky greenish-blue, sparkled with a deep sapphire

## Chapter Forty-Three

tint. It reminded him very much of Isabella's eyes.

*Should I mention that?*

Stop!

Alistair gave his head a frantic shake. Why was he so nervous all of the sudden? This was *Isabella*. They had shared so much together this last fortnight.

*Perhaps it is because you are still a titleless second born, and she is the daughter of a duke. Will she even accept my proposal when she has a viscount waiting for her hand?*

The duke...

Alistair cursed under his breath.

He'd forgotten to get the duke's permission to propose to Isabella.

He had been so preoccupied with finding the perfect ring for the lady that he had completely forgotten to ask George if he could ask for his daughter's hand to begin with.

He brought his hand to his jacket pocket where Isabella's diamond and sapphire engagement ring waited in its box.

Perhaps he should wait to propose *after* he returned? Being the redeemer of her little sister would certainly make him seem more worthy of her. He knew Isabella claimed not to care about such things as titles and honorifics, but it could not hurt...

A flash of white caught his eye. And there she was, walking toward him on the crowded graveled path with two maids following behind. She weaved her way between the passersby, all the while keeping her gaze trained on him.

Alistair's heart thumped wildly.

*Right.* He should probably make his way to her instead of standing there like the muttonhead she had once accused him of being.

## *Meeting Mister Baston*

As he began the short walk to meet her alongside the shore, he noticed how particularly lovely the lady looked today, having only part of her hair pinned back, leaving the rest to flow freely past her shoulders. His eyes fell to the white lace detailing around her décolletage, which peeked out from under her yellow cloak, and he realized this was the first time he had ever seen her in yellow.

She looked ethereal, like an angel glowing in a beam of sunlight.

*Christ, I sound like a lovesick fool.*

Alistair reached Isabella's side and dropped a bow. "My lady."

"Mr. Baston." She gave him a quick nod, and he could not help but notice the tension gripping her features. Her lips, usually full and soft, were pulled taught. The space between her blonde brows wrinkled as if she were contemplating something very grave, indeed.

"How is your sister?" he asked. Mayhap she was the source of Isabella's tension.

Turning away, the lady spoke in hasty tones. "She took breakfast in her room this morn and is still recovering from her ordeal." Isabella dismissed the maids that were standing beside her with a wave.

They curtsied and hurried off in a bustle of skirts, eventually settling on a nearby bench.

"That is to be expected, I suppose." Alistair toyed with the daisy he was still holding. "I am sure a few days of rest will do her well."

He held the small flower out to her, and without looking, she heedlessly plucked it from his fingers. "Thank you."

Alistair raked a hand through his hair. This was not at all

## Chapter Forty-Three

how he was expecting this to go. Perhaps he should have had tulips imported from Holland, as so many lords do. "I-I thought they were your favorite." He motioned to the daisy she now held.

"Oh, they are." She turned to face him, flashing him a cold smile. "How very attentive of you."

"Right..." Alistair removed his hand from his hair. "Shall we walk, then?"

Perhaps the lady was just restless from standing in one place. A walk should do her well, one would think. He offered her his arm—

"No." She clasped her hands before her, the delicate daisy becoming tangled between her fingers. "No, I should like to say something."

Alistair grimaced at the sight of the small stem bending and twisting in her hard grasp. Had he done something to upset her? "Is something wrong?"

Had Callum returned? Did Blackburn threaten the family again?

*Has she accepted the viscount's offer?*

Alistair's chest tightened at the thought. She had said she was not interested in the viscount... Was her father forcing her to wed?

His eyes widened.

George was not one to force his daughter into an unwanted union, was he? Though Alistair did not think George was one to order someone dead either.

"How could you?"

A strong breeze tore those words from her mouth. He almost did not hear them.

"How could I..." Then it struck him. She must have found

## Meeting Mister Baston

out about him leaving with Captain Lucas. He shook his head and let out a relieved sigh. "Do not worry over me. I shall return in a few days' time." He lied. He was not sure at all when he would return, but he had to admit, the lady's concern for him pulled a bit on his heartstrings.

He reached out to tuck a lock of hair behind her ear that had been loosened by the wind.

She slapped his hand away. "What are you speaking of?"

"What are *you* speaking of?"

"As if you do not know." She scoffed.

"I *do not* know!" Alistair looked to the passersby, who were now whispering and pointing in their direction. He lowered his voice. "I thought we were speaking of your father's orders to track down Diggory and Blackburn?"

"You are going after Blackburn?" Concern flashed within her eyes... and soon disappeared. "I do not care about that."

Pain stabbed his heart so suddenly it nearly made him flinch. "You do not *care* about my risking my life for the sake of your sister?" What was she saying? How had they come to this?

Isabella took a step toward him. She slowly raised her palm to his cheek, nearly stroking the flesh. "Of course, I care," she whispered, dropping her hand to her side, then turned to face the waters of the Serpentine. "But that is not what I wish to speak of."

"Then what—"

In a flash, she whipped back to him, throwing the crumpled daisy to the ground. "You knew of my brother's debts!" She lowered her voice to a harsh whisper. "You knew of Blackburn's threats toward our family and that *he* was the one to orchestrate Violet's kidnapping. You knew of Callum's

## Chapter Forty-Three

involvement. You knew *everything*, and you did not tell me. How could you keep this from me?"

*This? This is what she is angry over?* "I have not known nearly as long as your *brother*," he hissed.

Alistair did not know where Lady Violet was being kept or about Blackburn's involvement until recently, and now Reading was involving Alistair in his problems, yet again, forcing him to keep his bloody secret from his entire family until he was ready to confess. "He made me swear not to tell you." Not until he was ready to tell her himself, which apparently was this morn.

"Oh, he made you *swear*?" Her hands landed hard on her hips.

"He is my friend..." A gentleman never broke promises to a friend. Though the gentleman in question had not acted particularly loyal as of late.

Isabella's bottom lip began to tremble. The sight of it nearly killed him. "All those moments we shared together... I thought you cared for me."

*Christ.*

He more than cared for her. She was unlike any woman he had ever met. *She* was all he could think of. He loved every moment they had spent together. The good and the bad. He loved everything from the shine of her hair to the lonely freckle on her back. From the sapphire hue of her eyes to the sapphire-studded dagger she no doubt had strapped to her person this very moment. From the tilt of her nose to the curve of her lips.

He loved her when she laughed. He loved her when she cried. Hell, he even loved her now as she argued with him. He loved her fierceness and bravery, and how strong she was in the search for her sister.

He loved every inch of her being.

Alistair took the lady's cheeks between his hands and forced her to look into his eyes. Settling his forehead on her own, he whispered. "I do not care for you, Bella. I am in *love* with you."

Tears spilled from her eyes. He swept them away with the pad of his thumb. His heart pulsed with anticipation as he waited for the lady to respond.

Waiting…

Waiting…

Waiting…

*Say something.*

"Then how could you betray me?" Isabella's breath trailed across his lips.

That was not exactly the response he had hoped for.

He *loved* her, and nothing he kept from her changed Lady Violet's situation. If he had known her sister was being held in Guildford before they had even left for Derby… he would have told Isabella. If he had known from the beginning that Blackburn was the one to orchestrate everything, he would have gone to him first.

No—her *brother* knew of everything. *He* should have taken them straight to Guildford.

*He* should have settled his debts with Blackburn.

Simon betrayed her.

*Simon betrayed all of us.*

"I do not wish to see you when you return." Isabella slipped away from his hold. "Please do not call upon me again."

Alistair's hands fell to his sides as he watched the woman he loved walk away from him.

## Chapter Forty-Three

And he was letting her.

He just *stood* there, frozen—alone on the shores of the Serpentine, watching as Isabella sauntered away. Her maids hurriedly stood from their places on the bench and followed behind. One of the servants glanced back at Alistair with a flash of pity in her depths.

Alistair arrived in Hyde Park believing he'd be betrothed to the woman he loved... And now?

Now he would leave without that woman's hand.

*Please do not call upon me again...*

He should say something. He should go *after* her and explain himself. He should apologize.

But he could not. He just stood there, unable to move his legs, and watched as her form disappeared within the crowd of people.

What was he to do now?

*What am I do to with this ring?*

The tiny velvet box burned against his side. Rage, torment, sorrow—all built beneath his chest.

And the box...

In one swift movement, he yanked said box from his pocket and heaved it into the dark water before him. It disappeared beneath the surface with a loud *clump*.

"Ahhhhh!" With shaking fists, he shouted at the ripples of water that appeared after the ring box sank beneath its dark surface.

The gasps from innocent debutantes and their mothers brought him back to the moment. Alistair looked around and gave a slight wave to the gawking passersby.

*Bloody hell*. What would the *ton* have to say about this, he wondered. At least the burning in his pocket where the ring box had once sat had vanished, though his feelings for the lady were still very much present.

# Chapter Forty-Four

*I do not care for you, Bella. I am in love with you.*

Pish posh. What kind of gentleman made love to a lady, betrayed her, then confessed his feelings for her all in one week?

*A rake—that is who.*

And Alistair proved himself a rake time and time again, yet Isabella could not see it. She *refused* to see it.

Until now.

And, oh, how she thought the gentleman had changed, but he was still the very same dastard he was when they had first met at Ashbury Hall.

Still the same rake she had seen groping a young woman at Middleton Ball. And how *stupid* she was to fall into his trap.

She let Alistair touch her in ways no gentleman ever had. He touched her in ways she had not thought possible. He made her feel so warm and needed. He made her feel like a woman, rather than another innocent lady of the *ton.*

Isabella ripped off her cloak as she entered her London

home and handed the article to the nearest servant.

She would *never* be able to forgive Alistair's lies.

Yes, her brother lied as well, but such behavior was to be expected from her brother. Alistair was different.

*I love him.*

She stopped herself in her stride and laid her hand upon the carved oak railing that lined the grand staircase of her home. "No. Not anymore."

"What was that, my lady?" Her lady's maid, Bethany, appeared at her side.

"Nothing." Alistair kept information from her—from her entire *family*—that could have brought Violet home sooner. And for what? All so he could slate his lust and fulfill his own wants and desires? What a fool she was. "How is my sister? Has she left her chambers this afternoon?"

Bethany gave Isabella a sympathetic look. "I am afraid not, my lady."

"I would like to see her." All the better to get her mind off Mr. Baston and spend some much-needed time with her sister.

Bethany bobbed a curtsy. "I will let Lady Violet know."

Isabella stayed Bethany with her hand. "There is no need. She is my sister, after all." She gave Bethany a prim smile and sailed up the staircase toward her sister's chambers.

Butterflies began fluttering their proverbial wings within her stomach. Why did she feel so uneasy about visiting her sister? She supposed she wondered how Violet would be feeling. After all, it had been a full day since her rescue, which she supposed was not so very long. It would be normal for Violet to still be weary from her travels—and everything else she had endured.

## Chapter Forty-Four

Perhaps she was ready to speak more about what had happened?

Or mayhap Simon had already paid her a visit.

If *that* were the case, then Violet would be terribly upset, indeed.

Isabella arrived outside her sister's chambers and knocked thrice on the panel.

"Enter," Violet's muffled voice came from within.

Turning the handle, the door opened swiftly, and there Violet sat under her bed covers, still donning her chemise from the night before.

"Have you not bathed, dear sister?" Isabella closed the panel behind her. "Surely a warm bath will make you feel heaps better."

Violet watched as Isabella sat on the edge of her feather mattress, her hair mussed from spending the entirety of her day in bed. "I am afraid."

Isabella's heart sank, and she placed a comforting hand on Violet's shoulder. Violet flinched at her touch. "There is no need to be afraid anymore. You are home." Isabella slowly removed her hand from her sister's shoulder and held Violet's hand instead. She still looked very unwell. And so pale.

"I am here with you. I can even sleep here with you if you wish."

For the first time since Violet had returned home, her eyes brightened. "I think I would like that."

She should have stayed by her sister's side the night they arrived home, but Isabella thought Violet would want her space after what she had gone through. But now she understood that was the opposite of what Violet needed right now.

Violet needed her sister.

Isabella hopped down from the bed and made her way to the bellpull. "I shall ring for a maid to have a bath readied."

"N-no." Violet pulled the covers up to her chin and shook her head frantically. "Please, you do not understand."

Isabella wondered what the scoundrels could have possibly done to her sister to make her so terrified of bathing. "Help me understand." She returned to her sister's side. "I will stay in the room and will even wash your hair for you, if you like—just like when we were children."

She and Violet always enjoyed taking turns washing each other's hair when they were children. Their nursemaid was not too fond of their bath time bonding as they would always splash around far too much, creating very large and very wet puddles on the floor.

Isabella brushed her fingers through Violet's dark, tangled hair.

"You remember that?" Violet asked.

"Of course I do! Our nursemaid hated our bathtub antics."

Her sister let out a small giggle, which made Isabella's heart sing.

It was so lovely having her sister back home. And now that a certain gentleman did not so completely occupy Isabella's mind, she could focus her efforts on helping her sister heal.

"Has Simon visited you today?" Her sister did not seem as though she had had 'the talk' with their brother. Surely she would have mentioned it by now.

"He has."

A weight fell from Isabella's shoulders, which was surprising. She supposed now the task would not have to fall upon

## Chapter Forty-Four

her. She had feared Simon would try to keep his secrets, and Isabella would have to be the one to speak to Violet about their brother's treachery. "Did he... *say* anything?"

Violet's mouth turned up slightly at the corners. "Did he mention his debts to Blackburn?" She answered Isabella's query. "And how his debts caused my abduction and the attack on our family? Yes, he did say such things."

Isabella released the breath she had been holding. "I am glad—I mean, I am not glad about what happened; I am glad that he finally told you." Oh, how she wished she had been there for that conversation, to be sure their brother was telling the *entire* truth. "Did he say anything else?"

Then Isabella wondered whether Violet *should* know of their brother's deception. Would it hinder her healing process? Would it benefit anyone for Violet to know that Simon's lies and secrets kept Violet from being brought home?

"He knew where I was being held and decided not to act upon his knowledge so he could instead try to raise the funds himself without having to go to Father for money." Violet uttered those words in such a cold and empty tone it made Isabella shiver. "I do not know how I will ever forgive him." A tear ran down Violet's cheek as she fidgeted with her bedsheets. "I am sorry for what Callum did to you."

"Do not dare even think about such things. I am well." Isabella rubbed her palm over Violet's hand, attempting to distract herself from the memories of that night that were coming forth in her mind. "You must focus on your own well-being."

More tears streamed down Violet's cheeks. "I am trying, but it is so very hard. You..." Isabella took her sister into her arms, holding her so close she could feel the wetness of her tears. "You do not know what they did to me."

Isabella felt her chest crumple at Violet's words. She knew her sister was not yet ready to tell her story, but she would be there for her when she was. She would be there for her now, and she would do whatever it took to make her sister well again, to help Violet forget about all that happened, even though Isabella did not know precisely what her sister had endured during her time in Guildford.

*And I am not sure I want to know.*

## Chapter Forty-Five

Alistair soon realized his mistake of tossing Isabella's betrothal ring into the freezing depths of the Serpentine.

For he, being the stubborn gentleman that he was, did not want to give up on Isabella just yet. And so he had found himself knee-deep in the murky waters of the Serpentine, kicking up all sorts of muck that had settled at the bottom of the lake, trying his damnedest to find the meager velvet box that housed a very expensive ring.

He, unsurprisingly, had gathered quite the sizable audience. After all, what was more entertaining on a sunny afternoon in Hyde Park than to watch a gentleman sifting through the waters of the Serpentine in full dress?

Alistair knew he looked quite mad, but frankly, he did not give a damn.

"Mr. Baston!" A shrill voice greeted him, but it sounded more like a scolding.

Alistair paused his wading to meet the owner of said voice.

*Meeting Mister Baston*

It was the Countess of Hereford—Viscount Middleton's own mother—peering down at him from the shoreline.

"What on earth are you doing, boy?" She gazed down her nose at him, disapproval and disgust seeping from her features.

Alistair knew he looked ridiculous, but he did not need a scolding from his competition's mother. Luckily, the viscount was nowhere in sight. "I dropped something quite precious to me, Lady Hereford."

The woman arched a blonde brow. "All the way out there?"

The countess clearly did not believe his story. "I was out rowing earlier, and it fell from my grasp."

Clutching her elaborate gold-encrusted cane, she replied with a *humph*. "Edward!"

Alistair's stomach immediately clenched at the name that came from the countess's lips.

The viscount appeared from behind a small grouping of birch trees with two young girls in tow. "Mother?"

"Mr. Baston," the countess called out. "I am sure you are acquainted with my son, the Viscount Middleton?"

"Indeed!" Alistair shouted from his place in the water, and Lord Middleton eyed him strangely from his dry position on the shore.

"These here are my daughters," the countess continued. "Lady Olivia, my youngest daughter, and Lady Georgiana, my eldest."

The two young ladies curtsied, and the youngest tried to cover a giggle with her hand. Countess Hereford looked to Alistair expectantly, as if it were the most proper of time as any to make formal introductions.

Alistair swept into a deep, exaggerated bow, which made

## Chapter Forty-Five

young Lady Olivia giggle all the more. "Ladies."

"Edward." The countess thumped her cane.

The viscount leaped forward like a loyal dog. "Yes, Mother?"

"Aid poor Mr. Baston here in retrieving his precious item," she demanded, and Alistair wondered whether the countess was actually attempting to aid him, or whether, like most of the peerage, she was more interested in the item in question for gossip's sake.

Middleton's shoulders hunched over. He obviously did not relish the idea of wetting his expensive buckskin trousers.

The gentleman removed his decorated topcoat and handed it off to their footman, who was standing just a few paces away. He removed his boots and stockings, and approached the shoreline, eyeing the water warily. "Best get on with it, then," he grumbled to himself. "Baston! What exactly are we searching for?"

Alistair groaned to himself. The last thing he needed was for one of Isabella's suitors to know of his plans to propose to the lady. "A jeweler's box."

"Wonderful," he said on an exhale. Middleton then proceeded to step into the water. "You are certain you lost it about here?"

"Indeed." Alistair continued feeling around the slimy sand with his feet, hoping he would feel the small velvet box with his toes instead of having to plunge headfirst into the Serpentine.

Middleton reached his side. "How exactly did you lose this jeweler's box?"

He could not very well say he threw it into the lake in a fit of rage. "Erm... rowing."

*Meeting Mister Baston*

Middleton gave him a look that suggested he did not quite believe Alistair. "Rowing?"

"It fell from my pocket." Alistair continued kicking up dirt and muck, which made it all the more difficult to see through the already dark waters.

Watching Alistair kick about, Middleton raised a brow. "I am not entirely certain that is the best way to go about searching for a little box."

Alistair stopped his efforts. "And what do you suggest?"

The viscount placed his hands on his hips and searched the area with narrowed eyes, then, to Alistair's surprise, he swan dived straight into the Serpentine, sending a splash of water into the air.

Alistair watched in confusion, and he had to admit, in amazement as well, as the gentleman disappeared into the cloudy depths. He could not help but count the seconds that passed while the other gentleman was underwater.

Five seconds, ten, twenty-two, thirty-eight. When Alistair reached ninety-seven seconds, he began to worry. How long could a man hold his breath? He had heard of a Serbian man who had once held his breath for nearly fifteen minutes, but that particular man had trained in the art—if one could call holding one's breath an art form—for years. And who knew if the story was actually true?

Just as Alistair considered diving into the water himself, the viscount finally emerged with a loud gasp. He swept a hand over his eyes to clear the droplets from his face, his blond hair now dark with moisture. "I found it!" Middleton raised an arm into the air, waving about something that looked very much like a jeweler's box.

"Well done, Edward!" the countess shouted from the

## Chapter Forty-Five

shoreline.

Alistair's eyes flew open at the sight. He was astounded. He could not believe the blighter actually found it. "I have to give it to you, Middleton, I am impressed. Give it here." He motioned to the box in question. He had to see if Isabella's ring was still intact and had not fallen out of the box when it hit the water.

But instead, Middleton took it upon himself to open the box to check its contents. The viscount's face became alight with astonishment. "Baston! Who is the lucky lady?"

Alistair's heart pounded with both nervous energy and relief. According to Middleton's reaction, the ring was most definitely still safely nestled inside its box, but now the gentleman knew of Alistair's plans to propose. "You would not know her," he lied.

"Oh, come now." The viscount handed him the now soaked through velvet box. "Try me."

Alistair took the box and opened it, just to be sure the ring was safe. "As I said..." He then securely tucked it away in his jacket pocket. "You would not know her."

The viscount followed Alistair ashore. "Boo! You are a lout."

"And what did we find?" the countess asked as Alistair and Middleton stepped foot on land.

As if Alistair would ever tell—

"A betrothal ring," the viscount answered for him.

The countess's eyebrows flew up, nearly meeting her graying hairline. "Who is the lucky lady?"

Alistair sighed. Like mother like son, he supposed. Both of them were proving themselves to be meddlesome individuals. "I am afraid I must bid you all adieu. I am late for a meeting."

*Meeting Mister Baston*

Which was not untrue. He was meant to be meeting Captain Lucas at the Avery House that afternoon. He turned to Lord Middleton and bowed. "I thank you for your assistance in retrieving my box. Ladies." He tipped a proverbial hat toward the young Middleton daughters, gathered his boots and stockings from the ground, and took his leave.

## Chapter Forty-Six

The cramped space within the duke's carriage was unforgivably cold. Alistair still felt the chill from his soaked-through attire. Though he had already gone to his apartments for a change of clothing, he just could not shake off the frozen, wet feeling in his bones.

He rested his chin in his palm and rubbed the stubble on his cheek, eyeing Captain Lucas who was currently sitting across from him.

How was the gentleman so calm and composed? Alistair's skin crawled at the thought of killing a man. Yet Lucas was sat there aloof, bobbing his foot atop his knee and whistling a merry tune.

"Hey." Lucas's voice cut through the silence.

He looked up as Captain Lucas leaned forward to place a hand on Alistair's shoulder.

"You do not have to do this, you know."

*He did.* He needed to confront Blackburn for his misdeeds. What he had done to the Avery family was unforgivable, and

*Meeting Mister Baston*

the man needed to pay with blood. And Alistair was going to be the one to do it.

For George, Lady Violet, and the blameless servants who had lost their lives protecting the duke and his children.

For Isabella.

He would never forget the night Callum attacked Isabella and her fierce inclination to fight back. He would never forget the grief she experienced when she believed her father to be dead. "I do." Alistair brought his elbows to rest on his knees. "I have to do this for her."

Lucas leaned back against the seat, his hand slipping from Alistair's shoulder. "Revenge is a dangerous game."

"It Is not revenge," Alistair snapped. "It Is justice."

"Well, then." Their conveyance rolled to a halt outside the Fox's Den. "That is an excellent mindset to have." Captain Lucas gave an approving nod. "Are you comfortable approaching Blackburn yourself? The gentleman is already familiar with you, and it will be easier for you to gain access to his offices."

Without giving Alistair a moment to answer, Lucas pulled a pistol from his within his jacket and handed it over.

Alistair inspected the flint and barrel. It was loaded. The cold metal seared against his skin. *You can do this, Baston. Think of Isabella.*

"I will distract any security outside his offices then join you as soon as I am able."

Alistair gave Lucas a silent nod in response, still staring at the weapon in his hands. He'd fired pistols and rifles in the past, and he was a bloody damned good shot, if he said so himself; that was not the problem.

*What is the problem?*

## Chapter Forty-Six

"Baston?" the captain called out, immediately capturing his attention. "Are you ready?"

He sighed and placed the weapon inside his jacket pocket. He was as ready as he'd ever be.

*Bloody, bloody hell...*

The two gentlemen stepped inside the smoke-filled room at the Fox's Den. The place smelled of cheroots and cheap perfume. Patrons filled their bellies with whatever garish ale the establishment had on offer and were more than happy to throw their entire family's fortune onto the gaming tables.

Alistair shook his head in disgust. To think he used to frequent clubs similar to the Fox's Den.

Captain Lucas nudged Alistair's side and motioned to a blackjack table. Alistair nodded his understanding as Lucas ventured off into the crowd of patrons.

Alistair approached the guard standing at the back of the room near the velvet rope that kept gentlemen from wandering upstairs. The guard arched a brow in recognition. The burly man unhooked the velvet rope and let Alistair pass without a word.

In the upper quarters of the Fox's Den, the air was thick and smelled like sex. He could use a good tupping after this, Alistair thought. But that life was not for him anymore. After this meeting with Blackburn, he would return to Isabella and win her back. He was not precisely certain how he was going to accomplish that feat, but by God, he would do it, even if it killed him.

Alistair arrived at Blackburn's office. This time, the scoundrel's door was wide open.

Blackburn looked up from his missive with a crooked grin. "You again." He dismissed his security with a wave of the

*Meeting Mister Baston*

hand.

A mistake on his part.

"Did Reading not give you the answers you sought?" He leaned back against his leather chesterfield chair and flashed Alistair a questioning look.

"Oh, he did." Alistair closed the door behind him then approached Blackburn and settled his palms on the front of the blackguard's desk. "That is why I am here."

A scuffling noise came from outside the door.

Blackburn's smirk vanished, and the gentleman moved to open the top drawer of his desk.

Alistair withdrew his pistol and pointed it at the man in front of him. His heart was pounding against his chest and sweat began to bead at his brow. He tried his damnedest to keep his hand from shaking.

Blackburn stopped his movement and instead, raised both hands into the air. "Now, now…" The cad slowly rose from his seat, another damned annoying smirk planted over his face. "Let us settle this like gentleman, shall we?"

"You are no gentleman," Alistair spat.

He watched Blackburn slither around his desk like the snake he was. Alistair pulled the hammer into place with a decisive *click*.

Blackburn halted his steps.

The blaze from the hearth burned against Alistair's back. The sweat beading at his brow was now dripping down his temple.

*You can do this, Baston.*

The lowlife in front of him deserved all that was coming to him. He just had to bide his time until Captain Lucas was finished with the guards—

## Chapter Forty-Six

A loud bang came from behind the office door, momentarily capturing their attention. Alistair flinched at the sound and turned his head toward the door. Distant shouting came from beyond the panel—

*"Christ!"* A sharp pain stung his outstretched hand. Blackburn struck Alistair's hand, causing the pistol to fall from his grasp. Time slowed as Alistair watched the pistol hit the floor—

*Craaaack!*

The pistol fired from the impact. A cloud of white smoke filled the room. Alistair brought his hands to his ears. The ringing instantly demobilized him, bringing him to his knees.

Blackburn's boot collided with Alistair's jaw, effectively ridding him of the ringing in his ears.

"Come on, Baston!" Blackburn lifted Alistair by the lapels of his jacket, his black eyes crazed with... excitement? "Is that the best you've got?"

*The bastard was enjoying this!*

Alistair slammed his skull into the other man's nose. Blackburn stumbled backward and gripped his now bloodied nose with his fingers. His gaze met Alistair's, the man's lips raising into a deranged grin. Blood trickled over the whites of his teeth. "That is more like it."

Alistair brought his fists to each side of his face. If the blackguard wanted to fight like gentlemen, then by God, he was ready.

With a maniacal laugh, Blackburn gripped the ridge of his nose and snapped it back into place. Alistair watched as the man wiped the blood from his nose and rubbed his blood-soaked palms together. He then dragged his hands down the front of his face, leaving a stream of red to cascade down his

*Meeting Mister Baston*

jaw. "Come on!"

The lord beat his fists against his chest like an enraged gorilla, and Alistair would be lying if he said he was not slightly frightened by the sight. Blackburn swiftly closed the distance between them, allowing Alistair to take the next move.

Alistair composed himself and inhaled a gasp of air.

He jabbed left.

Blackburn dodged his attack.

He jabbed right.

Blackburn stepped to the left.

Alistair moved to strike the man's face, but Blackburn blocked Alistair's blow with his arm.

His eyes widened as he lost all faith in himself. How would he ever be able to protect Isabella from a miscreant such as Lord Blackburn if he could not even land a single blow?

A chuckle fell from the other man's lips. "Ready to call it quits?"

Rage revealed itself from deep within Alistair's person. A searing heat pumped through his veins as images of Diggory flooded his mind: his filthy hands groping and gripping at Isabella; his foul mouth coming down on hers hard enough to leave a bruise. All because of Blackburn. "Never."

The other man lunged at him with a loud grunt, and Alistair lurched to the side, evading his opponent's attack. Out of the corner of his eye, he spotted a small iron shovel leaning against the fireplace. He snagged the heavy piece and swung it like a cricket bat. Straight into Blackburn's back.

The gentleman fell to his hands and knees. He looked up to Alistair with a derisive smile. "That is cheating."

Alistair raised the shovel once again, getting into batting

## Chapter Forty-Six

position. "I do not care," he said and slammed the iron piece against the man's ribs.

Again. And again.

Until the blackguard fell to the floor.

Alistair stared down at Blackburn and waited. His breath came quickly as he struggled to catch his breath, questioning his role in all of this.

"I cannot." What was he thinking? He could not *kill* a man, even evil scum such as Blackburn.

He tossed the shovel into the burning hearth and fell to his knees next to the battered man on the floor.

Why was he not angrier? Where was the rage he felt when he beat Callum to a pulp that night at the inn? Alistair's shoulders slumped forward as the feeling of defeat fell onto him. He should have let Lucas handle it. Where was the bastard anyway?

He dragged a hand over his face. What was he to do now? Just get up and leave? Tell Lucas to finish the job because he himself was too cowardly to do so?

A rustling noise came from beside him. It was Blackburn pushing himself up from the floor. Alistair watched as he struggled to bring himself to his feet and contemplated helping him, but Alistair stayed in his place and continued watching as Blackburn fell to his backside and lazed against the wall beside the hearth. "Truce?" The lord held out his hand in accord.

Could he trust Blackburn to keep his word? Or would the man simply stab him in the back as soon as Alistair turned to leave? Was the lord's beating enough? Was that *justice*?

He was tired and out of breath, and he just wanted to return home.

## Meeting Mister Baston

"Truce." He decided to trust Blackburn. He was *technically* a gentleman, and a true gentleman always kept his word.

Alistair leaned forward to place his hand in Blackburn's when the shine of a blade caught his eye.

Blackburn caught Alistair's wrist and sliced the dagger through the air. In one quick movement, Alistair twisted his wrist free, took the iron shovel from its place in the hearth and swung blindly.

A bloodcurdling scream came from Blackburn. Flaming red ash fluttered to the floor. Alistair pulled himself up to standing, shovel still in hand. He stared down at the iron tool. It was glowing orange from its heat—charred skin stuck to the metal.

He looked to Blackburn. The man still shrieked with pain, his hands cradling the blistered skin of his face.

The shovel fell from Alistair's grasp. He backed toward the door while Blackburn howled and wriggled across the floor of his office. "I will kill you for this!"

Blackburn's words sounded distant to his ears. Alistair exited the office and slammed the panel closed behind him.

*You are useless!*

*What have you done to her?!*

*It is all your fault!*

*You should have never been born!*

His father's words clamored for attention in his mind. He needed to get out of there. He needed to leave *now*.

Pain arose in his skull as the excitement from the fight began wearing off. He just had to focus on getting out of the Fox's Den. He wanted to leave all of this behind and never think of it again.

A crack of a whip sounded, and he was not sure if it was

## Chapter Forty-Six

real or if it was a memory. He stepped over the bodies of Blackburn's unconscious security guards, which littered the corridors—or were they dead?

*Just one foot after another. Keep walking.*

*Craaaack!*

*Father, please. I did not mean to hurt her!*

*Get out of my sight... I never want to see your face in my household again—*

"Baston?"

The captain's voice came forward, and Alistair found himself outside the Fox's Den, standing next to their carriage. "Where the bloody hell were *you*?"

Captain Lucas shrugged. "I heard the shot, so I figured you handled it."

"And what if Blackburn was the one who did the shooting?"

Lucas shrugged again. "I would have come to your aid eventually." The gentleman rapped on the door of the carriage, signaling to the groomsman they were ready to depart. "It is done, then?"

The groomsman swung open the carriage door, allowing the gentleman to step inside. Once Alistair and Captain Lucas were seated, the door slammed closed.

Alistair swiped a hand over his face, breathing in the cool evening air. "It is done." *He* was done. Blackburn was far from dead, but he would just have to deal with that later.

Now they just had to find Callum.

## Chapter Forty-Seven

Barely a week ago, Isabella was certain she'd never be able to escape the haze left by Alistair's lovemaking. But there she was, just days after their meeting in Hyde Park, with her sister in the yellow drawing room, reading another Austen novel, and the gentleman hadn't even crossed her mind.

Well, except this present moment, of course, and it was almost as if they had never met at all. In fact, she had even accepted to go on an outing with Lord Middleton. After Alistair's deception, the idea of being Edward's wife was not such an abominable idea.

Yes, the gentleman was a bit more traditional in the ways of society, but that did not make him a bad person. He was not a rake nor a rogue. He was a viscount and future earl, which made him an ideal match for anybody.

Her mother would be elated when Isabella told her that she had decided to accept the viscount's proposal. But she need not make her mother aware of that fact *now*. She could use

## Chapter Forty-Seven

a bit more time to breathe easy after all that had happened over the last few weeks, and she was not quite ready to be thrust into wedding planning.

"Mama wants to throw a ball."

"What?" Violet's pensive tones cut into her musings. "Now? But you have only just returned—"

"Not now. In two weeks' time," her sister said, as if she did not care one way or another.

Isabella closed her book and set it down in her lap. "Surely Mother knows you are not ready to be thrust back into society?"

Violet shrugged a shoulder, sticking her nose back in her book. "Who is to say I will ever be ready?"

She was correct on that score, but it was still too soon. "I will talk to Mother." Isabella moved to stand, but Violet slammed her book closed with a loud *thwack*.

"It is fine," Violet blurted. "Let Mother throw her ball. Do you not see?" Violet's ice-blue gaze pierced her own. Her depths shimmered with so much sorrow that Isabella could feel her sister's pain deep within her bones. Violet's jaw tightened until her teeth audibly ground together. "I will *n-never* be fine. Those memories will always be *here*." Violet pressed her fist hard against her temple.

Isabella understood.

With each tender caress from a gentleman, the memories of Callum's cruel touch would forever be glaring in the back of her mind. Every time she took hold of her blade, the dark crimson color of that man's blood doused her thoughts.

Isabella reached over and gently took hold of her sister's hand.

Violet slipped away from her touch and opened her book

once more. "Mother will want us to begin writing the invitations."

"Yes." Isabella's voice emerged breathy and soft. "Of course." Perhaps it was better for Violet to resume as normal. Mayhap Violet did not want to sit in her bedchamber and wallow in self-pity like most delicate ladies of the *ton*.

"I assume your Edward will be making an appearance? Perhaps he will announce your engagement at the ball—if you have decided to accept his offer that is." Violet's aura shifted. It was as though she could change her mood with the snap of her fingers, which was not unusual, as she had done similar such things in the past.

"I have decided, and I will inform him of my acceptance this afternoon."

Violet reached over and laid her hand atop Isabella's knee. "How wonderful for you, dear sister. The rest of the Season will be very busy for us, indeed."

To Isabella's surprise, there was not a sense of nervousness or relief at her deciding to marry Edward… but a sting of guilt. "Indeed."

A footman appeared in the doorway, causing Isabella's person to jump with alarm. "Dear Jacobs." Isabella placed a hand over her now pounding heart. "You startled me."

"Apologies, my lady." Jacobs inclined his head. "You have a visitor. A certain—" the older man attempted a wink "—viscount."

"Speak of the devil," Violet muttered. "I shall leave you, then." Book in hand, she sprung from her place on the gold leaf sofa.

"Oh, there is no nee—"

"Do not be silly, Bella." Violet squeezed Isabella's shoulder.

## Chapter Forty-Seven

"You will want this time alone."

A suggestive grin stole over her sister's features, and it seemed, at least for now, Violet was back to being... well... *Violet*. Isabella shook her head as she watched her sister saunter out of the room, and but a few moments later, Jacobs returned with Lord Middleton trailing at his rear.

"Lady Isabella." The viscount approached her with a wide grin.

"My lord." She stood and curtsied, then offered him a seat beside her.

Lord Middleton held out an enormous bundle of very expensive tulips that varied in shades of pinks and purples. "They are lovely." Isabella took the sizable bouquet into her arms and scanned the room for a vase. Normally, her maid Bethany would handle such things, but she was busy doing whatever else it was maids did around the house, and so Isabella chose to keep hold of the tulips and took her seat on the sofa.

She glanced down to the flowers, and her heart sank a little. Tulips were beautiful, indeed, but they did not bring her the joy daisies did.

The viscount sat down beside her. "I thought we might spend the afternoon at the London conservatory, then meet my mother and sisters at Almack's for ices."

"That sounds wonderful." Isabella attempted to make eye contact with the viscount, but it was quite difficult to see over all the bright petals.

"Right." Edward stood and smoothed out his buckskin trousers with his palms. "I shall ring for your maid, then we can set off."

"Wait!" She would much rather accept Edward's proposal

here in the comfort of her own home. There would be no point in putting it off any longer—now that a certain gentleman was out of the picture. She stood, fumbling with the hefty tulips in her arms. "I would like to speak to you about something."

"Oh." Edward moved toward the bellpull, but instead, closed the door to the drawing room, leaving just a few inches open for propriety's sake. He turned toward her and combed his fingers through his dark blond tresses. "Nothing too grim, I hope." He flashed her a boyish smile.

In this moment, with Edward standing before her with his hands in his pockets—in a much more relaxed manner than she had ever seen him in before—she could almost imagine a happy life with the gentleman. He seemed so much more at ease, there in her family's drawing room, than he was when she had socialized with him at societal events. And in this moment, Isabella knew marrying Edward was the right decision.

*The safe decision...* a voice taunted her.

Isabella peered over the flowers before her. "I have decided to accept your proposal."

The gentleman looked to her with wide eyes. "This is wonderful news, indeed!" He snapped his fingers in a show of realization and began to pace. "We must inform my mother—" He paused his pacing and turned to her. "We must inform *your* mother!"

Closing the distance between them in two long strides, he plucked the bouquet from her arms and tossed it aside. He took her face between his hands. "My dear Isabella…"

Isabella could not help but laugh at the viscount's excitement. She had not known how much her decision had

## Chapter Forty-Seven

meant to the gentleman, and it almost seemed as though the gentleman did, in fact, care for her.

"You have no idea the joy this brings me." He brought his lips to hers with an eagerness and enthusiasm that nearly made her stumble.

And almost as quickly as he planted his kiss, Edward stepped away to resume his pacing. "Forget about the conservatory." He rubbed at the slight stubble on his jaw. "We have a wedding to plan."

"Actually." Isabella clasped her hands before her. "I was hoping we could wait a while longer?"

Edward stopped himself in his stride and tilted his head in question.

She toyed with her cerulean skirts. "Being as my sister has just returned from York, and with my mother planning a ball for later in the month... I was hoping to keep this quiet for now." Of course, Isabella could handle such chaos, but she was worried Violet could not. Her sister needed more time.

With his arms akimbo, Edward nodded. "A long, romantic engagement, then. I approve." He approached her and took her fidgeting hands in his. He raised them to his lips. "We will take as much time as you need," he whispered.

Isabella relaxed her shoulders and smiled. Life with the viscount would not be at all as terrible as she had once imagined it.

## Chapter Forty-Eight

*The Duke and Duchess of Waverly request the honor of your presence at Avery House to celebrate the return of their youngest daughter, Lady Violet Avery...*

"Sister!"

Dropping her quill on the desktop, black ink splattered over a number of Isabella's neatly written invitations.

Her maid, Bethany, let out a snort beside her.

"Simon!" Isabella screeched then helped Bethany work on clearing the desk, hoping to save as many invitations as she could. "You knew I was writing out the invitations! Why would you come barging in here like a mad bull?"

Leaning against the doorway, Simon shrugged. "It is my way."

"Then make it your way to enter a room *quietly*." Now she would have to rewrite at least ten invitations, and with her slow penmanship, it would take hours.

"I wanted to be sure you remembered to invite Baston to the ball."

## Chapter Forty-Eight

Isabella stood from her seat and glared at her brother. "Why would I invite Mr. Baston?"

Simon stuck out his chin. "Why ever not?"

Ink-spattered invitations in hand, Isabella made her way to the hearth. She chucked them into the fire one by one. "*Perhaps,* it is because he *lied* about knowing Violet's whereabouts." Isabella threw the remaining invitations in Simon's direction, but being as they were made of parchment, they spun and fell to the ground just a few feet in front of her. "Just as *you* had."

Simon's face blanched, but he quickly recovered his rakish demeanor. "So *that* is why I have not seen Baston around."

Isabella crossed her arms in front of her as Bethany picked up the remainder of the invitations off the floor. "I do not know what you speak of."

Waving a finger in her direction, her brother pushed himself off the wall and marched toward her. "You and Baston are in a quarrel, and *that* is why he has not come to call on you."

Isabella tapped her toes in annoyance. She was engaged to the viscount so it did not matter whether herself and Mr. Baston were *quarreling*. And Mr. Baston was away tracking down Callum and Lord Blackburn, though her brother may not know that. "I know not what you speak of."

"*I know not what you speak of...*" Simon mocked her in a silly boyish tone. He flicked her nose then turned to Bethany, who was now tossing the ruined parchment into the hearth. "Bethany, be sure to invite Baston to the ball."

Bethany faced him and gave a polite curtsy. "Yes, my lord."

If Bethany wrote out an invitation for Alistair Baston, she would be sure to rip it into pieces.

*Meeting Mister Baston*

Simon strode over to the doorway of the drawing room and paused. "Oh, and one more thing." Her brother turned to face her. "Alistair never knew of Violet's whereabouts. I had only told him just before we left for Guildford." Simon winked before disappearing into the hallway.

Isabella released her clenched fists. Her entire body went still. Even her heart felt as though it had ceased beating. Alistair did not know of Violet's whereabouts? The gentleman did not lie? He did not betray her?

Why did he not say something?

*Why did he not tell her?*

Instead, he let her rattle on like a fool.

*You did not let him speak!*

She gasped. That little voice in her head was correct. She *hadn't* let him speak.

"Blackburn." She brought her hands to her lips. Alistair was leaving to confront Blackburn that day. Even her brother, Alistair's *friend,* had not heard from him since then.

"Pardon, my lady?" Bethany questioned from beside her.

"Nothing." Isabella waved off her lady's maid. "Go and rest now, Bethany. You have done enough for today."

Bethany curtsied, "Yes, my lady," then exited the room.

And soon Isabella began to pace.

Mayhap something went wrong. Mayhap Alistair was injured or… She gasped once more. Mayhap Blackburn *killed* him. After all that she had said to him? She told Alistair to stay away even though he was going after Blackburn to seek justice for her sister.

*For me.*

Such a fool she was!

Perhaps she should speak with her father. He would surely

## Chapter Forty-Eight

know of Alistair's whereabouts. Hiking up her skirts, Isabella hurried to her father's offices. "Papa!"

*I have not known nearly as long as your brother...*

Isabella skidded to a halt in the corridor. Stumbling over her slippers, she placed a hand on the wall to steady herself. He *did* tell her he had not known of Violet's whereabouts.

*You just refused to listen.*

She was so heightened with rage at what Simon had told her that morning that she did not even stop to think over Alistair's own words. With a renewed vigor, she quickened her pace down the west corridor. She would make this right. She would force her father to tell her where he was, and she would bring Alistair back herself.

As soon as she reached his door, she began pounding on the wood panel. "Papa!"

"Yes, come in!" Her father answered from within his office.

Isabella hastily turned the handle and marched inside. "Papa..."

"Bella." Her father rose from his seat. "What on earth is the matter?"

Struggling to catch her breath, she placed both hands upon her father's desktop. "Have you heard from Alist— Mr. Baston?" she corrected.

"I sent him away on business." Her father gave her a confused look. "What is going on, Bella?"

She brought her arms akimbo. She knew exactly what *business* her father had sent him on. "You mean, confronting Lord Blackburn?"

Sighing, the duke returned to his seat. "He told you."

Not wanting to give her father the satisfaction of an answer, Isabella just glared at him.

He let out an exasperated sigh. "What is this about, Bella?"

"You sent him to his deathbed!"

"Isabella Elizabeth!" Her father's booming voice caused the entire room to rumble. "He has only just left. Alistair could be away for *weeks*. Captain Lucas is with him, and they will *both* return safely. I assure you."

Tears pricked her eyes. "You cannot possibly know that."

"But one can hope."

She had never seen her father so cold. *But one can hope?* This was Alistair! Not a stray dog no one had a care for. Isabella firmed her jaw. "Tell me where he is," she ordered.

The duke raised a single brow. He settled his ice-cold stare on her. Would that be his only response?

Clutching her fists at her side, she stomped her slippered foot hard against the wood of the floor. "Tell me!"

"Do you really think I would let my daughter go out into this world to chase down some boy?" He shook his head. "Really, Bella? And here I thought you were the well-behaved child of the bunch."

Swiping a tear from her cheek, she whispered, "I just need to know he will come home unharmed."

As much as it hurt her to admit it, her father was right. She could not go after Alistair—not after what had happened to her sister.

She just had to have hope.

# Chapter Forty-Nine

*Two weeks later*

It had taken far longer to track down Callum Diggory than either Alistair or Captain Lucas had anticipated, especially since Alistair was so wound up before meeting Blackburn, he had actually forgotten to get the information he needed from the gentleman.

After leaving Blackburn's establishment, they scoped the back alleys of the Seven Dials for days. They even visited the underground fighting rings that Alistair thought Callum might frequent.

After almost a week of false leads, Captain Lucas thought perhaps Callum was not fool enough to return to London after escaping the authorities—and so off they went to Guildford as the duke originally commanded, to the exact place where they had found Violet and the miscreants that had kept her captive.

*Meeting Mister Baston*

As far as Alistair knew, Captain Lucas still believed Blackburn to be dead, and Alistair also knew that such misinformation would most assuredly come back to bite him on the ass.

Lucas readied his stance. *"One, two, three!"*

Both gentlemen sprinted toward the locked door in front of them and rammed into the panel with their shoulders.

*Thwack!*

A sharp pain surged through his shoulder and neck. He gripped the base of his neck in the hopes of stopping the pain from ripping into other parts of his person.

*Bloody hell.* That was far more painful than he thought it was going to be, but luckily the door flew open on their first attempt.

And there he was, lazing over an aged chaise in the corner of his rented rooms at the Whispey Wey Inn, the very same inn Blackburn's gang of bandits had been keeping Lady Violet captive in.

"Diggory." Captain Lucas greeted the former servant with the barrel end of his pistol.

"Come to lock me up?"

"Not exactly." Lucas responded to Callum's query.

"What about you?" Diggory pointed his chin in Alistair's direction. "Come to enact revenge for your L-Lady Isabella?"

Catching that slight stammer, Alistair glanced about the room. Empty bottles of liquor littered the space, and a strong smell of spirits singed his nostrils. The lad was drunk.

He wondered how long the boy had sat in that room drinking himself to oblivion. Alistair almost felt sorry for the bastard.

Callum staggered from his seat on the chaise. He raised

## Chapter Forty-Nine

both arms in the air—one hand holding a half-empty decanter of auburn liquid. "Go ahead." He swayed. "Do it! I have nothinnn left anyway."

Alistair set his hand on Lucas's outstretched arm, forcing the gentleman to lower his weapon. "Why did you do it?" Alistair questioned the drunkard before them.

Callum brought the decanter to his lips and took a long swallow. "Me maw was ill. I n-needed the money."

Alistair was set aback. He did everything... for his mother? He shook his head in frustration. "Why did you not ask the duke? He would have helped you."

Pointing the decanter in their direction. Callum stumbled again. "Y-your kind d-do not care about *us*." He let out a maniacal laugh. "It does not even matter anymore... Me maw's dead now!"

Alistair raised his fingers to his forehead and rubbed vigorously. He turned to Captain Lucas. "This is not right—"

"Baston." Lucas cut in. "I think it is best if you leave the room."

Alistair stood stock still. Lucas would kill this boy, no matter what the reasons were for his actions? At that moment, Alistair lost all respect for the captain.

Shaking his head in disgust, Alistair stepped out of the room and closed the panel behind him. He slumped his frame against the door and rubbed his face with both of his hands. What would Isabella think of what was happening here? Would she act as cold and careless as Captain Lucas had? Or would she sympathize with the boy in that room?

It was not even a question. He knew what she would do.
*Craaaack!*
The sound of the pistol firing made Alistair flinch. The

*Meeting Mister Baston*

smell of the burning powder stung his senses, and after a moment, he heard the echo of footfalls coming from behind the panel. He stood, waiting for Captain Lucas.

The gentleman turned the handle and appeared before him, cleaning the barrel of his pistol with a white cloth.

Lucas sauntered past, making his way down the hallway. He paused. "Shall we stay in Guildford for the night or would you like to return to London?"

Alistair's mouth tasted of acid. The captain's frigid tones made him feel sick to the core, and he could not take one more minute of it.

"I would like to return to London."

He needed to put all of this behind him. *This...*

What happened here… was not justice.

# Chapter Fifty

Standing at the entrance of her family's ballroom, Isabella so desperately wished she could shield herself behind one of the many satin curtains that lined the grand space, as she so often did at the many balls and soirees she attended since her coming out.

Alas, it was the Duke and Duchess of Waverly's event, and so she had the pleasurable task of greeting guests as they arrived alongside her mother, father and both of her siblings.

"Bella, do stand up straight, dear," her mother whispered in her ear.

*A lady does not slouch...*

Her mother's lessons on decorum would never fail to amuse her. Isabella straightened her shoulders with a slight roll of her eyes.

"I saw that."

Ah yes, how could she ever forget about her mother's third eye? Her mother saw and heard everything.

"Did you forget about Mother's third eye?" Violet murmured at her side.

Isabella fought to hide the smile creeping over her lips. "I thought perhaps she had lost it, seeing as you have been able to slip from her sights so very often."

"I am merely good at avoiding it."

A snort escaped Isabella, which earned her a glare from the duchess.

Her sister shot her a look, and Isabella darted her tongue out in return.

"George!" her mother hissed. "Control your children."

The duke sighed. "They are your children too, dear."

It was rather delightful having her family together again. Though their lives would never be the same after the events of the last few weeks, it was nice to pretend, at least for a moment.

Her chest squeezed as Alistair's face flashed in her mind's eye. He had never responded to her invitation to the ball.

*I do not wish to see you when you return...*

She really should not be surprised after how she had treated him that day in Hyde Park. How she wished she could take back those cruel words. If she had only listened—

"Edward Middleton, the Viscount Middleton."

Isabella looked up from her musings when the viscount's name was announced. Edward stood tall in the doorway with his dark blond hair neatly slicked back as he so often wore it. His plum-colored silk waistcoat shimmered in the candlelight, and Isabella would admit that Edward always looked particularly handsome in such lighting.

The viscount approached their party and greeted each of them with a bow. After exchanging pleasantries with the duke, duchess, and her brother, Edward's chestnut eyes fell

## Chapter Fifty

on her.

"My lady." He brought her gloved fingers to his lips and lingered there for longer than was proper.

Isabella cleared her throat, the action prompting the viscount to lower her hand. "Good evening, my lord."

But instead of releasing her hand, he caressed her wrist before taking her dance card in his hand. "May I claim a set, my lady?"

Isabella gulped. Edward's touch made her feel... uneasy. It was not at all the same uneasiness she felt when Alistair caressed her skin, or pressed his lips against hers. This was... *different*. She shook those musings from her mind. She should not be thinking of Mr. Baston anyhow. Alistair was not there, and Edward—her betrothed—was. "Of course you shall, my lord. I very much look forward to it."

Edward signed her dance card then turned to Violet. "My lady, how lovely to see you again."

Violet dropped into a pretty curtsy. "You as well, my lord."

"My night would not be complete without a dance from *both* Avery sisters." Edward winked, causing a little giggle to burst from Violet's lips.

When had Edward become such a charmer? He took Violet's dance card in his hand and signed his name with the small pencil attached. When finished, he gave a regal bow. "Ladies."

Isabella and Violet curtsied in unison, and when Edward disappeared into the crowd, Violet nudged her with her elbow.

"Do *not* say a word," Isabella warned. "We are not officially announcing our engagement until *after* the ball." It was bad enough that Edward's proposal at Hyde Park had witnesses.

*Meeting Mister Baston*

She did not need her sister making their engagement even more public than it already was.

Violet frowned. "Whatever for?"

Because... she did not wish to overwhelm her sister with so much excitement. A ball and a betrothal all within a fortnight of her returning home? It was too much.

*That is what you tell yourself...*

"And what do we have here?" Simon asked as he approached. He took hold of Violet's wrist to inspect her dance card. "A reel with Violet." Then he moved to reach for Isabella's. "Interesting... *very* interesting."

Isabella yanked her wrist from her brother's grasp. "And what, dare I ask, is so *very* interesting?"

Simon crossed his arm over his chest. "It seems the viscount has claimed one dance with Violet and—" he lifted his middle and forefinger in the air "—*two* dances with you. I dare say our dear Bella is well on her way to becoming a viscountess. Have you accepted his offer yet?"

"You know," Isabella drawled. "Being that you are the heir to a dukedom, you have your own marriage prospects to worry over. You need not worry so much over *mine*."

"Ah, but you are my sister." Simon laid an arm over Isabella's shoulder, pulling her close. "It is my duty to fuss over your marriage prospects. Baston will be very jealous, indeed."

Isabella slipped out of her brother's hold. Her pulse skipped at the sound of his name. "Is he here?" She glanced about the ballroom, searching for his familiar auburn hair. She sighed. Isabella knew very well Alistair was not there. She had been standing at the entrance to the ballroom for nearly an hour, greeting guests as they entered.

## Chapter Fifty

"What do you mean?" Violet cut in.

"Oh, surely you remember Mr. Baston?" Simon teased.

"Of course, he is Papa's—" Violet's mouth fell open. *"Noooo! Papa's man-of-affairs fancies Bella?"* Violet turned to her and slapped her shoulder. "Why did you not tell me?"

"Because she fancies him as well," Simon quipped. "I do not know why she is marrying the viscount when she is *clearly* in love with Alistair."

Violet's mouth fell open even wider than before, and Isabella brought two fingers to Violet's chin, pushing her mouth closed.

Why must her brother speak of such things? She did not *love* Alistair. She simply... well... perhaps... She may have at one point... but now? Isabella gave her head a mental shake. Her thoughts were all jumbled. "I haven't a clue what you are speaking of, brother."

Simon just winked and continued sipping his spirits.

Where was Alistair anyhow? It had been over a fortnight since his departure with Captain Lucas. Surely he would have returned by now?

*Surely he would have responded to my invitation.*

Isabella had, of course, written out an invitation to the gentleman herself once she had learned the truth. She had even apologized to the gentleman for what was stated in Hyde Park and then spent the next *thirteen* days waiting for a response.

She attempted to keep busy, helping plan Violet's ball, but after four days of silence, she made sure to spend her mornings in the parlor, peering out at the busy London streets awaiting his arrival. But once again, he did not come, and once again, knowing what Blackburn was capable of,

*Meeting Mister Baston*

Isabella feared the worst.

On the eighth day of silence, Isabella went to her father to ask if he had had word from Alistair or Captain Lucas, but there was nothing.

Edward, of course, had called upon her. He proved himself to be sweet and caring during that time. He could barely control his excitement about their betrothal, and he would tell her of all of the ways he wanted to announce their union, but Isabella found she was not be able to share in his excitement until she knew Alistair was safe.

After a number of dances, including a reel with Edward, Isabella was physically and mentally exhausted. She made her way to an alcove at the back corner of the ballroom, removing her satin-clad slippers one at a time as she approached.

With a low moan, she dropped onto the soft cushioned bench within the small space, and reaching down, she took one of her very sore feet in her hands and massaged the aching flesh.

The clinking of silverware against crystal rang in Isabella's ear.

"If I could have everyone's attention!" a familiar voice called out over the roar of patrons. Isabella's head tilted toward the opening of her little alcove. Edward? Surely that was not Edward's voice...

The hum of chatter quickly died down, and the small orchestra ceased its playing.

"I have happy news to convey."

Isabella fell from her seat on the bench. *He would not!* She had made it very clear that she wanted their betrothal to remain a secret until *after* the ball, and he had agreed! The gentleman was even thrilled by the prospect of a secret

## Chapter Fifty

betrothal. *Secret!*

Righting herself, Isabella pulled back the velvet curtain. Edward stood upon the gilded platform, with the musicians at his back and the crowd of patrons at his front.

*Bloody hell.*

"I have asked the lovely Lady Isabella Avery…"

*No…*

"…to be my wife…"

*No, no, no!*

"…and I am happy to say, she has accepted!"

The guests burst out into cheers and applause as they all looked around in search of— Countess Hereford pointed in Isabella's direction. "She is there!"

She gasped. They were looking for *her*. Isabella stood paralyzed in the opening of the alcove. Her pulse quickened tenfold as she looked out to a sea of colorful gowns rushing toward her.

*"How wonderful!"*

*"Future viscountess!"*

*"Invite us to the wedding!"*

The uproar of congratulations that was launched in her direction was overwhelming. She had not even had time to don her slippers. "Th-thank you… thank you… Oh, of course! Yes, I am thrilled…"

"Pardon me! Step aside please!"

A sense of reprieve came over her at the sound of her mother's voice. *Oh, thank the heavens…*

"You will all have time to speak with the future viscountess *at the wedding!*" The duchess stood at the opening of the alcove and slammed the curtains shut. "Oh, for the love of…" Her mother turned to her with a hand fluttering at her breast.

"Why the viscount thought *here* of all places would be the best place to inform the entirety of the *ton* of his engagement, I will never know."

Isabella let out a nervous chuckle and fell back in her seat. Her mother joined her at her side. "Darling, what of…" Her mother's words trailed off into nothing.

"What of…?" Isabella urged.

Angling herself toward Isabella, her mother took hold of her hands. "What of Mr. Baston? I saw something there… I am not often wrong about these things, you know. I hope you did not feel pressured to accept Middleton's proposal because of me. I wanted a match between the two of you, yes… but that was before I saw you and Alistair together."

First, her mother wanted a union between the Averys and the Middletons, but now that Isabella was finally betrothed to Edward, her mother wanted to see her engaged to Alistair, the gentleman she *loved*.

There was no denying it now.

She, Isabella Elizabeth Avery, was in love with her father's man-of-affairs.

Isabella let the back of her head fall against the wall as she released a long exhale. It did not matter anymore. "I fluffed it up, Mama. And it is too late to fix things now."

## Chapter Fifty-One

Alistair found himself pacing the floor of the gentleman's retiring room like a nervous cad. Then again, he supposed he *was* a nervous cad, being as he was about to ask the woman he loved to marry him.

*Again.*

Well… he had actually never got around to it the first time—the stubborn minx had not let him.

In fact, he would not even be at the Avery House this very moment if it were not for Isabella's invitation and the small note she had scrawled at the edge of the parchment.

> *The Duke and Duchess of Waverly request the honor of Mr. Alistair Baston at Avery House for a ball to celebrate the return of their youngest daughter, Lady Violet Avery on 20$^{th}$ May 1817…*

And at the very bottom, there it was…
*I am sorry. Please come to me.*

## *Meeting Mister Baston*

It was so minute that he had almost missed it, and being as he had only just returned from Guildford the very same day the ball was being held, he hadn't much time to prepare his proposal.

Alistair paused his pacing and let out a curse, realizing he still hadn't asked for her father's blessing.

"Bloody idiot," he muttered to himself. There was no possible way he could propose to Isabella in a ballroom without asking the duke's permission.

The party was in full swing, so Alistair hoped George would have retired to his offices by now.

He yanked open the oak panel that lead to the hallway. The duke's office was straight down the hall, so it would only make sense for him to start there. And to Alistair's relief, George was lounging comfortably in his leather armchair with a small glass of spirits in hand.

"Baston! You made it back in time for Violet's ball." George greeted him with a friendly smile. "How did everything go with Blackburn and Diggory?"

"Fine, fine." Alistair waved off the duke's query. He would tell of his mishap with Blackburn later.

*How did one start a conversation such as this?* Asking one's employer permission to marry his daughter. He had to be completely mad. "I needed to speak with you on a different matter."

George motioned to the wingback chair opposite him. "Nothing too serious, I hope."

"It is a bit serious, actually." Alistair took the seat offered, even though he much preferred to stand.

George nodded, his features turning to stone.

Alistair cleared his throat.

## Chapter Fifty-One

The duke arched an impatient brow.

Alistair coughed into his fist.

"Get on with it, boy," George groaned. "I have never known you to be the timid type."

"Right." As the duke said, it was best to get on with it. "Over the last month, I have spent a great deal of time with your daughter."

"Which one?"

Alistair stammered. *Which one?*

George swiped a hand over his face. "I jest…"

Alistair let out a quiet sigh as he tried to remember what he had wanted to say. "Over the last month, I have spent a great deal of time with your daughter, *Isabella*." Alistair flashed the duke a glare.

The duke grinned in return.

"And I have grown very attached to her." Alistair's eyes fell to the floor. He could not remember the last time he'd blushed, but he was certain he felt his cheeks burning.

"Not only is she beautiful, she is intelligent, funny, independent—"

"Stubborn," George supplied.

*Lord knew the lady was stubborn.* "And she knows how to handle a dagger, thanks to you…" Alistair met the duke's expressionless gaze. He cleared his throat, continuing his speech. "She is unlike any woman I have ever met, and I have come to the realization that if I do not spend every moment of the rest of my life with her, my life will be truly and utterly meaningless. And so I come to you today to ask permission to marry your daughter."

After a few moments, George stood from his chair and slowly made his way toward Alistair. The duke towered over

*Meeting Mister Baston*

Alistair's seated position and took in a long breath. "I am sorry to hear that, boy."

*Sorry to hear it?* Perhaps Alistair had overstepped his bounds. Perhaps he and the duke were not as close as he had thought. George must have been expecting more for his daughters—*more than he could ever give.*

"I-I do not understand…" Alistair's words trailed off as George turned away, returning to his seat.

"You should have come to me sooner." Alistair looked up. "Viscount Middleton just announced his betrothal to Bella."

His stomach dropped, and it felt as though someone had punched a hole through his chest, grabbed onto his heart, and squeezed it with all their might.

"But I do very much favor your reasonings for wanting to marry my daughter over the viscount's."

The grip on his heart slowly released, and Alistair attempted to hide the grin that began to creep over his lips.

"What are you still doing sitting there? Go get her!"

Alistair rose from his seat and shook the duke's hand.

"Just be sure she wants to marry you as well before you go off and make a fool of yourself," George added slyly.

Alistair strode into the ballroom using one of the side entrances. He scanned the crowd in search of any of the Averys. Surely they stayed close to each other. Weaving his way through the small groups of elegantly dressed ladies and gentlemen, he spotted a familiar blonde head.

He quickened his pace until he could clearly see her through the crowd.

Isabella stood along the front entrance next to her brother. She was wearing a dark blue satin gown that seemed to make her golden hair stand out that much more.

## Chapter Fifty-One

Their eyes met as he closed the distance between them. He exhibited one of his boyish grins she seemed to adore and she—

*Ducked?*

Indeed. The lady ducked behind her brother, which was *not* the look of longing he had hoped to see. "Good evening, my lady," he said over Simon's shoulder, causing the lord to stumble with confusion as Isabella continuously attempted to dip away from Alistair's stare. "You look stunning."

Isabella let out an audible sigh and stepped around Simon. "Good evening, Mr. Baston." The lady's eyes glanced about the room, and she seemed to be trying so very hard to avoid his gaze.

"Good of you to show your face, Baston." The marquess gave him a friendly slap on the shoulder.

"And good evening to you, Reading."

"And where have you been?" Simon asked. "Bella has been sulking about all week. She was beginning to drive me mad."

Alistair's eyes grew wide as he watched Isabella land a hard punch on her brother's arm. "Hush," she warned.

Though he should not be surprised that the lady could throw a punch. He moved to stand next to Isabella. "And what has had you sulking about?" he murmured into her ear.

"I have not been sulking."

"Mhmm..." Alistair gave her a sideways glance. "Why are you not dancing?"

"Chaperoning." She gulped.

"Should that not be Simon's responsibility?"

The lady huffed. "The last ball we attended ended so badly, it is now *my* responsibility."

"I am standing right here." Simon waved a hand through

*Meeting Mister Baston*

the air. "Now that Isabella is officially betrothed, she qualifies as a chaperone."

"When my mother is too busy, that is," Isabella added, evading Alistair's gaze yet again.

"Oh! Baston, you were not here. Bella is now publicly engaged to Viscount Middleton. Lord knows why…" Simon groaned then sipped his glass of spirits.

"Indeed, I have heard." Rage began to build in his chest—or was it jealousy? Alistair leaned in. "And where is your dear sister?" he asked, changing the subject of conversation.

"Dancing with Lord Middleton."

*Middleton*. That bastard. "I see." Alistair's blood burned through his skin. He needed to speak with Isabella *alone*, and he had to convince her to break off her engagement with the viscount. It seemed his proposal would have to wait a few more minutes. "May I have the next dance, my lady?"

"No."

"No?" The woman was really making this deuced difficult.

"I have promised the next set to the Duke of Chesterfield." She shrugged.

"All right," he said through gritted teeth. "What about the dance after that?"

"Chaperoning."

Alistair's jaw jutted out as he clenched his teeth even tighter together. "And the dance after?"

Isabella sighed. "If you insist, that dance shall be yours." She handed over her dance card and Alistair quickly jotted down his name. He was disappointed to see it was a country reel.

Just then, a very tall, blue-eyed and brown-haired gentleman approached. "Reading." He greeted Simon with a nod.

## Chapter Fifty-One

Turning to Isabella, he gave a regal bow. "Lady Isabella, or should I say, future Viscountess Middleton?" The gentleman purred as he brought Isabella's knuckles to his lips, and—in Alistair's opinion—the gentleman lingered for far too long…

"Baston." Simon nudged his elbow. "May I introduce Alexander Widley, the Duke of Chesterfield?"

Alistair attempted to hide his grimace as he greeted the duke. "Alistair Baston of Sussex, Your Grace."

The Duke of Chesterfield gave a curt nod before turning back to Simon. "I am afraid I have come to steal your lovely sister from your company."

"Steal away…" Simon waved them off with an imperious smile.

As Alistair watched the lady he loved stroll off with the Duke of Something or Other, Simon quickly came to his side. "Baston, where on earth have you been this last fortnight?"

Alistair's stomach did a roll as a rush of disturbing memories came forth. Blackburn's burnt flesh… Callum's death…

Simon narrowed his eyes at his duress.

"I was conducting business on your father's behalf." Which was a half truth at least.

"Does *she* know that?" Simon inquired, stealing another glass of spirits from a passing servant.

"Of course she does. Though I suppose she may not have known how long it would take." And after their meeting in Hyde Park, Alistair had no plans of visiting Isabella so soon, at least not until her note… And why would she ask to see him if she had already accepted Middleton's offer of marriage?

Perhaps he had looked too deeply into its meaning. Perhaps her scribbled words of apology were just that? An apology and nothing more?

Alistair gave his head a mental shake.

*Nay.*

Something about her engagement did not make sense. His skin began to burn with unease as he came to the realization that he *must* rectify the situation—*now.*

"Well." Simon swirled the contents of his beverage. "I suggest you explain yourself to Bella. The only reason she accepted the offer from Middleton was because of *your* absence."

"She said this to you?"

"No." Simon slapped Alistair's shoulder with the back of his hand. "I am her brother. I just *know* these things."

Alistair felt a bolt of newfound courage surge within him and as soon as the Duke of—Acresfield?—returned Isabella to her brother's side, Alistair quickly took her by the arm and whisked her off to the dance floor.

"I am meant to be chaperoning," the lady said through gritted teeth.

Alistair's nostrils flared. "Are you *that* determined to keep away from me?"

Isabella glanced toward the plastered ceiling. "I am *engaged*, Alistair. We have nothing more to say to each other."

The low hum of violins slowly filled the room, signaling the start of a waltz. Alistair smiled inwardly. A waltz would allow them to have a somewhat private conversation without hopping about and changing partners like one did in a country reel.

Placing his hand on Isabella's lower back, he pressed her body boldly against his. "Why are you angry with me?"

She avoided his gaze. "I am not—"

## Chapter Fifty-One

"Yes." His grasp tightened around the lady's delicate digits. "You are."

Her eyes dropped to their hands as they fell into the rhythmic 1,2,3 step. "Very well. I am angry with you," she fumed, finally giving in to his questions. "I was worried sick over you. Why would you go after Blackburn?"

"I could not let him get away with what he did to your family. I did it for you."

"I did not ask you to!"

Alistair grimaced, knowing very well she was right.

"And why did you let me believe you knew Violet was in Guildford?" she continued, and her voice dropped to a barely audible whisper. "After you... after we..." She lifted her chin to meet his gaze. "I felt betrayed... so I accepted Lord Middleton's offer of marriage."

"Oh, Bella..." He removed the hand that was resting at her back and slowly brought it to the lady's reddened cheek. "I tried to explain..." That her brother was the one who knew everything from the beginning. *Not him.*

She removed his hand from her face, and Isabella's expression turned somber. "It is too late to fix things now."

*Christ.*

He would have to make this up to her somehow.

As the music began to slow, Alistair steered them in the direction of the French doors that led out to the garden. Once the music came to a halt, he placed her hand in the crook of his elbow and led her toward the exit.

"What are you doing?" she seethed, attempting to pull away from his grasp.

He leaned in, gradually pulling her toward escape. "You do not wish to cause a scene, do you?"

She released a fiery exhale from her nose and relaxed her posture. Alistair took that as a sign of her compliance.

"Good."

Leading the lady through the double doors, he brought her behind a small row of hedges, just out of view of the ballroom. Alistair positioned her body to face him and took her face into his hands. "I am so sorry."

"I am sorry too. But as I said—" she turned away "—it is too late for us."

*Stubborn minx.* "It is not too late—"

"It. Is." Isabella moved to make her escape, and Alistair swiftly took hold of her wrist. "Let go of me."

"No." Yanking her body into his, he met her angry gaze with equal ferocity. *She will hear me out.* "You will not marry that bastard Middleton. I will bloody kill him before you even have a chance to walk down the aisle."

"Edward announced our engagement *here.* The entirety of the *ton* knows we are due to be married. If I break it off now, I will only bring shame to my family." Her nostrils flared and she continued to struggle against his hold.

Alistair let out an exasperated sigh and gripped her free hand, pulling both of the lady's small wrists into his chest. Her sapphire eyes sparked with fiery passion, causing desire to burn through his veins.

He would remind this woman just how much he loved her and just how much *she loved him.* He pressed his lips hard against hers, holding her wrists tight against his chest. Now was not the time for sweet, tender kisses. Alistair needed to remind her of what they had together.

And he was *not* going to lose her to the viscount.

## Chapter Fifty-Two

One moment, Isabella was arguing with Alistair, and the next... he was kissing her.

She quickly turned her face away in an attempt to dodge his kisses, but he slyly moved his lips to her jaw, her neck.

"Is this all you want me for?" Her voice cracked with emotion.

"Do not be ridiculous," Alistair drawled, placing a kiss at her temple. "You know I love you. How many times do you wish me to say it?"

She wished him to say it again. Over and over until she could finally let herself believe it. Until she could trust he was not just another rake that used women for his own pleasure.

"We needed this time apart," he murmured, his breath hot against her skin. His lips fell to her neck, then to her collarbone, causing her once tight and angry fists to go limp. "I cannot trust myself to be alone with you."

And *she* could not be trusted to be alone with *him*. There

*Meeting Mister Baston*

she was, a betrothed woman, letting another gentleman kiss her in her mother's gardens. He had made her wanton.

Releasing one of her wrists, he moved his hand to the small of her back.

Isabella gasped at his touch, and the gentleman used that moment to capture her lips with his. He waited for her to open her mouth to him, almost as if he were asking her permission.

Using her free hand, she snaked her palm over the strong muscles of his chest before gripping the back of his neck, and she was gone. Her body simply melted into his. She wanted his mouth between her thighs again. She wanted Alistair to bring her to the heights she had experienced with him.

She parted her lips, allowing his tongue to dart inside. His tongue softly tickled and caressed as he explored the inner workings of her mouth. She let out a moan, and Alistair deepened his kiss. As he did so, Isabella nipped his lip. She quickly pulled away. "I am sorry…"

"Do not be." His low, husky baritone wrapped around those words. "I enjoy it."

With his words, passion exploded to life within her, booming like thunder in the night. She crushed her body against his, needing to be closer, and no matter how close she was to Alistair, it still was not close enough.

He softly nipped and nibbled at her jaw, causing a familiar throbbing between her legs. The feel of him brought forth memories of them at the inn. She remembered how she so willingly gave herself over to him—and how he so willingly took what she offered.

"Do you know what you do to me?" Alistair murmured against her lips, rousing the swirling, burning feeling at her

## Chapter Fifty-Two

center. And feeling his hard length against her belly, she knew perfectly well what she did to him.

Isabella remembered the first time he had touched her cheek, the night he had snatched her sketchbook from her hands. She thought of how close to her person he had been and just how aware she was of the gentleman's nearness.

So aware it made it difficult to breathe.

Her breath caught as Alistair's hands slid to her buttocks, pulling her into him.

"*This* is what you do to me." He rubbed the evidence of his arousal against her belly. "*This* is why I cannot stay away from you."

His voice wrapped about her senses, and she felt herself falling deeper into this rake's spell. Was it a spell? Or was it love?

In that moment, Isabella definitely believed it was love.

Alistair's lips pressed against hers once more as a small moan escaped her. He pressed his length against her center, stroking her in the most intimate of ways, which brought her back to the present.

The truth of their situation she had so easily let escape her.

"We cannot," she whispered between kisses. "We have to stop."

"I do not want to stop," he groaned.

"You have to."

A sharp ache needled at her chest. If they were to continue as they were, anyone could walk into the garden and find them. And it did not matter that her reputation would be ruined, because Alistair would marry her. It mattered that her *sister's* reputation would be ruined as well. And Isabella would not allow that to happen.

Alistair slowly pulled away, leaving Isabella's body cold and shivering. He let out a heavy sigh and rested his forehead on hers.

"Have you mussed my hair again?" Isabella thought back to their interlude in the library.

He pulled away in order to assess her appearance fully. "Not at all," he said with a sly smile before pulling a leaf from her hair. A small chuckle escaped her.

She studied the green of his eyes, the dark auburn of his thick, tousled hair, the red undertones that shimmered brightly against the candlelight.

She choked back the tears that drew a thick haze over her eyes. She brought his hand to her lips and kissed the warm flesh. "This will be the last we see of each other, Alistair." Her voice cracked on the gentleman's name.

Bringing his hand to her cheek, he caressed her gently. "What are you on about?"

He could not possibly be so daft. "I am to be married to Lord Middleton." She turned away from his caress and made to leave, hating the thickened quality of her voice.

Alistair stayed her by taking hold of her hand. "Leave him," he commanded.

She whipped around to face him. "It is not that simple!"

"Yes, it is!"

She forced a cynical laugh. "You are not a woman, therefore you will *never* understand."

Isabella hated how unfairly society treated women. While men were free to do as they would—have relations with whomever they liked, visit their wicked clubs and lay with as many women as they pleased—ladies of the *ton* were forced to hide away in their homes, learning how to be respectable

## Chapter Fifty-Two

in order for society to accept them. Forced to be clean and always proper, for if a lady even took *one* misstep, she was immediately cast out from society.

"I will protect you. Society be damned. We will leave London and move to the country. We can be *together*, Bell—"

"It is not about me." She yanked her hand from Alistair's grasp. "It is about my sister." It would *always* be about her sister. "*She* would be ruined as well as I, and she did not ask for any of this to happen to her." She did not ask to be abducted and tied to a bedpost for days on end. She did not ask for her life to be set aflame.

Isabella's life be damned if it meant her sister could live a happy one.

"I will *not* ruin Violet's happiness for the sake of my own."

Knowing Alistair would try to convince her to stay with him, and terrified that he would succeed, Isabella left him standing alone in the garden, just as she had left him in Hyde Park.

## Chapter Fifty-Three

That had marked the third time Isabella had rejected him.

Or mayhap fourth. Honestly, Alistair had lost count of the number of times the lady had wanted to be with him... and then did not.

He had decided he would give the lady ten minutes. Ten minutes to return to the ballroom, compose herself, and return to her chaperoning duties or dancing or *whatever* it was she had planned for the rest of the evening—and then Alistair would propose.

Yes, she was already engaged to be married, but as far as he knew, nothing official had been signed. Even if they had signed some sort of official document, Alistair did not care. He would take said documents and throw them into the fire if it meant Isabella could be his forever.

This evening was decidedly not the grand and romantic evening he had hoped it would be, but it would have to do. And Alistair decided he was going to propose in front of

## Chapter Fifty-Three

*everyone.* Perhaps if the lady had an audience, she would not reject him *again.* Or perhaps she would, and he would make an even bigger ass of himself than he already had.

Alistair pulled out his timepiece. It had been *exactly* ten minutes since she had left him abandoned in her mother's gardens. He tucked the watch fob into his jacket and strolled into the ballroom through the French doors.

Walking the perimeter, he searched for her familiar gold tresses, but instead, found the Duchess of Waverly. "What a marvelous party you have put together, Your Grace." Alistair placed a small peck on the duchess's gloved hand.

A blush stained the older woman's cheeks. "Oh, Alistair, you needn't call me 'Your Grace.' Mary will do just fine."

"As you wish." Alistair released her hand and moved to stand by her side, facing the swarm of dancing couples. "Chaperoning duty?"

Mary let out a small sigh. "Yes, I figured I would give Isabella and Simon a break. They are all out dancing now." A wistful smile appeared over her lips. "It is lovely seeing my children so happy, although quite sad now that they are grown and will soon be starting families of their own." The duchess fluttered a hand about her breast. "Did you hear that Bella is now engaged to the Viscount Middleton?"

Alistair's jaw tightened. "Indeed."

"I was really quite shocked, given how long it took her to give the gentleman an answer." The duchess gave him a sideways glance. "In fact, she had only started spending more time with Edward over the last fortnight, this last fortnight in which *you* were *away.* How interesting…"

Was the duchess alluding to something?

Mary sipped at her beverage, eyeing Alistair accusingly.

*Meeting Mister Baston*

"We did miss your company while you were away."

He felt a pull of his heartstrings. "I was quite busy with… paperwork," he lied.

Mary gave a shake of her head. "It is *so* strange. I really thought Isabella fancied a *different* gentleman."

It seemed every one of Isabella's family members worried over her happiness, everyone except the lady herself.

He supposed she had a point about the possibility of her sister's ruin, but in all honesty, being the daughters of the Duke and Duchess of Waverly, Isabella *nor* Violet had anything to worry over. For if society wanted to cast out the Avery sisters, that meant the loss of a connection with a dukedom, and no sane persons of the *ton* would ever give up such a powerful connection *or* go against a family of such influence in society.

Just then, Alistair spotted Isabella jumping and twirling to a Scotch reel. "If you will excuse me," he said to the duchess, never taking his eyes from Isabella. "I must ask your daughter to marry me."

As Alistair took his leave of the duchess, he could have sworn he heard the woman mutter, *"Finally,"* to his back.

With quick, confident strides, he focused his gaze on the lady's golden, bouncing curls. Everything and everyone around him became a blur of movement and color.

Once he reached Isabella's side, thoroughly interrupting her dance, he took the lady by the hand and guided her away from her dance partner.

"Get your hands off her!" Alistair's gaze locked with Isabella's dance partner—Lord Middleton.

Alistair let out a curse.

"I said—" Middleton took a step forward "—take your

## Chapter Fifty-Three

bloody hands off her. *Now.*"

The orchestra faltered to a stop, causing the couples around them to cease their dancing.

"Alistair, what are you doing?" Isabella implored, her cheeks burning red. "Everyone is staring."

Indeed they were. Just as he want—

With a grunt, Alistair hit the ground.

*Hard.*

Pain swept through his skull. His head was in a daze, and his vision was like a cloud of smoke.

"Alistair!" He heard a shriek come from his side.

He blinked away the fog and looked up to see the viscount hovering over him with his wrist pulled back, ready to deliver a second blow.

That bloody bastard struck him! And without the decency to give warning first.

Alistair made to lift himself from the ground, and Edward landed another hard blow on his mouth. Bringing his fingertips to his lip, Alistair let out a string of curses as the warm red liquid trailed down his fingers.

"Edward, stop!" Isabella came between them, blocking Lord Middleton's forward motion.

She fell to her knees and took his face into her hands. "Are you all right?" she asked with concerned eyes.

Alistair glanced toward the viscount and then to the surrounding peers. Staring. Whispering. There was no doubt they were thoroughly enjoying the spectacle... And it had all better be worth it, for his sake.

"Isabella." Middleton reached a hand toward the lady. "Come. Step away from him."

For the love of— The bastard was already ordering her

*Meeting Mister Baston*

about like some puppy dog.

Looking between herself and the viscount, Isabella quickly dropped her hand to her side, leaving Alistair's skin cold and desolate, like a frozen lake in the midst of winter.

"Baston! Middleton!" Simon entered their grand circle of turmoil. "What on earth is happening here?"

If Alistair had wanted an audience full of Averys... well, he certainly had one. He watched as Mary, George, and Lady Violet arrived just behind Lord Reading. He was actually quite surprised to see the duke return to the party. Perhaps he was there to see if Alistair's proposal had been successful.

Well, the duke would soon find out, along with the rest of the *ton*.

"Ah, Reading." Middleton stood before them with his arms akimbo. "Perhaps you can ask the gentleman what was going through his mind when he snatched my betrothed from the dance floor?"

"I prefer the term: *whisked away.*" Alistair winked.

With a growl, Middleton leaped forward and would have landed another blow had Simon not intercepted.

A giggle came from Lady Violet, causing Mary to whack the young Avery sibling with her feathered fan.

"What were you thinking?" Isabella asked, appearing quite unamused.

Right. He supposed it was now or never.

With slow, pained movements, Alistair climbed to his knees. He took both of the lady's hands into his, and thinking the better of it, brought her satiny soft gloved hand to his cheek, returning that warmth to his skin.

"Alistair?" The soft, breathless query escaped her.

He reached into his jacket pocket and pulled out the slightly

## Chapter Fifty-Three

mussed velvet box—

"Are you bloody serious?" Lord Middleton let out a contemptuous laugh. "*She* is the '*lucky lady?*'" Edward stepped around Simon. "Well, I regret to inform you, it is too late. The lady is betrothed *to me*," he spat.

Edward made to grasp Isabella's arm, but Reading stopped the viscount's movements once again. "I believe that is up to *the lady*."

"Isabella." Edward offered his hand. "Come now, this is madness!"

"I should like to hear what Mr. Baston has to say." Isabella kept her gaze trained on Alistair.

Gulping past the newly formed lump in his throat, Alistair opened the slightly dirtied jeweler's box before her. "Isabella Elizabeth Avery. I will go mad if I am not able to spend every day of the rest of my life with you."

She crossed her arms over her chest. "And?"

Was she enjoying this? Enjoying Alistair embarrassing himself in front of high society? *The minx.*

He managed to grin through the throbbing pain in his lip. Her blue eyes glistened with amusement. "You are intelligent and witty and daring." He arched a mischievous brow. "Mayhap a bit unconventional…"

A guffaw bubbled past the lady's lips.

"… and you could best anyone here at knife throwing."

She gave him an arrogant nod.

"But, beside all of that, you see that there is more to me than my lack of title. You make me feel as though I am *more* than just a spare." His breath hitched as emotion built up in his throat. "You see *me*."

Alistair grasped the small diamond and sapphire ring from

*Meeting Mister Baston*

its place in the box, his heart racing with anticipation as he held it before her. "Will you please do me the honor of being my wife?"

The only thing he could hear in that moment was the loud beating of his heart.

*Thump-thump.*

*Thump-thump.*

*Thump-thump.*

And it was as though the entirety of the room held their breath along with him... waiting for her answer.

Isabella's hands slowly dropped to her sides, her expression turning very serious. She looked to her sister.

*Blast and damn.*

The lady was still worried about her sister and what their relationship would do to Violet. Alistair looked over to Lady Violet, who had a huge grin on her face, a grin that soon faded after noticing Isabella's hesitance.

With quick shallow steps, Lady Violet made her way to her sister's side. "Whatever is the matter?"

Isabella took her sister's hand. "If I were to accept him—" she lowered her voice to a whisper "—such a scandal could ruin our family."

Violet scoffed. "If what happened to me has not already ruined our family, then nothing will. Stop worrying over me and think about your own happiness for a change." Leaving a kiss on Isabella's satin-clad fingers, Violet returned to the duke and duchess's side.

Alistair's body began to relax a little. Surely with her sister's approval, she would have no reason to refuse him.

Isabella took Alistair's hands in hers and aided him to his feet. She placed a hand upon the stubble of his jaw, and he

## Chapter Fifty-Three

leaned into her touch. "Yes," she said on a gasp. "Yes, I would love to."

"Unbelievable," Middleton muttered from somewhere in the background.

He let out a breath, as what felt like the weight of one thousand elephants fell from his shoulders. But before he could slide the ring on to the lady's finger, a loud squealing came from nearby.

It was Isabella's mother, and it had to be the most comical thing he had seen in his nearly thirty years.

The duchess came sprinting from across the room, her arms flailing about in the air. Isabella's hand flew from his as the duchess yanked her daughter into her arms.

"I must apologize for the confusion, Lord Middleton." The duke approached the viscount with an extended hand. "I hope this does not damage our families' relationship in any way."

The viscount eyed the duke's hand but eventually accepted his gesture. "Of course not, Your Grace." Middleton gave the duke's hand a hard shake. "I wish your daughter all the happiness in the world."

Alistair watched as Middleton stormed off without a second glance. He supposed it could have gone worse.

"My eldest daughter is finally getting married!" the duchess declared to the entirety of the ballroom, and the crowd, slowly, began to applaud, a messy, muted sound with a significant lack of enthusiasm.

Though Alistair supposed he could not blame them. It was not every day a lady of the *ton* found herself betrothed to two different gentlemen in the same evening.

"Why has the music stopped?" Simon shouted over the

*Meeting Mister Baston*

roar of the crowd as he reached Alistair's side.

The orchestra promptly resumed their low bellows.

The duchess released Isabella from her hold and turned to her son. "Your sister just got herself engaged! Again…"

"Yes, I saw," Simon drawled then swiped a glass of champagne from a passing servant.

Stepping forward, Alistair cleared his throat. "May I give my future wife her ring now?"

"Oh, of course!" the duchess squealed. "I had almost forgotten."

Alistair dabbed his bloodied mouth with his kerchief before returning it to his jacket pocket. He took in a breath of air and turned to his betrothed. Her pink lips turned up into a grin, her eyes glowing with anticipation.

Alistair slowly slid the small golden ring on to the lady's finger and led her off the dance floor.

Isabella inspected the glistening sapphire stones and diamonds. "It is beautiful," she whispered.

"It was my mother's." Alistair smiled thoughtfully to himself. He truly wished he had known more about his mother, more than the fact that she had died while giving birth to him—and that his father hated him for it. "I had a jeweler add the sapphires though… to match your dagger."

She smiled and placed a hand over her heart.

"Bella, dear!" Mary shouted from a few paces away.

*Good Lord.* Alistair had the feeling that he was never going to get another moment alone with Isabella until their wedding night.

"Have you seen Violet?" the duchess asked with labored breaths, making her way to their side. "She seems to have disappeared."

## Chapter Fifty-Three

Isabella motioned toward Alistair. "Apologies. I have been a little distracted." She waved her left hand through the air. "Getting betrothed and all that."

"Yes, yes." Mary waved them off and glanced about the room. "Simon!"

"I am here, Mother." The marquess appeared at their side.

"Where has Violet gone off to?" The duchess wagged a long finger at her son. "You were supposed to be watching her."

"No, Mother." Simon propped himself lazily against the wall. "*You* were supposed to be watching her. And no, I do not know where she is."

The duchess stomped her foot hard against the floor and huffed.

"Enough of this." Enough hiding, enough bickering. Isabella was finally his, and he wanted the entire world to see.

He took her in his arms. "Alistair, what are you doing?"

Isabella eyed him warily, and before she could stop him, Alistair pressed his lips against hers, treasuring her every taste. He would never take the feel of her for granted. He would never let her leave his arms—or his bed, for that matter. "I love you so much," he muttered on a break in between kisses. "I need you like my lungs need air."

"And that would be my cue." Simon pushed himself off the wall and stalked off, champagne flute in hand.

Isabella chuckled, then placed her fingertips over her well-loved mouth. "You just kissed me in front of my brother. I am surprised he did not pummel you."

He smirked. "I am certain he will later."

Bringing her fingers to the corner of his mouth, Isabella grinned. "I love your smile." She brushed the pad of her thumb across his lower lip, sending a rush of desire through him. "I love *you*—ever so much—and I am sorry for waiting until now to tell you."

Alistair's heart jumped from his chest and soared into the heavens. She loved him.

*Of course, she loves you. She agreed to marry you, did she not?*

Indeed she had, and now she was his to cherish for the rest of their lives. He would make it his life's ambition to make this woman fall even *more* in love with him. He wanted her to fall in love with him again and again.

Day after day.

Month after month.

He was not even sure if it were possible for one to fall in love with the same man over and over and over again, but he knew it was quite easy for him to fall in love with the same woman day after day—for it had already happened. Now, while he kissed her in front of the entirety of the ballroom, he loved her even more than he had a mere moment ago.

And he would keep loving this stubborn minx, more and more, for the rest of his days.

*Lord help him.*

# Epilogue

*One month later...*

"Are you ready to see your new home, my lady?" Alistair peeked out the carriage window as they made their way down a cobbled drive.

*Our home*, she corrected for him in her mind. This would be *their* home, together as husband and wife. She could hardly believe it. If one had told her she would end up married to Alistair Baston the first day they had met at Ashbury Hall... well, she would have simply laughed in their face.

"Very much so." Small, nervous tingles fluttered around Isabella's belly. She had lived so very long in the same set of properties, with the same family and the same servants... The house in Littlehampton was going to be entirely new—an entirely new set of staff with entirely new surroundings.

And not a soul but herself and Alistair.

It was true, their relationship had been complicated from

the very beginning. But the complications were soon overlooked, and they had formed a friendship of sorts... with an attraction. There had *always* been an attraction, no matter how fiercely she had tried to deny it.

A familiar yearning stirred low in her belly as she settled her eyes on her new husband. The carriage began to slow, and Isabella opened the curtain to catch a glimpse of her new home—

"Ah-ah-ah." Alistair's hands instantly shielded her eyes. "No peeking, young lady. I want it to be a surprise."

The warmth of the gentleman's touch, her husband's touch, made her stomach do little flips. "Surely it will be a surprise either way—"

"Shhh." In the blackness caused by Alistair's hands, she felt him turn her face toward him, and then his lips were on hers. Before she had time to react, he had already pulled away. "I want it to be extra surprising," he teased.

Alistair's teasing used to frustrate her beyond belief, but how she loved it now. She could not imagine him being anything but the playful rake she had grown to love.

"Just promise me you will not be disappointed if it is not as grand as what you are used to."

Isabella felt a pull of her heartstrings. Would he always feel as though he was beneath her? Because of his lack of title? "Do you really think that low of me, Mr. Baston?"

"Oh, definitely," he baited her. "In fact, I am not even certain why I married you."

She smiled at the amusement in his voice.

Alistair's hands suddenly slipped away as he jumped to the front side of the carriage. "Cartwright!" He pounded against the wall. "Turn this carriage around at once!"

## Epilogue

Isabella quickly reached out to tug his arm. "Alistair," she laughed. "Stop it!"

"I wish to be rid of my new bride immediately!"

A muffled voice came from outside. "Erm, sir?"

"I said—"

She jumped to cover the gentleman's mouth with her hand. "He is jesting, Mr. Cartwright!"

Alistair fell backward into his seat, his body shaking with mirth. He slid her gloved hand from his lips. "Your new home *is* quite small," he warned, pulling Isabella onto his lap. "Like a cottage."

She leaned into his embrace. "I am sure it is lovely." She would be happy with wherever they lived, as long as she was with him.

"Actually." Alistair quirked a brow. "It is more like a shack."

She struck him with her satchel.

As the carriage rolled to a stop, Alistair warned her not to peek through the curtains. She sighed but ultimately agreed.

Her husband quickly jumped from his seat, not bothering to wait for the groomsman to open the door. "Close your eyes," he instructed.

Ridiculous as it was, she did as he asked, and she listened as Alistair opened the carriage door. He tugged at her hand, signaling for her to move forward, leading her down the small steps.

Taking both of her hands in his, he led her forward. She felt the crunch of the gravel under her slippered feet and smelled sea in the air. The squawking of seagulls assaulted her ears, but she could not help but smile. One did not hear seagulls very often in London.

"Open your eyes."

## Meeting Mister Baston

It took a moment for her eyes to adjust to the evening sunlight, but as soon as the fuzziness faded from her vision, she let out a gasp. Before her stood a three-story Elizabethan wonder. With its towering walls of windows, glowing ham stone, and perfectly symmetrical exterior, it was most definitely not a cottage.

*Or a shack.*

It was rather large, actually. Not as expansive and extravagant as her family's country seat, to be sure, but she did not need such extravagance. This home, *their home,* was truly stunning, and she could even see a glimpse of the bright turquoise blue water of the sea. "Alistair, it is beautiful…" She could very much see herself out sketching by the sea in the early morning hours. She did not have much experience sketching birds, but now she would have an infinite amount of time to practice.

"Welcome to Isabella Manor."

Her head whipped around to face him. "What…?"

Alistair shrugged. "I changed the name."

She moved her hand to rest on her chest. "You did not have to do that." The name could have been Clam Cottage and she would have loved it.

"I wanted to," he said simply. "The name it held before was terrible."

She gave him a sideways look. "What was it?"

"Little Baston—as my brother so graciously called it."

Isabella's hand flew to cover her mouth—an attempt to hold in her laughter, but it was unsuccessful. Her shoulders began to shake with her amusement. "Oh my…" she laughed. "That is actually quite adorable. Can we change it back?"

Alistair swiftly took hold of her wrist and yanked her

## Epilogue

body into his, causing her to stumble. He rightened her. "Absolutely not."

"Please," she whimpered. Isabella Manor was beautiful, but Little Baston was so much better.

"Do not make me punish you, dear wife," he growled, bringing his lips closer to hers.

Her gaze dropped to his mouth, completely and unashamedly transfixed by Alistair's crooked, half grin. She reached up to caress the dark auburn stubble of his cheek, and he let out a husky moan.

"I took the liberty of giving the servants the day off." He placed a kiss at her temple, her cheek, her ear. Isabella's center began stirring with desire. "I wanted you all to myself," he whispered.

A flutter of nervousness sailed through her. This would be the day Alistair would have her, truly and fully. He already had her heart. She had handed it over to him alive and thumping the day he had swiped that purple daisy from the public gardens.

Once inside, Alistair gave a tour of their new home, which included two parlors, three drawing rooms, an elegant dining room, breakfast room, a beautifully mature garden with a footpath that led down to the sea—she would make great use of that every summer—music room, billiards room, a small library, and his study. Then, of course, nine bedrooms. *Not including his.*

He saved that for last.

"And *this*—" he pressed the handle and swung open the heavy oak panel "—is our room. You may decorate it however you wish."

Isabella took a hesitant step inside. The room was quite

## Meeting Mister Baston

masculine, decorated in dark maroons and blues, with a large four-poster bed in the middle of the room. "It will do." Turning to face Alistair, his large frame leaning lazily against the door, she added, "For now."

Pushing himself off the door frame, her husband began to move with slow, languid steps. She took in a deep, unsteady breath. Alistair removed his topcoat and hat and tossed them onto a nearby chair. His hair was mussed from the day's journey, and his eyes... his eyes were alight with fire.

She retreated, holding her arms to her chest in a protective embrace. The back of her knees hit the hard mahogany of his bed.

*Their bed*.

Taking her bottom lip between her teeth, she slowly sat on the soft, feathered mattress. When Alistair reached her front, his well-muscled frame radiated heat and desire. Her pulse quickened—as if it were not already fast enough. He took another step forward.

"*Wait!*" Her hands flew forward to stay his movement, her fingertips pressing against the hard muscles of his abdomen.

Alistair paused his movements. "What is it, love?"

"*Just wait.*" She did not know what had come over her. But suddenly she felt dirty, unworthy of the gentleman before her.

"Is it... Callum?" He brought her hands to his lips and left soft kisses on each knuckle.

"N-No." Her voice cracked. No, she had not had nightmares of the attack since Alistair had proposed. But... a vice clenched around her heart. "May I ask you something?"

Turning her hand over, he left a featherlight kiss on the inside of her wrist. "You may ask me anything, my love."

## Epilogue

That endearment sent shivers down her spine. "It is not Callum, *per se*."

Alistair gave her a sideways look, his green eyes glinting with curiosity.

She took in a steadying breath. "Does it... does it bother you that..."

"What is it?" He took her face into his hands.

"Does it bother you that I was touched by another?"

His eyes narrowed. "Is that what is bothering you?" Alistair fell to his knees, making his gaze even with hers. "If such things bothered me, we would not be here, and do not ever—" he kissed her forehead "—feel ashamed for what happened. You are stronger now because of it, and do not dare have regrets about anything."

Isabella's heart soared. Some gentlemen would find what happened to her repulsive. They would assume it had happened by her own doing. They would assume she was wanton. Not Alistair. Alistair admired her for her strength and resilience, and she loved him so deeply for it.

Alistair's emerald gaze intensified. "If Simon hadn't owed his debts... if Blackburn hadn't ordered Violet's abduction... we may not be together today." He returned her hands to his lips. "Lady Isabella may have never had the pleasure of meeting Mr. Baston." He waggled his dark brows, causing a laugh to burst from her lips.

He was right. Although she could never—would never—forgive Callum or Blackburn for what they had done to her family, she could at least let go of her anger. And speaking of anger... "Are you still angry with me for being betrothed to Edward?" She flashed him a sly smile.

Alistair slowly rose from his knees and answered her with

a searing kiss. The feel of his mouth on hers stole away any fear she had inside her. And heavens help her, did it feel good. The expert ministrations with his tongue brought back memories of his mouth between her thighs. She burned there, pulsated with a need for him to be there again.

His hands slid down the length of her, leaving a trail of fire along the silk of her wedding gown. "I will make this good for you," he promised.

"I trust you." And she did. She trusted him with her entire being.

He moved his lips to her neck. Isabella let her head fall back, giving him more access to that sensitive skin. She snaked her hands around his neck and pulled him closer, needing him closer. His hands worked the back of her laced gown.

The moment reminded her of when she had asked Alistair to assist her with unknotting her corset. He had been so gentle then—reluctant even. Now his fingers were fast and fumbling.

Alistair nudged her legs apart and shoved her gown up and over her hips. Their eyes met, and he gave her a suspicious look. That is when she felt the cold metal at her calf, and she gave him a soft smile.

He yanked the dagger from its holster and eyed it questioningly. "Really? On our wedding day?"

"One can never be too prepared." She was actually quite happy that she was no longer afraid to have the dagger on her person. Instead of the blood dripping down from its blade infecting her mind, she now thought of her father and how the blade her father had gifted her had saved her life.

Alistair tossed the dagger to the side and slowly removed the holster strapped to her leg. He slid his fingers along her

## *Epilogue*

calf. "I have never met a woman quite like you." He squeezed the muscle of her thigh. "But that is one of the many reasons why I love you."

With strong hands at her waist, Alistair lifted her from the bed and placed her in the middle of the mattress.

Heart racing, she scooted herself backward until she felt the soft, satin pillows against her back. She watched as Alistair slowly crawled onto the bed, his eyes hot and primitive with need.

*I do this to him.* A strange, feminine satisfaction filled her. And with a newly found confidence, Isabella bit her lower lip as she drew out her leg, pressing her white-stockinged foot against Alistair's hard chest, staying his movements.

He arched a playful brow.

Isabella let out a shriek and fell backward as Alistair yanked at her ankle and pulled her toward him, causing her skirts to once again pool at her waist.

His gaze fell to the heap of fabric, and her pulse tripled its beat. He let out an animalistic growl. "I will show you just how much I love you." And she wanted him to. *Oh, how she wanted him to...*

Alistair came to hover over her, his forearms and knees bearing all of his weight. One of his hands found the edge of her stocking and traced small circles on the skin of her upper thigh. With hooded lashes, he drew his fingers closer and closer to her most feminine place.

Wonderful burning energy swirled at her core. "Please," she begged. "I want to feel you."

Alistair let out a groan and immediately did as she asked, and she nearly bucked off the bed as soon as the gentleman's fingers began their tantalizing teasing of her feminine place.

Closing her eyes, she let a moan escape her lips. Here, in their home, they did not have to worry about being caught. Here, she was free to be herself and feel any way she pleased. And right now, she felt like the wanton woman she had never dared to be.

Alistair placed open-mouthed kisses along her neck, collarbone, and the swell of her breast. Using his teeth, he removed the thin strap of the gown from her shoulder. A slap of cool night air hit her skin where the fabric had been. With trembling fingers, he pulled at the edge of her bodice, slowly revealing the hard nub of her nipple. She gasped as he took the tip of her breast into his mouth and suckled, all the while continuing his sensual circles on the folded flesh at her center.

Isabella entwined her fingers into his dark auburn hair. "I need you." She needed him in every possible way.

Alistair brought his lips to her ear and whispered, "You will have me." He slipped two fingers inside of her.

She cried out his name, over and over, as he stroked her lovingly. His fingers felt enormous as she stretched around him. And just as her world was about to spiral out of control, Alistair removed his fingers.

"*Nooo.*" She let out a whimper.

He laughed as he removed his cravat. "We are not finished yet, my love." That smooth baritone contained promises she was not sure she was ready for.

With heavy breaths, she watched as her husband removed all of his clothes, including his breeches… She let out a gasp, her fingers flying to the edge of her mouth. "Where is that going?"

Alistair flashed her one of his lopsided grins as he lowered

## Epilogue

his body onto hers. "Trust me."

She did. She trusted him, but *this*... She had seen him nude before, but he was soft then. Soft and flopped over like she had seen on so many statues before. Now Alistair was alive. Hard and erect.

She reached out to touch him, testing the size and length of him in her hand. He pulsated against her grasp and let out a tortured moan. "Bella..."

At the sound of her name, she drew back her touch. "Did I hurt you?" Heat stained her cheeks. How she wished her mother had told her more of what a gentleman desired in the marriage bed.

"No," he breathed against her skin. Taking her hand in his, Alistair placed her fingers on the tip of his shaft. He moved her hand along the hard length of his erection, back and forth.

Isabella quickly realized that what Alistair was feeling at that very moment must have been what Isabella herself felt when he had his fingers inside of her. She continued her movements, and Alistair's guiding hand slowly retreated.

With an innocent uncertainty, she grasped his shaft and slowly began stroking the entire length of him. She circled his tip with her thumb, and Alistair began to move. "My God, Bella."

He thrust himself against the palm of her hand, over and over. The scandalous friction caused her center to burn with a need for something more.

With blunt fingers, Alistair pushed against her wet folds. "Place me here."

At first, she did not quite understand. *Place what where?*

"Right here." He pushed two fingers inside of her, and she

soon interpreted his meaning. Without another thought, Isabella placed him at her opening. The size of his fingers were a mere blade of grass compared to the size of... *him*.

But she was so wet between her legs. Surely that meant she was ready for him. And the feeling of his erection against her opening was pure bliss.

With sweat beading at his brow, Alistair pushed her gown up and over her head and tossed the article to an unknown destination. The fit of her gown had not allowed her to wear a chemise, so she was now completely and utterly bare to him.

Alistair nudged her legs further apart as he settled himself comfortably between her thighs. "I will try not to hurt you."

She gave him a hesitant nod. Her mother had told her that her first time in the marriage bed may be painful, and she almost wished her mother had not said a word about it. Expecting pain had made her limbs stiff with anticipation.

Then Alistair slowly began sliding himself within her. Inch by inch. His lips met hers with a burning intensity as he swallowed down the moan escaping from her lips. He moved his hands to her backside and pulled her hips into his. He pushed forward slowly, letting out a low cry of pleasure when her inner muscles tightened around his length.

"Oh, Christ, Bella," he grunted, pushing himself even further inside. She was not certain how much further he'd be able to go. She felt so full already.

She went stiff, digging her nails into Alistair's back as he pushed inside another inch.

"Shhh," he crooned. "You must relax."

"I am trying."

Placing one hand at the edge of her lower back, Alistair

## Epilogue

slowly moved against her. He used his hand to press at her spine, teaching her to move with him, and those motions made her body soften in response. She moved with him in a carnal rhythm until it felt like he had reached a barrier within her.

She could feel the wall against him, and her muscles began to tighten. *The pain will come soon.* She could almost already feel it.

"This may hurt a little," he warned.

Swallowing past the lump in her throat, she placed her fingers along the stubble of Alistair's cheek. "I trust you."

Alistair stared down at her, his auburn tresses hanging over his brow, and he had never looked as handsome as he did in that very moment. She watched him as he closed his eyes and sent a prayer skyward.

He then thrust hard against her, breaking past whatever barrier had blocked him from entering her fully. She let out a groan when she felt that barricade break. And if she was not full of his length before, then she certainly felt more than full now.

"I am so sorry." He placed his forehead against hers. "It will never hurt like that ever again."

"It was not too bad. I was just... surprised."

Alistair pulled her close then continued his rhythmic movement. And this time, it was different. Her muscles tightened around his shaft, causing waves of pleasure to stir throughout her body. Pushing forward and pulling back, her need for Alistair intensified.

Isabella's fingers tangled themselves into his hair. Her legs wrapped about him on their own accord, with a need to feel closer to him. She matched his thrusts perfectly, and they moved together in a primitive dance full of lust and love.

Alistair let out small moans of pleasure that drove her wild. "I love you," she whispered. He pressed her lips against hers in return, causing her heart to soar.

He grabbed at her hips and pulled her against him again and again, harder and harder until the sounds of their naked skin slapping against one another filled the room.

Tears leaked from her eyes. But not from pain, no; it was not painful at all. What they were sharing was the most beautiful thing Isabella had ever experienced. And then her muscles clenched around his length as waves of pleasure moved through her, causing her entire body to shake. "Oh God, Alistair."

And he kept riding her, riding her waves of ecstasy in a passion-driven frenzy, his hips circling and thrusting until he let out a cry of emotion. He tangled his fingers into her hair and collapsed on top of her. His chest heaved with large breaths as he rested his head next to her own.

Once Alistair's breathing settled, he rolled on to his side, taking her with him in his arms. She let out a sigh and looked to him. His eyes glistened with love, happiness and promise. "That was…" She gasped. "That was—"

"Just lay with me," he purred. And she did. Tonight was the first night Alistair would not have to sneak away after making love to her, and she was going to take full advantage. Letting out a peaceful sigh, she closed her eyes and fell asleep in her husband's arms.

\* \* \*

## *Epilogue*

Isabella woke to the feel of her stomach beginning to devour itself. She clenched her fingers over her rumbling belly and turned over to face Alistair.

He was sound asleep, his dark lashes settling atop his cheeks.

A soft smile crept over her lips, and her stomach let out another fierce growl.

Alistair looked so peaceful when he slept. She truly did not wish to wake him, but... "Alistair?"

Nothing.

"Alistair?"

He let out a sleepy grumble, but still, did not move from his lifeless position on their bed.

Reaching out, she softly caressed his cheek and repeated his name in a sing-song manner. "All-is-staaairrr."

His eyelids slowly fluttered open, and a barely there half grin fell over his lips. "Hullo, my love," he said, his voice quiet and groggy.

"Alistair." Isabella frowned. "I am famished." She clutched at her belly through the thin bedsheets and gave him the saddest puppy eyes she could muster.

Alistair let out a groan and rubbed his eyes awake. Throwing the bedsheets off himself, he rose from their bed and made his way to the bellpull, stark naked.

She watched her husband yank at the bell string, letting his manhood dangle freely in front of her. Her hand flew to her mouth.

"What is so amusing?"

Isabella stifled a laugh. "You are naked."

*Good heavens.* She sounded like a schoolgirl.

Alistair arched a brow and flashed her an aloof smile. "As

are you," he pointed out.

Her hands flew to her chest, being sure she was fully covered by the thin white satin sheet.

"I am covered— Oh!" How had they forgotten? "We seem to have forgotten that you have dismissed the staff for the day."

Alistair cursed under his breath, returning to his spot on the mattress. "Do you know how to cook?" He gave her a sideways glance.

Cook? Well, she supposed she had observed the kitchen staff now and again when they were making her favorite dessert: heavenly raspberry tarts.

Isabella quirked a brow. "I am offended that you think me so spoiled with my servants that I have never learned to cook." She threw a cushion toward his face.

The gentleman caught the cushion midair. "Well, do you?"

"I used to watch our cook prepare raspberry tarts as a child." She shrugged. "It cannot be so difficult."

Standing from their large four-poster bed, Alistair yanked on his breeches. "Good enough for me." And he promptly disappeared through the door.

He returned holding a silky garment in his hands.

"What is this?" she asked after Alistair tossed the small piece toward her.

"Clothes," he answered simply.

She lifted the garment from the mattress and held it out in front of her. It appeared to be a rose-brown silk nightgown with thin straps and opulent lace detailing at the bodice. The item also seemed to be about half the length of her white cotton nightshirt she usually wore abed. "You call these clothes?"

# Epilogue

"Yes."

"I will freeze!"

"It is almost July!" Alistair tossed her a boyish grin and shrugged. "You could always wear nothing at all. Your choice."

Isabella grimaced. "Where did you get this?"

"The trunk in your room."

Confused, she narrowed her eyes into thin slits. Her mother must have taken a visit to the modiste without her knowledge. "I thought *this* was my room?"

Alistair sat on the edge of the feathered mattress. "Technically, you have your own room, but I assure you, there will be no need for it." He winked then placed a light kiss on her forehead. Rising again, he made his way to the door. "I will leave you to dress in private. I shall be in the hall when you are ready."

With that, Alistair left the room.

Not bothering to don a shirt.

Once dressed, Isabella stood in front of the large beveled mirror, removing what was left of the pins in her hair. With a relieved sigh, she let her golden tresses fall freely over her shoulders.

*My God.*

Isabella studied her reflection in the mirror. What was her mother thinking of dressing her in such a way?

The silk nightgown, though beautiful, was rather provocative. The soft material was sheer to the point where one could clearly see the rouge of her nipples peeking through the fabric.

She reluctantly stepped into the hallway where Alistair was waiting.

His eyes grew dark with promise as he devoured her with his gaze, causing Isabella to instinctively shield her breasts from view.

Alistair closed the distance between them and took her face into his hands. "If we were not so famished, I would make love to you all over again."

Isabella turned away with burning cheeks. "Alistair, you are making me blush."

"Good." His voice was rough with desire.

They soon made their way down to the kitchen where they searched through the pantry. Isabella pinched her chin as she looked for something particularly simple to prepare. "What about eggs?" She turned to Alistair. "They should be easy enough."

He offered her a debonair smile. "Anything you prepare, I am sure to enjoy." He winked.

Isabella grimaced in return. "Do not say that! You will put far too much pressure on me."

"Do not worry." He held her cheek in his palm. "I am here to help." She was not so sure Alistair's assistance would make the task of cooking any easier.

Isabella lifted a basket full of eggs off its shelf, a bit too forcefully, causing an egg to roll out and smash into a sticky mess on the floor. "Oops…" She had to admit, she had never cooked eggs before in all her life, but how difficult could they be?

The simplest way to cook them was to fry them in a pan. All one had to do was crack the egg open, plop it in the pan, and leave it cooking until it was finished.

Feeling somewhat more confident about her endeavor, Isabella set the basket down next to the cooker. Turning

## Epilogue

to her husband, she asked, "And how do you like your eggs, Alistair? Cooked well and through? Or a bit runny?"

He tilted his head in thought. "I prefer when the yolk is a bit runny. How about you?"

Isabella beamed. "I like them just the same."

"With toast," they said in unison.

Alistair barked with laughter. "It seems my new wife and I have much in common." He placed a featherlight kiss on the tip of her nose.

"It seems we do, Mr. Baston." With a proud smile, Isabella turned toward the black behemoth of a stove and *hmm'd*. "Now, how do we work this infernal contraption?"

"Not a clue." Alistair leaned lazily against the work table.

Isabella planted her arms akimbo. "You can at least fetch some bread instead of standing there like a ninny."

With a wink, Alistair pushed himself from the table and disappeared into the pantry. He returned with a large loaf in his hand.

"You do know how to slice bread, do you not?" she drawled.

Alistair located a serrated bread knife and waved it toward her. "Do not make me hurt you, my lady," he teased.

Isabella glanced toward the gentleman's bare chest. "Do be careful, Mr. Baston. We would not want you to hurt yourself."

He stalked toward her. "It is not often I can walk around my own home shirtless." Alistair dragged the tip of the blade along her collarbone, which caused goose pimples to form along her naked flesh. "I must take full advantage of this rare occurrence."

Isabella gulped down the lump beginning to form in her throat, praying that her husband would not get the idea that,

*Meeting Mister Baston*

she also, should be shirtless.

Her erotic nightgown was bad enough.

Turning her attentions back to the cooker, she began examining all of the small knobs and handles. Eventually, Isabella found a compartment that stored firewood. "Aha! Alistair, would you be so kind as to light a fire?" When he did not respond, she turned her head to face where the gentleman stood.

Meeting her stare, her husband crossed his arms and offered the most rakish smile she had ever seen. "I am quite enjoying my view from here."

Realizing that she was bent over with her backside in the air, her body burned with embarrassment.

She immediately stood upright and took an egg into her hand. "You fiend!" Pulling her arm back, Isabella threatened to toss the egg.

The gentleman pointed a staying finger. "Do. Not. Dare."

She narrowed her eyes, and after a moment, returned her egg to the basket. There would be plenty of time to splatter her new husband with eggs later.

Right now, she needed food.

They managed to light the stove, place four slices of bread into the oven, and Isabella even managed to crack six eggs into a pan, enjoying the sizzling sound they made as they cooked.

Spatula in hand, Isabella soon began work on removing the eggs from the pan. "*Oh, no...*"

"What is it?"

"The eggs..." Isabella turned to Alistair and frowned. "I forgot to add lard to the pan. They're sticking."

"Let me see." Alistair took a step toward her and reached

## Epilogue

for the spatula—

"No!" she shouted, pulling the utensil from his grasp. "You will be sure to ruin them."

"Says the young miss who forgot to add lard to the pan."

Isabella's brows came together, and in two swift movements, she grabbed an egg from the basket and launched it into the air.

It exploded on impact, directly in the center of her husband's bare chest.

Alistair's jaw went slack as he peered down at the yolk, which had created a sticky trail of slime down to his navel.

Isabella attempted to stifle her laughter. Alas, she failed.

The gentleman took a step toward her and reached for her arm, but she was too quick, and dashed around to the opposite end of the table.

Which left Alistair within reach of the basket...

He sent an egg flying toward her, and Isabella could not help but let out a loud *yelp* as she ducked away.

Alistair took hold of another egg, but instead of throwing it, the gentleman decided to make a mad dash toward her. And this time, her reflexes were not quite fast enough. Her husband took her by the waist and smashed the egg atop her head.

"*Nooooo!*" she cried as the gooey substance dripped down her hair and onto her naked shoulders.

"What on earth?"

A plump, middle-aged woman appeared in the doorway.

Both Isabella and Alistair froze in their current position, which happened to be with Isabella's back to Alistair's front, his arm wrapped seductively around her waist, with his free hand planted on her head.

*Meeting Mister Baston*

"Sir!" The silver-haired woman placed frustrated hands on her plump hips. "What are ya doin' in me kitchen?"

"Cooking eggs," Alistair answered plainly, not bothering to remove himself from where he held her.

The cook sniffed the air. "What on God's green earth is that smell?"

Isabella took that moment to remove Alistair's hold and attempted to brush some of the slime from her hair.

"I believe our food is burning." Alistair nodded toward the stove, which was now letting off dark puffs of smoke.

The woman waddled over to the cooker, removed the pan from the hot surface, and took the bread slices out of the oven, which—Isabella must admit—she had completely forgotten about.

"Erm." Alistair cleared his throat. "May I introduce our cook, Mrs. Hollands. Mrs. Hollands, this is my wife, Isabella."

"Nice to meet you." Isabella's voice shook as she nervously attempted to cover her bare self behind Alistair's form. Heat stained her cheeks. This indeed was a most unusual introduction.

Mrs. Hollands curtsied and gave her a bright smile. "Lovely to meet ya, m'lady. I am very much lookin' forward to workin' for ya." The woman's hands quickly returned to their place on her hips. "Now, if yous would please leave my kitchen before ya both burn the house to the ground, that would be grand. I will prepare ya's a meal."

*This Mrs. Hollands is quite intimidating, indeed.*

"My apologies, Mrs. Hollands." Alistair gave the woman a regal bow and then took Isabella by the hand, escorting her out of the kitchen.

## *Epilogue*

"I will be sure to have one of the maids prepare a bath for ya as well," Mrs. Hollands added before they left.

A bath sounded wonderful.

Once they stepped out of the kitchen, Isabella could not help but laugh at the entirety of that exchange.

Alistair tilted his head and smiled. "What is so amusing?"

"Us." She combed her fingers through her sticky hair. "We look ridiculous."

Alistair stopped them in their stride and cupped her face with equally sticky hands. "Mmmm, but I think you look lovely."

His emerald gaze sent her heart soaring. "I love you."

The gentleman's eyes flickered with delight. "And I love you, my lady."

A giggle slipped past her lips. "Mr. Baston?"

Alistair brought his lips to her ear. His warm breath sent shivers through her body. "Yes?"

"You are getting egg on my face," she whispered.

Unperturbed, he cupped the nape of her neck, tangling his fingers through her knotted tresses. "I shall wash it off during our bath."

Isabella stiffened. "*Our* bath?"

"Of course." He brought her hands to his soft lips. "We are man and wife now. We shall sleep together, bathe together..." He dropped her hand and placed his forehead against hers. "But never again cook together."

Amusement filled her. "Oh, but I was very much looking forward to cooking with you again," she teased.

"Hmmm..." He pursed his lips to the side. "I will have a talk with Mrs. Hollands. Perhaps she would be willing to provide lessons."

"I very much doubt that."

"You are probably right. Come." Taking her hand in his, Alistair led her toward the stairs. "Let us rid ourselves of our failed attempts at cooking."

Joy and contentment filled her soul as her new husband led her up the steps. Life with Alistair, she thought, would prove to be very wonderful, indeed.

# *More*

Did you enjoy **Meeting Mister Baston**?
Please leave a review!

Be on the lookout for Violet's story, **The Marquess Behind the Mask**
*Coming soon!*

# About the Author

Jodi is a hopeless romantic who fell in love with Regency-era England while watching the movie Pride and Prejudice (2005). After moving from America to the Netherlands in 2016 (and after reading every single one of the BRIDGERTON novels) she began writing her own stories.

Jodi is now living with her husband and fur babies in southern England. She spends her time writing, reading, singing, and creating videos for her YouTube channel.

Having just finished her debut novel: *Meeting Mr. Baston*, she is now writing its spin-off sequel: *The Marquess Behind the Mask,* and has plenty more story ideas for the future!

**You can connect with me on:**
- http://www.linktr.ee/jodimariemackin

Printed in Great Britain
by Amazon